CLAIRE ASKEW

Cover Your Tracks

HODDER

First published in Great Britain in 2020 by Hodder & Stoughton
An Hachette UK company

This paperback edition published in 2021

1

Copyright © Claire Askew 2020

The right of Claire Askew to be identified as the Author
of the Work has been asserted by her in accordance with
the Copyright, Designs and Patents Act 1988.

A CIP catalogue record for this title is available from the British Library

Paperback ISBN 978 1 529 32737 3

Typeset in Plantin Light by Hewer Text UK Ltd, Edinburgh
Printed and bound in Great Britain by Clays Ltd, Elcograf S.p.A.

Hodder & Stoughton policy is to use papers that are natural, renewable
and recyclable products and made from wood grown in sustainable
forests. The logging and manufacturing processes are expected to
conform to the environmental regulations of the country of origin.

Hodder & Stoughton Ltd
Carmelite House
50 Victoria Embankment
London EC4Y 0DZ

www.hodder.co.uk

For Dom

I

It wasn't that DI Helen Birch *hated* Monday mornings, per se. She just wished they didn't have to be so full of emails. Every Monday morning, she drove towards her office at Fettes Avenue police station with a mounting petulance: she didn't *want* to do emails. She had so many other things to do. It wasn't fair. It certainly wasn't what she'd signed up to the police force for, over fourteen years ago. And on this particular Monday morning, she'd rather have been anywhere other than in front of her computer screen. It was the second day of September, and still summery. Leaving her little house on the Portobello promenade earlier had felt like a real bind, with the sun already shining full on the beach and the wet sand reflecting it back in stripes of pinkish gold. As she'd driven through town, Birch had passed fluorescent-vested men working in teams to take down Fringe Festival posters and dismantle hoarding. Edinburgh was basking in a quiet, post-Festival glow.

'And what have I got to do?' Birch muttered to herself as she flopped into her office chair. 'Bloody emails, is what.'

She nibbled at the edge of her cardboard coffee cup as she waited for the inbox to load, and show her this Monday's figure of doom. Seventy-six unread.

'Really?' Birch leaned forward and squinted at the number. She hadn't misread it. 'Haven't people got better things to do with their weekends?'

'Everything okay, marm?'

Birch jumped, then felt herself blush. She'd been caught talking to herself. 'Jesus, Kato. You ever thought about switching to the other side? You'd make a great cat burglar.'

DC Amy Kato was standing in her office doorway. 'Sorry,' she said. 'I did knock.'

Birch blinked. Amy was wearing her trademark high heels. She must have made a racket, in fact, walking up to the door.

'Seems I was miles away,' she said. 'But don't worry, nothing's up. Just . . . having a coffee and feeding my resentment over the great injustices of this life, you know?'

Amy smiled, but then frowned, worried that her boss might not be joking. 'Yes, marm.'

Birch laughed. 'Ignore me,' she said. 'I'm just being daft. What can I do you for?'

Amy glanced back over her shoulder. 'I've just come through reception,' she said. 'There's a bloke downstairs wanting to report two missing persons.'

'Two?'

'Yeah, that's what he said. Desk sergeant's sent me up to find someone to talk to him. He says he'll only speak to someone senior. He seems a bit . . . well, belligerent.'

Birch rolled her eyes. 'Oh great, one of those.'

''fraid so, marm. And you seem to be the only DI in the building who isn't terribly busy.'

Birch fluttered her eyelashes at her friend. 'Who, me?' she said. 'I'm busy! I'm tied in absolute *knots*, in fact.'

Amy grinned. 'You literally just said you were sitting drinking coffee and . . . erm—'

'Resenting the great injustices of this life, yes, Kato. That's very important work.'

'I don't doubt it.' Amy was still grinning, but she'd begun to back out of the door again, beckoning Birch to follow. 'I'm just not sure this gent downstairs would see it that way.'

Birch downed her coffee. 'All right, all right,' she said. 'I'll just nip to the Ladies and make myself look a little more *senior*. Tell this guy – what's his name?'

'Robertson Bennet.'

Birch raised an eyebrow. 'Wow, okay, quite the handle. Tell him I'll be down in five.'

*　　*　　*

Birch flopped down the stairs, having tucked some stray wisps of hair into her ponytail and wiped the lipstick off her front teeth. Waiting for her in reception was perhaps the widest-set man she had ever seen. He wasn't fat, rather his body looked triangular: huge shoulders and a barrel chest tapered down to a pair of surprisingly small feet. He was also ginger-haired, though more tawny than carrot-topped. He was well groomed, but looked about as Scottish as it was possible for a person to look.

'Mr Bennet?'

The man looked in her direction. Birch walked across the lobby, her hand extended.

'DI Helen Birch,' she said. 'I came down as soon as I could.'

With some difficulty, the big man unfolded himself from his chair. These days, thanks to Anjan, Birch knew a made-to-measure suit when she saw one. She also noted the giant Rolex on Mr Bennet's wrist.

'At last,' he said, and shook her hand. 'Robertson Bennet.' The man paused, and then, as if he couldn't help himself, added, 'ReadThis CEO.'

'Pleased to meet you,' Birch said. She glanced over at the desk, catching the eye of the custody sergeant on duty.

'John,' she called over, guessing at the name and apparently getting it right, as the sergeant looked up. 'Do you have a room free?'

Robertson Bennet didn't seem too impressed by the tiny meeting room Birch had squeezed him into, and he sighed his way through her preliminary questions about his own personal details.

'In the event that we open a case on this, we need to be able to contact you,' she said, trying to keep her voice light. 'I promise you, this is standard procedure for everyone, Mr Bennet.'

Bennet huffed a final time, but coughed up the required information. His accent was unusual: he was Scottish for sure, but with an American inflection. Some of his *t*s came out like *d*s. The home address he gave was in California.

'Now,' Birch said. 'I'm going to take notes while you talk, and I may well ask questions as we go to make sure I have all the information I need.'

'That's fine.'

'Great. So, tell me why you've come in to see us.'

The man shifted in his seat, settling, showing her he meant business. 'I want to report two missing persons,' he said. 'My parents. They've both disappeared.'

'I'm sorry to hear that,' Birch said. She was doing maths in her head: Bennet's date of birth made him fifty-eight, though he looked younger. That meant his parents could be pretty elderly. 'Can you tell me the last time you saw your parents, or had contact with them?'

'Yes: 1986.'

Birch blinked. She'd been expecting him to say *last week*. 'Nineteen eighty-six,' she said, stringing the words out a little, to check she'd heard him correctly. 'Over thirty years ago.'

'That's right. We're, ah, we have been . . . estranged.'

Birch was trying not to make a face at the man. Is this a wind-up? she wondered. But no: Bennet looked serious.

'Tell you what,' she said. 'I'm just going to let you talk for a bit. Tell me what's happened.'

'Well, basically . . . I'm a computer nerd, Detective Inspector,' Bennet said. Birch tried to keep her expression even: this wasn't where she'd expected him to start. 'One of the original nerds. Bill Gates, Steve Jobs, all those guys – I'm one of those guys.'

Oh God, she thought, this is a wind-up. But Bennet was still speaking.

'This all started,' he said, 'because as a teenager I was all about computing. I read up about it in the library, could see the potential where most people couldn't – my teachers, the school careers adviser, they all thought it was a fad. I wanted to build robots, that was the dream, had been ever since I was a little boy. So I knew I needed to get into computer programming. When I left school I decided I was moving to the USA. That was where it was all going on back then. My parents were dead against the idea. They were sheltered folks, and they had ambitions for me that they thought were grand: teacher, accountant. They didn't believe that robotics engineer or computer programmer were real jobs. They were small-minded people, and we got into a lot of fights.'

Birch was nodding. She couldn't really see where this was going, but Bennet didn't show any signs of pausing, so she let him speak on.

'I was still living under their roof in my mid-twenties, and I'd had enough. I was doing menial, meaningless jobs, earning barely anything. They made me pay rent – *rent*, to live in the family home – deliberately, I think. They didn't want me saving enough money to move to America. But one day, after a particularly bad fight, I'd had enough. I went to the building society and talked the clerk into letting me empty my father's account. I used the money to buy a one-way ticket to California. San Jose, to be precise. Silicon Valley.'

'You stole from them.' Birch gave him her best *let me remind you that you are speaking to a police officer* face.

'Borrowed,' he said. 'I even said that to them at the time. That I was going to make something of myself in the US, and I'd be able to pay them back a hundred times over. They didn't understand.'

He waited, as though expecting Birch to reprimand him. Once upon a time she would have done, and would have repri-manded his parents, too: she used to hate cases where people failed to report obvious, open-and-shut crimes. But these days – thanks to her little brother, Charlie – she felt less able to pass judgement. She understood the logic of covering for a family member.

'So you left.'

'I did. That was 1985. I tried to keep in contact with them for the first few months – called home a couple of times, and then later I wrote letters. My mother would talk to me if my father was out, but if he was there he'd make her put the phone down. I never got a letter back from either of them.'

Birch made a note, in shorthand: mother forgave him, father did not. 'Then what?' she asked.

At this, Bennet's face lit up. He sat back in his seat, and spread his hands. He suddenly looked rather like a Bond villain. 'I made it big, Detective Inspector.'

'In . . . robotics?'

He laughed. 'No. No, I never did get to live out my childhood fantasies. I went to work for Xerox, initially.'

'The photocopier people?'

He laughed again, and pointed a finger at her. *Good one.* 'That's what they're famous for now, but in the eighties they were all about programming. I worked with them alongside 3Com on Ethernet.'

Birch realised her face must have gone blank.

'Don't worry,' he said, 'most people react that way. I worked in . . . connectivity. The early internet. After a while I moved to 3Com itself, then I went solo. Got into dot-coms in the nineties and made my first big money, then went on to start-ups after the bubble burst. These days I'm an apps man.'

Birch's head felt like it was spinning. 'Okay,' she said. 'I should tell you I can barely work my phone. Is it important that I understand this stuff?'

Bennet's smile faded a little: he'd encountered a Luddite. 'Not at all,' he said. 'In fact, I ought to get back to the point. My parents.'

'Yes.'

'I tried to get back in touch with them, in the early nineties. By that time I'd stopped the calling and the writing. I was busy, and I guess I was mad at them, too, for not understanding. But I decided to get back in touch and pay back what I'd borrowed.'

Stolen, Birch thought, but she didn't say anything.

'I called their home number but they never answered. I wrote. I asked them how I could wire them the money. I wrote maybe four times. I never got any reply.'

'And after that?'

Bennet drew himself up a little taller in his chair. 'After those four or so letters, I stopped,' he said. 'I figured they'd made their decision. They'd cut me off. They didn't care that I'd done it, that I'd made my way in the world like I always said I would. They never wanted that for me.'

My heart bleeds, Birch thought, looking again at the man's tailored suit, diamond-studded watch, spotless brogues.

'That was the last contact I ever made, or tried to make,' he said. 'Until now.'

Birch scribbled a note. 'That was the early nineties, you said? Any chance you remember what year?'

'It was 1992,' Bennet said. 'Maybe.'

'Okay, Mr Bennet.' Birch took a deep inhale. 'Now you've decided to make contact with your parents again, can I ask . . . how extensively have you looked for them?'

The man frowned. 'What do you mean?'

'Well, given that you haven't seen them in over thirty years, isn't it possible that they've simply moved away? Rather than being officially missing, I mean.'

Bennet blinked at her. 'Well, I hoped you'd find that out for me.'

She fixed him with a look. 'With respect, Mr Bennet,' she said, 'you've come to Police Scotland, not Friends Reunited.'

Stop it, Helen, she thought, you'll end up with a complaint made. But to her surprise, the man smiled.

'Lordy, your tech knowledge really *is* rusty, isn't it, Detective Inspector? Friends Reunited? Really?'

Birch realised she was blushing again, and hated herself for it. 'What I mean is,' she said, 'finding out where people have moved to in recent times doesn't really fall under the sort of investigative work we do. Perhaps American police officers have the resources at their disposal for such things, but I'm afraid we really don't.'

Bennet sighed. 'I've done all I can to find them,' he said. 'I've visited the house. The people living there now have no forwarding address. The real estate agent who sold the house won't tell me anything because of your data protection laws over here. I've tracked their online presence, both of them, not that it amounts to much. They don't seem to have active social media accounts, no surprise there.'

'Do you have siblings?'

'Only child,' Bennet said.

'Aunts, uncles? Friends?'

He shrugged. 'My mother had a sister, but she died when I was a kid. I've found a handful of the friends I remember my father having – found them on Facebook, I mean, and tried to get in touch. No dice: mostly their accounts haven't been logged into in years, so they haven't seen my messages, or if they have they don't seem to want to talk. No doubt my parents let them know *their* side of the story. Maybe they've all just died.'

Birch winced. 'I was going to ask, Mr Bennet,' she said. 'I'm sorry to have to do so, but – is it possible your parents could be deceased? I imagine they'd be quite elderly now.'

'Don't be sorry.' Bennet waved a hand. 'It was the very first thing I checked myself. But I can't find any death records, any obituaries. Nothing like that. They'll both be in their eighties now, so, sure, I knew that was a possibility. But they're not dead, more's the pity.'

Birch started. Bennet noticed, and let out a short laugh, as though trying to pass the comment off as a joke.

'Why do you say that, Mr Bennet?' Birch rolled out the *you're speaking to a police officer* face again.

Bennet squirmed. He held up his hands. 'All right, all right,' he said. 'It's about money, okay? Everything seems to be about money when it comes to my parents. I haven't been back in Scotland for thirty years or more, never wanted to be – pardon me for saying this, Detective Inspector, but it's a damned parochial country. So no, I'm not here for some tearful reunion. The fact is . . .'

He was sweating. Birch glanced at the box of tissues on the table between them, but thought better of suggesting he wipe his brow.

'The fact is,' he said, 'I'm here for my inheritance, okay?'

2

'So how did you leave it?'

Amy was sitting on the other side of Birch's desk, warming her hands around a polystyrene cup of canteen soup. She was so engrossed in the story that she hadn't so much as taken a sip, though her lunch break was almost over.

'I sent him away with a flea in his ear,' Birch said. She glanced up at her office door for about the sixth time, checking it was still closed. 'Told him his parents were probably in a lovely retirement home somewhere, having a grand old time.'

'If that's the case, a private investigator's what he needs,' Amy said. 'Not us.'

Birch nodded. 'I did hint at that,' she said, 'though not in so many words. But I also said that people have a right to privacy. He was a bit upset about data protection. I think he thought he'd be able to sweet-talk people into telling him more than he's entitled to know.'

Amy did a theatrical eye-roll. 'Americans,' she said. 'Plus, he works in tech, right? The internet? Those guys like to think they can poke into anyone's business. It's creepy. I'd swear blind that my phone listens to me. Like, I'll mention something really random to someone, something I haven't thought about in years or typed into a search engine maybe *ever*, and what do you know? The next time I open Facebook there's an ad in the sidebar for that exact thing. It freaks me out.'

Birch grinned. 'The wonders of modern technology,' she said. 'But yeah, he seemed irritated that his parents weren't, I don't know, putting their wee caravan trips to Troon up all over Instagram, or whatever.'

'Now now, marm.' Amy wagged a finger. 'There're plenty of older people on social media these days, doing all sorts of cool stuff, I'm sure. Don't be ageist.'

'Wouldn't dream of it.' Birch flipped open her sandwich, and wrinkled her nose. 'But answer me this, Kato: why do they put cucumber in every single sandwich in that bloody canteen?'

Amy was frowning. 'I wouldn't be surprised if they'd done it deliberately,' she said.

'The canteen staff?'

Amy's frown disappeared, and she raised an eyebrow at Birch. 'Sure, them too – but I meant Bennet's parents. Maybe they made themselves un-findable. I sure as hell wouldn't be interested in hearing from someone who'd nicked all *my* savings, only son or not.'

'Hmm.' Birch was thinking about Charlie again, of the things she'd forgiven her brother for. But not all families were the same.

'Anyway,' Amy said, finally taking a mouthful of her soup. 'One less thing to add to the workload, eh, marm?'

Birch glanced up at the door again. 'You're not wrong,' she said. 'Like I say, none of this goes any further. I know it hasn't turned into a case, but you know . . .'

'Oh come on.' Amy snorted. 'You know you can trust little old me. If anyone asks – and nobody will – you told me nothing. He showed up, I came to get you, you talked to him, he left. I'm pretty sure anyone who saw him here would assume he was a crank anyway. That or a lawyer, dressed the way he was.'

Birch allowed herself to think of Anjan Chaudhry – her personal favourite lawyer – and smiled.

'Oh don't,' Amy said. 'You bloody loved-up types make me sick. Don't you know I'm perpetually single?'

Birch laughed. 'Single my eye. You're out on dates every other night!'

'Dating doesn't mean you're not single.' Amy looked at her nails. 'Perusing the menu isn't the same as eating, is it?'

'You're terrible. Those poor men.'

Amy grinned. 'It's their own fault for being so disappointing.'

Birch waggled her eyebrows at her friend. 'Maybe it's your fault for being so picky?'

'Pfft, nonsense. You may not realise this, but there aren't all that many tall, smart, handsome lawyers around. You just got lucky.'

Birch tried not to preen. Amy's dating record was, admittedly, disastrous. She opened her mouth to wisecrack back, but before she could speak, the phone on her desk rang.

'DI Birch.'

It was John, the desk sergeant. 'I'm sorry to bother you, marm,' he said. His tone was pointed: he was saying it for someone else's benefit. 'But your . . . visitor, from earlier. He's back at reception, and asking to speak to you again.'

Birch's heart sank, and her face must have done the same, because Amy frowned at her and mouthed, *What?*

'There in two shakes, John,' she said, and put down the receiver.

'Everything okay?' Amy asked.

Birch dumped her sandwich on the desk, and stood up. 'I'm afraid Mr Robertson Bennet is downstairs once more,' she said.

'Oh God. Persistent, isn't he?'

Birch squinted at her laptop to check the time. Bennet had only been gone a couple of hours. 'Looks to be,' she said. 'Come down with me, would you? I'd like a partner on this one, just in case things get . . . vexatious.'

Amy jumped to her feet, and a little splat of soup landed on her jacket sleeve. 'Damn it,' she said, swiping at the wet patch. 'Sorry – I mean, with you all the way.'

This time, Bennet didn't want to wait to be shown into another room. He began speaking as soon as Birch rounded the corner into reception.

'What if I told you,' he said, 'that I believe my mother's life to be in danger?'

Birch threw a glance to John: *we might have trouble on our hands here.* He took the hint, and stepped out from behind the desk.

'I want to report my mother missing,' Bennet was saying, his voice raised. 'And I have reason to believe my father may have hurt her.'

Birch had crossed the lobby now, but Bennet didn't wait for her to speak. Instead, he thrust his mobile phone out towards her, roughly at eye level. 'A local news report,' he said, 'detailing that police were called to a domestic disturbance at my parents' house, while they still lived there. My father was taken into custody, and my mother to hospital.'

Birch squinted at the screen.

'In addition,' Bennet said, 'I have personal testimony, years of it. My father is a domestic abuser, and I believe that if something bad has happened to my mother, he's at the bottom of it.'

He was still holding the phone in Birch's face. She looked past it, fixing her gaze on him. 'If that is the case, Mr Bennet,' she said, 'why didn't you tell me earlier?'

Bennet lowered the phone. 'Because I thought you'd help me,' he said, 'without needing to know that sort of personal information.'

Birch glanced around. Bennet didn't seem to grasp the irony in the fact that he was speaking, loudly, in a public space that, along with police personnel, contained a handful of members of the general public. She tried, in her head, to accuse him of fabrication; of nipping out for an hour or so to spin a yarn that might make his case more credible. But she couldn't.

'Yes,' Bennet said, 'my tech company's sinking. Yes, I need money. Yes, that's why I came back to Scotland. But the longer I look for my parents and can't find them, the longer I think about it, the more I fear that my father has done something to my mother. Something bad. I need to find out if she's okay. And to do that, you have to let me report her missing.'

Amy was at Birch's side. John was standing close to Bennet, having placed himself within cuffing distance. Birch looked at all their faces, Amy's last. The *Edinburgh Evening News* article that was still visible on Bennet's phone screen was dated 2013. A while ago, but not ancient history. Bennet's mother would have been in her seventies then. In her seventies, and hospitalised by her husband.

Birch closed her eyes. *Shit.* 'John,' she said, 'show Mr Bennet back to Room 03, will you? I'll nip back to my office and get his previous statement.'

Bennet turned towards John, ready to be led away.

'Here we go,' Amy whispered.

Birch gave a grim nod. 'Oh, and get him a cup of tea, will you, John? This may be a long interview.'

3

'George MacDonald,' Bennet said. 'M-*a*-c. Like the writer.'

This time, Amy was in the little meeting room with them, and she took the notes. She was faster at it than Birch, and used real shorthand, rather than Birch's own half-made-up version. Birch, meanwhile, asked the questions, and scrutinised Bennet as he spoke.

'You don't have the same name as your father,' she observed.

'I changed it,' Bennet said, 'by deed poll. It wasn't working for me in America. My birth name was Robert MacDonald. Sounds like a geography teacher. I needed something more . . . tech. More memorable. Google-able.'

'Interesting,' Birch said. The name-change sounded like vanity, but then, she'd never had any business sense. 'And your mother's name?'

She prayed it was something less ten-a-penny than George MacDonald.

'Phamie,' he said.

Amy paused in her scribbling. 'Spell that for me?' she said.

'P-h-a-m-i-e,' Bennet said. It's short for Euphemia. But she never went by her full name, always Phamie.'

'Maiden name?' Birch asked.

'Innes.'

Okay, thank goodness. There wouldn't be all that many Euphemia Inneses around.

Birch nodded to Amy. 'I have the last known address from Mr Bennet's previous statement. Morningside, you said, Mr Bennet?'

'Yes. It's a terraced house, smallish. Nothing fancy.'

I'll be the judge of that, Birch thought. Morningside was the city's most affluent area.

'Tell us about your father,' she said.

Bennet took a deep breath. 'Okay. Well, he was kind of an asshole. I mean, fathers *were* back when I was growing up … they'd got rid of the belt in my school, but you bet your ass it still got used in plenty of folks' homes.'

Amy scribbled.

'But in my dad's case, it was manipulation. My mother didn't work when I was a little kid, and she had no money of her own, except what he gave her. So he had power over her. She'd get worried sick about him, 'cause he was always disappearing. Sometimes just for an evening, and he'd come back late at night. But sometimes for days at a time. I think he did it just to scare her. Just to remind her that without him, she'd have no way to live.'

'Where did he go?' Birch asked. 'Was he drinking?'

'Sure, sometimes,' Bennet said. 'But no more than most men drink. Mainly he was down at the railway.'

'The railway?'

'He was obsessed with trains. He was one of those guys who stand on train platforms and write down when trains come in and go out. I think you still have them here, right? They must be real lone wolves now. But back then it was a hobby. My dad had a bunch of friends who did it.'

'Trainspotting,' Amy said, and Bennet laughed.

'Yeah, that has a whole new meaning now, right? But I swear to God, that's where he used to go. Hang out with a bunch of other grown men and look at trains. Then go to the pub and talk about trains. He had train sets at home – kids' toys, though I was never allowed to touch them. He pored over those notebooks of his: stations, engine numbers, timetables. I never understood it. Still don't.'

Birch wrinkled her nose. She didn't buy this, entirely. In her experience, men didn't disappear for days at a time solely because of a hobby. That might be the excuse they gave, but there had to be more to it. Bennet was a kid at the time, and likely to swallow whatever line he was fed.

'Do you think there might have been anything else keeping your father away from home?'

Bennet sighed. 'My mother was certain there was another woman, other women, whatever. I don't think either of us ever saw any evidence of it. She just couldn't believe he was *that* fanatical about trains.'

Her and me both, Birch thought.

'Honestly? Maybe there was other stuff. Women, drink, whatever. But whenever my mother confronted him, she'd get backhanded. Meant she stopped asking where he'd been, pretty quick.'

Beside her, Birch could feel Amy's resentment towards Bennet's father glowing, like the heat of a small flame.

'He always came back, though. It sounds twisted, but I believe he loved my mother more than anything. He was a little obsessed with her, in fact. He'd buy her red roses, treat her like porcelain, especially after . . . they'd fought. He called her his princess. That's what makes it hard for me to believe there were other women. He loved her so much, in spite of everything.'

You don't hit someone you love, Birch thought. But Bennet's father did sound fairly textbook. Domestic abusers often showered their victims with adoration, especially in the wake of an attack.

Across the table, Bennet was musing. 'I believe,' he said, 'that the reason we never got on, my old man and me, was 'cause he was jealous of me. I came along and took her away from him. Took up so much of her attention. He wasn't the apple of her eye any more.'

Of course, Birch thought. Bennet lived in America: he'd have been to therapy. He had it all figured out. But how could he have left, when he knew his mother was at risk from this man?

'He wasn't unusual, you know.' Bennet had seen what she was thinking. 'Most of the kids I hung out with, their dads were like him. Bitter. Sometimes violent. Liked to keep to themselves and not be questioned. It was just how men *were*. Part of the reason I left was, I could see myself getting like that, getting like him, if I stayed working in dead-end jobs, giving up the dreams I had. He was normal, the default. I remember when I was maybe eight, our next-door neighbour had had enough and called the police, saying she'd heard a ruckus. My mother answered the door with a fresh black eye. The policeman said someone had complained about noise, and could you please keep it down in future, Mrs MacDonald? It was that normal of a thing. *Expected*, even.'

Birch winced. She gave thanks for the past five decades of progress in policing.

'What did your father do for a living, Mr Bennet?'

Bennet grimaced. 'Sanitary inspector,' he said. 'We did all right financially 'cause he got danger money. Going down in the sewers and stuff.'

'He worked for the council?'

'Yes. All the time I lived with him, anyway.'

'And your mother? You said she didn't work.'

Bennet nodded. 'She did after I went to high school,' he said. 'She worked for the post office, part time. For pocket money, my dad used to say, though he took it all off her anyway. She'd get paid in cash, and didn't have a bank account of her own.'

'Which post office, do you remember?'

'Bruntsfield,' Bennet said. 'I used to walk there and meet her after school sometimes. I went to James Gillespie's.'

Amy scribbled.

'Okay. We're nearly done here, I think. Can I just ask, did either of your parents have any haunts? Places they went often? Places they made an effort to go on trips to, things like that?'

Bennet thought for a moment. 'My dad went to all sorts of stations,' he said. 'Sometimes on his own, and sometimes with his pals. I used to look at his notebooks occasionally, when he was out. Trying to figure out the appeal, or something. He liked to go out to Carstairs, though. He went there most often.'

'Carstairs?'

'Yeah. Don't ask me why.'

'Any other haunts? Particular pubs?'

'I know he drank in a pub with a weird name, near Waverley Station – could it be Jingling Georgie?' Bennet hazarded. 'He took me in there a couple of times, when I was small.'

'Geordie.' Birch sighed inwardly. The Jinglin' Geordie had cleaned up its act a lot in recent years, but it had been the site of plenty of trouble in its time. It made sense that George MacDonald might drink there. It was the pub historically favoured by railwaymen.

She glanced over at Amy, who'd paused in her note-taking. Birch would fill her in on the pub's chequered past later.

'And your mother?'

Bennet laughed. 'My mother was a home bird,' he said. 'Didn't like to be out on her own, except to take me to school, and then when I was older, to go to work. But those were duties to her, you know? Duty was all she really did. Housework. Gardening. She did love her gardening. But that was pretty much her whole life.'

Honestly, Birch thought. The things women used to have to settle for.

'The only haunt she had, if you can call it that,' Bennet said, 'was the next-door neighbour's house. Mrs . . . oh, something, it's too long ago. Next door at number 24. She'd go round there for a cup of tea quite often. They were pals.'

'You're sure you can't remember this woman's name?'

Bennet frowned, but then shook his head. 'Nope, it's gone,' he said. 'For ever into the mists of time. Like so many things.'

Edinburgh Evening News

77-year-old man taken into custody following 'domestic disturbance' in Morningside

ROBIN BLAKE   Published 11:44   Share this article
Email   18 December 2013

Officers were called to an address near Craigs Park Road following reports from neighbours of a 'serious domestic disturbance'.

When police arrived on the scene, an ambulance was called and a 78-year-old woman was taken to the Edinburgh Royal Infirmary.

A 78-year-old man has been taken into custody. Police Scotland have declined to comment at this time.

4

Birch left the office a little early that night, to allow for the drive to HMP Low Moss. She didn't usually go to the jail on a Monday: the Sunday Family and Friends session was her favourite. The prison wasn't as busy on a Sunday, and something about the sabbath day seemed to leak in through the high fences and concrete. From 3.30 p.m. to 4.30 p.m. every week, inmates from all halls of HMP Low Moss were ushered into the Visit Room, and allowed to sit with their mammies and aunties and weans in a special kind of Sunday afternoon hush. Birch was there every week, without fail: as faithful to the jail as her mother had been to the good old Church of Scotland. But that Saturday afternoon, she'd received a phone call to say that Charlie wouldn't be available for his usual Sunday visit, and would she be able to attend one of the week-night visits? Birch had pressed for a reason, but the prison officer was tight-lipped. She had no choice but to agree to it, but as she locked her car in the prison car park she felt a sting of irritation. She didn't like having to cut out of work early, but she was always there for the full hour of visiting. She was, after all, the only visitor her little brother ever got.

'Evening, Tommy.'

Birch approached the reception desk with her well-practised smile pasted on. The screws weren't keen on her: as a police officer, she was tricky to accommodate. She knew more about how prisons worked than the average visitor. She wasn't intimidated by the metal detectors and the keyfobs and the doors upon doors upon doors. Trickiest of all: there were men in this prison that she'd put away. A couple were good-natured about it: one would even smile and wave if he was there when she walked into the Visit Room. But her presence in the jail each week made the screws stand up just that little bit straighter, hands hovering near their radio packs, just in case.

Officer Tommy Swinton sometimes manned the reception on Sundays, so knew her well. He gave her a tight smile. 'Inspector Birch,' he said, and held out his hand.

Birch passed over her ID to be logged in the system, and then stood still. There was a click as Tommy took her photo with the little webcam-style camera suspended over the reception desk.

'Handbag,' he said. 'Pockets.'

He placed a grey plastic tray on the desk in front of her. This part always reminded Birch of going through airport security. It was warm – September had decided to start out kind this year – and she'd left her coat in the car. She fumbled in her jeans pockets: keys, her phone, a few coins. She dumped her handbag into the tray, too, then turned away and stepped through the metal detector. *Clean*.

Tommy handed her a locker fob with a number on it. 'We'll call you through,' he said.

Birch zipped away all the change but for a pound coin, which she inserted into her allotted locker's coin slot. Other visitors were arriving, too: to her right, a young woman with three small children in tow was trying to cram the last of her possessions into one of the narrow lockers. Tommy had tied a tag to the pushchair she'd brought, and sent for another prison officer to put it somewhere secure. Birch wondered where. The woman clanged the locker door shut, but it ricocheted back open, and a tiny backpack, red with black spots like the wings of a ladybird, fell out on to the floor.

'Shit fuck,' the woman said, and the children gasped in unison.

'Mammy, you said a swear.' The biggest of them, a boy, was laughing as he said it. He looked like he'd been sweeping a chimney: below the miniature buzzcut his neck was practically black.

The woman reached down past her son and snatched up the backpack. As she straightened, she caught Birch's eye.

'Bastards, eh?' she said. She was speaking loudly, aiming her words at the reception desk and Tommy. 'Wan locker fer me an aw these weans! Fit barely anything in these. See wintertime, wi' the thick coats an that? Ye jist cannae.'

Birch opened her mouth to speak, but Tommy called out across the reception hall. 'You can have another locker, Mrs McGuire. You can have as many lockers as are free.'

The young woman half spat her reply. 'Aye, bit they're no free, are they, ya bastard. Nine outtae ten times ye dinnae get yer money back. Ye think I've pound coins coming oot ma ears? I've the bus hame tae think aboot, pal.'

Tommy simply shrugged.

Birch held out her hand towards Mrs McGuire. 'Let me take that,' she said, gesturing at the backpack. 'There's plenty of space in mine.'

The woman cocked her head. She looked at Birch's outstretched hand, her expression at once surprised, grateful and suspicious.

'Naw,' she said, after a moment. 'Naw, I'll manage.'

The Visit Room reminded Birch of a service station café. Everything was plastic but for the carpet tiles, and the walls were unadorned. There was only a whiteboard, near the main door, where a few posters for forthcoming activities in the prison were pinned. Reading group in the library, places limited. Induction for PIP prisoners, Monday 10.15 a.m. The week's visiting schedule: a laminated Excel spreadsheet. Every week she felt a pang of horrible sympathy for her brother, shut up in this place, and every week she had to remind herself why he was here.

The prisoners were shown in first, and seated at their assigned, individual tables. Birch waited with the other visitors – almost all women, as usual – behind a door with a glass partition, through which she could see a snapshot of about twenty men, though not her brother. At this distance, they all looked alike: the prisoners here wore black sweatshirts, unless they were on remand, in which case they wore green. The prison barber seemed to offer one style of haircut only. Everyone was pale, whether from limited diet or lack of sun, Birch wasn't sure.

A buzzer sounded and the door opened. The assembled women filed in carefully: you could always tell a new prisoner, because his visitors displayed more emotion, hadn't yet learned to keep their gestures small and deliberate. Charlie was always seated in the far corner, and each week Birch skirted the room in an L shape to reach him. She didn't make eye contact with anyone: didn't even look Charlie in the face until she'd sat down opposite him. This time, she'd barely found her seat when she jumped out of it again.

'Holy *Jesus*,' she said. 'What the *hell* happened?'

Her brother's mouth tightened. People were looking. Birch glanced up, and saw one of the prison officers gesturing to her to sit, and quiet down. She obliged, mouthing, *Sorry*.

'It's all right, Nella,' Charlie said. His voice was thick, a little slurred. 'It's not as bad as it looks.'

Birch leaned forward over the table. Half of Charlie's face was purple. His right eye was swollen shut, and his cheek looked weird, somehow wrong. His bottom lip had been split on the right-hand side, and he worried at the dry cut with the tip of his tongue. So *this* was why he'd been unavailable for her usual visit. He'd had the shit kicked out of him.

'Really,' he said. 'Don't freak out, it's fine.'

'Charles Arthur Birch,' she said. 'You can't downplay *that*.'

Charlie replied softly, wanting her to lower her voice. 'It was a wee scrap. You know it's not the Hilton I'm staying in. This is just the jail.'

Birch raised an eyebrow. 'That' – she pointed to his swollen eye, the lashes jagged between folds of bruised flesh – 'was not *a wee scrap*. You're going to tell me what happened.'

'You sound like Maw.' Charlie attempted a smile, and Birch saw he had teeth missing.

'*Char*lie!'

'Shh, Nella. Keep your hair on. They're saying I'll see the dentist in a few days, when the swelling goes down. Like I said, it's just the jail. Stuff like this happens.'

Birch deliberately hadn't looked at the other inmates, but nevertheless, she gestured vaguely at the general congregation. 'Really? I don't see anyone else in here looking like they got hit by a car.'

Charlie shrugged. 'Well, I guess my number was up this time.'

Her brother was maddening. She sat back in her chair, folded her arms, and fixed him with her best scowl. '*Tell* me,' she said, through her teeth, 'what happened.'

Charlie sighed. 'I'll make you a deal,' he said. 'I'll tell you what happened, as long as you promise not to make a *thing* of it.'

'Make a *thing*? I—'

'I mean it, Nella. No writing to the governor or demanding an audience with the screws, or – any sort of preferential treatment, okay? I'm trying to fit in here, get on with it, you know? It's bad enough that every fucker in here knows my sister's a DI. I'll tell you, but you have to let me handle it.'

Birch raised an eyebrow.

'My*self*, I mean,' her brother added, 'on my own.'

She tutted. 'By handle it, I expect you mean you'll do nothing.'

'Probably.'

Birch snorted. Looking at Charlie's mashed-up face was hard, so she risked a glance to one side. Mrs McGuire was a few tables over. Her prisoner – husband? Cousin? Brother? – was dandling the smallest of her children on his knee, while she repeatedly shushed the other two. Looking at the younger woman did make Birch realise her privilege: if Mrs McGuire's prisoner was beaten in jail, she'd never think to talk to an officer about it, or write to the governor. She wouldn't be listened to, and she'd know that. Things would just have to work themselves out, or not.

Birch turned back to her brother. 'Fine,' she said. 'Just tell me.'

Charlie huffed out air. It whistled in the gap where one of his teeth used to be. 'Okay. There's this lad in here – I'm not going to tell you his name, so don't even ask – who's always giving it the Barry. Stirring shit, starting fights, intimidation, you know. Prison stuff. Power games, I guess. Anyway, he must have got interested in me, because lately he's started . . . well, they've all got nicknames in here, you know. He decided mine ought to be *Cucumber*. And he's got all the lads calling me it. That's how it started.'

Birch frowned. Her slang was a little rusty. 'Cucumber?'

'Yeah, took me a while to figure it out too.' Charlie winced. 'It means a grass. One who gets extra protection for his own safety.'

She felt her frown deepen. 'But you don't,' she said. 'We tried to make the case, but—'

'You and I know that,' Charlie said. 'This guy doesn't. Or he doesn't care.'

'So . . . your face?'

Charlie shrugged. 'He's in my hall,' he said. 'They were moving us, yesterday morning. I got in the middle of the pack. He cornered me, him and some pals of his. He . . .' Charlie trailed off, cringing a little.

'Tell me,' Birch said, 'I'm a big girl, I can handle it.'

'He got hold of my neck,' Charlie said, 'and slammed my face into the wall. A few times, fast, like *wham wham wham wham*.'

Now it was Birch's turn to cringe. Her own neck retracted into her shoulders.

'Then they took off, yelling this *cucumber* shite. 'See, that's what happens, ner-ner, giving it all that.' Charlie flapped one hand, *yadda yadda*. 'It was so quick, no one saw. Or no one's saying they saw.'

Birch felt like her insides were boiling. '*Bas*tards,' she spat.

'Yeah.' Charlie looked down at his lap. He was quiet for a moment, letting his sister fume.

'He's not even that old,' he said, after a moment had passed. 'He got starred up from the young offenders just recently.'

'Little shit. Absolute little—'

'Nella.' Charlie put one hand, palm down, on the table between them. 'Calm down. You promised.'

Birch bit her lip. She made herself count to ten, though it didn't much help. She wanted to know if the kid who'd done this to her brother was in the room with them, right now, breathing the same air. She knew that if he was, Charlie would never say so.

A thought occurred to her. 'Did you retaliate at all?'

Charlie looked a little shamefaced. 'Didn't get a chance, did I? They just jumped me. Like I said, it was fast.' He straightened up in his chair. 'But besides, I'm trying to keep my nose clean, remember? Good behaviour.'

Birch nodded. 'I remember,' she said.

He was attempting to smile again. 'It's almost a relief, in a way,' he said. 'I mean, we knew this was coming. I grassed out the biggest crime fraternity in Glasgow. I got Solomon Carradice locked up. It's a wonder I've lasted this long without getting malkied.'

She couldn't believe her brother was so sanguine, though she had to admit there was some truth in what he'd said. 'But—' The protestation sounded feeble, but she ploughed on. 'That's why you're in here, and Solomon and his lot are in Barlinnie. You were supposed to be *safe*. You were given a deal . . .'

Charlie was laughing at her, as much as his battered face would allow. 'Nella, you know fine well that some jumped-up Billy Bigbaws in the jail gives precisely no fucks about what deal I got. Like I said, this isn't the Hilton.'

She was starting to get a headache from frowning. 'You think this is Solomon's doing, though? That he put the kid up to this somehow?'

Her brother shrugged again. 'It's possible. There's plenty of chat between this place and the Bar-L. But to be honest with you, I reckon if this was a message from Solomon.' Charlie pointed at his face. 'I'd know about it. He'd want me to know, for sure, that it had come from him. And for Solomon's boys, this is playground stuff. Amateur. If it came from Solomon I'd expect the lad to've chibbed me, at least.'

Birch shuddered. This phrase she did know: *to chib*. Slang for a stabbing.

'Jesus, Charlie,' she said.

He was still smiling. He leaned back, and spread his arms, imitating the shrug emoji. 'And yet, here I still am,' he said. 'Not dead yet. That's a silver lining, right?'

5

Birch had driven for over an hour, but she was still troubled when she arrived home. She understood Charlie's attempt to shake off what had happened, knew he was probably right, it was the only thing to do. It might even be the right thing to do: for Charlie to show the guy that he wasn't getting to him. But she hated feeling so powerless. Charlie was her little brother, her *baby* brother, and she'd always protected him ... until she hadn't. Before he was sent down for his involvement with Solomon Carradice's organised crime ring, he'd been lost to her for fourteen years. Missing, presumed dead, but in fact just underground, working in a dark and dangerous world. She didn't like that he was in prison, but for the first time in all those years she knew where he was. And she'd hoped, rather than believed, he'd be safe.

'He *is* safe.'

Anjan was sitting on her couch, his laptop on his knees. The coffee table was covered with papers. She'd scolded him more than once about working in the evenings, but he always just shrugged, and told her this was the lawyer's lot in life, the terrible bargain he had regrettably struck, or something. But he'd closed the laptop and listened, with his head cocked towards her, as she told him about what had happened to Charlie.

'He's in the safest place he could be,' Anjan added. 'And he knows better than you how things are in there.'

'I know, but Solomon—'

'Charlie says this young man is a known bully. He thinks it's a random attack. He's in a better position to know that, Helen. Maybe you should trust him on this?'

Anjan was speaking gently, but Birch felt nettled. This was the problem with dating a lawyer: presenting the other side of something was all he knew how to do.

'I mean.' Anjan had noticed her crestfallen face. 'The problem is, even if Solomon *was* behind this, if he somehow made this happen from inside Barlinnie—'

Birch snorted. 'No *somehow* about it; you know how prison whisper networks are.'

'Okay, true. But even if he did, there's no way to prove it at this point. Anything we did at this juncture would probably only serve to single Charlie out even more. From what I hear, prisoners who get special treatment are never desperately popular.'

Birch went quiet. Anjan was right. Charlie had been right. She'd have to do nothing, and she hated doing nothing.

Anjan shuffled the laptop on to the sofa beside him, stood up, and crossed the room towards her. She still had her coat over her arm, and was standing beside the living room window, looking out at the Portobello prom and the last light lingering on a strip of grey-brown sea beyond her front garden. Anjan slipped an arm around her waist, and she leaned into him.

'I know it's hard,' he said. 'I'm sorry this has happened.'

'It hard enough him just being in there, without this . . .'

'I know.' Anjan planted a kiss on the top of her head, tickling her scalp. 'And we'll keep an eye on it. You ought to note it down, record the date this happened. Keep a log of anything else. A contemporaneous note.'

Birch nodded. 'That's something,' she said.

Anjan squeezed her waist, then slid his arm away. 'It is,' he said. 'Now, I believe a cup of tea is what you need.'

She watched as he strode towards the kitchen.

'And I'll see if I can rustle up a biscuit.'

Birch inched round the coffee table, so as not to cause an avalanche among Anjan's papers. She finally dumped her coat and sank into the armchair. She couldn't quite believe how good it was to have Anjan around. They'd only been able to be *an item*, as her mother might have put it, for a couple of months, as Anjan had been Charlie's legal counsel for his trial, and a relationship with Birch – the defendant's sister, a senior police officer and a key witness – would have been a gigantic conflict of interest. But once Charlie was sentenced, they'd been able to start seeing one another: properly, not just the polite, professional discussions she'd had with Anjan over her brother's case. Anjan was kind and, like her, he understood what it meant to be married to his job. She teased him about working too much, but liked that he felt comfortable enough to come over and do admin on his cases while she was out visiting Charlie. They went out for dinner sometimes, but Anjan was just as happy to collapse on to the sofa with her at the end of a long day and eat pasta in front of the TV. They didn't make demands of each other. They both had enough demands to deal with already.

'Besides, Solomon's an IPP prisoner.' Anjan was back, a steaming mug of tea in each hand.

He liked to do this – pick up a conversation she'd thought was finished. Sometimes he'd wake in the morning and resume a train of thought from the previous evening, as though no time had elapsed. She tried to imagine what the inside of his mind must be like. Busy, she guessed.

'They'll be keeping a very close eye on him,' he said.

Birch leaned over and made a small clearing in the briefing documents on the table. Anjan laid the mugs down in the space, and headed back to the kitchen for biscuits.

'You're right,' she called after him. 'It's just my protective mama bear instinct at work. Or . . . sister bear, or something.'

Anjan returned, passing her a Tunnock's wafer. 'Charlie is his own bear,' he said. 'He's a gangster, remember? He knows how to handle himself.'

'*Ex* gangster,' Birch said, but she could feel herself smiling. Yes, Anjan was good for her. She stretched, feeling her shoulders pop with tension from her day, and the het-up drive home.

'Oh,' Anjan said, sitting back down among the chaos of his papers, 'before I forget. Someone phoned, maybe an hour ago. A man, asking for you by name.'

Birch closed her eyes for a moment. She hoped very much the call hadn't been from her boss.

'Was it McLeod?'

'No,' Anjan said, 'that's the thing. I asked who was calling, if I could take a message, and he just said he'd call back. Then he hung up.'

Birch shrugged, blowing the steam away from the top of her mug. 'Weird,' she said. 'But at least it wasn't a work thing. I thought you were going to tell me I had to go back to the office, then.'

Anjan shook his head, smiling. 'Heaven forfend,' he said. 'I've been looking forward to seeing you all day.'

'I wonder who it was, though,' Birch mused. 'Maybe just a sales call or something.'

'Maybe. Probably.'

There was a moment of quiet, in which Birch made the decision to file any further thought of the phone call away. She didn't need anything else to worry about right now. 'Tell me something good,' she said.

Anjan looked down at the coffee table, crossing one leg over the other as he did, and settled back into her sofa with his tea. 'Hmm, something good,' he said. 'Tricky. I've been looking at this fraud case all day. Little old ladies groomed for their pin money, thousands embezzled. I'm afraid it's been wall-to-wall depressing stuff today.'

Birch grinned. 'But you'll stand up for them, the old wifeys, won't you? You'll see them right.'

Anjan nodded. 'Oh yes, and then some.'

She felt a patter of butterflies in her stomach. 'You're a hero,' she said.

Anjan was still thinking. 'Something good,' he said. 'Oh, I know. I did have the thought, earlier: La Favorita for dinner? I'm buying.'

'Takeout?'

'If you'd like.'

Birch smiled. 'I love you.' She hadn't even realised what she was saying, and for a second, her heart clutched. *Too much?*

Anjan raised an eyebrow. 'Cupboard love,' he said. 'I know you, Helen. You'd say anything for a La Favorita pizza.'

Birch relaxed again. It was such a relief to be in a relationship with someone who could see things the way they were intended. Another lawyer trick, maybe.

'Exactly,' she said soberly. 'It's the most powerful love there is.'

6

As DI Birch had suspected, Robertson Bennet was being a little disingenuous in his description of the former family home. Craigs Park Avenue was indeed a terrace, but the houses were pretty sandstone cottages with stained-glass porches, balconies, gardens front and back: a far cry from the pebbledashed two-up-two-downs that Amy had imagined. The road itself was privately maintained, or rather not maintained. Amy had no sooner turned her car in off Craigs Park Road before she realised she'd made a mistake: the street had once been cobbled, but over the years it had fallen into disrepair and now resembled a farm track, full of ruts and puddles. A sign at the turn said the road was a no-through, but at the far end Amy could see a municipal-looking building with a curtain-sided lorry parked outside. No wonder the little road was in such a state, with freight rattling up and down it. She reverse-parked a few yards up from the house she'd be visiting, and wondered if there were neighbourly disputes here, some reason why the various homeowners hadn't banded together to pay for the road to be properly paved. Such things made houses difficult to sell, after all.

The inhabitants of number 23 were expecting her: Bennet had already been round, asking about his parents, and Amy had called ahead using the details he'd given. A Mr and Mrs Ross, a young couple with a small baby. The man answered the door, the baby propped up in his arms.

'DC Amy Kato,' Amy said.

The baby looked at Amy, its little face opening into a gummy laugh.

'Oh,' the man said, 'you're an instant hit! I'm Abe.' He squirmed one hand out from under the baby and Amy shook it. 'Please come in.'

Amy followed the man as he backed away from her through the porch, into the hall, babbling to the baby.

'Who's this lady, then, Belah? Who's come to visit us?'

Belah hid her face in her father's shoulder, pretending to be shy.

Mr Ross waved Amy into the living room. In the centre of the room was a huge playpen, filled with soft toys, blocks, things that rattled. Some items had clearly been thrown out of the pen's confines: the floor was also littered with brightly coloured toys.

'Excuse the mess,' the man said, as Amy skirted the playpen and settled demurely in a clear space on the sofa. He lowered Belah into the playpen, and she flopped on to her stomach, grabbing at a squishy plastic ring and immediately putting it into her mouth.

'Don't worry,' Amy said. She nodded at Belah. 'She's a very good baby.'

Abe Ross flushed with pride. 'She's a peach,' he said. 'She loves new people. I started working from home since she came along, and I have meetings here quite a lot. We joke that she's my PA.'

As if on cue, Belah clapped her hands: once, twice.

'Can I get you a cup of tea, er . . . marm?'

Amy laughed. 'Just call me Amy,' she said. '*Marm* is promoting me rather above my station. And no, I'm fine. I'll be out of your hair shortly. Just a few quick questions.'

Abe nodded. He picked up a pile of tiny garments from the armchair across from Amy, and shifted them carefully on to the floor before sitting.

'It's about the lady who lived here before,' he said.

'Yes,' Amy said. 'Or rather, the family whose house this was, the MacDonalds. I know you've already had a visit from their son.'

'Yes. I'm afraid I couldn't really help him. I might not be able to help you either, to be honest.'

Amy fished out her tablet, and flipped it open. 'The MacDonalds didn't leave a forwarding address, after you bought the house?'

Abe shook his head. 'Well, no. I mean, we had no dealings with them at all. I don't know if you know this already, but we bought the house at auction. It was never on the market in the traditional sense. That's why we were able to afford it. We were incredibly lucky.'

Amy tapped in a few notes. 'I didn't know that,' she said. 'That's unusual, isn't it? An auction for a house like this?'

'It is,' he said. 'Toni and I – Toni's my wife – we were looking at auctions because we thought a fixer-upper was all we could afford. The other properties we saw were nowhere near in the same league as this place. They generally had a lot wrong with them, or they'd been flooded, or the person who'd lived in them had died and there was no one to inherit them, or no one who wanted to. We couldn't believe when this place came up.'

'Do you know why the house was auctioned?'

Abe shrugged. 'I mean, the road was certainly a factor,' he said. 'I'm sure you noticed.'

'I did.'

'It's a drag,' he said, 'but it wasn't a deal-breaker for us. You just learn to perfect your rally-driving skills. And the house was kind of old-fashioned when we moved in. Still is, really, but we've started to modernise. New kitchen, that sort of thing. But there was nothing about its condition that would have prevented a conventional sale, I'm sure.'

In the playpen, Belah murmured to herself.

'So you had no knowledge of the MacDonalds at all?' Amy asked.

The man shook his head. 'We knew the old lady's name,' he said. 'But everything was done through the auction firm. She was – or the family was, I guess – already gone. I was pretty surprised when the son turned up the other day. He worried me, to be honest, I wasn't quite sure what his deal was.'

Amy looked up from her screen. 'In what sense?'

'Well.' Abe looked down at Belah, who was closely examining the plastic ring in her hands. 'I was worried about what he might be after. He seemed kind of . . . belligerent. I thought he might be going to try to make a legal claim for the house, like he thought it ought to have been left to him, or something. I don't know much about that stuff, and I was a bit concerned.'

Amy frowned. This hadn't been in the version Robertson Bennet had told them. 'Belligerent?'

Abe seemed to remember who he was talking to. 'Oh,' he said, holding up his hands. 'Nothing I'd call you guys about, nothing like that. He was seemed sort of . . . well, entitled, frankly. He seemed quite affronted that we were living in what he obviously thought was *his* house.'

Amy resisted the urge to respond, but tapped out a note on the tablet.

'He calmed down a bit after a while,' Abe went on. 'I gave him some things. Bits and pieces we found when we were doing up the kitchen. That seemed to placate him.'

Amy stopped dead, her fingers still resting on the screen. 'Do you mind if I ask what things?'

The man looked a little sheepish. 'I – to be honest, I regret giving them to him now I know the police are involved. They were notebooks. Diaries, I think.'

'You think? Did you ever open them?'

Abe shrugged. 'Couldn't,' he said. 'Well, we could have, but it would have meant forcing them open. Each one had a little brass padlock on it . . . the sort of thing I remember girls having back when I was a teenager. When we first found them, Toni was dead keen to break the locks and have a look, but there's something wrong about that, don't you think? Besides, I always thought someone might come back, and ask for them.'

'Did Mr Bennet ask for them? Did he know about them?'

Abe shook his head. 'He didn't seem to have a clue. I asked him if he had a sister, and he said no, but he suspected they were his mother's. I felt like once I'd mentioned them, I had to hand them over. Do you think they could be important?'

Amy was typing again, but tried to talk as she made notes. 'There's no knowing until we see them,' she said. Abe's face was stricken, and she added, 'Don't worry. I'll follow up with Mr Bennet. You haven't done anything wrong.'

Abe seemed to relax a little.

'Where did you find these diaries – if they are diaries?' Amy asked.

'Oh. We pulled the cooker out to replace it. It was like the cooker out of the ark – and there was this lump, covered with a flap of lino. It was these diaries, absolutely filthy. They must have been there ages. Probably a fire hazard, too.'

Amy laughed. 'You're probably right. But anyway, where were we?' Amy scrolled backward on her screen. 'Yes. A minute ago you mentioned that you knew the name of the woman who lived in this house, back before her son appeared.'

'Yes, I remember it from the auction paperwork. I noticed it because she was called Euphemia. I didn't think anyone was really called that.'

'Was there a man's name listed, or mentioned? A Mr MacDonald?'

'I don't remember. But I do know whenever we talked to the auction people, they'd talk about *the old lady*. It was never *the old couple*, you know?'

Amy typed. 'So if I were to ask: do you have any knowledge of the whereabouts of either George or Euphemia MacDonald?'

'I'm afraid I'd have absolutely no idea,' Abe said.

Belah suddenly twisted her tiny body and pointed directly at Amy. Her face lit up. 'Ba!' she declared.

Amy laughed. 'You're quite right, Belah,' she said.

Abe shifted in his seat. 'I told the son that I'd look out the details of the auction company,' he said. 'They'd have more details about all this, I'm sure.' He got to his feet.

Belah looked up at him, and cackled.

'It worries me,' he said, 'that I'm apparently so hysterical. Anyway – I could give that stuff to you, if that'd help? It's in the kitchen.'

Amy glanced down at the baby.

'She'll be fine in there, don't worry. She's tried her level best, but she's yet to stage a successful escape.'

Amy stood up, smiling. 'Keep practising, kiddo,' she said, following Abe out of the room.

The hallway was narrow, with steep stairs leading up to the first floor. Amy noted old-fashioned wooden banisters with twisty spindles, painted a rustic white. Under the stairs was a void which had been stuffed with a pushchair, a rain cover, a snowsuit, coats, nappy bags and other baby-trappings. Tiny shoes were lined up against the skirting boards.

The kitchen was at the rear of the house, dominated by a large picture window. Amy gasped as she stepped into the room. It was flooded with green light from the garden, which sloped up from the back of the building in steep tiers. A stepped path had been cut into the sandstone retaining walls between each level, making a path that led from the back door to a tiny shed on the very top. The garden was a late summer triumph: dwarf apple trees surrounded by windfalls, berries fat and purple under their netting. Spires of red-hot poker and Michaelmas daisy rose above the greenery, and aubretia tumbled in purple waves down the retaining walls. Amy looked at the garden and felt instantly calm.

'Never mind Robertson Bennet,' she said, '*I* want to move in. That garden is incredible.'

Abe was rustling around in a kitchen drawer, but now he turned, a sheaf of paper in his hands. 'Quite the thing, isn't it? We can't take credit for any of it though, except for the weeds. It was all like that when we moved in. The MacDonalds must have been amazing gardeners.'

'They really must.'

'To be honest, I did wonder if the garden put some folk off in the auction. It's a lot to take on. I'm ashamed to say, Toni and I haven't tended it as much as we'd thought we would.'

'You can't tell,' Amy said, 'it looks fantastic.'

Abe shrugged. 'It's well planted,' he said. 'Whoever planned it out made sure it could look after itself, bar some pruning here and there. It sounds like the MacDonalds were older. They'd maybe prepared for being less able to manage it.'

'Maybe,' Amy said. 'And Belah must love it.'

At the mention of his daughter's name, Abe stilled for a moment, listening for her. There was the distant sound of plastic ball bearings, rattling around inside a toy. He relaxed. 'Well,' he said, 'we don't take her out there much, yet. With it being quite steep, and the steps and everything. It's many things, but it isn't exactly baby-proofed. But I hope she'll get green-fingered when she's older. Anyway – here's some of the paperwork.'

He handed a couple of A4 sheets over to Amy. 'That was the original print-out we got off the auction site,' he said, 'in 2015, but the contact details are probably the same, right?'

Amy looked down at the papers. 'We'll track them down,' she said. 'Don't worry. I'm okay to keep these?'

'Sure.'

Amy folded the papers in half, and closed her tablet around them, like closing a book on a bookmark. She took a last look at the garden: the pillars of blown foxglove losing their last flowers to the wind.

'Final question before I go,' she said. 'Do you know of any neighbourhood disputes in the street? Any animosity, old feuds? The state of the road made me wonder . . .'

Abe nodded. 'Made us wonder, too,' he said. 'But we're not aware of anything. Mary next door would have known about that – number 24. She'd lived here pretty much her whole life.'

Amy had a spark of recollection: Robertson Bennet mentioning his parents' next-door neighbour. 'She *had* lived there? Did Mary pass away?'

Abe blinked. 'Oh no,' he said. 'The house just got too much for her, and she was getting a bit forgetful towards the end. She told us she was moving into a home.'

'I don't suppose you know which one?'

'I don't,' he said, 'but Toni will know. They liked a good gossip over the garden wall. I know we sent her our Christmas letter last year, to tell her the baby had been born.'

Amy fished in her pocket for a business card, and handed it to Abe. 'Could you ask Toni to call me, please? It would be great to chat to Mary if we can. Do you know her last name?'

'It's McPherson,' Abe said. 'I always said to Toni, she has a name like a grandma in a fairy tale.'

Amy smiled. 'Thank you, Mr Ross.'

She turned away from the swimmy green light of the kitchen window, back into the dim hall with its little row of Mary Janes, jelly sandals, tiny Ugg boots. At the living room doorway, Amy paused. Belah had levered herself into a standing position, and was holding on to the side of the playpen.

'Ba!' she said again, as Amy came into view.

'You're a clever wee scone,' Amy said. She turned to Abe, who'd followed her to the door. 'Thank you so much for your help, Mr Ross. If you could have Toni call me.'

'No problem,' the man said. 'Thanks for coming by. The neighbours will have all sorts to say about a police car in the street.'

Amy grinned, unlatching the front door. 'We aim to please,' she said.

7

'Well.'

DCI McLeod's new haircut didn't especially suit him. Birch had noticed it as soon as she'd walked into his office, but it had taken her too long to formulate a suitable comment, and now, after she'd summarised her two meetings with Bennet, she felt it was too late. Instead, she tried not to look at it.

'You want to know what I think?'

That's the reason I came in here, Birch thought.

'Yes, sir.'

McLeod pressed the end of his index finger on his desk, as though it were a cigarette being stubbed.

'This man is leading us a merry dance, Birch, that's what I think. I think he's tanked his company, he's probably got a list of bad credit as long as your arm, and this is his last resort. Come home with his tail between his legs and beg Mummy and Daddy for money. He sounds like a man who's used to getting his own way, and when you didn't give in the first time, he fabricated this story about his father.'

It sounded callous coming from McLeod's mouth, although this had been Birch's own train of thought at first, after Bennet's exclamation in the lobby.

'I ran a search on George MacDonald,' she said. 'Obviously there are hundreds and hundreds of George MacDonalds out there, but *this* George MacDonald popped up a couple of times. There's the incident that Mr Bennet mentioned, from 2013. His father was brought in overnight but then released: the wife didn't press charges. Then way back in 1979 there's a fine for trespassing on railway property: no surprise there, we know he's a gricer—'

'Gricer?'

'Train buff. I, er – did a bit of a Google.'

'Gricers, they call themselves?'

'They do, sir. Anyway . . .' Birch was trying not to blush. She didn't want to fess up to the fact that after Bennet had left, she'd fallen down something of an internet wormhole about trainspotters – though they found that term pejorative and preferred *gricer* or *buff*, she'd discovered – and their habits. 'The other one is rather more unexpected. In 1999 MacDonald was cautioned for being in possession of stolen property.'

McLeod frowned. 'Railway property?'

'No, sir.' Birch handed him a print-out of the report she'd found. 'It was jewellery: an emerald bracelet and earrings, as you can see. They'd been reported stolen by a woman who believed her daughter had taken them. The girl was a runaway: the mother reckoned she'd stolen them with the intention of pawning them. A tour of local pawnshops turned up a guy who said George MacDonald had come in trying to flog a very similar-sounding jewellery set.'

McLeod was scrutinising the pixelated 1990s photo of the jewellery: the three items inside a plastic evidence bag, with a numbered sticker on the corner.

'Anyway, he received a visit at home,' Birch went on. 'Claimed he'd found the set under a bench on the station platform at Carstairs Junction. The report says he was deeply remorseful for trying to pawn them, rather than handing them in. The attending officers seemed to think he was harmless. He was cautioned, the jewellery was returned to the mother, no harm done.'

'Interesting,' McLeod said. He passed the print-out back to Birch. 'Unexpected, but . . . well, plausible. With the exception of the 2013 incident, there's nothing other than Bennet's testimony to suggest his father had a history of violence?'

'No, sir.'

'So.' McLeod sat back in his chair. 'It's entirely possible that what happened in 2013 was a misunderstanding, or a one-time lashing-out. Bennet, frustrated by your lack of assistance, went away and, after a brief dig, constructed a story around it in order to get our help. Wants us to do the job of a PI so he doesn't have to pay for one.'

Birch was quiet for a moment.

'That's certainly possible,' she said. 'However, I think that, unfortunately, we need to pursue this. Bennet may well be stringing us along, and if it turns out he is, then he's bang to rights for wasting police time. But if we do nothing, and then it turns out that something *has* happened to his mother . . .'

McLeod sighed.

'I'm just saying, he seems like the litigious type, sir. Better safe than sorry.'

McLeod flapped a hand at her. 'Fine, fine,' he said. 'But given that this is most likely nothing, I don't want a whole lot of resources wasted. Light touch, okay?'

'Way ahead of you, sir. I was going to assign DC Kato to make preliminary enquiries. Just her, no team at this point. I thought we could assess her findings and decide where to go from there.'

Her boss was nodding.

'She's been out to the former MacDonald home,' Birch went on. 'Mr Bennet had already been there, rattling his cage at the new owners, from the sounds of it.'

McLeod lifted an eyebrow. 'Anything we need get involved in?'

'I don't believe so,' Birch said. 'Although apparently the new family had found some items belonging to the MacDonalds while doing renovations, and Mr Bennet walked off with them. I've sent DC Kato to meet him and get the items back, in case they turn out to be useful.' Birch glanced at her watch. 'That's probably happening as we speak, in fact.'

'Good,' McLeod said. 'The more I hear, the more convinced I am that this is a wild-goose chase we're being led on. This man sounds like a right royal pain in the backside, to be perfectly frank with you. Let me be clear: light touch only. I don't want *you* on this, Birch. You've got more important things to do, and Mr Bennet has wasted enough of your time already.'

'Yes, sir. Is that everything?'

McLeod raised an eyebrow. 'Well,' he said. 'Apart from the fact you haven't complimented me on my new look, yes. That's everything.'

Birch walked back to her office slowly, daydreaming a little. She'd need to stop at the Portobello Aldi on the way home, she thought, to pick up some things for dinner. Anjan was out at some sort of function that night, and she was trying to convince herself that they each needed to maintain their independence. She did feel a small thrill as she thought of the evening to come: she could potter around a bit tonight, do some laundry, and have the whole bed to herself. But she also found herself wishing she could bounce her thoughts about the Bennet case around with Anjan: he always had such a clear head. She had questions – do you think the parents don't *want* to be found? Could George MacDonald possibly still be a threat, now, at eighty-odd? – and Anjan would, she knew, have thoughtful answers to them. Still, it wasn't the sort of case that developed overnight: it was likely to be a slow burn. She'd chat to Anjan when she saw him.

She was nearing the office door when a strange, stray thought struck her. Bennet had said he'd checked his parents weren't dead, but . . . his lack of findings only meant they weren't *officially* dead. Had the couple been murdered, there would be no record, and—

Oh for goodness' sake, Helen, she thought. Where the hell did that come from?

Maybe from thinking about Charlie, the particular line of criminal work he'd been involved in. It was hard to disappear under your own steam these days, what with social media, mobile phones, electronic banking and CCTV. But it was still possible to *be disappeared*. To have someone else come along and erase all trace of you. The thought made Birch shiver.

No, she thought, unlocking her office door. It'll turn out that the MacDonalds are just in some nursing home somewhere, or they've found themselves a nice expat villa in Spain. *It'll be fine.*

Still, as she settled back behind her desk, Birch made a mental note: she'd get Amy to ask Bennet if he knew of any enemies his parents might have made. It was like she'd said to McLeod: better safe than sorry.

8

Birch looked up from the glowing screen of her iPad. Amy was hovering, tapping her fingertips on the edge of Birch's desk.

'Like I say,' she said, 'there wasn't much to note about the meeting with Bennet. He was huffy, but he handed the diaries over readily enough.'

Birch scanned down the document Amy had sent her. 'You're sure they're diaries?'

Amy shrugged. 'I assume so,' she said. 'They've got little padlocks on them, all three. I used to have a diary like that myself, back when I was about thirteen. If you scroll to the bottom, I've attached a photo. Or I can run back to my desk and grab them, if you'd like?'

Birch swiped to the photograph: three tatty card-backed notebooks in an evidence bag. The brass hasps and padlocks were green with corrosion, and the books themselves looked warped with age, possibly damp.

'The photo's fine,' Birch said.

'I thought I'd hand them over to one of our resident geeks,' Amy said. 'See if they can pick the wee locks? It shouldn't take long.'

Birch laughed. 'You can if you want, Kato,' she said, 'but you have my full permission to just bust them open. It's the contents we want to preserve, right? Plus, I doubt they'd take much breaking.'

Amy was nodding, but her nose was wrinkled: she didn't like the idea. 'True,' was all she said.

'I have to admit,' Birch went on, 'the Rosses are better people than me. If I found three locked diaries under *my* cooker, there's no way I'd just hang on to them without opening them.'

Amy laughed. 'Sure,' she said, 'but you're a police officer.'

Birch grinned. 'So they keep telling me.'

'You want to read them, then?' Amy asked. 'Once I get them open?'

Birch hesitated. The temptation was strong. 'I'd better not,' she said. 'McLeod doesn't want me on this case, really. He reckons it'll all turn out to be nothing, so we're not to waste resources. You just have a flick through, see if anything leaps out as important?'

'Will do, marm.'

Birch studied Amy: wasn't she pleased to have kept hold of this particular assignment? Maybe it's the big sister in me, Birch thought, who likes the idea of nebbing at someone's diary. Maybe I'm nosier than the average person.

Amy's face remained impassive. 'There *are* a few other things to fill you in on,' she said, 'since I wrote up my notes from the Abe Ross interview.'

'Oh yes?'

Amy handed over a photocopy. 'That's the paperwork Mr Ross gave me with details of the auction company. I've called them and requested that they look out the file on the MacDonalds' sale of the house. We'll need a warrant to collect, of course.'

Birch nodded. 'Happy to sign off on that,' she said.

'And Toni Ross called me back. Mary McPherson hasn't moved far. The building I saw, at the far end of the street? It's a nursing home. That's where she's moved to. I thought I'd head back there tonight. The home's website says visitors are welcome till seven.'

Birch glanced at her watch: 4.30 p.m.

'Give me half an hour,' she said, 'and I'll come with you. I'm hoping Mrs McPherson will know exactly where the MacDonalds are, and we can get this whole thing tied up in one fell swoop.'

Amy grinned. 'And home in time for tea,' she said.

'Something like that, yeah.'

The visitor section of the nursing home car park was largely empty, though the spaces were narrow. Birch pulled up next to

Amy: they'd come in separate cars, though McLeod would have disapproved of the double mileage claim, so each could go their separate ways afterwards. Amy was already locking up, having experienced the rutted track of a road once already. Though Birch had been warned, she'd found herself slowing to a crawl in order to protect her CID Mondeo's suspension.

'Christ,' she said, opening the driver's door. 'I see what you mean.'

Amy was looking back down the road, shaking her head. 'I don't understand,' she said. 'I know it would cost a bit to fix, but if everyone in the street chipped in their share . . .'

Birch shimmied along the gap between the two cars.

'There has to be some sort of ill feeling,' Amy was saying. 'That one person who refuses to pay up because *their* bit isn't so bad, or whatever.'

Birch followed Amy's gaze. 'Maybe,' she said. 'But each house's share would still be pretty hefty, I imagine. You think the Rosses have a four-figure sum to spare?'

Amy shrugged.

'It might be as simple as that,' Birch said.

But Amy was frowning. 'Even so. Why auction your lovely family home for way less than it's worth?'

Birch studied the houses in front of them. Apart from the state of the road, they were beautifully positioned: a line of mature trees grew opposite them, and the hill rose sharply behind so they were overlooked by nothing but their own steep little gardens. In the early evening sun, they looked as quaint as a scene painted on a chocolate box. Amy was right: auctioning such a house off cheap made very little sense.

'It's fast,' she heard herself saying. 'An auction is fast. If you needed to do a moonlight flit . . .'

Amy was looking at her. 'What are you thinking, marm?'

Birch shook her head. 'I just think it's a quick way to liquidise your assets,' she said. 'And if the MacDonalds really did go missing right after selling up . . .'

At the far end of the road, a squat truck pulled in, and began to jostle its way along the rough road towards them. Birch realised she'd tailed off.

Amy nudged her. 'Nah,' she said. 'This neighbour lady, she's going to whip out her address book and tell us exactly where they are, remember? Open and shut case.'

Birch smiled. Maybe they would be lucky, and it really would be that simple. 'Oh,' she said. 'Yeah, totally, you're right. Home in time for tea.'

The truck slid through the boundary gates, and chugged past them. The side-panel read *Industrial Laundry Services*. Birch shuddered. She remembered bagging up sheets from the hospital bed in her mother's little bedroom, waiting for the laundry truck to come for them. Waiting for the NHS people to come and dismantle the bed and take it away to be used somewhere else. Waiting for someone to tell her it had all been a bad dream.

'Marm?'

Birch shivered, though the sun was still warm on her back. 'Sorry. I'm afraid I hate nursing homes. I always said I'd never put my mum in one.'

Amy had begun to walk towards the front door, and Birch found she was following.

'They're not like they used to be,' Amy said. 'Some of them are quite fancy now. This one looks all right, doesn't it?'

Ever the optimist, Birch thought.

The nursing home foyer was empty, and the reception desk unmanned. As Amy pushed open the front door, a buzzer sounded, presumably to indicate that someone had walked in. The noise didn't stop when the door swung closed behind them.

A clipboard with a sign-in sheet sat on the reception desk, facing outward, and beside the sheet was a chewed biro pen attached by a piece of string and sellotape. At the top of the sheet, someone had written VISITORS PLEASE SIGN YOURSELVES IN in thick black marker pen. The buzzer sound droned on.

Birch scribbled herself and Amy down on the sheet.

'What's your car reg?' she asked, twisting round. Amy was examining the various health and safety certificates displayed in clip frames on a nearby wall.

'SG08 OXJ,' Amy said.

Birch wrote it down. 'You need a new car, Kato.'

Amy threw her a hammed-up, wounded look. 'I *love* that car,' she said, clasping one hand to her chest. Then she just as quickly dropped it, and straightened up. Birch turned back to the desk. A large man had walked into the foyer, and now slid in opposite her.

'I can help you ladies with something?' The man had tired eyes and an eastern European accent. He was wearing a light blue nurse's tunic with a name badge: *Patryck*. As he spoke, he pushed a button on the wall behind the desk, and the buzzer noise stopped.

'You can. I'm Detective Inspector Birch, this is Detective Constable Kato, Police Scotland.' Birch placed her badge down on the sign-in sheet, and tried to ignore the fleeting look of panic that crossed the man's face. 'We'd like to speak with one of your residents, a Mary McPherson. We're hoping she can help us with some information pertaining to one of our investigations.'

Patryck's brow unfurrowed slightly. 'McPherson,' he said. 'Yes, Mary. I will take you to her. She is a lovely lady, but she has some problems with her memory, Inspector.'

Birch glanced back at Amy, but Patryck had set off, and the younger officer was already making to follow him. Birch brought up the rear, and as Patryck led them through what seemed to be the building's main corridor, she glanced left and right, through the various doors leading off into the ground-floor rooms. On one side, a series of lounges, in which residents were watching TV, eating food from trays, some of them talking. On the other, there was a long conservatory filled with faded wicker couches and patio chairs. A couple of older people, presumably residents, were sitting with visitors. Birch caught sight of a little boy cuddled on an old lady's knee, his fist tight around the long beads she wore. Patryck began to climb a flight of stairs, and Birch stopped looking. The home smelled of soup and carpet and disinfectant, but also somehow like her mother, the way her skin had smelled towards the end.

'Here is Mary,' Patryck said, gesturing to an open door at the top of the stairs. It was marked by a small slide-along plaque that read *McPherson, Room 1/7*. Patryck stepped on to the threshold and poked his head inside. 'Mary? I have some special visitors here.'

Amy walked into the room first, and Birch followed. She had expected Patryck to stay, but he didn't follow them in.

'Any of you need me, just press the button.' He gestured to a flat white box on the coffee table, which looked rather like a TV remote. The buttons on it read *Emergency*, *Call* and *Reset*.

'Thank you, Patryck,' Birch said.

Mary McPherson was a small woman, with delicate hands and feet. She was nestled in a wingback armchair that looked too large for her. Her hair was pure white, and hung in a long, straight sheet across one of her shoulders. She was dressed in a Winceyette nightie and dressing gown set so old-fashioned that Birch wondered where the hell it had been bought from.

'Mrs McPherson,' Amy said. 'We're so sorry to disturb you when you're all ready for bed.'

When Amy spoke, the old woman's eyes seemed to focus properly for the first time. She smiled broadly. 'Hello, hen,' she said. 'Are you new?'

Amy smiled back, and stepped a little closer. 'No,' she said, 'I don't work here, I work for Police Scotland. I'm Amy, and this is my boss, Helen. We've just come to have a quick chat with you, is that all right?'

Birch relaxed a little: Amy was good at this. She shuffled further into the room.

'Nice to meet you, Mary,' Birch said.

'Well, away in properly, then,' Mary said. She seemed unfazed at the presence of two policewomen in her room. She gestured at Amy. 'You, young one, you sit on the bed there, and' – Mary waved a hand at Birch – 'there's the stool, there. Just put those magazines anywhere.'

'Thank you – we won't stay long,' Amy said, settling on to the bed as though trying not to leave a wrinkle. 'As I say, we're just here to ask you a few questions regarding . . .'

Birch let her colleague talk, and allowed herself to study Mary McPherson. The woman's face was heavily lined but pretty and girlish, and her hands sparkled with old-looking rings that she obviously never took off. Her room was small but neatly kept. On the bedside table was a knitting project made of pale grey yarn on four fine needles: a sock in progress, Birch guessed, though she was no knitter. There was also a Venetian glass frame with a black and white wedding photograph in it: the slim, petite bride was Mary. Outside the window, Birch could hear a blackbird singing, and she found herself thinking that nursing homes might not be all that bad after—

'That *brute*,' Mary said. 'That absolute *menace*. Poor Phamie.'

Amy shot Birch a look. 'What can you tell us about George MacDonald, Mary?'

The old lady's expression was fierce. 'Oh, some tales,' she said. 'Some tales that would make your hair curl.'

Birch shook herself a little, remembering the tablet in her handbag. She flicked it on to her lap, and tapped it into life.

'Start at the beginning,' Amy said. 'When did you first meet the MacDonalds?'

Mary's face crinkled. 'It was ... Oh. It was – what year did I marry Donald, hen? When was that?'

Amy glanced at Birch again. 'I'm afraid I don't know,' she said, 'but don't worry, I don't need exact dates or anything.'

Mary was still frowning. 'I don't remember. I don't remember many things, these days – it drives me round the bend. But Phamie ... I've known Phamie a long, long time. She lives next door, just through there.' Mary made a vague gesture.

'Used to, you mean,' Amy said. 'At number 23.'

'Just beyond the wall there,' Mary went on as though Amy hadn't spoken. 'We'd talk over the wall. She was always in that garden. Always lugging big bags of soil about, Phamie was. I used to say to her, you'll do yourself a mischief, girl. But she loved her garden. Put mine to shame.'

Birch made a note. It was clear they weren't going to get a clear chronology from Mary: whatever they could glean would have to do.

'How often did you see Phamie?' Amy asked.

'Oh, most days. Some days it would just be a wee *cheerie!* over the garden wall, but other times we'd spend all day together: walk down into Morningside, or get on the bus to Princes Street. We'd go to the café at Jenners and get tea and iced buns, if we'd time. And Donald and I would mind the wee one for her, when she needed it. I used to tell her she was the sister I never got to have.'

Amy smiled. 'Did you keep in touch, after . . . you moved here?'

Mary's expression changed. She looked puzzled. 'Keep in . . . touch?'

'I mean, have you heard from Phamie? In recent times?'

The older woman looked down at her lap. 'Oh,' she said. 'Oh, I don't . . . I'm sorry, I don't know.'

Birch saw Amy squirm a little, and decided to step in. 'Mary,' she said, 'do you know where Phamie lives now?'

Mary looked up at Birch for the first time since she'd sat down. Her eyes were wet: not being able to remember had upset her. She didn't speak, but shook her head.

'That's okay,' Birch said. 'You're doing so well. You're being so helpful.'

The old lady smiled a thin, watery smile.

'We would like you to tell us what you remember about George, though, if you can. Phamie's husband.'

Upon hearing the name, Mary's face darkened once more. 'A *brute*,' she said again, her inflection identical to the last time. 'That man wasn't welcome further than my doorstep. I always said that to Donald, I said, *He is not to come into this house.*' She stabbed the tip of one gnarled finger into the arm of her wingback, and glanced at the open door, as though she thought George MacDonald might walk into her room right then.

'I know it might be hard,' Birch said, 'but can you tell us what it was that George did, to . . . make you feel that way about him?'

Mary stuck out her chin, defiant. 'He hurt Phamie,' she said. 'He hurt her, my beautiful friend. She was so good, so gentle with the wee one, she loved growing things, she'd give you her last penny if you needed it. And he bullied her. He threatened her.

Threatened to kill her, sometimes. He saw she was good, and he knew she couldn't fight back, or wouldn't. I mean, me and Donald, we had our ding-dongs over the years, but he knew I'd give as good as I got, and he was a gentleman. A true gentleman, he never raised his hand to me, not once. Not like that *George*. He'd a temper on him like I'd never seen. She'd be black and blue after, sometimes, poor Phamie, and frightened half to death.'

Amy's eyes were wide. 'Did you report George's behaviour to the police?' she asked.

Mary laughed a cold laugh. 'Oh yes. The polis came by sometimes. Give George a talking-to if they thought it was too late for the noise to be going on. But there was nothing to be done. You young ones, you don't know how it was then. It was just the way of things. After a while it was just *oh, the MacDonalds again*, and no one would come. No one would say anything. And I'd have Phamie in my sitting room next day, black and blue, telling me he'd swanned off.'

Birch paused, mid-note. 'Swanned off?'

'Oh yes. He liked to take off, did George. Sometimes for a night, sometimes for a week at a time. Phamie would get distraught worrying where he was. I used to send Donald out to drive around looking for him, or down the hill to the Canny Man's to see if George was drinking in there. Usually he didn't want to be found. But he'd always come back, usually with a bunch of roses and a gallus swagger. I'd say to Donald, *Why can he not just leave her be?*, but he never would. He'd always come back and she'd always open the door and let him in, and there was no telling her. Poor Phamie.'

Birch thought back to the news article Robertson Bennet had shown her. 'Do you remember Phamie being in hospital?'

Mary looked at Birch, and in the quiet that followed the question, blinked her girlish eyes once, twice. Then she carried on speaking, as though she hadn't heard.

'He had fancy women, did George. Phamie was convinced of it, and I was too. I can't see any other reason a man would leave his wife and son like that, for days at a time. When she'd set her face to forgive him, Phamie would say it was just him and his trains.

But when she was crying at midnight on my sofa with my Donald out there driving through the night searching, then she'd say to me, *There's a woman somewhere, Mary, and he's with her right now.*'

Birch looked at Amy. She was unsure whether to repeat her question or not, though she suspected Mary didn't remember, and didn't want to have to say so again. The pattern of her memories seemed to fit with what little Birch knew about early dementia: recollections from long ago are clear and detailed. The short-term memory falls away first, recent years swallowed by fog. The 2013 incident was recent enough that Mary might have forgotten it.

Amy was speaking. 'Did you or Donald ever confront George about his behaviour, Mary?'

Mary looked at Amy, and let out a sort of snort. 'George knew what I thought of him, that's for sure,' she said. 'He . . . made a pass at me once, you know. Phamie was working in the post office, but I'd nipped round. There was washing on the line, so I thought she'd be in. But it was him. Didn't see him until I was in the kitchen. I'd gone through to the back door, thinking she might be out in the garden, but the door was locked. When I turned round, he was there. Standing in the hall passage, so I couldn't get out.' Mary shivered. '*Brute.*'

Amy's face had gone pale. 'Mary,' she said. 'Did George . . . did he attack you?'

The older woman gave Amy the same sort of look she'd given Birch: heavy-lidded, slow-blinking. For the first time since they'd walked in, Mary looked tired. Without answering, she turned and fixed her gaze on Birch once again.

'You young ones,' she said, 'you don't know. It wasn't like it is now.'

'*Bas*tard.' Amy was stomping across the car park, her shadow spiky in the long evening light. 'Absolute swining bastard.'

Birch caught her up as they reached the cars. 'You're not wrong, Kato,' she said. 'He sounds like a piece of work. Looks like Bennet wasn't embellishing.'

'And he's how old now, eighty? It's bloody true that only the good die young.'

Birch laid a hand on her colleague's arm. 'Okay,' she said. 'Just take a breath or two. I know that was hard to listen to, in there.'

Amy closed her eyes, pulled air in through her nose, and straightened up. When she opened her eyes again, she looked a little sheepish. 'Sorry, marm. That just got to me a little, you know? She's such a sweet old lady.'

'I know.' Birch opened her car door. 'And her friend Phamie will be much the same age. Hop in for a minute? We'll debrief properly tomorrow, but . . . while it's fresh, yes?'

Amy nodded, rounding the back of the Mondeo. Inside the car, the air felt stuffy and tight.

'Right.' Birch flipped open the tablet and rested it against the steering wheel. 'It's not the most credible statement, unfortunately, simply because of the memory issues. It seemed to me she remembered very little of what's happened in recent times, including the MacDonalds leaving the street.'

'Yeah,' Amy said. 'And she was foggy on details, too – no dates or anything. I couldn't really get a handle on what happened when, or in what order.'

'I don't think she could, either. Dementia's a bitch of a thing.'

'It really is.'

They were quiet for a moment.

'So, what do we know?' Amy said into the silence.

'For sure? Not a lot more than we did before, annoyingly. Bang goes the idea that we'd walk out of there with the address of George and Phamie's retirement bungalow. But we know that Bennet's story about his parents' relationship holds water. We know that George MacDonald's outburst in 2013 wasn't his first domestic abuse rodeo, not by a long shot.'

Amy grimaced. 'God,' she said, 'to think . . . he'd been at it decades by then.'

'Maybe,' Birch said. 'I mean, probably – but like I say, we don't have a clear timeline. It sounds like his attacks may have got worse as the years went on: Phamie had never been hospitalised before, until 2013. But I suppose we don't know that for sure. We don't have a whole lot, really. Except for a few suspicions.'

'Oh yes?'

Birch nodded. 'I suspect that Robertson Bennet was being naïve when he said his father didn't see other women. Mary's version of events rings far truer to me. And if he hurt Phamie, and he hurt Mary, then it's likely he hurt other women around him, too. We might be able to find some other folk who'll be able to tell us about him.'

Amy was staring through the windscreen. 'True,' she said.

'Unfortunately, though,' Birch went on, 'I suspect Bennet was right about one thing.'

'What's that?'

Birch looked up from the tablet and its few meagre lines of text. 'Call me alarmist if you want, but this doesn't feel like an ordinary missing person case. I suspect that Phamie MacDonald really is in danger.'

Amy was nodding. 'Me too,' she said.

'We've now got a witness – I mean, admittedly not a very reliable one, but still – saying he threatened to kill his wife.'

'I know,' Amy said, her face troubled. 'I know.'

'We need to get out there and find her,' Birch said. 'And I mean *yesterday*.'

Edinburgh Evening News

OUR REGION ¦ EDINBURGH ¦ LEITH ¦ NEW TOWN ¦ STOCKBRIDGE
PORTOBELLO ¦ CORSTORPHINE ¦ MORNINGSIDE ¦ CITY

Police ask witnesses to come forward in search for missing teen

ROXANNE GILLIES   6 November 1996   Share this article

RETURN TO ARCHIVE
SIGN UP TO OUR DAILY NEWSLETTER

Lothian and Borders Police are asking anyone who may have seen 17-year-old Suzannah Hay to come forward.

Suzannah, known as Suzie, disappeared following a night out with friends in Edinburgh on 31 October. She was last seen walking through Edinburgh Waverley railway station. CCTV from the station shows that she was wearing a black dress with a red coat over it, black boots and a black Halloween witch hat.

Police have launched a fresh appeal for anyone who may have seen Suzie at any point that night, but who has not yet come forward, to contact their local police station or call Crimestoppers.

A Lothian and Borders Police spokesperson made the following statement: 'We are growing increasingly worried for the safety of 17-year-old Suzie Hay, as she has now been missing for five days. We would ask that anyone who has any information about Suzie's whereabouts please pass that information on to the police. We are also keen to hear from anyone who saw Suzie, or talked to her, on the night of 31 October 1996.'

The Crimestoppers telephone number is anonymous and any information passed on is treated confidentially. The number to call is 0800 555 111.

9

Birch was glad to escape the city, and get home to her little house by the sea. She'd tried not to show it to her colleague, but Birch felt as rattled as Amy had been by the interview with Mary McPherson. It wasn't just Mary's revelations about George MacDonald that were unsettling, but Mary herself. She seemed so small, so vulnerable, and so much at the mercy of the dementia that was beginning to unravel her memory. Birch let herself in through the front door and dumped her belongings at the bottom of the stairs. She walked into the living room and picked up the photograph of her mother from its place on the gas fire's mantel. At times during the interview, Mary had gone quiet, as though physically absorbing whatever question had been asked of her. In these pauses, Birch realised she'd held her breath, waiting for the reply – but then Mary went on with what she'd been saying, as though the question had never existed. At other points in the conversation – like when she'd asked Amy the year of her own marriage – Mary wore the expression of a person hunting through their mind for a piece of information that feels just out of reach: that *it's on the tip of my tongue* face. Birch looked down at her mother's photograph, and forced herself to think of a memory of the two of them together.

The first that sprang to mind was a recentish one, and a fairly mundane one at that: Birch recalled walking along Johnston Terrace on a frosty winter evening, the floodlit castle a cold cliff rising up beside her. She walked to the top of Castle Wynd South, the close that jackknifes down through the tenements on to the Grassmarket via a set of stairs. Birch would do this many times subsequently, but this was the first time she'd approached her mother's flat from this angle: the reason why was lost to her now. But she remembered pausing at the top of the stairs, and realising that from her vantage point, she could see the lit windows of her mother's retirement flat: the warm orange glow of its lamps diffuse behind gauzy nets. Birch had pulled out her phone, dialled the number she knew by heart, and waited, imagining her mother hauling herself out of the armchair to cross the room and pick up the receiver. 'Look outside!', Birch had said, excited as a child seeing the first snow of the winter. Again, she'd waited, knowing her mother would need time to cross the room, the phone's flex trailing behind her. Then, she could see the shape of her, fiddling at the hem of the net curtain: her mother, lifting the fabric up over her own head as though it were a veil. Birch had extended her arm and waved a big, sweeping wave with her free hand. 'I can see you!' her mother had exclaimed into the phone, delighted. 'I can see you!'

Birch set the photo back down on the mantelpiece, grateful to have been able to call up such a memory without effort. She couldn't imagine what it was like to be Mary: a woman with so many more years of memories to choose from, finding herself increasingly unable to access that precious archive. Birch hated the feeling of knowing something, *knowing* that she knew it, but being somehow unable, momentarily, to call it to mind. The idea of finding oneself so often in that space – increasingly often, as Mary was – felt intolerable. Birch brushed the photo's frame with her fingertips, and sent up a silent prayer that, were she lucky enough to live until she was old, she'd be spared such difficulties.

She shook herself, and turned away from the fireplace. In the hallway, she could see the haphazard pile of things she'd dumped: among them an Aldi shopping bag. Birch realised with some alarm that she'd been on autopilot since she'd left the nursing home: the drive home, parking in the Aldi car park, buying whatever the hell was in that bag – she'd done it all without really thinking, musing as she was over Mary's testimony and the increasing anxiety she felt about Phamie MacDonald's whereabouts. As she retrieved the bag and carried it through to the kitchen, Birch noted – not for the first time – her own subconscious biases rising up, trying to prod their way into her conscious mind. She had a mental block around domestic abuse, she knew: even now, having worked on cases, met survivors, undertaken training, Birch still found it hard to understand why people whose partners were abusive didn't leave. She understood it, but it was an effort for her to understand, in that she couldn't imagine herself acting that way in the same scenario.

It turned out that the plastic bag contained pasta, pasta sauce, a bottle of wine, a bag of salad, and a pale brick of cheese. As Birch unpacked these items into the fridge, she realised there was a small part of her that was angry with Phamie MacDonald: she'd withstood decades of abuse from this man. Why did she never leave, when he'd literally threatened to kill her? But at the same time, she chastised herself. Because Phamie had no money of her own. Because she had no family. Because her only friend lived next door: not far enough to run. Because her son abandoned her, helpfully taking the family savings with him. Because it would have meant leaving the only life she'd ever known. Birch slammed the fridge door.

'Don't be an idiot, Helen,' she said.

She unscrewed the cap of the wine, because she'd read somewhere that red wine was meant to 'breathe' before you drank it. Birch wasn't sure if this applied to an Aldi screw-top, but she'd give it a try. She clinked a wineglass down out of the cupboard and found herself thinking, perhaps Phamie *did* leave. Perhaps the incident in 2013 was one too many: she'd had enough, so she left him. She was elderly, yes, but that didn't mean anything. Birch recalled a story she'd been told as part of a training course on working with survivors of domestic abuse, delivered by Scottish Women's Aid. They'd supported a woman in her seventies who'd finally left her husband after decades of psychological abuse. The husband had always made sure, the trainer said, that his wife only ever owned one pair of shoes. Every day, he'd take those shoes to work with him, so she couldn't leave the house. He relied on the rather old-fashioned idea that no one would take seriously a woman who went outside with bare feet in the middle of the day.

For decades, this had worked: the woman had assumed she'd be written off as mad if she tried to go anywhere, or talk to anyone, with bare feet. But one day, something had happened – Birch couldn't remember what, but there was a *final straw* moment, and the woman had gone next door in bare feet, and told her neighbour all about her husband's treatment of her. The neighbour had, of course, believed the story and called Scottish Women's Aid, who helped the woman to leave. Who could say that the same thing hadn't happened with Phamie? Maybe she'd disappeared to get away from George, and George had gone looking for her?

The thought wasn't even complete before Birch realised she didn't believe it. It was depressing, but the statistics were against Phamie. The most likely thing that had happened was George had done something to hurt her: almost everything Birch had learned and experienced on domestic abuse cases told her that. She sloshed out a glass of wine and drank the first inch of it, standing at the kitchen worktop, waiting for the first little buzz to kick in. Outside, she could see the light turning in the back garden, the very last of it falling pink on the stone walls, the unruly grass. Birch carried her wineglass through the house, back to the hallway, and propped open the front door. This side of the house faced roughly east, and the front garden was deep in shadow now, chilly as night began to come on. Birch unhooked an old fleece from behind the door and put it on, swapping the wine from hand to hand, her tongue out, concentrating. Then she stepped over the threshold and out, crossing the wild front garden in four paces. At the gate, she paused and looked both ways along the Portobello prom: she knew how quickly cyclists could whip by, their lights flickering in the dusk. But it was quiet, so she crossed the narrow tarmac strip of the prom, and settled down on the low concrete wall that separated her little row of houses from the beach.

The novelty of living right by the sea hadn't worn off in almost two years, and Birch hoped it never would. She realised it had been weeks since she'd sat out here with a glass of wine, watching the waves, and she'd missed it. Most of her neighbours had benches in their gardens, perfectly angled for maximum sunlight and the view. Birch's own garden was too overgrown for a bench: it had been neglected by the old man who lived in the house before her, and now it was neglected by her. She'd get round to clearing it one of these days, she told herself, and besides, this wall was the best seat she could ask for.

Out of nowhere, she found herself thinking about Charlie, wishing he were able to sit there with her. They'd come to Portobello a lot as children, to paddle in the sea, bury each other up to their necks in the sand, and feed copper coins into the machines at the arcade. Thinking about her brother now, in this place, felt like a dull kind of pain. How long would it be before he was freed, and able to do things like sit on a wall by the sea and watch the clouds turn pink in the last of the light? How long before he could come and visit her here? How old would she be? Would she even still live here? Birch felt a deep shiver pass through her. Would she even still be alive? Who could know?

Further down the beach, a dog-walker threw a stick out to sea, the dog charging into the surf after it and then charging back out again, shaking off the spray. Behind her, beyond the row of houses, Birch heard the distant chug of a number 26 bus as it pulled away from a stop, headed for Seton Sands. Then there was another noise, one she didn't immediately recognise: a high trill. She jumped, slopping wine on to the sleeve of her fleece. Inside the house, her landline was ringing.

Birch swung her legs back over the wall, flinging the last of the wine out on to the sand. The glass dangling from her fingers, she dashed back over the prom, in through the front gate, and across the garden. How many times had it rung, four? Five? Six, she realised, as she reached the phone: it made a quiet clicking sound, and she knew she'd just missed the call. Birch rolled her eyes, and wandered back to the open front door, the stem of the wineglass still wedged between her fingers. She looked out at the beach once more, but the light was well and truly gone: over Fife, the moon had begun to rise. She shivered.

'Time to come in, then,' she said, her voice bitter as she closed the front door and locked herself in.

Birch took off the fleece, ignoring the wine stain she'd made on the sleeve, and hung it up. She'd long ago designated it her 'gardening coat', though she'd yet to do any gardening – the stain wouldn't matter. She crossed back over to the phone and lifted the receiver, listened to the soft burr of the dial tone for a second or two. Then she dialled 1571, expecting nothing.

'You have – one – new message,' the robotic answer-machine woman informed her. 'To listen to your message, press one.'

Birch frowned, and hit the key. Then she stiffened.

'Helen, are you there, hen? Hope I've got the right number for ye. It's – it's Jamieson, here. Jamieson Birch. It's your father.'

Birch dropped the phone. It hit the carpet with a thud, but she could still hear her father's voice, distant and reedy, piping out of the receiver.

'I jist . . . wanted tae . . . I read about Charlie, hen, in the paper, a wee while ago. I ken he wis involved wi some bad folk, but. I wanted tae see if . . .'

For a moment, there was silence, and Birch wondered if the recording had cut out. She bent down to pick up the phone, reaching out for it gingerly, as though she expected the plastic would be hot to the touch. But then her father's voice ebbed back.

'This isnae how . . . okay, look. I'll ring ye again, right? Hope tae catch ye in.'

This time, she heard the scrunchy sound as he hung up, and then the answer-machine woman said, 'To listen to the message again, press one.'

Now she knew her father was definitely gone, Birch snatched up the phone and slammed the receiver back into its cradle. Then she stood staring at it for a long time, as though she expected it to ring again, or perhaps to burst into flames.

Her father. Her *father*. She felt as though her internal organs were boiling up together in a stew of anger, fear and something else she couldn't quite place. Her pulse chugged in her ears. She tried to remember the last time she'd seen him: was she twelve or so? He'd come over one day, seemingly out of the blue, but her mother must have known ahead of time and assented to the visit, because she let him into the house. Birch remembered getting into the car with him and going somewhere, though she couldn't remember where. It was summer, and hot: she remembered winding the back window right down and sticking her head out, like a dog trying to keep cool. He'd yelled at her not to do it, and she'd kept doing it, because she hated him and because she hadn't signed off on this reconciliation attempt, or whatever it was he thought he was doing. *That* was why she remembered the car ride and not the rest of the trip: because he'd yelled at her, she'd defied him, and so he'd yelled more, and she'd defied him more, though she grew more afraid the longer she did. Her cheeks burned again now, recalling it. Paul Simon's *Rhythm of the Saints* was in the tape deck. Twelve, yes – she'd have been twelve then. There were no more visits after that. He'd barely been around before then, and he never came back.

Birch counted backward in her head. That day was almost twenty-eight years ago. How had he found her, now? How had he got her number? And why in the hell was he rearing his ugly head again? Birch plucked up the phone again, dialling 1471 this time. She was going to call him back, and tell him exactly what she thought of all this, which was —

'The last person to call you withheld their number.' The answer-machine woman sounded so smug that Birch nearly threw the phone across the room. Instead, she put the receiver down, realising she felt relief at having got out of it – at not having to interact with Jamieson Birch.

'Well, isn't that just *typical*?' she spat, her own voice sounding loud after the thin simulated voice of the phone. 'He gets to call *me*, but makes sure I can't call him back. All on his fucking terms, as usual.'

Birch sat down on the chair next to the coffee table where the phone sat not ringing, a newly threatening presence in the room. She looked at the mantelpiece, and the photograph of her mother. After a few minutes of trying very hard not to, Birch allowed herself to cry.

10

The following day was another bright one: Edinburgh basked in what would likely be its last, late summer spell of warmth. As Birch turned right on to Waverley Bridge, her favourite view in the city opened out before her. The Old Town, rising up out of itself in layers, like a jagged wedding cake: one long crow-stepped line of sunlit sandstone buildings running all the way from the Scotsman Hotel to Ramsay Gardens and the Castle Esplanade. She glimpsed the panorama for only a few seconds before an airport bus pulled out in front of her, and she swore.

'Watch the bloody road, woman,' she muttered, thankful that Amy wasn't in the car. She'd left her at Fettes Avenue, following up on the warrant they'd need to discover more about the sale of the MacDonalds' house. Birch hadn't yet told McLeod of her fears over Phamie's safety. As far as he knew, the case was still just Amy, doing quiet, necessary grunt work. McLeod wasn't the sort of person to get ruffled by the testimony of an old lady with dementia, no matter what she'd said. If he found out that Birch was following up leads based on nothing more than *a really bad feeling*, there could be hell to pay.

Besides, she needed to be alone. Last night's phone call had unsettled her more than she could ever have prepared for. She'd sat for a long time next to the phone after she'd listened to her father's message, waiting to see if he would call back: wanting him to, but also hoping he absolutely never would. After a while she'd replayed the voicemail he'd left, and then replayed it again. Before she knew it, Birch had listened to the message over ten times, listening for something, some clue – though what that clue might be, or what it might reveal, she didn't know. Eventually, hunger had forced her up out of the chair, and she'd put together her Aldi meal via a series of tiny, delicate movements. She didn't want to crash pans around or even run the tap too hard in case the phone rang and she failed to hear it. She'd eaten standing up in the kitchen, leaning in the doorway so she could see the phone, her thoughts running at ninety miles per hour.

Her mother had been anxious – as she came to the end of her treatment and realised that nothing more could be done – about her own funeral. As she and Birch had gone through the difficult process of making arrangements, her mother had stated emphatically that she didn't want Jamieson to be there. Alone and floundering in the wake of her mother's death, Birch hadn't known how to broach that: how to find her father to let him know his ex-wife was dead, but that he wasn't welcome at the funeral. In the end, she did nothing, and it worked. Jamieson Birch did not show up. Birch found herself wondering now, as she drove through sunny Edinburgh on what ought to have been an ordinary Wednesday morning, if her father had ever heard about her mother's death. Perhaps he assumed she was alive to this day.

Birch parked on East Market Street, across the road from a bubble tea bar with a chalkboard that exclaimed, *Hello! Is it tea you're looking for?* She tried to summon a smile, but it was hard work. She'd finally fallen into bed the night before and surprised herself by dropping off to sleep almost immediately. But then she had dreamed long, stressful, complicated dreams all night: her father in every one of them. She rubbed her eyes for the fiftieth time that morning. It was going to be a difficult day.

The platforms of Waverley Station were still far below, but Birch could feel the chug and pulse of the trains through the soles of her feet on the pavement as she walked towards the Market Street entrance. She passed under the long shadow of North Bridge, and pattered down the station steps into the concourse.

Commuter time had passed, but the station was still busy with newly arrived visitors and folk with wheeled suitcases running to catch their departures. On the footbridge, Birch collared a platform guard in a ScotRail uniform.

'Excuse me,' she said. The man looked down his nose at her, annoyed at having been stopped. Birch flashed her ID. 'I'm from Police Scotland.'

She watched him wind his neck in. 'Oh,' he said. 'How can I help . . . officer?'

Birch pushed a smile around on her face until it settled. 'I'm looking for . . . I think they call themselves *gricers*? The group of men who come here to look at trains. Can you tell me where they like to hang out?'

The man rolled his eyes. 'Is it too much to hope you're going to arrest them?'

'Yes, I'm afraid so. I'm just looking for a quick chat.'

'Okay.' He pointed along the concourse, the way Birch had come. 'There are a few platforms they favour, but 8 and 9 are your best bet. They're usually way out at the far end, on the east side. That's where the big Pendolinos come in from London.'

'Thanks,' Birch said.

'No problem. Careful they don't bore you to death, though.'

Platform 8 was a long platform, and although most of its length was covered, the roofing ran out before the concrete underfoot, and at the far end there was a sunny, exposed patch where the whole thing tapered off into the tangle of tracks. A gaggle of four men were standing in this little triangle of sunshine, with their backs to Birch as she approached. They were looking eastward, in the direction of the tunnel cut into the foot of Calton Hill: a narrow double-barrelled passageway that carried trains out of Waverley and on to the East Coast Mainline south, through Newcastle and York to Newark, Peterborough and eventually London. Beyond the shoulder of the hill, the sun sparkled on the higher points of the skyline stretching to Abbeyhill and Portobello. The Firth of Forth was a hazy blue strip on the far horizon. Birch rubbed her eyes a final time, and tried to shunt her brain fully into work mode.

'Good morning, gentlemen.'

When they turned, Birch was surprised to note that two of the men were much younger than she'd expected: perhaps only eighteen or so. All four wore backpacks, and the two youngsters carried expensive-looking cameras around their necks.

'Morning,' said one of the older men. His tone of voice was bemused, and he took a couple of swaggering steps towards her. Birch held out her ID: she wanted to cut off any tedious banter before it started.

'Detective Inspector Helen Birch,' she said, and the man stopped walking. She nodded in the direction of the tunnel. 'Nice day for it.'

'It certainly is.' The other three were eyeing their de facto leader. 'How can we help you, Detective Inspector?'

Birch drew level with the four men. The two younger ones shuffled instinctively away from her.

'Don't worry,' she said, 'no one's in any trouble. I'm looking into a missing person case and witnesses are thin on the ground.' She glanced at the nearest of the young men, the camera slung against his chest. 'You must see all sorts, doing this.'

The boy nodded.

'Come on now, Jason.' The older man who'd spoken first gave the boy a playful cuff on the shoulder. 'What have we talked about? Use your words, son.'

'Yeah,' Jason said.

'Nice to meet you, Jason,' Birch replied. 'And you are . . .?'

The group's leader held his hand up, rather than out: opting for a wave instead of a handshake. 'Geoff,' he said. 'This here's Drew.'

The other older man also raised his hand. Birch tried not to laugh: they were like boy scouts, saluting her. She wondered if this was how they greeted one another.

'And this is Matty, our young protégé,' Geoff said. The other young man threw Birch a beaming smile, which she couldn't help but return, in spite of her rather cloudy thoughts. She noticed for the first time that he had Down's syndrome.

'Hi, Matty,' she said.

Matty turned away from her, but spoke, pointing eastward. 'That's the Calton Tunnel,' he said. 'This line was built in 1846, and the second track was added in 1902.'

Geoff smiled. 'Matty knows his stuff,' he said. 'Keeps the rest of us right.'

'Which train are you waiting for now, Matty?' Birch asked. She felt a rustle of amusement pass among the men.

'We're not waiting for any specific train,' Matty replied. 'But the next one to come through will be the southbound 10.50 from Aberdeen to Penzance. That's the longest end-to-end train journey in the UK, and it takes thirteen and a half hours.'

'Whoah,' Birch said. 'I'll remember that for future pub quizzes. Thanks.'

'You're welcome,' Matty replied.

Down to business now, Helen, she thought. Keep your mind on the job. 'So, gents. Like I say, I'm investigating a missing person case, and I think the four of you might know the individual I'm keen to find. His name is George MacDonald, and I believe he is, or was, a keen train buff himself.'

As she spoke, Birch glanced at each of the men's faces in turn. Matty and Jason looked blank, but Geoff and Drew, she could see, both recognised the name.

'George,' Geoff said, after a moment. 'Yes, I know George. He's gone missing?'

'His son believes he has, yes. Have you seen him in recent times?'

Geoff looked at Drew. 'When would the last time be?' he said. 'It's a few years ago now, Detective Inspector. Could be five years ago? You think?'

'Aye,' Drew said. 'Could be.'

Geoff looked back at Birch. 'I always just assumed he was getting on a bit, didn't want to be out in the elements any more, you know? I hope he hasn't come to any harm.'

Birch tried her best to keep her face blank. 'That's what we're trying to find out,' she said. 'Five years ago, you say? That would be, what? 2014?'

'Or so,' Geoff said. 'Yeah.'

Birch took her phone from her pocket. Behind her, further up the platform, the 10.50 pulled in. Matty and Jason aimed their cameras at the locomotive and began taking photos.

'Would the two of you mind if I take a few notes, while we talk?'

The two older men shook their heads.

'Great. So, before he stopped turning up, was George a regular? Did you see a lot of him?'

Geoff waved a hand. 'So-so,' he said. 'He could be a bit moody, to be honest with you. Sometimes he'd daunder along all hail-fellow-well-met, and have a chat. Other times I'd be stood here and I'd look up and see George away over on platform 2.'

Geoff and Drew both looked northward, and Birch turned her head.

'You can't see it now,' Geoff added. 'They've built a whole new piece of station just recently. But it's over yonder. George could be a funny one.' He looked to Drew for confirmation. 'Right? It was like sometimes, he just didn't have the time of day for anybody.'

Drew made a sort of snort sound.

'What am I missing?' Birch asked.

'Well.'

Birch was realising that Drew was a man of few words. She looked at him until he felt obliged to speak again.

'Always hud time fer the ladies.'

Geoff laughed. 'True, that's true.'

Bingo, Birch thought. I knew it.

'But you know, this wasn't really George's station,' Geoff went on. 'He used to start here, but he'd get bored after a while and head out to Carstairs Junction. That was his real stomping ground.'

Yes, I knew that, Birch thought. Robertson Bennet had said the same.

'Why Carstairs?' she asked.

'Oh' – Geoff was suddenly animated – 'it's a fascinating wee station. Out in the middle of nowhere, but it has all sorts to recommend it. It's got an important triangular junction to the south. If you've ever been to Carlisle on the train from here, or to Manchester, you'll have passed through that junction. It's where the West Coast Mainline divides. The Caledonian Sleepers go through Carstairs. There are also what we call Up and Down Loops, where some services are stopped to allow others through.'

Birch frowned. Geoff took this to mean she needed more information.

'For example,' he said, 'there's an early service from Glasgow Central to North Berwick.' He raised one hand to signify the train he meant. 'It's slow. But over here' – Geoff raised his other hand – 'there's a faster service to Manchester. Carstairs Junction is where the slow train will be held while the fast train passes.' Geoff glided his hands past one another, through the air.

'Plus,' he said, 'there's a big curve in the line at Carstairs Junction. The trains come in slow, and you get a really good look at them.'

'Sounds great,' Birch lied. 'Are there others out there, who might know of George?'

Geoff frowned. 'Maybe one or two,' he said, 'but it's a pain to get to. Once you're there, you're stuck there for a while, unless you drive, which is rather against the spirit of the thing. It's a lonely sort of place, a bit of a ghost station really, as far as footfall goes. From what I know, George was the only one who went out there very regularly.'

'Handy fer him,' Drew said.

Birch blinked. 'I'm sorry?'

'I say it wis handy fer him. Playin away. Naebody around tae see whit he wis up tae.'

Birch paused in her note-taking, her finger hovering over her phone screen. 'Just to be clear,' she said, 'are you referring to women again? You think George was having an affair? Or affairs?'

Geoff was giving Drew a look, but Drew didn't seem to have noticed. 'Aye,' he said. 'Or he wis tryin'. Saw him head oot oan the Carstairs train wi' some lassie a few times.'

'One lassie in particular?' Birch asked.

'Naw.' Drew chucked. 'George didnae discriminate.'

God, I hate when I'm right, Birch thought. She looked at Geoff. 'Were you aware of this?'

The man squirmed. 'I mean, I didn't know George all that well,' he said, still looking hard at Drew. 'I didn't feel it was any of my *business . . .*'

'I'll take that as a yes,' Birch said. 'These lassies, Drew. Were they *lassies*, as in, younger women? Or is that a catch-all term?'

Drew shrugged. 'Think he took all sorts, did aul' Ginger.'

Birch froze. Behind her, the 10.50 set off, hissing and heaving its way out of the station. Matty and Jason's camera shutters clicked. She waited for the final roar of the rear locomotive to pass before she continued.

'Did you say *Ginger*?'

'George's nickname,' Geoff chipped in. 'In fact, we all knew him as Ginger. When you said George MacDonald, it took me a moment to connect who it was you meant.'

'Ginger Mack,' Drew said. 'We aw called him that.'

'An alias,' Birch said quietly.

Geoff shifted his weight. 'I suppose you could call it that.'

'These women.' Birch glanced at Drew. 'Do you know any of them? Could you tell me how I'd find any of them?'

She knew from the look on his face what the answer would be.

'Not a scooby,' he said.

'And for all we know,' Geoff cut in, 'they might all have told George to get lost. He did a lot of chatting up, for sure, but we don't actually *know* he ever had affairs.'

He looked again at Drew, a look Birch didn't like.

'Geoff,' she said. 'This has been so helpful, but I might have follow-up questions. Might I take your contact details? It may be necessary for us to have another chat, at some point.'

At this, the man rallied. 'Of course,' he said. 'Let me give you my card.'

Birch and Drew both watched as Geoff took off his backpack and rummaged in several of the pockets. At last, he retrieved a business card, slightly bent, which he handed to Birch.

Waverley Model Trains, it read. *Bought & Sold, Restoration & Refurbishment.* There was a URL for an eBay shop, and Geoff's contact details at the bottom. He still had an @lycos.com email address.

'Great,' Birch said, pocketing the card. 'Just a couple more questions. First, did either of you ever meet George's wife, Phamie?'

The men looked at each other. 'There's erm ... there's a no wives or girlfriends policy here,' Geoff said. He had the decency to look shamefaced, while Drew simply nodded. 'We don't even tend to talk about our partners, really.' He glanced over at Jason, who was flipping through photos on his camera screen. 'If we have them,' he added.

'But you knew that George was married?' Birch asked. 'Which made you notice that he was chatting up other women?'

'Yes,' Geoff said. Drew was nodding. 'Though I don't know how I knew. He must have mentioned it at some point.'

Birch looked at Drew, too. He didn't say much, but what he did say came out ungilded, which was helpful.

'These women,' she said, 'this was going on for the whole time you knew George? Right up until you last saw him?'

Drew shrugged. 'It wisnae some big thing,' he said. 'He wis just a flirt. But aye, it got embarrassin', a man o his age.'

You're saying he was a dirty old man, Birch thought. Great.

'Okay,' she said. 'Last question, and I think I know how you're going to answer it, but I have to ask anyway. Do either of you have any idea as to the whereabouts of George MacDonald, or his wife Phamie MacDonald?'

Neither man needed to speak: their blank expressions were genuine.

'I hope you sort this out, Detective Inspector.'

Birch gave Geoff her best professional smile. You and me both, pal, she thought.

The thought of breaking open another person's diary gave Amy a feeling of mild horror. She'd been avoiding doing it all morning, though she couldn't really put her finger on why. She'd noticed, when she and her boss talked about the diaries, that DI Birch had seemed almost envious of this particular task. The three scruffy notebooks sat on top of Amy's in-tray, their covers flaking on to the white paper memos and photocopies underneath. She wondered if her reticence about opening them was something to do with being an only child: her teenage peers had often griped about their siblings stealing and reading their diaries, then threatening to spread the sensitive information therein around the school playground. Amy had no siblings to worry about, but had never kept a diary anyway. She'd lived in fear throughout her teenage years that someone far worse than a pesky brother or sister might learn her innermost thoughts.

Amy's mother would, she knew, have *loved* to have come across a little padlocked notebook whose contents might help her to figure out her quiet and fastidious daughter. She would have relished the opportunity to sit Amy down and say, 'I'm so glad I finally know what's going on in your head.' The truth was, there was nothing going on, and never had been: Amy just never got interested in the things most teen girls got interested in. Boys were immature and annoying, parties were mildly frightening, and beer tasted so dreadful that neither teenage Amy nor adult Amy could understand the hype. Far better were books: especially non-fiction books, and especially true-crime books about serial killers or famous real-life mysteries. Amy spent time with these books whenever she could, though she had to trek to the public library to get them, because the school library deemed them unsuitable and the adults in her life sure as hell would not have bought them for her. Her mother would crease up her face and tell Amy that her obsession with *this stuff* wasn't healthy. Why couldn't she make some friends, get out there, have some fun?

Amy found herself rolling her eyes, and reaching for the first of the decrepit notebooks. She'd had friends, they were just bookish types like herself. Amy suspected her mother felt short-changed: she'd wanted a daughter who'd confide in her over boy drama, not one who retreated into a paperback at every possible opportunity and asked for a fingerprint dusting set for Christmas. But perhaps also, Amy thought as she ran one manicured nail around the fixings of the notebook's little padlock, her mother was a bit afraid. It was true that at fifteen, Amy knew more about dead bodies and how to dispose of them than any teenage girl really ought to. Perhaps when her mother said, 'I don't know what's going on with you sometimes,' she was really saying, 'I don't like that I don't know what you're capable of.' Amy slid open her desk drawer, smiling. Her parents must have breathed such a sigh of relief when they found out she was going into policing. Using her powers for good, as Amy liked to think of it.

At the bottom of the desk drawer was a pair of metal scissors. Amy grasped the scissor points together, and jammed them into the loop of the little padlock fastening the first of the diaries. The loop didn't so much break as crumble, rusted green and crusty as it was. Flecks of that crustiness scattered across Amy's desk, and she wrinkled her nose, reaching for the second diary. It took her less than a minute to break open all three, and she felt glad that Birch had encouraged her to do it herself. She realised the locks had never been a barrier to opening the notebooks: it was just her own weird mental block.

As she opened the first of the diaries, the spine made a crackling sound, and she felt the cheap glue binding of the book give out. She flicked through the first few pages. They were filled with dense text in a small, neat hand. There were no dates written anywhere, but a slip of paper fell out on to Amy's computer keyboard. It was a newspaper clipping, yellow-brown with age, dated May 1977. The headline read: *Whizz kid's letter lands brand-new tech for school.* In the accompanying photo, Amy recognised a very young Robertson Bennet. He was teenaged and awkward, sporting what looked like an attempted Elvis quiff. He was grinning, holding up a piece of paper that Amy couldn't really make out in the black and white photo. She skimmed the article, and learned that Robert MacDonald, 16, of James Gillespie's High School in Edinburgh, had written an impassioned letter to Apple Computers. To the delight of his teachers, Apple had responded by offering to send the school an Apple II computer, fresh off the production line. Amy smiled at the fact that Phamie had saved this, and wondered if Robertson Bennet remembered it, now he was a software big shot. She tucked the clipping back into the notebook, and reached for another.

All three diaries were much of a muchness: no dates, just that neat, close-packed handwriting, looping on and on, sometimes for pages at a time. Amy fanned out the pages of each one, but nothing more fell out. She studied the paper – cheap and translucent, its edges browning – and hazarded a guess that the diary with the newspaper clipping inside was the oldest of the three, the first in this weird, private trilogy. Now, she realised, there was nothing left to do but read what Phamie had written. She turned to the first page of the oldest notebook, and began.

Mary says I should keep a diary. Phamie wrote. *She showed me hers, and said it keeps her company sometimes. I asked her what on earth she puts into it, and she said, all the thoughts I don't share with Donald. I'll admit, I was surprised to hear that. I assumed Mary shared everything with Donald. It looks from the outside as if they tell each other everything. Mary laughed at me, and asked if I share everything with George. Well, of course I don't. But George is different, not like Donald at all. George wouldn't thank me for telling him my thoughts, I suspect.*

I'm not entirely sure what a diary is for, but I promised her I would make one. She thinks it might be good for me. Mary really is a good friend, and I feel very lucky to have her. I know that she worries about me, and I wish she wouldn't. I don't like the idea of her worrying. But I know that sometimes I lose control of myself and tell her too much, and give her cause to worry. Perhaps that is why she wants me to write in this diary, so that I will have an outlet for my feelings, and I won't go round and bother her with them as much! Not that she'd ever say that to me. But that does seem like as good a reason as any to carry on writing here.

Here, the entry ended, leaving a few blank lines at the bottom of the page. Amy looked up from the notebook, and frowned. It felt strange to meet Phamie MacDonald for the first time in this way: intimately, but not in person. She sounded like a straightforward sort of woman. But it was also mildly upsetting to hear Phamie gaslight herself the way she did. Amy felt sad for her: she'd assumed her friend's suggestion that she keep a diary was an act of self-preservation on Mary's part. Amy suspected that Mary had in fact advised Phamie to start a diary for the same reason that people in violent partnerships were still advised to do so: because it would create a timeline of George's outbursts, develop a log of evidence against him. Amy wanted to believe that Mary had been canny, had hoped that something could perhaps be done about George's behaviour. She smiled a bittersweet smile, thinking of the little old lady in the nursing home. Then she gave her head a quick shake, and turned the page to read the next entry.

A difficult day today. This morning, a man walked into the post office and refused to leave. He was what my great-aunty Isobel would have called 'a gentleman of the road'. He wanted money, he said it was for a train ticket. First he went down the queue, person to person, asking for loose change. Then he came up to the counter. He could see my change dispenser and demanded I give him some money from it. I tried to stay calm but he was rather frightening. Joyce was working in the back room, and came through to help me, but there was no man on the premises to assist us. The man began to shout and most of the customers who'd been waiting left.

In the end, Joyce had to telephone for the police. Unfortunately, the man overheard her, and ran away before the officers arrived. When they did, I felt awfully guilty. The man hadn't committed any real crime, and it was hard to give a description beyond his dishevelled appearance. Joyce and I talked it over all the rest of the day. Had we wasted the officers' time? I worry that we did, but calling them seemed the only way to be rid of him.

Oh Phamie, Amy wanted to say. You did all the right things. You really did.

Once Robert had gone up to bed, I told George about the incident. I expected him to be sympathetic. I know he gets terribly angry about tramps and people like that, their behaviour. And he did get angry, but not the way that I thought he would. He was angry with me. He said I didn't do enough to deal with the man – said he was probably drunk or high on something and therefore no match for Joyce and me. He was insistent that we ought to have frogmarched him off the premises, the two of us, and said that we failed the Post Office and our customers by not doing so. I tried to explain to George how frightening the man had been, but he was having none of it. He said he was ashamed of me for being such a shrinking violet. That's something he says a lot. 'These things wouldn't happen to you so often, Phamie, if you weren't such a bloody shrinking violet!' Then he went out. That was several hours ago now, and as usual he didn't tell me where he was going. I know that George is a grown man, that he needs his freedom from me and from Robert. I really do listen when he says that to me, and I really do try to understand. But I do so wish he would tell me where it is he goes. I do so wish I didn't have to sit up into these small hours, looking every two minutes at the bedside clock, wondering if he's all right. Wondering where he might be. Wondering when he'll come home.

12

Birch was disobeying orders, she knew: McLeod had said, *I don't want you on this.* What she ought to be doing was feeding back to Amy, and then getting on with her other cases – all of them somehow at the dull, deskwork stage, all at the same time. It should have been Amy who went to see the gricers, too, but Birch was glad she'd gone in person. As she drove back towards the station, she kicked herself for not thinking about possible aliases sooner. Right turn at Jenners department store, where a woman in a purple tunic was arranging glinting perfume bottles in the window display. Along St Andrew Square and a left on to Queen Street, where the sun gleamed off the railings at Queen Street Gardens and the leaves of the big trees were just beginning to turn. Birch felt her face getting red: *check for aliases* should have been the first three words she said to Amy, or just about. *Perhaps I was distracted by the son's nom de plume,* she thought. *Perhaps I assumed that, with a name as common as George MacDonald, a man might feel he could get away with anything.*

Right turn down the hill on to the cobbles of Howe Street: beyond the black block of St Stephen's Church tower, Birch could see Warriston, Trinity and a glittering strip of the Firth of Forth.

'Ginger,' she said aloud. She pictured Robertson Bennet, his tawny hair. Ginger might have been less an alias on his father's part, and more a nickname: given to him by other people, against his will. Maybe he'd decided to make use of it, make what might have started as a taunt into a persona he could slip on and off.

'We'll soon find out,' Birch said to the empty car.

Raeburn Place was quiet – in fact, the whole city was quiet. Though she routinely changed her mind, Birch would often tell people that this was her favourite time in the Edinburgh year. Early September: the Fringe all finished up, most of the tourists gone, and the students not yet back at their lectures. After the excesses of the Festival, there was an earnest, back-to-school feeling about the place. She usually felt peaceful at this time of year, but not today. Her mind churned with the possible new discovery she'd made, tinged as it was with guilt and annoyance at not having thought of it sooner. And behind all that, the spectre of her father loomed. She realised she was fretting about what might be in her voicemails when she got home.

Birch turned off Comely Bank Road on to Fettes Avenue, then slowed down to nose her Mondeo into the police station car park. She walked into the building as briskly as she could, determined to get to a computer without running into Amy. If her colleague had a chance to ask her how it went, Birch would be forced to fess up about the alias, and Amy would take over running checks on Ginger Mack. It was a weird thrill Birch felt, stepping into her office and closing the door behind her. A butterflies feeling, but sickly, not-quite-right. She knew a hunch when she felt one, and didn't want to waste any time in being proven right.

She ran searches for *Ginger Mc*, *Ginger Mac* and *Ginger Mack*, and the last turned up gold. *Mack* wasn't desperately common, but it was a real surname. It was also unique: though *Ginger* and *Mack* both turned up on profiles under *also known as*, there was only one man in the system who'd reported his given name as Ginger Mack. Born 1935, the same year as George MacDonald. Married, resident in Edinburgh, and, seemingly, not yet deceased.

The crimes fitted, too. Whereas George MacDonald had received a single slap on the wrist for trespassing on railway property, Ginger Mack had done it numerous times. He'd parted with a lot of cash: the fines for his offences got higher as he repeated and repeated them. Birch skimmed the files: *Carstairs Junction*, always there. *Witnessed walking the trackside adjacent to Strawfrank Road. Witnessed in the sidings below Eskdale Farm.* George MacDonald, glimpsed through trees; standing in the wagon yard;

walking off the platform's end, into the dark. George MacDonald, wearing his other name like a gallus coat. Birch scrolled.

'What the hell were you *doing* out there?' she said, and her own voice spooked her in the empty room.

That wasn't all. Ginger Mack had been questioned in relation to several missing person cases. The word *suspect* was used more than once. At one point, way back in 1979, he'd appeared in a police line-up. The files showed interview transcripts (bland: *I'm sorry, officer, I've no idea*), the checking in and out of personal possessions, a description of the outfit he'd worn for the ID parade. Rather ancient now: some of the files were scans of yellowed memo sheets, typewritten and scrawled upon. Relics from back in the day, when a given name was a given name, and ID checks wouldn't be run until someone was in proper trouble. Nothing had stuck to Ginger Mack, but a cold feeling was spreading through Birch, making her hands and feet prickle. The missing person cases were all women, some *in suspicious circumstances*. She clicked through each one, then clicked through again. Unsolved, the lot. Gone cold long ago.

Birch picked up the phone and dialled Amy's mobile. Two rings, and then, 'You've reached Amy.'

'Oh God, Kato,' Birch said, by way of greeting. 'George MacDonald. I think we were right about him.'

'Okay,' Amy said. She was sitting opposite Birch, looking down at her lap. The tissue she had pulled from her sleeve as her boss began to speak was twisted into a tight coil and shedding, little white flakes scattered all over Amy's smart pencil skirt. She swatted at them now, as though noticing them for the first time. 'Okay.'

'Tell me your thoughts, Kato.'

Amy seemed to shake herself a little. 'Well,' she said. 'I mainly have questions, I think.'

'Fire away.'

'Right. First, how sure are you that Ginger Mack and George MacDonald are one and the same?'

Birch shrugged. 'Officially,' she said, 'not very. I haven't cross-checked anything yet, so I've no proof. But unofficially? I'm about as sure as I can be. We know George MacDonald went by that name in his wee railway club. We know that George MacDonald and Ginger Mack both frequented Carstairs Station: a place I've been precisely once, by the way, and I can tell you there was absolutely nothing and no one there. It's like the station that time forgot, so it's a bit of a coincidence if these two men of the exact same age went there regularly, but aren't the same person. Though he's less prolific than Ginger, George also has previous with trespassing on the railway. And the very reason we're looking at him at all is because he's mixed up in the case of a missing woman. This one just happens to be his wife, but what if this weren't his first go-around? What if he's been involved with disappeared women before?'

Birch dropped her hands. She realised she'd been counting off the similarities on her fingers.

Amy was nodding. 'There's also the jewellery,' she said.

Birch blinked.

'Remember, marm? George MacDonald was in possession of jewellery belonging to a missing girl. A runaway.'

'Shit,' Birch said. She rummaged on her desk for the photocopies she'd made for McLeod. 'You're right. You're bloody right.'

Papers slid around, and out of the corner of her eye, Birch saw Amy tilt her knee up slightly, preventing an avalanche of files off her side of the desk.

'Aha.' Birch slid her copy out of the mess, and scanned it for the name of the runaway girl. 'The jewellery belonged to the mother of one Maisie Kerr.'

Amy leaned in to peer at Birch's screen, trying to find that same name among the list of cases Ginger Mack was linked to. Birch didn't need to look far. Maisie Kerr disappeared in 1999: Ginger Mack's last ever mention.

'It's him,' she said. 'Ginger Mack was questioned about Maisie Kerr's disappearance, and then George MacDonald tried to pawn her jewellery. They're the same man. Surely . . . they have to be.'

The two women looked at each other across the desk. On the wall, the clock ticked. From beyond the closed door came the muffled trilling of phones in the bullpen, the occasional bark of a laugh.

'I think I have even more questions now,' Amy said at last.

Birch raised one hand and rubbed at her face. 'Yeah,' she said. 'Like, where did all these women go to?'

Amy shivered.

'Some of them are written up as runaways here,' Birch said, her hand still worrying at her face as she looked at the screen. 'Younger women. Wanting to get out from under their mothers.'

Amy was nodding. 'So did Ginger George help them? Get on a train with them, like your guy Drew said, and help them disappear? Or did he . . . disappear them himself, in some way?'

Birch snorted, but there was no mirth in it. 'How many ways can you disappear a person?'

At this, Amy shrugged. 'You've heard of those cases,' she said. 'Older guys who kidnap young women – runaways, often – and lock them in a basement, or somewhere. Decades go by and eventually one escapes, and there's a whole bunch of them, and they've been living with this one psycho bloke.'

'I guess.' Birch looked down again at the photocopy: the grainy black and white photo of the jewellery, the little spikes of the earring backs needle-thin and lethal. 'That, or we've got a serial killer on our hands.'

As soon as the words were out of her mouth, Birch regretted them. In her head, she flicked through the roster of infamous names: Manuel. Tobin. Bible John. Across the desk, Amy's eyes had widened.

'Sorry,' she said. 'Forget I said that. I'm getting very, very ahead of myself. After all' – Birch nodded towards the screen – 'according to this, Ginger Mack is an innocent man.'

'Till proven guilty,' Amy said, but her voice was quiet. Birch's outburst had unsettled the air between them.

Another silence fell. Birch was thinking about Peter Tobin, thinking about all the years he'd managed to get away with it, the lives he'd—

'Do we go to McLeod?'

Birch almost jumped. Amy's train of thought had clearly been more practical.

'I think . . . not yet,' she replied, drawing out the words so she could think as she said them. 'We've got to get this into better shape before we take it beyond this room.'

Amy sat up a little. 'What can I do?' she said.

'Well.' Birch scanned the list on her screen for what felt like the hundredth time. 'We need to link Ginger Mack and George MacDonald, and be *sure* they're one and the same. If they're not, I'll want to see Mack's birth certificate at the very least before I'm convinced. That might take a little while, so first up, get Robertson Bennet on the phone. See if he can remember his father going by that name, or any other for that matter.'

Amy's back was straight, and her head was tilted, listening. 'Yes, marm.'

'Meanwhile, I want to follow up on these missing persons. Mack's last appearance here is 1999, before my time and yours. But not so long ago that no one will remember him. I might go and knock on some doors.'

Amy was nodding.

'And not just police,' Birch went on. 'I think we should go and see some next of kin. Starting with Mrs Kerr, Maisie's mother. Maisie's case is the only one where Ginger Mack *and* George MacDonald are both involved – as well as being the most recent. Guess what the Kerrs' address is written up as, in this file?'

Amy raised an eyebrow. 'Somewhere in Carstairs?'

'Carstairs Junction,' Birch replied, pointing at the screen. 'Ginger George's favourite place.'

The two women looked at one another, their faces grim. Birch let out a long sigh. This case was about to grow arms and legs. McLeod would be livid. And her father was trying to phone her, trying to reinsert himself back into her life. Her *father*. Just exactly what she didn't need right now.

'Marm?'

'Yes? Sorry, I was drifting into my own wee world, there.'

'It's okay,' Amy said. 'I just – I thought you might want an update on Phamie's diaries.'

'You've opened them?'

'I have. You were right, it didn't merit any serious lock-picking.'

Birch smiled. 'So they are diaries, then, as we thought?'

'Yes,' Amy said, 'and definitely written by Phamie. They seem to go back as far as the late seventies. I haven't got very far in yet, but they back up Robertson Bennet's testimony about his father's abuse.'

Birch pulled air in through her teeth. 'Anything significant leap out at you?'

Amy laughed. 'An old newspaper clipping *literally* leaped out at me,' she said, 'but it was just a memento from Bennet's school days. Thus far, I haven't learned anything we didn't already know. Except that Bennet had a terrible hairdo when he was sixteen.'

Birch smiled, but the smile faded fast. 'Keep at it, Kato,' she said. 'I'd like you to read through the whole lot, and note anything that might lead us to Phamie's whereabouts. Any time she mentions a friend or relative, going on holiday, a particular haunt – and you've got initiative, you know how this is done. Anything that raises a red flag, note it down. I don't think McLeod can object to you preparing me a memo with the pertinent information, can he?'

Amy shook her head. 'No, marm. I'll get that done asap.'

Birch nodded. 'Besides,' she said, 'I think McLeod's *light touch* isn't going to cut it on this case any more. I have a feeling we're about to get in deep.'

Edinburgh Evening News

Missing woman case re-prioritised in hope of potential DNA breakthrough

ED LAING   10 March 1998   Share this article
Email

RETURN TO ARCHIVE
SIGN UP TO OUR DAILY NEWSLETTER

Lothian and Borders Police have re-prioritised the case of missing nursery teacher Christine Turnbull, almost 33 years after she went missing.

Christine Turnbull was last seen in Glasgow on 1 June 1965. An Edinburgh resident, she was visiting her aunt who lived in the city. At the time of her disappearance, she was 23 years old.

The circumstances surrounding Christine's disappearance have remained a mystery for over thirty years, but police are shining new light on the case in the hope that advances in DNA testing may turn up new evidence.

Christine's empty handbag was found shortly after she disappeared, leading police to believe she may have been robbed or even kidnapped. They have now revealed that DNA swabs have been taken from the handbag and could be used to track down a new suspect or suspects in the case.

Read more Christine Turnbull stories in the Edinburgh Evening News online archive.

13

With only a limited amount of her Wednesday left, Birch did the one thing she felt she could to move the investigation along: emailed Al Lonsdale, custody sergeant and her former colleague at Gayfield Square police station. Al had been around for ever, and his elephant's memory was legendary. She kept the details light: *Wanted to pick that giant brain of yours about something that might turn out to be nothing. Also, it would be lovely to see you.* Once she'd hit send, Birch refreshed her inbox about once every minute, and resisted the urge to text Amy and ask how things were coming along. Instead, she tried to focus on her paperwork: the pressing cases that were based on more than just speculation and doubt. But she found she couldn't stop thinking of George MacDonald, of Ginger Mack, of what Drew the trainspotter had said about trains out of town and random women. Of Carstairs Junction: a dot on the map, just train tracks, a haulage yard, a few houses. If she tried to stop thinking about all that, she just found herself thinking of her father, and at least mulling over the investigation still counted as work, and didn't make her feel quite so sick with nerves.

She Googled, but Birch found no hotels or B&Bs near Carstairs Station, nowhere obvious to conduct illicit affairs or stow newly departed runaways. He might have had friends there, she thought. An address he used. Perhaps Ginger Mack had a whole life: a house out there by the railway, mortgage, bank account, papers in his name. That idea was worth following up: she tapped out an email to Amy. Perhaps George had just decided to become Ginger permanently, and he'd taken Phamie with him. Did she have another name, too? All afternoon, Birch chased the thoughts in circles around her head. She only knew one thing for sure: no one ever just disappears. She, of all people, ought to know: her own brother came back from the land of the missing, though it took him fourteen years. Her father wanted to reconnect after twenty-eight. Phamie MacDonald had to be out there somewhere. George too: still sitting by a railway track, watching trains go by. Still daundering up to women, aged eighty-three. Still at large.

Finally, 5 p.m. came. It would be reasonable for Birch to stop struggling on with her cases, and go home. As she began to pack up, her phone pinged: a text from Al Lonsdale.

Free tonight, love? Pub?

Birch paused, smiling, her phone hovering over her half-stuffed laptop bag.

It's on me, she wrote, *if you'll meet me at the Jinglin' Geordie, Fleshmarket Close?*

She waited: message read.

We going to arrest someone? Al eventually wrote back.

Birch smiled. *I hear it's much better than it used to be.* She added a tongue-out emoji. She couldn't imagine Al ever using an emoji, or knowing what one was. She was amazed to find he'd joined the world of texting.

Believe it when I see it, he replied. *See you there.*

It felt like a long time since Birch had stood in Fleshmarket Close. She had memories of it from her uniformed days: it was a dark, steep close, but sheltered, the tenements towering high above. The stone steps were broken up by wide landings, some with lees and doorways favoured by the local homeless population. Fleshmarket Close was the handiest shortcut down through the Old Town buildings to Waverley Station, and many a weekend drinker ran its gauntlet faster than was really advisable. Birch remembered it as a place where she'd broken up fights, piled drunks into her panda car, and issued on-the-spot public urination fines: the bad old days. Now, there was a fancy brewpub at the foot of the stairs, and the tiny Halfway House pub – which nestled on the first landing

– had received a hipster refit. The close also housed a barber shop, a hole-in-the-wall kebab place, and the Jinglin' Geordie.

The pub was and was not as Birch remembered. There were still the quaint stained-glass windows, crossed saltires painted at their centres, dimming what little light leaked in from outside. There was still the copper-topped bar, the scalloped seating booths around the walls. But someone had given the place a lick of paint, some new upholstery. The floor was clean, and the optics behind the bar gleamed. Birch even spotted tall glass jars of bar snacks: wasabi peas among them. The twenty-first century had arrived.

There were a few other folk dotted around the place, including three men propping up the bar, wearing the orange boiler suits of Network Rail. Al was nowhere to be seen. Three TVs were positioned around the bar like a panopticon in reverse: no one in the room could avoid looking at them. An episode of *Pointless* was playing, unmuted, competing with the background muzak: Al would hate this, Birch knew. She walked up to the bar, where the three railwaymen were sitting ignoring one another.

'Hedwig,' one of them said, as she approached, and Birch saw his pal jump, just slightly.

'You what?'

The first man pulled his gaze from the TV they'd all been watching. 'Hedwig,' he said. 'I bet that's a pointless answer.'

The other two said nothing, but the man in the middle of the trio snorted.

'Look,' the first man said, 'it's the name of the fucking owl, okay? Don't you have kids? Back me up here, love.'

It took Birch a moment to realise she was being spoken to. 'Oh,' she said. 'Yeah, Hedwig. Hedwig's the owl.'

The trio turned back to the TV, the matter settled.

'What can I get you?'

The barman was young, which annoyed Birch. She'd hoped for some old-timer with a long memory and a loose tongue. This guy was perhaps thirty, and wearing a Guns N' Roses T-shirt apparently without shame. His arms were heavily tattooed. On one forearm he bore a design of a bottle with the words *Mother's Ruin* snaked around it.

'Gin and tonic,' Birch said, and placed her Police Scotland badge on the bar. 'I'm off duty. But I wondered if I could have a few words?'

The young man looked down at the badge for what felt like a little too long. Birch hoped she wouldn't have to explain to him what it was.

'Sure thing,' he said at last, jerking his head away and reaching for a glass. He threw it up in the air, where it spun, before catching it deftly.

'Jesus fucking Christ, Tom,' one of the railwaymen said. All three had turned to look at the barman's trick, and Birch saw the one closest to her clock the badge as she tucked it back into her jacket. 'What is this, Stringfellows?'

Tom the barman laughed. 'Weekends, I work in Frankenstein's,' he said to Birch. 'Gotta practise.'

Birch smiled, and tried not to think of the antics she'd got up to in Frankenstein's pub as a feckless youngster.

'Hendrick's okay?' Tom asked, brandishing a bottle.

Birch prayed he wouldn't throw it in the air. 'Yep, ideal.'

He held the steel measure over her glass, and she watched as he let it overflow.

'What did you want to ask about?' he said.

Birch found herself wishing she'd got hold of a photograph of George MacDonald. She made a mental note to talk to Amy about it. Robertson Bennet might be able to provide a picture of his father: even an old one would do.

'A regular of yours,' she said. 'One Ginger Mack. Name ring a bell?'

The barman frowned. 'Not sure,' he said. 'More likely I'd know him by sight than by name.'

Birch scratched around for the little she knew about George MacDonald's appearance. 'The name isn't ironic,' she said. 'Red hair. Although possibly grey now, if he still has any. An elderly man, in his eighties.'

Tom was still frowning. 'And he's a regular?' he said.

Birch winced: this was a brick wall. 'Is, or was for a long time,' she said. 'He's a big train buff. Used to hang around on the station, taking notes.'

The railwayman closest to Birch – the one who'd noticed her badge – cleared his throat. He turned on his barstool to look properly at her. 'Ah ken him,' he said, nodding at her. 'That gadge. Ginger, you said?'

Birch took a risk: it was all but confirmed anyway. 'Also goes by the name George.'

The railwayman raised a hand. Birch could see every crease in the palm, filigreed in muck and grease.

'Big guy,' the man said, waving his raised hand. 'Or he wis. Shrunk a bit these days, bein the age he is.'

She felt her pulse speed up, just a little. 'You've seen him? In recent times?'

The railwayman dropped his hand. 'Depends whit ye mean by *recent*,' he said. 'Come tae think o it, it's been a while since he's drunk in here. This yin' – he gestured at the barman – 'he's new since I last saw that gadge, I reckon. That'll be why ye dinnae remember, Tammy.'

Birch watched Tom the barman colour slightly at the nickname. He placed a fizzing glass in front of Birch.

'That's three fifty.'

Birch dug in her pocket for change. The railwayman materialised a five pound note from somewhere inside his boiler suit.

'On me,' he said.

Birch looked up from her scrabbling, her face clearly saying, *That's not appropriate.*

'C'mon,' the man said, smiling. 'Ye're off duty, ye said.'

A large hand reached between Birch and the railwayman and settled on the bar. It, too, was clutching a five pound note.

'Sorry, sunshine. You'll have to wait in line.'

The rest of Al Lonsdale materialised, very close to Birch. She'd forgotten what a bear of a man he was, until he leaned over for an awkward hug.

'Fantastic to see you, Al,' she said, into his shoulder.

'Likewise.' Al swayed backward to look her up and down. 'How're you keeping, lass? Looking after you at Fettes, are they?'

Birch shrugged. 'Mostly,' she said. 'I do miss the old place, though.'

Tom the barman had extricated Al's fiver and now handed him the change.

'Keep that, kid,' Al said, 'and pour me a seventy.'

There was a pause. Tom looked puzzled. 'Seventy?'

The railwayman Birch had been talking to laughed. 'Shilling, ya daftie. It's a beer.' He nodded to Al. 'But they havnae served it in this place for years, pal.'

Al huffed playfully at Birch. 'Well,' he said, 'there goes my nostalgia trip, eh? 'scuse me, young lady.'

He manoeuvred his large bulk out from beside Birch, and moved along the bar to inspect the various taps.

'If I could . . .' Birch was keen to keep the railwayman's attention just a little longer. He blinked at her. 'Could I ask what you remember about Ginger Mack? How well did you know him?'

The man looked down at the bar's shining top. 'Gave each ither the time o day,' he said. 'I'd see him aboot the station as well as in this place, so I'd gie him a wee hullo an that. *How's things the day? Aye, pal, no so bad.* Ken, jist small talk.'

Birch nodded. 'Anything you particularly remember about him?'

The railwayman rubbed his neck, and Birch heard the rasp of his hand on the skin.

'He'd a laddie,' he said. 'An they fell out. I remember that fae years ago. One night he wis in here an he'd fair hit the drink, got so's he could barely stand, an I decided tae huv a wee word. *Whit's this in aid o, then,* I ask him, an he tells me his laddie, his son, went an stole aw the money fae his bank account. Sounded like a lot, too.'

Another domino falls, Birch thought. Another fact from Ginger Mack's life that matched George MacDonald's exactly.

'Did you ever meet his wife?' she asked. 'Did she ever come in here?'

The man raised an eyebrow. 'I saw him wi' plenty o' women over the years,' he said. 'Couldnae tell ye which wan was his wife, though.'

Al shuffled past them, pint in hand, heading for a table. He threw Birch a wink.

'I'd like you to think as hard as you can,' Birch said, 'about the last time you saw him. He's missing, you see, and it's becoming quite urgent that we find him.'

The man looked down at the bar again, frowning. Then he looked up. 'I'm sorry,' he said, 'but I'd be lyin' if I even said whit year it wis. He wis just . . . part of the furniture, ken? In the station, an' in here. Wi' someone like that, it takes a while fer ye tae think, Och, ah huvnae seen that gadge aboot in a while. Ken whit I mean?'

'I do. But you've been very helpful, thank you.' Birch flicked a business card out from the breast pocket of her jacket. 'If you happen to remember anything, particularly the most recent time you saw Mr Mack, I'd be grateful if you'd give me a call.'

The railwayman looked at the business card for a moment before taking it out of Birch's hand. 'I hope ye find the auld gadge,' he said. 'He wis gettin a wee bit unsteady oan his pins as I recall, and that wis a while ago, ken?'

Al had settled at a small table, as far away from the trio at the bar as he could get. Birch sipped her gin and tonic, and then placed the glass down again, trying to fit it exactly over the wet ring it had left on the wood.

'Ginger Mack,' Al said. His West Yorkshire accent made the *a* in *Mack* sound both deep and wide. 'Can't say I remember him, though it's a daft name.'

'He wasn't really a perp, as such,' Birch said. 'He just seemed to end up helping us with our enquiries an awful lot.'

Al nodded. 'One of those,' he said. 'Well, you know they're ten a penny. And he was last through my door in 1999?'

Birch grinned. 'That infamous memory starting to fail you, Sergeant?'

He batted at her with one huge hand. 'Now then,' he said, 'don't start with the verbal insubordination, madam. You may be DI Muck these days, but remember and respect your elders.'

'I've missed you,' Birch said.

'So you should,' Al shot back. 'You've nothing like me at Fettes Avenue.'

She smiled. It was true. 'That's why I wanted a chat,' she said. 'This guy I'm looking for is actually called George MacDonald. But I've all but confirmed that he and Ginger Mack are one and the same. I'm starting to think he might be connected to some cold cases I've dug up.'

Al threw her a theatrical eye-roll. 'Now, what have I told you about doing that? Dig up the past . . .'

'And you just get dirty, I know,' Birch said. 'I didn't go looking for this. It's one of those ones where you're minding your own business, and then all of a sudden you get a guy called George who might also have been a guy called Ginger for a while. And Ginger's nose is nowhere near as clean as George's.'

Al leaned over the table. 'Let's have it, then.'

Birch took a long slug of her gin and tonic. Tom had made it strong, and she was glad she'd bussed into town. After this she'd head to Anjan's smart flat in the Quartermile, where she'd try not to feel insecure about her own scruffy house, its constant state of disrepair. At least she'd be away from her landline, and wouldn't have to decide whether or not to answer if it rang.

Al listened as she spoke in a low voice about Robertson Bennet, about Phamie MacDonald, about the visits to Mary McPherson and the Waverley gricers, at which she'd pieced together a picture of George. She told him about Ginger Mack's file and the disappeared women. Halfway through her description of Mack's unscrupulous railway activities, she saw a light go on in Al's eyes.

'I remember him,' he said.

Birch clapped her hands once, twice. 'I knew you would,' she said. 'You remember everyone.'

Al was shaking his head. 'What a funny one he was. I couldn't tell you exactly how many times I processed him – not many, but it was always the same. Lateish at night he'd be picked up, always the weekend, Friday night or Saturday. Right when every custody suite in the city was bloody heaving. Pain in my arse, frankly. I remember saying to him, *There's other places to take a walk, sunshine.* He didn't seem to care. Reckoned it was worth it to look at his bloody trains. I rather hoped one might flatten him some bright day.'

Birch frowned. 'I don't buy it,' she said, 'the train thing.'

Al waggled his eyebrows at her. 'All right, so maybe he was off wooing some lady love,' he said. 'Bloody mad place to do it, on the side of a railway track, but I'm not one to question the proclivities of others. Maybe he was one of those exhibitionist types. Anyway, all I know is Sunday morning would dawn bright and early and I'd give him back his worldly goods and let him go. There's a standard fine for those sorts of offences, usually. But you know that.'

Birch looked hard at Al. His expression was blithe.

'You think that's it,' she said. 'You think that's all there is to it?'

Al shrugged. 'I'm not so bold as to think anything, *marm*,' he said, with a smile. 'But I'm telling you that, having met the gent in question, I wouldn't have him down as the dangerous sort. Boring, yes. He once near enough chewed my ear off about the various merits of Wakefield Westgate Station. But a danger to the general populous? I wouldn't say so, personally.'

Birch looked down at her drink, tiny slivers from her slice of lime swirling through the liquid like glitter in a snow-globe.

'No one's seen him,' she said, 'no one knows where he is. Everyone's saying it's been three, four years since he was around. The wife, too. How do two old folk pushing eighty just vanish? *And* I've got a lady in a nursing home telling me this man made murderous threats. No, Al – there's something to this alias thing.'

Al took a gulp of his pint, and smacked his lips. 'And you're sure they're not just no longer with us? Shuffled off this mortal coil, as it were?'

Birch shook her head. 'If they're dead,' she said, 'they're not officially dead. No paperwork.'

Al reached across the table, and put a hand on her arm. 'Listen, lass,' he said. 'It's hardly unheard of for two old folk to hole themselves up somewhere and just live off the cash under the mattress. So they auctioned their house, got themselves a bungalow and settled into their decrepitude – I can believe it. Eighty-three is *old*, love. If no one's seen the old bloke in four or five years, it might be because he can't make it out of the house any more, you ever think that?'

Birch looked down at her drink.

Al nodded at her. 'I know if *my* son had pinched all my savings, I'd be less than keen to see him when he reappeared, that's for sure and certain. I'm telling you, they'll be living off meals on wheels in some bungalow in Ratho, love.'

Birch forced herself to meet Al's eye. He was right: she had nothing. Or almost nothing. 'All I have,' she said, 'is this really, really bad feeling. Don't you ever get that? Something's just not right.'

Al lifted his hand off her arm, and slapped the top of the table, making the surface of the drinks shiver. 'I long ago learned,' he said, 'to put *that* down to indigestion.'

Birch laughed a frustrated laugh.

Al nudged her again. 'Come on,' he said. 'Lighten up. It'll all turn out to be nothing, this business. You mark my words.'

14

Amy stood on the pavement outside the Safari Lounge, waiting for an Uber. There was just the slightest bite of cold in the air, and she felt for the first time that the season was beginning to turn, and autumn would soon be here. She'd spent the last two hours making her mind up about the man she'd come for a drink with: it was their second date, because she hadn't quite been able to get the measure of him on the first. He was a Canadian named Alex, currently still inside the bar, in the bathroom. Amy hadn't waited for him to come back out again before leaving. Her mind was made up now: it was a no. He was in banking, had his own flat near the Scottish Parliament, his own car, and a big annual bonus. The problem was, he only ever seemed truly engaged when he spoke about that small list of things. Whenever Amy tried to draw him towards other topics – current affairs, his family, his hobbies – he seemed to shut down, become blank. At times, she hadn't even been sure he was listening when she spoke.

Suddenly, there was a hand on her arm. *Damn.* He'd emerged before the Uber had arrived.

'Hey,' he said, leaving his hand there just a little longer than necessary. 'You sure you don't want to stay for one more?'

Amy put on her best polite smile. 'I'm sorry,' she said. 'I have to get home and do some work before tomorrow. Like I said, I'm on this big case at the moment.'

If Alex sensed she was lying, he didn't show it. 'Come on,' he said, 'you'll be fine. I'm sure you're great at bullshitting.'

Amy blinked, unsure whether or not this was a compliment. She shifted her phone so the screen faced up, and he could see the Uber app open on it.

'Oh,' he said, noticing, but then rallied. 'Hey, we could get a lift into town, go somewhere a bit more . . . upbeat. Maybe Cowgate somewhere? Opium?'

Amy wrinkled her nose. 'Clubbing?' she said. 'It's a Wednesday.'

Alex shrugged, unperturbed. 'Great drinks deals, midweek,' he said.

Amy resisted the urge to sigh audibly. *This* was the problem. This guy had his own money, an education, a complicated job, and yet sophistication had escaped him. The Safari Lounge wasn't a bad place, but Amy knew he'd only suggested it because it was within reasonable walking distance for him to get home. Opium was, too – it also had a sticky floor, and the midweek crowd would be mostly undergrads. Both places were cheap. Alex was looking for a good time with minimum inconvenience or effort for him. Amy, meanwhile, would have to pay for an Uber both ways. He'd even had them split the bar tab.

'It's a cute idea,' Amy said, not caring if she sounded condescending, 'but I really do have to work.'

They both watched as her Uber swung out from Marionville Road and slowed as it approached. Alex opened his body up, expecting a hug.

'It's been a lovely evening,' Amy lied, and stuck out one hand for a handshake. They shook – Alex too Canadian to make a fuss about it – but she saw the penny drop.

'It really was,' he said, the edge of his voice bitter now.

The Uber pulled up at the kerb and Amy jumped to open the back door before Alex could reach out and do it for her.

'For Amy?' she called through to the driver, even though she could see on the app that this car was hers. He nodded. She turned back to Alex, the car door between them now like a shield. 'I hope you have a great night,' she said.

Alex's shoulders sagged. 'You too,' he said, but his heart wasn't in it. 'Give me a text, yeah? I'd really like to see you again.'

Amy felt like saying, *You and I both know that's never going to happen*. Instead she said, 'Thanks. Get home safe.'

She was in the car and the door closed behind her before he could say anything else.

The driver made it as far as the traffic lights at the top of Easter Road before he glanced back and asked, 'Bad date, eh?'

Amy cocked her head for a moment, thinking. 'Not the worst,' she said, 'not *bad*. Just . . . depressingly average.'

Amy was glad to find she'd left the hall light on when she got home. As she climbed the stairs, it shone out through the little window above her front door, making the flat look welcoming. Once she got inside, she let out a long exhale – not a sigh so much as a little bit of breath she'd been holding all night, in the top of her lungs, the way she always did on a date. Maybe this will be the start of something exciting, she always thought. It hadn't been so far, but she wasn't going to let herself get maudlin about it.

Amy hung up her coat on the back of the door and stepped gratefully out of her high heels. She picked each one up to inspect it for scuffs or marks before placing both shoes in their rack. Then she crossed the hall to the bedroom, fished in her top drawer, and unballed a pair of fluffy socks. They were white and fleecy with a repeating pumpkin motif. She stretched her feet out in them and felt deeply glad that she wasn't currently squished into a booth in Opium, having some neon-coloured shot placed in front of her by a grinning Alex. Home was good, she thought. Alone was good.

Amy *had* lied to Alex: she didn't have any work to do, as such, but she knew that Phamie's diaries were still sitting where she'd left them, on the edge of the breakfast bar that separated her tiny kitchen from the living room. She walked back through the hall – skating a little on the laminate floor in her soft, slippy socks – and stopped in the living room doorway. The diaries seemed to eye her from their vantage point on the counter top. Amy looked past them at the darkened kitchen beyond, remembering the half-bottle of white wine chilling in the fridge. She didn't *have* to read the diaries now: she could always lose herself in some crap midweek TV, or dip back into the Helen Sedgwick novel she was keen to keep reading. But now she'd entered Phamie's world, her feelings about the diaries had changed. She'd been reluctant to open them, and now she wanted to get through their contents quickly, to see the job done. The sooner she read them, the sooner they could see for sure if Phamie had left behind any clues that might lead them to her whereabouts. Like DI Birch, Amy also felt it was urgent that they find the old lady, though they still had no proof that she'd come to any harm. Amy walked into the kitchen without turning on the overhead light, and poured herself a glass of wine in the glow thrown by the opened fridge. Then she carried the wineglass and the first of the diaries over to the sofa, where she flipped a table lamp on, and settled down to read.

You're a useless woman, that's what he said to me today! I know it's better to keep quiet when he's in one of his rages, and I did. But my goodness, did that make me cross. I am not a useless woman, I know I'm not. I have birthed a child! I have raised a beautiful and intelligent boy! Even if my life has meant nothing else, I did that. And with very little assistance from George, at least at times.

But he's like a child himself, George, especially when he gets worked up. I remember the tantrums Robert had when he was little, the times when his whole body seemed so full of energy that he couldn't stand it, and he had to let some of it out by shouting or flinging himself to the ground. Robert has grown out of that now, but it feels like a part of George never did. I have to admit that I feel for him, when he flies into a temper. He seems so like a child that I want to fuss around and comfort him. I've learned now that he hates that, it makes him even more angry, and usually if I get too close he lashes out and I end up hurt for my efforts. Thankfully today was not one of those days. But the words can wound me more, sometimes.

He knows how frightening he can be. In the moment, I think he forgets it – he shouts and lashes out and hits and kicks, just like a little toddler having a tantrum, only with so much more power, of course. But afterwards, when he's calmed down, he's so terribly remorseful. He hates that he's struck out in his rage and hurt me. He sees that I was trying to comfort him, trying to be caring.

Sometimes he puts his head in his hands and cries, and he says sorry over and over. Sometimes he goes to the cupboard and gets out the first aid kit and helps me clean myself up: he gets the frozen peas from the freezer and holds them on whatever part of me he managed to hit. It's like this real George, the one who cares, disappears inside the rage, and when he comes out again he can't stand to see what he's done. How can I help but forgive him when he seems so gentle? When he talks about feeling like a man possessed, doing things that are out of his control?

The worst times are the times he leaves. Then I don't get to see the gentle George return. I don't get to see him come back to himself, and he doesn't take care of me afterwards. He just walks out, and then I have to worry about where he's gone. Then, like now, the words he's said hurt the most, because he isn't there to say sorry for them or to talk to me about what happened. He's just gone, and the words go round and round in my head, along- side all the worry about where he might be and if he's all right. I'm not a useless woman, I know I'm not. But the words are there all the same, beating around my head like the beat of a terrible drum.

Edinburgh Evening News

OUR REGION ¦ EDINBURGH ¦ LEITH ¦ NEW TOWN ¦ STOCKBRIDGE
PORTOBELLO ¦ CORSTORPHINE ¦ MORNINGSIDE ¦ CITY

Trainspotter given 'final warning' in trespassing case

ROBIN BLAKE
Email

20 May 2004

Share this article

RETURN TO ARCHIVE
SIGN UP TO OUR DAILY NEWSLETTER

An Edinburgh man has been given a 'final warning' after being repeatedly fined for trespassing on private land owned by Network Rail.

The 68-year-old man was issued a £1,000 fine for his latest offence of walking around, unauthorised, in a secure railway yard on the western outskirts of Edinburgh.

His fine was issued with a 'final warning' that he could face jail time if he commits any further offences.

A representative of Network Rail could not be reached for comment.

15

Birch sat in Anjan's living room, watching the early morning sun stream across the Meadows Park. She hadn't slept well, but the coffee Anjan had brought her was helping. She sat close to the huge, plate-glass window and looked down at the dog-walkers with their zippy little dogs, the runners, the early commuters. It wasn't yet seven o'clock, but Melville Drive was already studded with cars.

'If it's bothering you so much that you can't sleep, then you need to take it to McLeod.' Anjan was behind her in the spotless kitchen, rattling crockery, opening and closing the fridge. Birch could smell toast. She watched him, wondering whether or not to tell him the real reason she'd lain awake much of the night: she was thinking about her father again, wondering what he could possibly have to say to her after all these years.

'McLeod's just going to say what Al said,' Birch replied. 'That it's nothing. Man has nickname, so what. It's not a crime.'

'It's not nothing,' Anjan replied. 'It's more than a nickname if you use it as your given name at a police station when brought in for questioning. Then it's an alias. Unless the name Ginger Mack is actually on this man's birth certificate, which I doubt. Marmalade? I'm out of jam.'

Birch shuddered. 'God no,' she said. 'Sorry, I mean, no thanks. Just butter is fine.'

Anjan laughed. A moment later, he leaned down to place a white plate with two slices of buttered toast on it next to her elbow, and hovered there. She kissed him.

'You're a star,' she said.

He moved to the armchair opposite Birch, and settled into it, balancing his own plate of toast on one knee. Birch fretted about the white button-down he'd put on, but then remembered that Anjan was always neat, careful. Crumbs didn't seem to stick to him the way they did to her.

'Just standard boyfriending,' he replied. 'And I'm with you on this one. It's weird. Why adopt an alias if you've nothing to hide? If you're so determined to wander around on the railway that you're happy to pay the resulting fines, why bother giving a made-up name to police? I suppose if he *was* having affairs, he was ensuring he'd never be found out by Phamie. After all, if he'd had to explain those trespassing charges he might have had to answer other questions about where he'd been, and with whom. An alias would protect you from that, somewhat. How many women did you say he was connected to?'

'The missing persons? A few. Six or seven,' Birch said. 'Between 1965 and 1999. The last one, Maisie Kerr, is the one whose mother's jewellery George MacDonald tried to pawn.'

Anjan was chewing on his toast. 'So, what's the bad feeling?' he said. 'What is it that's stopping you from sleeping – specifically, I mean.'

Birch winced. Just tell him, she thought. But she couldn't, not yet. She didn't know what this *was* yet, this thing with her dad. She decided to let Anjan keep believing it was the case that was bothering her, at least for a while.

'I'm not even sure,' she said. 'All I know is, everything I learn about George MacDonald leads me to believe he's a real mean swine of a guy. The fact that we can't find him is annoying the hell out of me. And the fact that we can't find his wife, who we know he was violent towards, who we believe he threatened to kill, is concerning. Especially as he's been connected – or his alias has – to other women who've disappeared in the past, and never been found.'

Anjan looked down at his plate. 'Of course,' he said, 'there are different angles to this. Yes, he's the common denominator. But have you considered the possibility that those six or seven women all disappeared *themselves* so he couldn't find them any more?'

Birch blinked. She hadn't.

'We know he was violent to his wife,' Anjan went on. 'So chances are he was pretty dreadful to his mistresses, too. They might all have gone into refuges, and been supported to get away from him.'

Birch could think of nothing to say to this. *Fuck*, Anjan was a good lawyer: able to pick up everything and inspect it from so many different angles.

'I'd never even thought of that,' she said at last. 'But . . . seven girlfriends all on the run from you? That'd be a hell of a streak.'

'Possibly, yes. But I see why you're worried about the wife,' Anjan went on, clearly deep in his own train of thought. 'About Phamie. It sounds like she lived with his bad behaviour for over fifty years. It's not impossible, but it does seem less likely that she'd break the cycle after such a long time.'

'Yeah.' Birch took a sip of her coffee. 'It's based on nothing more than a hunch, but I'm certain: wherever they are, they're together. Find him, and we find her, and vice versa.'

On the coffee table between them, Birch's mobile rang, and they both jumped.

'Early, isn't it,' Anjan said, 'for you to be in demand?'

Birch swiped to pick up. It was a landline, a number she didn't recognise.

'This is Helen Birch,' she said.

'DI Birch, good morning.' As she tried to place the familiar voice, Anjan threw her a smile and stood, glancing at his watch. 'This is Tommy Swinton from HMP Low Moss. I'm sorry to disturb you so early in the morning.'

Anjan didn't seem to notice Birch stiffen. He reached over her, scooping up her plate and coffee mug.

'I'm afraid there's been an incident involving your brother, Charles. Charlie.'

Birch was on her feet. Beside her, Anjan flinched.

'What's happened?' she demanded.

'Please don't panic,' Tommy said, 'it's all being dealt with. Are you . . . able to talk right now?'

'Tell me what's happened.' Birch felt her back teeth grind together.

'Okay. In the early hours of this morning, Charlie was jumped in his cell. It was a targeted attack that we believe his cellmate helped to plan.'

Birch opened her mouth to speak again, but no sound came. Anjan was still beside her, his face confused, worried.

'Your brother was asleep,' Tommy was saying. 'And sustained some quite serious injuries. He's been taken to the infirmary.'

She swallowed hard on the last of her toast. She felt like she might be sick. 'What's his condition? Is he . . . stable?' She didn't really know what she was asking, but she also didn't like the way Tommy had said *quite serious*.

'We discussed sending him to the Royal,' Tommy said, 'but the staff here have managed to get things under control. He's been sedated and they've made him as comfortable as they can for now.'

Birch began to look around. Keys, she needed her car keys. 'Shit fuck,' she said aloud. She'd left her car at work.

'DI Birch?'

'Sorry, Tommy. I'm just . . . I'm on my way.'

There was a pause on the line. 'We haven't decided yet if visitors—'

'Don't finish that sentence,' Birch said. She realised her voice was raised. 'Just don't. I'm coming to see my brother and then I'll want to sit down with the warden and find out just exactly how you allowed this to happen, is that clear?'

Tommy was quiet for a moment, and then said, 'Yes, marm.'

'Good. I'll be there as soon as I can. You've got an hour or so to get your stories straight.'

Birch walked through the door of reception with her badge already raised. The female prison officer on the front desk looked alarmed.

'Detective Inspector Helen Birch. Tommy Swinton's expecting me.'

She slapped the badge down in front of the woman, and hoisted her handbag on to the desk beside it. The prison officer looked blankly at her.

'Come on,' Birch said. 'Give me a tray. Let's get this dog-and-pony show over with.'

'If I can just call Tommy . . .'

'Do that while I check myself in, yes?' She was being needlessly snippy, but it seemed to be helping with the panic. The prison officer eyed her for a half-second, before placing one of the grey plastic trays in front of her. It nudged her bag ever so slightly, sending it careening on to the floor.

'*Jesus*.'

Birch scrabbled for her possessions. Back at the flat, she'd stuffed everything into her handbag blindly while Anjan called her a cab. It seemed to take for ever for the vehicle to pick its way out of the maze of the Quartermile and on to the main roads: she had used the time to leave voicemails for McLeod and Amy, explaining where she'd be that morning. At Fettes Avenue, she'd crossed the car park at a flat sprint. It took all the strength she had not to put the siren on as she drove out of town and towards Charlie.

The prison officer behind the desk was speaking on the phone in hushed tones. Birch straightened up and poured the haphazard bag into the plastic tray. Her keys clattered in after it, and the badge too.

'Tommy says you're clear for entry.'

Birch spattered a handful of pocket change into the tray. 'You're damn right I am.'

The officer's face had coloured, and Birch felt a sting of remorse.

'My brother is an inmate here,' she said, knocking the edge out of her voice. 'He's in the infirmary. I'm here to see him.'

The woman straightened up, took hold of Birch's tray of items and placed them on the conveyor for x-ray. 'Well,' she said stiffly, 'Tommy will be right down.'

*   *   *

The infirmary was harder to get to than the Visit Room: there were more corridors, more keyfobs. Birch had only ever visited during designated hours before, and now the prison felt different. Tommy seemed jumpy, pausing at every door to look through its glass panel before opening it and showing her through.

'We'll be moving the route soon,' he said, as though he'd heard her thoughts. 'The prisoners start their work schedule at 8.30 a.m.'

Birch glanced at her watch. Less than five minutes. 'And?'

'*And,*' Tommy said, 'after what happened last night, they're excitable. Word's getting around. Last thing I want is you caught up in the move, getting their attention.'

They arrived at the door to the infirmary. Tommy peered through the door's glass strip, and seemed to give a high-sign to someone inside. Then he pressed his fob to the panel, and the door buzzed open.

Inside, another screw, a man.

'This is Charlie Birch's next of kin,' Tommy said, and then, quickly, 'Detective Inspector Birch.'

Birch nodded, and the man nodded back.

'This way,' Tommy said.

The infirmary was a strange place, though elements of it were familiar: an eye-test chart, blue-roll dispensers, an NHS poster raising awareness about testicular cancer. Tommy tapped his fob at the door of Charlie's secure room, while Birch squirted antiseptic liquid on to her hands from a wall-mounted bottle outside. Through the door's glass panel, she could see only the small mound of her brother's feet under the bedsheets.

Walking in was like walking into a wall: Birch felt the air rush out of her lungs with the shock of seeing her brother. Her knees gave, and she was glad to sink into the chair Tommy dragged up to the bedside for her.

Charlie's face was barely recognisable. The wounds from his previous attack hadn't had a chance to heal, and Birch could see the skin was yellow in places from the older bruising. But at least that had only been on one side: now both eyes were swollen shut, and Charlie bore a nasty gash across his forehead, closed with white medical staples. More of those on his cheek, where the flesh had been sliced in three jagged arcs. His nostrils were flecked with dried blood, and she could see that since she saw him last his split lip had reopened. His left arm was pulled across his body in a sling, and both hands were bandaged. Charlie was snoring, and the breath whistled in his nose.

Behind Tommy, another man buzzed into the room. He wore the navy blue tunic of a ward-managing nurse, complete with the same kit belt as Tommy: keyfob, radio, baton, paraphernalia.

'This is Charlie's sister,' Tommy said. Then, rather pointedly, 'I told you she was coming in.'

Birch barely acknowledged the new man's arrival. She couldn't tear her gaze away from her brother's broken face. The nurse appeared at her shoulder, and ducked on to his haunches to look her in the eye.

'DI Birch, I'm Rob,' he said. 'I've been taking care of Charlie overnight.'

Birch forced herself to look at the man. He smelled scrubbed and clinical, the way nurses do, and he had freckles.

'Helen,' she said. Her voice was a wet croak.

'Good to meet you, Helen,' he said. 'I'm so sorry this has happened. I know it must be very hard to see Charlie this way.'

Birch nodded. There was a lump in her throat and she was determined to swallow it. 'Can one of you tell me what happened?'

Rob the nurse glanced backward towards Tommy.

'Like I said on the phone, it was a co-ordinated attack, very targeted,' Tommy said. 'They all did something to wedge their cell doors, so they looked closed but didn't lock. Fuck knows what, or how they did it, but the fuckers have time on their hands, pardon my French. Then at the allotted hour, which we reckon was three in the morning, six boys – three cell pairs – went to Charlie's room and were welcomed in by his cellmate.'

Birch let out a small, involuntary sound. 'There were *seven* assailants?'

'Six,' Tommy said. 'The cellmate swears blind he didn't partake in the attack itself.'

'Charlie was asleep,' Rob said, 'so obviously very vulnerable. It looks like he took some hits to the face before he knew what was happening.'

'We confiscated an improvised knuckleduster from one of the assailants,' Tommy said. 'It was made with fragments of snapped plastic which we reckon caused the facial cuts.'

'His arm . . .' Birch managed.

'I'm afraid it's broken,' Rob said. 'He also has some broken ribs on that side, but we don't think there's internal damage beyond bruising, fortunately. We know that Charlie was able to get up, and . . . protect himself, to some degree.'

Tommy made a sort of snorting sound.

'Protect himself?' Birch asked.

'Give as good as he got,' Tommy said. 'Or try to. The alarm went up and most of the boys scattered, but one . . . wasn't so lucky.'

Birch straightened up. 'This is the kid from Polmont, isn't it?' she said. 'The one who beat him up last week.'

She turned her head in time to see Rob and Tommy exchange a look.

'He told me about it on Monday,' she said. 'You should know I've spoken to Charlie's lawyer. A contemporaneous note has been logged.'

She hoped this sounded more official than what really happened: a cup of tea with Anjan and a few lines in a Word document.

'I can't comment,' Rob said.

'So yes, it's the same kid.' Birch screwed up her face. The hollowed-out feeling that hit her when she looked at Charlie was now being replaced by something else: a white-hot, seething anger. 'And Charlie retaliated?'

Rob nodded. 'That's why his hands are bandaged,' he said. 'We have the, um – assailant here, too. In the infirmary.'

Birch clutched the arms of her chair. The instinct to bolt from the room and find the man who hurt her brother was almost over-whelming. As though he'd felt its electrical charge pass through her, Tommy stepped a little closer to Birch, one hand near her shoulder.

'They'll both be up on review, once they're back in the hall,' Tommy said. 'This'll affect their sentences, I've no doubt.'

Birch whipped round. 'But it was self-defence!' It wasn't until the words came out that she realised they were almost a shout. 'You can't punish a man for fighting off a totally unprovoked attack.'

'No,' Tommy said, leaning towards her slightly, 'but when the attacker is curled up on the floor, begging for mercy, and four screws have to drag you off the poor cunt, I'm pretty sure you've crossed the border out of self-defence territory, don't you, Inspector?'

Birch blinked. 'Charlie did that?'

Tommy straightened up again. 'It's a good fucking job we arrived when we did,' he said. 'Your brother had been taken by the red mist, good and proper. Don't think he could see what he was punching, he was just punching. He'd have pounded the boy into the concrete given another sixty seconds.'

Birch felt her mouth fall open. She still forgot sometimes who her brother was, who he'd been, why he was in this hellish place to begin with. She looked to Rob for something, anything.

He shrugged. 'Your brother's a trained fighter,' he said. 'It does seem like some sort of instinct kicked in.'

Birch raised one hand to her face, pressed the hot palm over her eyes. *What were you thinking, Charlie?* she wanted to say, but she knew what he was thinking, because she was thinking it too: the little weasel deserved what he got, and more besides. In spite of her job title, in spite of all her training, there was a small part of her that felt a twinge of pride. *Good on you, our kid.*

'Tell me about . . . recovery,' she said to Rob, pulling her mouth into a straight line.

'Well . . .' Rob straightened out of his crouch position, and looked Charlie up and down. 'He'll need to see the dentist. He'd already lost a tooth in the first altercation, and now there are others loose or missing. We'll have to get his swelling down before that happens. The arm hasn't been set yet, that'll happen later today, on the next shift: it'll go in plaster. We still need to x-ray his hands, too. And we'll monitor the situation with his ribs, make certain there's no internal bleeding. He's going to be here a while, and he'll be very, very sore.'

'When might he be back in the hall?'

Behind her, Tommy shifted his weight. He was keen to know this, too.

'I can't say with certainty,' Rob answered, 'but we'll conduct reviews weekly.'

Birch nodded. 'I want the ringleader out of the hall before he goes back,' she said. 'I'll be working with Charlie's lawyer to ensure that he's moved. It's clear there's a vendetta there, and this cannot happen again.'

'You're fucking *right*,' Tommy said, almost to himself.

Birch levered herself up from the chair, and faced him. 'Officer Swinton,' she said, 'I'm unsure quite where you've dug up that brass neck, but I suggest you bury it again. It was *you*, and *your staff*, who allowed the security of four separate cells to be compromised last night. You created the conditions for this attack, and that won't go unchecked, let me assure you. This happened on your watch. If my brother is going to be punished for defending himself, then you're sure as *hell* not getting away with putting him in that position in the first place, you understand?'

The room seemed to reverberate in the silence that followed. Birch was breathing hard. She'd treated Tommy to her best *you're going down* voice, usually reserved for only the grossest of perps.

Eventually, Tommy looked at Rob. 'I think we're done here,' he said.

Birch glanced back at her brother, a red and purple mess in the tight-tucked bed.

'You'll not see him conscious,' Rob said, his voice quieter than before, as though he were trying to make up for Birch's outburst. 'Not today. He's well sedated, for the pain. It's better that way, at least until we set his arm.'

She nodded. The words made sense, but she couldn't seem to react to them. In that moment, standing in the close confines of the weird, white little room, she felt the whole weight of Charlie's incarceration tumble down on her, all at once. She hated that he was in here, she hated *why* he was in here, and more than anything, she hated that he was being hurt and she was powerless to stop it.

'Time to go,' Tommy said.

She wanted to touch him, just for a second, in case he might feel it and know she was there. She reached down, and let her fingertips brush the soft hill Charlie's feet made under the sheets. Then she looked at Rob.

'Tell him I was here,' Birch said, 'when he wakes up.'

Rob met her eye, and nodded. Then the door was making its buzzing noise, Tommy holding it open and watching her, and it was time to go.

16

'We were meant to set off for North Berwick today,' Amy said. She was reading aloud from one of Phamie's diaries, the spine crackling as she turned each page. 'But suddenly, everything went wrong. I had us all ready. I'd helped Robert to pack his suitcase, and then I'd done George's and mine. I'd phoned and checked with the B&B, they were expecting us, and everything was paid for. The sun was out. It was shaping up to be a beautiful day. I was excited, more fool me, for the three of us to get away together for a few days by the sea. Robert has been quiet lately, quite moody with me. I had hoped it would bring him out of himself. But then I noticed at the breakfast table that George had that dark look on his face. The one he gets when he's spoiling for a fight. To be honest, I knew then that everything was going to fall apart.'

Amy stopped, and let out a low whistle. 'He vetoed the family holiday,' she said, after a moment. 'Didn't care about losing the money, or any of it. I reckon he just didn't want Phamie out of the house. He didn't want her to have even a couple of days outside his control. It's gross.'

They'd parked outside the address listed in Maisie Kerr's file, and were sitting in Amy's car. Birch hadn't checked, but she assumed the address on file would still be correct. With missing person cases, the next of kin tended to stay in touch, sometimes to a distressing degree. They were so keen to find their missing loved one that they convinced themselves that any new development in their lives might hold the key to that person's return. Birch remembered it well enough herself: in the early days of Charlie's disappearance, before she became a policewoman, she'd probably been a bit of a nuisance. I'm going on holiday, here's where I'll be staying. I've got a new mobile number. I'm going slowly mad. Please find him. Please find him and have him call me . . .

'Marm?'

Birch jumped. 'Yes?'

Amy was frowning. 'You were miles away. Are you sure you don't want to take this afternoon off? Go home and rest up?'

Birch tried to pull herself together. 'No, no, I'm fine. I'd just pace back and forth if I went home, so it's better to be busy. But thanks. And keep an eye on me, will you?'

Amy grinned. 'Always do, marm.'

Birch returned the smile. 'Good to know."

The Kerr house was the very last one in Carstairs Junction: beyond it, the village gave way to fields. The street Amy had parked on was rather creepily called George Street, but there was nothing on it: it ran along the side of the Kerr property and then came to a dead end in some waste ground. There was a weedy turning circle and a wild hedge: above the hedge, Birch could see the tops of curtain-siders parked in the haulage yard.

'Nice view,' Amy said, ringing the front doorbell and standing back.

She wasn't wrong. To the right of the house there was nothing but fields: a meander of the River Clyde, reddish cows, the odd barn. Birch realised she didn't spend much time in the countryside, and felt a nostalgia for it that belonged to nothing: she'd always been a city dweller.

In front of them, the door opened. Behind it there was a woman who looked to be in her late sixties. Her hair was clipped into a severe pixie cut, and dyed a dull blonde, the colour of straw.

'Mrs Kerr?' Amy asked.

'Yes?'

Birch flipped her badge as Amy introduced them both.

'We're here to talk to you about Maisie,' Amy said.

The woman's face hardened. Birch recognised the expression exactly: it was a gathering of strength, a putting up of barriers.

I am going to have to talk about the one I've lost. She still did it herself when people talked about Charlie, though now he was lost to her in a different way. Mrs Kerr stepped to one side, and they filed past her into the house.

Birch wasn't sure what she'd expected, but she found herself blinking as she entered the living room. The house was small, but its decor was modern and chic: stripped pine, laminate floors, sheepskin rugs. On the mantel over the minimalist gas fire, Mrs Kerr was burning a honey-coloured candle, and the room was filled with the smell of cinnamon.

'You have a lovely home,' Amy said, settling on the couch.

Birch blinked again. She didn't think she'd ever said those words to anyone.

'Thank you,' Mrs Kerr said. Birch knew her name was Hazel, but she and Amy would wait to be invited to call her that. 'Can I get youse some tea, coffee?'

'I'm fine,' Birch said, and Amy shook her head.

Mrs Kerr sat down in an armchair that faced the fire. At her elbow was a nest of tables, and on it were three framed photos: school portraits, all from different years. A time-lapse of Maisie.

'Mrs Kerr, we're so sorry to interrupt your day,' Birch said. 'But we're in the process of investigating another missing person case, and we've come across something that we think may link it to Maisie's.'

Mrs Kerr just looked at Birch, without blinking. If this information moved her, she showed no sign.

'I know it's been a long time,' Birch went on, 'and I know you will have answered lots and lots of questions at the time of Maisie's disappearance. But I'd like to ask you again about a man named Ginger Mack.'

This time there was the slightest flicker of an eyelid. Mrs Kerr remembered the name.

'You said at the time that you didn't know anyone of that name, and didn't know that Maisie did, either.'

'Yes.'

'Okay. But we've discovered that Ginger Mack might actually have been an alias. Do you know the name George MacDonald?'

Birch watched Mrs Kerr's eyes unfocus for a moment while she thought. 'There was a teacher at Maisie's school,' she said, 'whose last name was MacDonald. I can't remember his first name.'

Amy had her iPad out, taking notes. Birch saw her tap something in. But that's not him, Birch thought. Robertson Bennet had said his father was a sanitary inspector.

'Can you describe Mr MacDonald?' she asked.

Mrs Kerr nodded. 'He was a young teacher,' she said, 'just out of his training I would say. But it's been decades, he'd be middle-aged now.'

Amy stopped typing.

'Okay,' Birch said. 'That can't be the man we're looking for, unfortunately. George MacDonald is in his eighties.'

She watched Mrs Kerr retreat back in behind the barriers she'd made.

'Sorry,' she said.

'Don't worry,' Birch replied. 'We're at that stage of the investigation where every conversation we have is useful.'

Right, Helen, she thought. You're going to have to ask the big one, now.

'I'm so sorry to have to ask this, Mrs Kerr,' she said. 'Please know that I've been where you are, I've had a family member go missing, and I know how hard it is to have to answer these questions time and time again. But I have to ask, have you heard from Maisie at all in the years since her disappearance? Have you had any contact, of any kind, that might perhaps have been from her?'

Mrs Kerr closed her eyes. Beside her, Birch could feel Amy holding her breath.

'If I had, I promise I would have told you.' The woman's voice was sad, rather than angry. 'It's coming up twenty years since she went, and still, every time that phone rings, every time the door goes, every time the postman brings a letter . . .' She tailed off, her throat beginning to rasp.

'I know,' Birch said. 'I absolutely do know.'

'It's never her,' Mrs Kerr went on. 'It never has been her.'

All three women were quiet for a moment. Outside, behind the haulage yard, a train rattled by.

'I'm so sorry,' Birch said.

Mrs Kerr looked at her then, her eyes sharp, like a bird's. 'Did you find yours?' she asked. 'Your missing person.'

Birch nodded. 'I did,' she said. 'He came back, after being gone for fourteen years without a trace.'

For a moment they sat looking at one another, Birch willing the other woman to take comfort from what she'd just said. But eventually Mrs Kerr's eyes dropped.

'That's not Maisie,' she said. 'Maisie's just gone.'

Birch glanced at Amy, but Amy was looking at the three photos of the smiling girl: each one in a white blouse, the same striped school tie.

'I'd like to ask,' Birch said, 'if Maisie ever spent time around the railway, to your knowledge? Did she walk over to the station much, or hang around there?'

Mrs Kerr shrugged. 'Once she got older, Maisie pretty much did what she wanted,' she said. 'I'd very little idea where she was towards the end. As you'll see there's no father here to discipline her. There's just me. And I was no match for her when she put her mind to something.'

Amy began to type again.

'The two of you argued?'

Mrs Kerr gave a short, bitter laugh. 'She was nineteen when she disappeared,' she said. 'What nineteen-year-old girl doesn't think they know better than their mother? I see now I was wrong. Too strict. I tried to give her a curfew, tried to stop her from gallivanting off at all hours of the day and night. I just wanted to protect her, stop something bad from happening. Then something bad happened anyway.'

There were tears in the woman's eyes, now.

'I'm sorry,' Birch said, 'I just have to ask a few more questions. Soon after Maisie's disappearance, some jewellery was found . . .'

Mrs Kerr nodded. 'My emerald set,' she said. 'I still have it, if you want it. It's still in the evidence bag they brought it back in. I hate the sight of it now. I hate that they found it, instead of her.'

She was pulling air in through her nose, seemingly determined not to cry.

'Did Maisie wear that jewellery often?'

Mrs Kerr looked sharply at Birch again. 'Oh come on,' she said. 'You must have read up on this before you came. She stole it from me.' Her expression softened again. 'Stealing had become a bit of a pattern with Maisie. First it was just food, the odd bottle of wine out of the fridge, and she'd tell me afterwards that she'd replace it or pay me back, though she never actually did. Then it was money out of my purse. Not lots, just a fiver here and there. Then suddenly it was more. And then I started noticing valuables were gone.'

'And you confronted her about it.' Birch *had* read the file.

'Yes. It was one of the things we fought about,' she said. 'I wanted to know why she was stealing. My first thought was she must have a drug habit, to be honest, though she never seemed like she was on drugs. But what else would she steal for? If she'd needed money for anything legitimate, I'd have found it for her somehow. But she never asked. And she never did confess, about the money or the valuables. It was all *you must just have lost it, Mum*. I did start to question my sanity after a while. The only good thing about that emerald set turning up was at least then I knew I'd been right about the stealing. Well, that – and I thought she might come back. If she didn't have the jewellery with her to sell, if she didn't have money, I thought she might come home.'

Mrs Kerr raised her hand, and ran the tip of her index finger along the table, as though drawing an invisible line between herself and the photos of Maisie.

'I've thought about it so many times,' she said. 'I've sat awake nights, and tried and tried to understand. Something must have happened. She was such a good girl, and then all of a sudden, she wasn't. It was as though she turned sixteen, and flicked a switch.'

Birch was nodding.

'That jewellery set,' Birch said. 'The person who . . . was found to be in possession of it. They said it was found under a bench at Carstairs Station. I'm just wondering . . . do you believe that version of events? Does that ring true, that Maisie just dropped it there?'

Mrs Kerr thought again for a moment, and then shrugged. 'I was told at the time it made sense,' she said. 'They reckoned Maisie got on a train. That she was at the station for that purpose. But whether she hung around there more regularly, I don't know. I don't know why she would, there's nothing down there. But like I say, she could just as well have been on the moon, for all she ever told me.'

Amy's car was tiny. Birch pushed the passenger seat back so she could stretch her legs out. They were still parked outside Mrs Kerr's house, the sun moving west, shining warm through the windscreen and on to their faces.

'Something happened when she was sixteen,' Birch said. 'What do you want to bet that the *something* was meeting Ginger Mack? In 1996, right?'

Amy looked down at the iPad, which she'd propped against the steering wheel. 'I wondered that, too,' she said.

They sat in silence.

'Maisie was nineteen when she disappeared,' Birch said. 'Ginger George would have been what . . . sixty-odd?'

'Sixty, when Maisie was sixteen,' Amy said, 'so sixty-three when she disappeared, if my maths is right.'

Birch shook her head. 'That's . . . still pretty old,' she said. 'I know it happens, but a teenage girl involved with a man that much older than her? Of her own volition? It doesn't add up.'

'I dunno, marm,' Amy said. 'I got a photo from Robertson Bennet, like you asked. George MacDonald was a handsome man. And it does happen. Teenage girls are a weird breed. And she'd no father figure at home.' Amy glanced behind her, to where Phamie's diaries were sitting haphazardly on the back seat. 'I haven't got as far as 1996 in Phamie's diaries yet. I'll keep an eye out for anything that seems like it might fit with Maisie's timeline.'

Amy looked back down at the iPad and swiped around.

Let me show you the photo of MacDonald. Birch recognised Robertson Bennet immediately, though he could only have been twenty in the picture, which bore the bright, bleached colours of a film photograph from the late seventies or early eighties. He stood stiffly, next to a man who was undoubtedly his father. They'd had the same barber: both wore their hair in a shock of mahogany-red curls on the tops of their heads, with short sides that accentuated their rather prominent ears. Both were that stocky shape Birch had noted the first time she met Bennet: wide shoulders and big arms, their large torsos tapering into long, slim legs and small feet. George MacDonald was taller than his son, and stood more confidently, feet apart, one fist on his hip so his muscled arm jutted outward. He looked like he was trying to take up space, while Bennet seemed to be trying to shrink. Amy was right: he was handsome.

'He'd be how old here?' Birch asked.

'MacDonald? Forty-five or so. Bennet reckoned this was around 1980.'

Birch nodded. 'Fair enough,' she said. 'I can see how fifteen years later he'd still be a handsome man. He clearly cared about impressing the ladies, so I guess he kept himself in trim.'

'Still creepy,' Amy said. 'If he was involved with a teenage girl.'

'Oh God, Kato,' Birch said, 'I'd never say otherwise. That'd be horrendous.'

Silence fell once again.

'But we don't *know*,' Amy said. 'We don't actually *know* that they ever even met.'

Birch screwed up her face. 'It's true,' she said. 'But it's some coincidence. Ginger Mack was asked for a witness statement at the time of Maisie's disappearance. Then, only weeks later, George MacDonald was caught trying to pawn her mother's jewellery.'

Amy was also frowning. 'Devil's advocate, though,' she said, 'Mack was often on the station ... and Maisie was believed to have got on a train. It does make sense to ask him if he'd seen her at all. And then ... he really could have just found the jewellery

under the bench. The only thing he did that wasn't right was failing to tell anyone about it, and trying to sell it. For which he was,
rightly, cautioned.'

Birch laughed. 'You sound like Anjan,' she said, 'you ought to
be a lawyer. But no, you're totally right. We've got nothing, unless
you manage to find something in those diaries. I don't know why
I keep chasing this.'

'You do,' Amy said. 'It's because you've got—'

'I've got a bad feeling, I know, I know. But I haven't managed to
turn anything up, anything extra I mean. I got nothing much from
Al and we've got nothing from Mrs Kerr that we didn't already
know. Mary McPherson isn't a reliable witness. The diaries only
confirm that George MacDonald was a pig, as you say. I don't
think I can take this to McLeod, in all honesty. I think I just have
to back off again, and you can get on with the MacDonald case.
A straight-up missing person, times two.'

Amy was looking at her. 'I know you're not happy with that,
marm.'

Birch sighed. 'I'm not,' she said. 'And I'm still worried about
Phamie MacDonald. But we can only work with facts. My weird
feeling is not evidence, is it?'

Amy flipped the case shut over the laptop screen. 'Sorry,' she
said.

'It's okay. Can't win 'em all.'

Amy looked around for the car keys, then began digging in her
pockets. Birch closed her eyes for a moment. Behind her eyelids,
she could see Charlie, lying broken in his bed in the infirmary. Her
father crept once again into her thoughts – if he phoned her again,
she now had the dilemma of whether or not to let him know about
the whole Charlie situation. The air in the car felt suddenly hot,
stifling. She snapped her eyelids open, just in time to watch as
Amy realised the keys had been in the ignition all along.

'Hang on, Kato. I'm thinking . . .'

'What?'

'Look, I know you'll think this is mad, but . . . I might get the
train back in. I want to go and have a look at this station George

MacDonald was so very enamoured with, see if I can figure out the appeal.'

Amy was smiling. 'I thought you just said . . .'

Birch waved a hand. 'We're still looking for the MacDonalds, aren't we? Besides, I'm not very good company after this morning. You'll have a better drive back in without me.'

'Not so,' Amy said. 'But if you're wanting some time to yourself, I totally get it.'

'Thanks, Kato.' Birch opened the car door.

'One thing, marm,' Amy said, as Birch unfolded herself from the small space. 'You might want to check there's actually a train you can get on. I don't want to leave you here if the next one isn't till tomorrow.'

17

The next train was the 16.37: half an hour's wait. Birch had insisted that was fine: it was a little walk out of the village to the train tracks, and she'd like a chance to look around the famed station, anyway.

'I doubt that'll take thirty minutes, marm,' Amy had said, but Birch insisted, and then stood on the kerb until the car was out of sight. It felt good to be alone for a while: roughly every thirty seconds she recalled either Charlie's broken face, or the sound of her father's voice on the phone, and wanted to cry, or scream, or throw something. Such feelings were easier to handle without Amy around.

Carstairs Station was very much as she remembered it: it sat between the twin villages of Carstairs Junction and Carstairs, not really a part of either one. From the platform, she could hear the occasional car passing on Strawfrank Road, but otherwise there was no sound of human activity. The land around the station seemed semi-wild: rosebay willowherb grew everywhere, the breeze flinging its seeds all over the steep cutting to one side of the tracks. A further barrier of undergrowth stood between the railway and the eventual fields on the other: the spires of rosebay; nettles; woody, years-old buddleia; brambles like long coils of barbed wire. From here, Birch could see the fat fruit ripening on the briars. The railway's overhead wires stretched as far as the eye could see, and on the distant hillside, the high fence and floodlight struts of the State Hospital were just about visible. This was the landmark Birch had most associated with Carstairs, prior to her current case: the State Hospital was Scotland's only high-security medical facility, made infamous in 1976 when two patients committed a triple murder as part of an escape attempt. She shivered. Had she been George MacDonald, she wouldn't have liked being here alone. Sure, an escape from that place was unlikely, but she'd bet that the train station would be the first place a patient on the run might head.

The station had little to recommend it in general. Birch couldn't remember what year she'd stopped there before, but she remembered the station having buildings. She knew she hadn't dreamed it: there had been a canopy over the platform with a rusted lattice of ironwork holding up the roof. The metal had been painted cream and was flaking: little stars of fallen paint littered the platform like blossom. Now, there was nothing in the way of a waiting room but the standard glass and steel box: the old buildings had been demolished, a criss-cross design on the overhead footbridge the only remnant of the flaky cream paint.

Cheaper, Birch thought. The station must have been unstaffed for decades, and who wants to be maintaining buildings that are never used?

She walked the length of the platform in one direction, then the other. It really was a lonely spot, and surely a boring place to sit for hours on end. In the distance, the red and white stripe of a train crawled past on the long curve of track that Geoff had described to her: Manchester to Edinburgh, Birch guessed. The train seemed miles away: no wonder Ginger George used to wander off the platform. She checked the time on her phone, and found she'd been there seven minutes. The idea of staying for a whole day made absolutely no sense.

A cloud passed in front of the sun, and Birch shivered. She headed to the glass box, and let herself in. It was warmer inside: that sort of stored-up sunlight warmth that a greenhouse has. The inside of the box smelled faintly of cigarettes and stale urine. She swithered, trying to decide whether to stay inside or continue pacing the station's short length. Then something caught her eye.

On the opposite wall of the glass box, someone had taped a Police Scotland poster. *Jewellery found near Carstairs Station*, it read. *Please telephone Lanark police station for further information.*

Birch fished out her phone, and dialled the direct line on the poster. The phone rang six times, and she was about to hang up.

'Police Scotland.' The voice of a man, though he almost sounded too young to be a police officer.

'Hi,' Birch said. 'Am I through to Lanark police station?'

'You are. How can I help?'

'This is Detective Inspector Helen Birch,' Birch said. 'Call sign CA38. I work out of Fettes Avenue in Edinburgh, but I'm standing on Carstairs Station right now, looking at your poster about a piece of missing jewellery.'

On the other end of the line, Birch *felt* the other officer stand up a little straighter.

'Ah yes, marm. That went up . . . a good few weeks ago now.'

'Can you tell me about it? I'm working on a missing person case at the moment, and the missing man spent a lot of time around the station, we're led to believe. We're struggling for leads, and I'm just hoping this might be in some way connected.'

'Oh,' the officer replied, 'it isn't men's jewellery. It's actually a small bag with a few pieces in it. A cloth bag, satin or something, though the bag itself is in a bad state. Inside there's a silver locket, some earrings, three or four rings. It's probably worth a bob or two, in all.'

'Can you tell me how it came to be found, and where?'

'Sure.'

Birch couldn't quite believe how easy this was: she could, after all, be anybody, and this wasn't her turf. But the guy was young. She imagined manning the desk at Lanark police station didn't give you all that many opportunities to chat.

'It was handed in by a railway worker,' the officer was saying. 'There's been some track maintenance going on a little way up the line, near the station, in the direction of Carluke. I don't know what they were doing, but the guy said he dug it up, the bag.'

Birch's heart kicked. 'It had been buried?'

'Perhaps. But it might also just have been dropped, and covered over by works on the railway, or whatever.'

'Is it public land, where it was found?'

'I don't think so,' the man said. 'It was found near a wee run-on that's used for railway vehicles to access the track. Opposite from there, the guy said. The area is wooded. You can get a car down close to the tracks, but to get to where the jewellery was you'd have to go on foot. The guy's theory was someone threw it from the window of a train, or dropped it, and that's how it got to where it was. Quite the mystery, though, eh?'

'Could be, yes. No one's phoned up about it yet?'

'Just yourself,' the officer replied.

'Okay,' Birch said. 'I know you don't know me, and I'm calling out of the blue, and what I'm asking is a massive favour, but . . . hang on to it for the time being, would you? I'd like to come in and have a look at it. I can give you a call back tomorrow to arrange a time.'

'No problem at all,' the man said. 'I'm PC Mitchell. John. If it's not me that answers, just say it was me you spoke to. I'll make a note of it.'

'Thank you so much,' Birch said. 'I really appreciate it.'

'Besides.' PC Mitchell laughed. 'No one's rushing to come and collect this stuff. The scaffy wee bag's been here weeks now, and it looks like it's been sat in the ground far longer. The locket's engraved on the back: a date in 1982. Could have been missing since then – I wouldn't be surprised.'

Birch's mind was racing. She tried to remember if 1982 was a significant year in any of the disappeared women cases she'd looked at in Ginger Mack's file. She hadn't paid much attention to dates, having been unsure what she was looking for. But it *could* be . . .

'Thanks again, PC Mitchell,' she said. 'I'll be in touch.'

Birch hung up. Almost immediately, an automated voice on the tannoy announced that her train would be arriving in five minutes, making her jump. She clattered out of the stuffy glass waiting room and pulled in a lungful of clean air. This could be nothing, she thought. It probably is nothing . . .

And yet, something made her begin walking along the platform, her back turned to the State Hospital and the junction curve and

Edinburgh. Towards Carluke, the man had said. But near the station, somewhere . . .

As she reached the end of the platform, Birch paused. The station tapered out into a sea of tracks. Two red signs were mounted on the fence that marked an end to the public right of way. One read: *Passengers must not pass this point.* The other: *Do not trespass on the Railway. Penalty £1000.* Am I trespassing, she wondered, if I'm investigating a lead? She heard McLeod's voice in her head: *A lead on a case I told you not to get involved in.* She shook her head, pushed the phantom voice away, and shimmied out past the fence into no-man's-land.

Getting to the track-side was hard going: Birch had to pick her way over several sets of rails. The tracks were set into chunky, hard-edged gravel that bit into the soles of her feet through the thin, flat shoes she was wearing. At least they're not heels, she thought, as she picked her way across. She headed diagonally, to a spot where the undergrowth beside the track was thinner: a place she could get off the gravel on to the verge without getting caught up in brambles. It took what felt like a lifetime, but she made it from the platform's end to the verge without – she thought – being seen.

Up ahead, she could see the wooded area the officer at Lanark had described: only a few yards away, really, though she had no idea how far along the spot she was looking for was. Beside her, the rails began to sing, and the overhead wires started up their *swick, swick.* Her train was coming.

Birch felt two things, then: one was a sudden panic at being seen, and reported for trespassing. If the train driver sounded the alarm and the police were called, she'd have to fess up to her flimsy reasoning. The other feeling was *shit, if I miss this train then the next one isn't till after 8 p.m.* She turned to look back at the station, and thought for a second about turning around. But even if she ran, she'd never make it back to the platform ahead of the train.

Instead, Birch found herself stumbling forward. There was an old line here, and a runway of tarmac beside it: a former siding, she assumed. A few feet ahead was a patch of hawthorn scrub, dense and woody. The *swick, swick* of the wires became more frequent. If she could just make it to those bushes, and get behind, she'd be screened from view. But it was easier said than done: though the cracked tarmac was easier to cover than the gravel had been, the ground around the bushes was thick with nettles, grown to thigh-height in the late summer. Birch paused to take a deep breath before plunging in, immediately feeling the stings on her legs through the cheap fabric of her trousers. Now she could hear the train itself: its engine, and the soft high whine of its brakes as it slowed towards Carstairs. Thrashing in the nettles – holding her arms above her head so her hands wouldn't be stung – Birch arranged herself among the hawthorn. She stood as still as she could, holding her breath, eyeing the dark, inch-long thorns on the branches around her. The train chugged past, and Birch turned her face downward. She half expected to hear shouts across the line from passengers as they alighted at the station, but of course, none came. It might be that no one had alighted at all. She waited, listening to the sound of the engine idling. Hours to wait now, she thought, for the next train. And here she was crouching in a bush: she could feel the stings on her legs turning white and raised. She felt ridiculous. All this over *a bad feeling*, Helen. Honestly.

The high-pitched beeping of the train doors carried down the line to her hiding place, and she listened as the train pulled away, the pinging of the wires starting up and then quietening again. With as much dignity as she could muster, she clambered back out from the nettle patch, and straightened up beside the tracks. The woods weren't far now, and the sun was behind them, so the trees reached towards her with their long shadows. Birch looked around: still no one about, no sound of cars or feet or voices. She'd done it now, anyway: she was committed. She stepped out of the sunlight and into the trees' shade, and began to walk.

For a while, she found she could walk with ease along the old siding. The ground was dry from the spell of warm weather, and raised a haze of dust around her shoes. She passed the skeletons of long-disused buildings: prefabricated concrete struts poked up into the sky, the roofs gone. Buddleia grew out of the foundations of these structures, and around the last of the summer's blooms, white cabbage butterflies were busy. By the time she reached the tree-line, she was almost enjoying the walk. But the terrain pushed her off the siding, and back to the track-side with its scrabbly gravel: the wood had a wire fence around it, which read: *No public access to plantation.*

Progress was slow, and the view monotonous: rails and gravel and wires to one side, dense trees to the other. Birch passed below a farm, high up on the bank on the other side of the tracks, and hoped she hadn't been spotted. Occasionally there would be movement in the wood, and she'd startle, hoping it was only a rabbit or a bird. The shade under the trees was chilly, though above the railway cutting the early evening sun shone bright and gold. As she stumbled on the gravel verge, Birch thought about Charlie. His arm would have been set in plaster by now. He might be awake, and probably alone in that weird locked room with nothing to do. He'll be livid, she thought, and she knew it was true because *she* was. Mostly livid with the boy who'd done it, but also angry with her brother for fighting back beyond mere self-defence. His sentence was too long anyway: years and years she'd have to wait before he'd be released. And now he'd almost guaranteed it would be made longer. She imagined them both as older people, meeting outside the prison for the first time. Where would she be by then, in her life? What might have happened to her, how might she have changed while her brother was forced to remain the same, as though preserved in aspic behind the prison's walls? It hurt to think about, though not as much as it hurt to picture Charlie's cut and bloodied face. If I weren't a police officer, she thought, I'd want to batter that boy, too. Given her brother's chequered career to date, she realised it was amazing the kid hadn't taken more damage. At least Charlie didn't kill him, she thought, and the relief of that realisation brought her to a complete stop, just for a moment. If he had, he'd be lost to her for ever. The prison would have swallowed him up and made him its own.

She was so lost in thought by the time she reached the run-on that she almost didn't see it. The rosebay was tall there, where the cutting grew shallower, but suddenly she saw it: a strip of pressed tarmac that joined the quiet road above to the tracks. There was space there for a few vehicles to park, and wooden sleepers were neatly piled at the end of the run-on nearest to the rails. Birch could see that workers had been there recently: a Portaloo had been placed beside the tracks, and an orange fluorescent vest was looped round one of the fence-posts, tied in a fat knot. The railway was wide here, but straight: easy enough to see in both directions and move back and forth without being surprised by a sudden train. This was it, she realised: this was the place the Lanark officer had described.

She could see where the railwaymen had been working. It was clear that a tree had fallen across the rails, and needed to be cleared: there were still little wood-shaving eddies scattered here and there. The wire fence around the wood had been crushed, and the railwaymen must have cleared away the broken section. For the first time, Birch was able to step away from the track-side and into the wood. A few feet in, she found the tree's stump, the undergrowth around it tramped down, the soil disturbed. Somewhere here, she thought. Somewhere here.

Under the trees, the light was low. Birch flipped out her phone and thumbed the torch on. It didn't do much in the half-light, but if she bent low to the ground, she could see a circle of the wood floor in detail. She felt more relaxed now that she was screened from the road, and began to shuffle around, bent over like an old woman. What are you even looking for, Helen? She had no idea. But she couldn't stop moving from one square foot to the next, shining her tiny light. Inside her, the bad feeling seemed to have grown, like one of those pellets of tea that flowers into an ugly, floating bloom. It sloshed around inside her. If I were George MacDonald, she thought, and I had things to hide . . .

She turned to go deeper into the wood. I'd go this way, she thought, further away from the tracks. It was darker further in, and the undergrowth thinner. Birch could feel a cold sweat

developing on her face. I'd look for a clear spot where I could bury
something, a place where the tree roots wouldn't get in the way,
she thought. She straightened up. Sure enough, only a few metres
ahead, there was a dappled patch of ground where the tree canopy
gave way and light filtered down to the mulchy floor. The plantation was pretty regular, but perhaps a tree had failed, or fallen and
been cleared, never replaced. Birch stepped into the light patch,
and bent down once again. There was greenery here: a few weak-
looking plants reaching up to the light. With no other tool at her
disposal, Birch cracked her baton, and scraped at the soil around
her feet.

You're mad, Helen, she thought, as she notched a small channel
into the earth. You're out in the middle of nowhere, scratching at
the ground in the middle of a wood. You've about ten different
cases sitting on your desk that you ought to be working on. This is
madness, it really is absolute—

The baton hit something. The channel was about three inches
deep, but something was preventing her from scoring it any
deeper. Now, she stuck the heel of her shoe in and dragged it
backward, widening the little ditch she'd made and bringing up
more soil. Still the hard thing got in the way: she reached down
and brushed away dirt and pine-needles. It was a rock, rough and
craggy-feeling. Birch set her heel to its protruding edge and tried
to work it upward, but it was too big to move.

Now she was on her hands and knees, scrabbling with the baton
to uncover more of the stone. You're excavating a rock, she
thought. McLeod is going to go insane if he finds out about any
of this. Before long, Birch's nails were ragged, and clogged with
soil. Her trousers were filthy: she couldn't really see in the dim
light, but she could feel that they were filmed all over with dirt.
But now when she stabbed at the rock with her baton, it moved,
ever so slightly. A little more digging, and she could get her fingers
underneath its bottom edge, and rock it back and forth. She did
this for a long time, her phone back in her pocket now and what
little light there was leaching away from the clearing, turning the
plantation grey and formless. But the rock was almost out now:

she could feel it was about a foot across, and underneath it the soil was damp and slimy.

Birch was sweating, her fringe plastered to her forehead, but she finally levered the big rock out of the ground and pushed it aside. The bad feeling was pulsing through her now, as she reached for her phone and lit up the torch beam once more. In the well the rock had left behind, pale roots snaked this way and that, a lattice made by the surrounding trees. Birch pushed her hand in among them, closing her fist around as much of the root network as she could. Then she pulled, and there was a delicious crackling sound as the roots strained and came away from the soil. Fucksake, she thought, this is like a horror film; I'm like the mad lab assistant sent into the woods to dig up mandrake. Below the stringy roots, there were more: some thicker, some nearly as fine as hair. Birch plunged her hand into the hole left by the rock once more. This time there was something else among the roots. Something slimy, or shiny, or—

She shone the flashlight into the hole with one hand, and pulled away soil with the other. After a few moments, she fell backward out of her crouch, recoiling from the muddy channel she'd made. She sat on the forest floor, breathless and filthy, for several minutes, waiting as her heartbeat slowed, settled.

'Jesus fuck,' she said, and her voice bounced back at her from the dark trees.

Edinburgh Evening News

BREAKING: human remains found near railway line near Carstairs

BREAKING NEWS TEAM   Published 21:35   Share this article

Email   Thursday 5 September   Live updates

SIGN UP TO OUR DAILY NEWSLETTER

BREAKING NEWS: The Edinburgh Evening News is receiving reports that human remains have been found in woodland close to the villages of Carstairs and Carstairs Junction, South Lanarkshire.

Police personnel are on the scene just west of Carstairs railway station, and a secure crime scene is being set up.

Police Scotland have yet to make a statement, and the exact nature of the police operation is not yet known.

More details here as they come in.

18

'Well, bang goes my evening, Helen. I had *plans*.'

McLeod had parked on the roadside, across the tracks from the woods. Now, he was sitting on the back bumper of his estate car, pulling on a pair of black wellies. Birch was silent, surprised that he owned wellies. Surprised that he'd come out to a crime scene at nearly 10 p.m. on a Thursday night. Surprised that she still hadn't woken up yet from what felt like a surreal and horrifying dream.

'Sorry, sir,' she said. 'But I'm glad you're here. I have some concerns, and I'm struggling to keep control of the crime scene.'

McLeod stood. 'Keep control? What's going on?'

Birch waved an arm in the direction of the woods. Below them, the access ramp that led to the tracks was covered with police vehicles. Their blue lights lit up the surrounding trees like strobes at a disco. In the woods around the clearing where Birch had dug, floodlights had been erected, and the white-suited figures of the forensics team could be seen flitting between the tree-trunks. The air fizzed with the static from dozens of police radios.

Birch took a deep breath. 'I'm worried that there might be other bodies,' she said. 'In the immediate area, in the woods. Everyone's trampling all over the place. I'm worried that evidence could be destroyed.'

McLeod frowned. 'Other bodies? What haven't I been told?'

Birch's first call had been dispatch, asking for the cavalry. She hadn't been desperately coherent. *I'm in the woods at – somewhere near Carstairs. Carstairs Station, only . . . up the line, towards Carluke. I've found a body. No, I've found . . . part of a body. I've found – I don't know. I need immediate back-up. Look, just get here, okay . . .*

Her second call had been an equally panicked one to Amy. Find McLeod. Tell him what we know about George MacDonald, and Ginger Mack, and everything.

'Ginger Mack,' Birch said. 'Also known as George MacDonald. His wife is still missing. I believe he's connected to several missing women, in fact, and—'

McLeod held up a hand. 'I've had this already,' he said, 'from DC Kato. You know I have to stop you, Helen. We don't yet have an ID on this body, we don't know if it's a woman, and we don't know why it's here. We don't even know if there's been foul play – although I'll grant you, being buried in the woods is a pretty strong indicator. I'm asking: do you have a single shred of evidence yet to link this body to your Ginger Mack?'

Birch bit her lip. All I've got is that bad fucking feeling, she thought. 'No, sir.'

'No. So I can assume you also have no evidence – actual evidence – that there might be more bodies in the vicinity?'

'No, sir.'

McLeod reached behind him and slammed the car's boot lid. 'Right then,' he said. 'Regular crime scene procedure it is, then.'

He locked the car, and began to stride down the hill, on to the access ramp, picking his way between the police vehicles while the personnel around him bobbed their heads in deference.

'Oh.' At the edge of the tracks, McLeod stopped, and turned back to look at Birch. 'Don't think I've overlooked the little wild-goose chase you were on when you came across this crime scene, either. We'll have words.'

Birch swallowed. 'Yes, sir.'

McLeod strode out across the tracks, and Birch followed. They paused for a moment before crossing the flattened boundary fence into the woods. Birch couldn't help but cringe at the trampled path that had already been created there: earth and undergrowth packed hard by the movement back and forth of many pairs of boots.

The burial site was about twenty-five yards in. It took so much less time to reach it now – with the wood eerily floodlit – than it had for Birch to skirt her way across, bent double, phone in hand. Over the grave – now much deeper and wider than the crap channel Birch had dug – the forensics team were erecting their tent. Everyone stiffened at the approach of McLeod.

'This is only just going up now?' he barked, nodding at the flimsy tent fabric.

It took a moment of awkward silence for Birch to realise he was addressing her. 'Yes, sir. It's pretty cramped here, as you see, but sheltered from public view, so I made the call for the work to be done in the open, as far as possible. But we're worried about a change in the weather.'

'Hmm.' McLeod watched as the white-suited officers struggled with fabric and poles in the hemmed-in space between trees. Eventually he stepped backward and said, 'Fair enough. Where have the remains been taken?'

Birch nodded to her left, in the direction she had come along the railway line. 'We've set up camp just beyond the woods,' she said. 'Back towards the station. There's a disused siding there, and a stretch of paving. All excavated evidence is being taken there for initial processing.'

Around them, SOCOs bustled, training their cameras at the ground. The flashes lit up branches and undergrowth like tiny lightning strikes.

'Take me there,' McLeod said.

The siding Birch had walked through that afternoon looked creepy under the sharp white light of the police floodlights. The broken buildings she had passed were all sharp edges and deep shadows, and the white forensic tents floated ghostly in front of them. Birch ushered McLeod into the first tent, where she knew they'd find Letitia Bland, the Crime Scene Manager, and some of her team.

'Hi, Tish,' Birch said.

Bland looked up from a small laptop where, a moment ago, she'd been typing something. She nodded to Birch, but extended a small, pale hand to McLeod. Bland was a petite woman, nearing retirement age, but incredibly sharp, Birch knew.

'Detective Chief Inspector,' she said. They shook hands briefly.

'We must stop meeting like this,' McLeod said, and Tish Bland let out a humourless laugh. Birch held back an eye-roll.

'Tell me what we know so far,' McLeod said.

Bland moved towards a table in the centre of the tent, where excavated items were being sorted into containers. Birch swallowed hard before following. She already knew what was in there.

'Our victim,' Bland said, 'has been in the ground for a long time. The remains are skeletal, as you can see.'

McLeod leaned over the plastic containers on the table. Inside them were human bones, sorted by type, each bagged and labelled. Though the remains were old, a smell hung in the tent and caught in Birch's throat. The smell of foul secrets, of things left to rot. Her first thought, when she'd realised there were only bones: it's not Phamie MacDonald, then – she was last seen too recently. I'll have to keep looking.

'Can you be more specific than *a long time*?' McLeod asked.

Bland cocked her head to one side. 'The body was wrapped in plastic bags,' Bland said. 'The outer layers had begun to crumble away, but the inner ones are being catalogued and sent for further examination. The logos aren't current. From the bags and the state of the body, I'd say we're looking at twenty years at least.'

Birch felt cold. Maisie Kerr had been missing twenty years: her mother had said so just hours ago.

'Obviously,' Bland added, 'that's a guesstimate.'

McLeod nodded. 'What else?' he said. 'Any leads on identification?'

'Well.' Bland looked down at the containers in front of her. 'We're still excavating, but so far we've turned up very little other than our victim here. No clothing, no purse or wallet, no jewellery.'

'But sir,' Birch cut in, 'DC Kato mentioned to you, I think, that jewellery was found near to the scene some weeks ago, and is being held at Lanark police station?'

McLeod nodded. 'She did say that,' he said. 'I've sent her to pick it up, in fact. But nothing found with the body, Tish? Nothing at all?'

Bland shrugged. 'Not yet. It's possible that the victim was moved, and separated from their personal effects. That might explain the jewellery found nearby.'

McLeod was still peering into the containers, each in turn, as though he expected something vital to leap out of one of them and make itself known.

'Cause of death?'

At this, Tish Bland shook her head. 'I can't say at all, at the moment,' she said. 'Given the age of the remains, it'll take time in the lab before we can determine that. But you'll see' – she pointed at the container on the far end of the table – 'that the skull is intact.'

McLeod glanced up at Birch. 'And you believe that all the bones you've found belong to the same corpse. That this is one person, yes?'

'We'll know that for sure once everything's in the lab,' Bland said, 'but as far as I can see, yes.'

Birch looked at the ground, to avoid seeing McLeod's expression. There was a moment of silence, and then he spoke again.

'Anything else you can tell me?'

Bland was still looking at the skull. Birch couldn't see it, from her position further back in the tent, though she'd looked at it earlier, when it was first exhumed. She couldn't hold its empty gaze for long.

'Interesting burial,' Bland said. 'Our victim was more dropped down a hole than buried in a grave. Whoever did this dug down, not out. Perhaps they hit a void, or something, but if not it would have been some work. Then it seems that the body was lowered into that deep hole, feet first. Buried standing up, as it were. A large stone was placed on top of the whole thing, and then everything covered over.'

Birch shuddered. She still remembered the heft of the stone in her arms, the wet dirt under her torn nails. She still remembered the moment she touched the plastic bags underneath, the sliminess of them as she fumbled to pull back the layers . . .

'The stone is in Tent B,' Bland said. 'We'll give it a proper examination, too.'

McLeod finally stepped back from the table, the pieces of what were once a person neatly laid out in their numbered bags.

'Okay,' he said. Birch could tell he was dissatisfied: McLeod was a finisher, he loved to draw a line under things. They could guess at only a little, and knew even less for sure.

A scene-of-crime officer Birch vaguely knew poked his head through the tent's entrance flap. 'Ah,' he said, 'you're here.'

Birch was unsure whether he was addressing her, or McLeod.

'Yes,' McLeod answered, deciding.

The SOCO looked harried. 'I'm afraid the press are here, sir.'

Birch winced. *The press are here* were McLeod's four least favourite words.

'Oh for fuck's sake,' he said.

The SOCO nodded, then ducked back out of the tent.

'Excuse us, Tish,' Birch said, and followed him.

The SOCO was standing outside on the tarmac, pointing into the night with one outstretched arm. 'Someone's been spotted over there,' he said. Birch followed the line of his arm to the farm buildings above the railway cutting. 'They've probably parked at the farm. I dare say they're walking down to where our vehicles are.'

He turned back to face the tents. 'There are buildings just behind us here, too,' he said. 'I wouldn't be surprised if someone didn't try to gain access from there. And as you can see, there's a presence on the station.'

Birch looked up the line. On the station platform, she could see dark figures. The flash from a camera went off, illuminating a gaggle of press.

'Oh for fuck's sake.' McLeod was behind her. He sounded identical to the first time he'd said it.

Birch unclipped the radio from her belt. 'All units,' she said into it, 'this is CA38, Birch. I need anyone who's in uniform and not busy to head to the crime scene perimeter. We've got company.'

She glanced at McLeod. 'We might need some more personnel here, sir.'

McLeod huffed. He hated wasting resources, but he also hated press intrusion. She watched him take out his phone, and begin to dial for help.

'Press are arriving,' Birch said into the radio, 'and it's vital that this crime scene is not disturbed. Anyone who isn't police person- nel sets foot anywhere they shouldn't, and I want you to arrest them for trespassing on railway property, over.'

Behind her, she could hear McLeod saying, *Uniformed back-up to Carstairs Road*, into his phone. She looked back at the woods, the floodlights pushing their white light out in weird beams between the trees. It looked like an alien craft had landed, like something out of the *X-Files*. She remembered Al, sitting opposite her in the Jinglin' Geordie – was that really just last night? *Dig up the past*, he'd said, repeating an old cliché, *and you just get dirty*. Birch looked down at herself. She couldn't see all that well in the dim light, but she could feel that the legs of her trousers were coated with mud. Twigs and burrs clung to her at intervals. Under her clothes, her skin was nettle-stung, and her hands were filthy. She'd have given anything for a set of nail-clippers right at that moment: every single nail was ragged from scrabbling around in the dirt. It was getting late, and she had no idea when she'd get home. Tomorrow would be hell, no doubt: whatever news came about this body, it couldn't be good. The best they could hope for was a connection to a killer already incarcerated for some other crime. But no: the bad feeling hadn't left when Birch had put in her mayday call. It hadn't left when forensics arrived and started to take things off her hands. It showed no sign of leaving now: like a plant, it seemed to be uncurling still further, filling up Birch's insides.

'There'll be more digging yet,' she said quietly, in the direction of her gravel-ruined shoes. 'At least if I've anything to do with it.'

19

'I'm not going to tell you where I've been,' was what he said, as though me asking was the most unreasonable thing in the world. 'I'm a grown man and I'll go where I want, for as long as I want, with whoever I want. Did you think when you married me you were marrying a lapdog who'd sit for ever at your feet? Did you, Phamie? Were you really that naive?'

Amy stood under the harsh lights of the lab, imagining the green tinge they must lend to her skin. She looked down at the metal tray in front of her, at each piece of jewellery in its own clear plastic evidence bag, and tried to push the voice of Phamie's diaries out of her mind. The little satin pouch the jewellery had come in wasn't there: its fabric could potentially give up more secrets than the hard metal of the jewellery, and so was still being assessed. The metal items gave off a dull glow in their strip-lit tray.

'DC Kato.' The voice belonged to Letitia Bland herself, which surprised Amy. 'Good of you to come over.'

Amy stood up straight. 'Of course,' she said. 'It's good to see you. I'd expected you'd be at the crime scene.'

Bland waved one dismissive hand. 'It's grunt work now,' she said. 'We've accounted for the whole of the body, so I'm more use here than there, and they've got me on call.'

Amy nodded, letting her eyes brush over the jewellery in front of her.

'So,' Bland said, approaching the table, 'you've come to find out what you can about this little treasure trove.'

'Yes,' Amy said. 'Whatever you can tell me.'

Bland poked a latex-gloved hand into the tray, shuffling the items around. 'Well,' she said. 'I can tell you that this jewellery did not belong to the woman whose body we've found; or if it did, she went to enormous lengths to keep it uncontaminated. It has none of her DNA on it whatsoever. I don't believe our victim ever touched it.'

Amy frowned, and then saw Bland notice.

'The date on the locket doesn't match, either,' she said. 'I think she was born before then, but murdered after then.' Bland was looking down at the locket, dull with tarnish, in its bag. 'Of course, it doesn't have to be her birth year, it could be some other significant date. But if I had to guess, I'd say this jewellery belonged to someone entirely different, and its proximity to our corpse is purely coincidental.'

Amy was nodding, though she was unsure whether this was good news or bad, as far as the case went. 'What can you tell me about the victim?' she asked.

Bland's eyes unfocused, as though she were consulting some mental chart. 'We're still early in our examinations,' she said, 'so this is, to a degree, guesswork. But it's my belief that cause of death was strangulation. There's no skin or tissue left to betray damage to the throat, but the victim had two broken fingers and a greenstick fracture to the wrist. That suggests a struggle, moving us away from, say, poisoning. The body, though very decomposed, bears no obvious signs of a beating. Just those injuries to the hand and wrist. So if I were a betting woman – which I'm not, mind – I'd say our victim was strangled.'

Amy felt her throat turning dry.

'We're taking soil samples from the burial site,' Bland went on, 'to see if we can find blood residue. If we find it, then it may be that it wasn't strangulation, but something else. But then, she could also have been killed elsewhere, and moved. It's a lot of guesswork with remains this old. We might never know the cause of death, or any kind of specific date. But I'll keep you updated on anything we turn up.'

'Okay.'

'As for our killer,' Bland said, 'we're doing everything we can to find something we could use to scrape up some DNA. Everything's been in the ground a long, long time. But our best chance is those layered carrier bags. We're hoping something might have survived on the inner layers that we can get a result from.'

'Anything you could contribute to a profile?' Amy asked. 'Hypothetically, even?'

Bland shrugged. 'Profiling is not my specialism,' she said, 'as you know. But this was a well-planned burial, I know that much. The grave goes surprisingly deep. It's unusual to find a corpse buried essentially standing up. Perhaps he'd thought it out: take an infra-red scan of that wood and you might see a hotspot there, but it would look like just that, a spot. Not a long stripe, like it might had he laid the body out in one piece. Either way, he'd need to be a big guy, to have the strength to dig a pit like that. And heft the big rock to top off the whole thing. It's concrete, by the way. I suspect it's railway rubble.'

'Pretty calculating,' Amy said.

'It was. Like I say, he'd thought about it. I wouldn't be surprised if this guy had had some practice.'

Amy blinked. 'You think he'd killed before?'

Bland shrugged. 'That,' she said, 'or he was just a meticulous planner.'

Amy could feel goosebumps rising on her arms, though the lab wasn't especially cold. 'DI Birch has a bad feeling,' she said, 'that there might be more victims out there.'

Bland put her palms down flat on the table in front of her, and leaned on them. Suddenly, Amy could see how tired she was, remembered that the older woman had been working through the night.

'I hope not,' Bland said, nodding towards the jewellery in its tray, 'but there is *that*. If it didn't belong to our victim, what was it doing out there?'

In her pocket, Amy felt her phone buzz. 'That's maybe a bridge to cross when we come to it,' she said. 'I'm charged with trying to identify its owner.'

Bland rocked back on to her heels. Her gloved hands left small, damp prints on the table top, which shrank almost as soon as they'd appeared.

'We've taken DNA from the earrings,' she said. 'And there's a lock of hair in the locket. Someone else's, not the same person as the earring-wearer. The earrings were worn by a woman, no surprise. But the hair belonged to a man. A ginger man, in fact. Good old Scottish red hair, perhaps?'

Amy felt her hearing stutter out. The word *ginger* clanged in her brain. Not just a hair colour, she thought. A name. In her pocket, her phone buzzed again, and she shook herself.

'Speaking of DNA . . .' Amy realised she'd been standing with Phamie's diaries hugged to her chest, as though she were protecting them. Now, she held them out towards Bland, self-conscious. 'I've brought you these.'

The diaries crackled in the evidence bag Amy had put them in as Bland reached out to take them.

'They're diaries written by our missing person, Phamie MacDonald,' Amy explained. She still had one hand on the parcelled notebooks, reluctant to let them go. 'They were found in the MacDonalds' former home. We were hoping you might be able to pull some DNA off them, too, or any fingerprints.'

Bland nodded, and Amy let go.

'DI Birch briefed me,' Bland said. 'There's no chance our Jane Doe is Mrs MacDonald. The remains have been in the ground too long.'

'No, I know,' Amy said. 'We're – DI Birch is just keen to confirm or rule out a link between the MacDonald case and this murder you're looking at. We figured, if you could join any dots . . .'

'I'll get someone on to it,' Bland said. 'But with all the evidence from Carstairs, it might take a day or two. Can you wait?'

Amy winced, but tried not to show it. 'Sure, no problem. Thanks, Letitia.'

'Tish,' Bland said, with a smile. But Amy was already backing away, planning the phone call she was about to make to her boss.

*   *   *

DI Birch was parked around the corner from Hazel Kerr's house, in the same place as Amy had parked the day before. Amy pulled her handbrake on, climbed out of the car, and walked round to the passenger side of Birch's Mondeo. Inside, her boss was asleep, her neck curled awkwardly, one temple against the window. Amy tapped on the passenger window, and Birch jumped.

'Jesus.' Her voice was muffled inside the car, but Amy could hear the spike of fear in it.

She opened the door. 'Morning, marm.'

'Get in, Kato. Bloody hell.'

Amy climbed in. DI Birch's car smelled like pumpkin spice: a novelty orange air freshener in the shape of an autumn leaf dangled from the rear-view mirror.

'I was just resting my eyes,' Birch said.

Amy tried not to grin. 'I never said a word, marm.'

Birch passed a hand over her eyes. 'No, but you were thinking it. Anyway. I'm with it now, promise.'

Amy eyed her boss for a moment. 'Are you sure you're okay? I tried to give you a call last night, but you didn't pick up.'

'Did you?' Birch reached for her phone. 'I could swear I didn't have a missed call.'

'No, marm. On your landline, I mean.'

Something flickered behind DI Birch's eyes, just for a moment, and then it was gone. 'I've unplugged my landline,' she said. 'Just . . . for the time being. I've been getting cold calls and I just can't be bothered to deal with them.'

There was something not quite right about the way this came out, and Amy didn't respond. She wondered whether she ought to probe further. Her boss had been the victim of malicious phone calls not all that long ago – calls that turned out to be connected to her brother's case, to the men who wanted to hurt Charlie. But Birch cut in before Amy could say anything more.

'Anyway, we're up to speed now, right?'

Amy nodded.

'Good,' Birch said. 'So. Maisie Kerr.'

Amy fished in her oversized handbag, and pulled out the jewellery. Each piece was still tightly sealed in its own little evidence pouch, but Letitia Bland had put the whole lot into one larger, more sturdy plastic bag.

'Keep them in here as much as you can,' she'd said. 'And obviously don't open the smaller bags. These things can be clearly identified through the plastic, okay?'

Amy had nodded solemnly.

'I figured we could start with her,' Amy said now, to Birch. 'Or rather, with her mother. We know Maisie had a habit of lifting jewellery . . . and the crime scene is what? Ten minutes' drive from here?'

'Yeah.' Birch rubbed one eye with a balled fist. 'And she knows our faces. Our little chat yesterday was excruciating, but we've laid the groundwork.'

Amy nodded. 'Stupid question,' she said, after a moment. 'But . . . you've not had much sleep?'

Birch shook her head. 'Basically none,' she said. 'I've got . . . lots to think about at the moment. Charlie, apart from anything else.'

Amy felt her face crease in sympathy. 'Any news?'

Birch let out a long sigh. 'I phoned the prison this morning,' she said. 'His arm is broken in two places. They've set it properly now, and he's been awake on and off. But they're keeping him pretty well sedated, it sounds like. Christ knows when I'll get to go and see him again, with all this going on.'

Amy waited, unsure what to say.

'Not that the screws want me there,' Birch added. Her eyes looked glassy. The quiet stretched between them.

'I'm so sorry, marm,' Amy said, unsure of what else would do. 'But . . . positive developments from the lab, no? Or . . . developments, at least.'

Birch seemed to snap back to the present. 'The red hair,' she said, 'yes.'

Amy swiped her phone open to show her boss the photo Letitia Bland had sent her. 'That's what the inside of the locket looks like,' she said, leaning over so Birch could see the screen.

Having peered at the photo for a moment, Birch straightened up. 'Okay,' she said. 'Let's go and see what Hazel Kerr makes of all this.'

'I'm going to hand you each of these items in turn,' Amy said, fishing in the big plastic bag for the handful of smaller ones, the jewellery inside.

Mrs Kerr was sitting across from her, in the same armchair, the three photos of Maisie at her elbow. It was like the past twenty-four hours had been erased, and Birch and Amy had never left this house. The only difference was that this time it was DI Birch who sat with the iPad open on her lap, ready to take notes if necessary.

'You can look at each item for as long as you like,' Amy went on. 'If they jog any memory for you, however distant, let me know.'

She reached across the space between herself and Hazel Kerr, and passed her the first pair of earrings. They were cream pearls on brassy gold studs, so small that they fell to the bottom of the evidence bag and lay in the crease at the bottom. Mrs Kerr put the bag close to her face, and peered at them. Amy fancied she could feel DI Birch holding her breath. Mrs Kerr's face was hard to read.

'Not sure,' she said at last.

'Okay,' Amy said. 'That's okay. They're quite generic, those. Let's try this.'

With one hand, she took back the earrings. With the other, she held out the bag containing the silver locket.

The recognition was immediate. Mrs Kerr's mouth twisted open into a sort of grimace. She let out a low, animal sound.

Amy glanced at Birch, but Birch was watching the reaction unfold.

'No,' Mrs Kerr said, her voice hoarse. 'No, no, no.'

Amy moved in a sort of crouch from her seat on the sofa, to kneel beside the stricken woman.

'Mrs Kerr,' she said quietly. 'Hazel.'

Mrs Kerr gulped in air, tears now running down her face. 'It's Maisie's,' she managed, between sobs. 'It's Maisie's christening locket.'

Amy closed her eyes for a moment. She was going to have to force herself to say two fairly terrible words. 'You're sure?'

When the woman didn't respond, Amy said, 'I'm sorry, Mrs Kerr, but . . . you're quite sure?'

This time, Mrs Kerr nodded. Behind her, Amy could hear the soft, slow thud of DI Birch's fingers on the iPad screen.

'This means . . .' Mrs Kerr was struggling to speak. 'This means the body you found. In the woods. This means it's Maisie.'

'No.' DI Birch's voice was urgent, behind Amy. 'No, I'm sorry, I should have been clear. The jewellery wasn't found with the body, and our lab results have shown that the victim never touched any of these pieces. We're still waiting for identification, but we don't believe the body is Maisie's.'

Mrs Kerr was clutching the evidence bag with both hands, pinning it in her lap, looking down at the locket. Amy could tell she was trying to bring her emotions under control.

'It was plain,' Mrs Kerr said, not looking up, 'when I got it. Cheaper than the fancy ones with the scrollwork on them, or whatever. I had the date engraved. Maisie was two by the time she was christened. I didn't get round to it till after . . .'

There was a pause so long that Amy thought perhaps Hazel Kerr wouldn't speak again.

'Till after her father left,' she said at last. Her voice had a new edge in it. Amy reached out and placed one hand over Mrs Kerr's nearest, the left hand. To her surprise, the older woman closed her fingers around it.

'Can I ask,' DI Birch said, 'what colour hair Maisie's father had?'

Hazel Kerr looked up from the locket for the first time. Her eyes were red, but her face was pale. 'Why?'

Amy stayed where she was, holding the woman's hand, looking down at the locket in her lap.

'Inside the locket,' DI Birch went on, 'is a lock of hair. It's been preserved in there, all these years. Our lab tests show it belonged to a man. We're keen to find out who that man might be.'

Mrs Kerr blinked. 'David's hair was brown,' she said, 'very dark brown, almost black. But I never put it in there. I don't think I've ever done that. That lock of hair thing.'

'Did Maisie have a boyfriend,' Amy asked, 'whose hair she might have put in the locket?'

Mrs Kerr let her eyes drop back to the evidence bag. 'Probably,' she said, tears returning to her eyes, 'but I'm afraid you're asking the wrong person. We grew so far apart. She never told me anything.'

'I need you to call Robertson Bennet.'

DI Birch was stony-faced, resolute, her seatbelt already fastened. Amy was in the passenger seat, still holding the bag full of jewellery. It was heavier now: before they'd left, Hazel Kerr had staggered upstairs and brought down the emerald bracelet and earrings, found in George MacDonald's possession almost twenty years ago. She hadn't been lying: the items were still in their own evidence bag, the way they'd been returned to her. The ID sticker on the bag was faded, handwritten in a jumpy scrawl.

'I think he needs to know,' Birch said, 'that his missing person case has ... evolved. I also want a DNA sample off him.' She sounded weary.

'What's your plan, marm?'

Birch glanced down at the emerald jewellery set in Amy's lap. 'I'm going to see if the lab can pull MacDonald's DNA off those emerald pieces,' she said. 'It's a stroke of luck she's never taken them out of that bag. Let's hope he handled them enough that we can get something, then we can cross-check against the hair in the locket. My bad feeling tells me that we'll get a match, they'll be the same person. And if Bennet will give us a swab then we can prove that person is George MacDonald. That Maisie Kerr knew him.'

'You want me to tell Bennet that's what we're doing?'

'He doesn't need the details,' she said. 'You can tell him that we're looking at his father for another case, but you can hopefully get away with not saying too much about why. Maybe say . . . we're working to eliminate him from our enquiries.'

Amy nodded.

'I need to take this to McLeod.' DI Birch sounded sick at the thought of it. 'If we get a DNA match, then we know George MacDonald was lying when he said he just found that jewellery. We'll be almost certain that he was involved with Maisie in some way.'

'And why would he lie, unless he was involved in her disappearance?'

'My thoughts exactly,' Birch said. 'But there's more to this. We now have a positive ID on jewellery that was found only yards from the body of a murdered woman. It belongs to someone else, but that someone else also happens to be missing. I'd bet everything I own that Maisie Kerr's body is also somewhere in that wood.'

Amy screwed up her face. She couldn't shake the feeling of Hazel Kerr's hand, damp from wiping away tears, curled around her own.

'It doesn't look good,' she agreed.

'McLeod won't want to,' Birch went on, 'but I think I can convince him that we need to widen the search area. We need to be looking for Maisie Kerr.'

Amy nodded again slowly. 'And you want me to tell Robertson Bennet?'

DI Birch looked down again at the tangle of evidence bags across Amy's knees, weak sunlight caught in the surface of the plastic like water.

'Not in so many words,' she said. 'But I'm afraid so.'

Edinburgh Evening News

BREAKING: Carstairs forensic net to widen in hunt for further evidence

BREAKING NEWS TEAM   Published 17:27   Share this article
Email   Friday 6 September   Live updates

SIGN UP TO OUR DAILY NEWSLETTER

BREAKING NEWS: Following the discovery of human remains in woodland near Carstairs railway station, South Lanarkshire, Police Scotland have announced that further excavation will take place in the hunt for evidence relating to the discovery.

The body, found in woodland near the villages of Carstairs and Carstairs Junction yesterday evening, has yet to be formally identified. Police Scotland forensics teams will now widen their search area in the hope of unearthing further clues.

Speaking at a press conference this afternoon, Detective Inspector Helen Birch told journalists at Fettes Avenue station: 'We anticipate that this excavation will cause some disruption to local rail services, as trains running between Carstairs and Carluke stations will have to be temporarily suspended. This is necessary to ensure the safety of our officers on the ground. Police Scotland would like to apologise in advance for any inconvenience this may cause.'

DI Birch also said the police are doing all they can to identify the remains, which they can now confirm are human. However, she could not release any further information regarding the investigation at this time.

More details here as they come in.

20

Birch hadn't felt like going home – hadn't wanted to have to plug her phone back in and listen to see if there were voice-mails. Instead, she pointed out that it was Friday night, and suggested the pub. To her surprise, Amy agreed, and together they drove back towards the city. At Hermiston, as they passed signs for Ratho, Birch was reminded of Al Lonsdale and his assertion that George MacDonald would be living off meals on wheels in a bungalow there. If he is, Birch thought, he's got some brass neck.

Amy suggested the Raeburn: it made sense to go somewhere near to Amy's flat, and there were plenty of places to park nearby. Birch disliked the Raeburn for a variety of reasons that weren't really its fault: it was a five-minute walk from Fettes Avenue, for example. Birch didn't fear running into colleagues – the place was too upmarket and pricey for that. Rather, it was like she could just *feel* the proximity of her office, all her paperwork, and all the questions she still couldn't answer about George and Phamie MacDonald.

Nevertheless, she'd parked on Comely Bank Road. They'd found an empty table in the beer garden, and decided to sit outside under the big trees.

'The weather's been so nice lately,' Amy said, waving away Birch's offer to go to the bar. 'It can't last much longer. We ought to make the most of it.'

While Amy was inside, Birch tried to drag her mind out of her increasingly knotted tangle of thoughts. Look at this place, she thought. The Raeburn had once been semi-derelict, a former hotel fallen into disrepair. The beer garden in which she was now sitting had been hired each November and December by a Christmas tree company. Every year, Birch would pick a night after work to drive down the road and choose a Christmas tree. She'd stand in the cold, floodlit yard, the empty skull of the Raeburn looming up in front of her, while the men wrapped her tree in spidery white netting. The building was barely recognisable now, repointed and sandblasted and sporting a fancy gilt sign. The Raeburn had been little more than a rain shelter to the Christmas tree men: they'd stamp in and out of its unheated rooms, blowing the pale smoke of their own breath into their hands.

'Here you go, marm.' Amy shook Birch out of the memory, placing a tonic water down in front of her. Amy brandished a large glass of white wine. 'I hope you don't mind.'

'Don't be daft,' Birch said. 'Drink up, you're done driving.'

Amy settled on the bench opposite Birch. 'Right,' she said, flattening both palms against the table. 'Now you can tell me what's going on.'

Birch flinched, and stared at Amy for a moment. 'What do you mean, going on?'

Amy dipped her head to one side, studying her boss. 'You seem awfully distracted, is all,' she said. 'And I don't mean the way you usually are, with a case. When a case is getting to you – and don't get me wrong, I know this one is – you talk about it. You sort of . . . think aloud, you process. But now you're zoning out. You're going very quiet for long spells of time. It's like you're going somewhere inside your own head, and . . . well, I'm worried about you.'

Birch looked down into the vortex of her glass. She watched the tiny bubbles rise to the surface, colliding and exploding. She had a choice here. She could say to Amy, Look, my brother just got beaten up in prison. I'm worried about him, that's all. Saying that wouldn't be a lie: she *was* worried. But Amy was right, of course. There was more.

'Okay,' Birch said, after what felt like a long silence. 'You got me.'

'Tell me,' Amy said.

Birch took a deep breath. 'It's . . . God, it's hard to even say the words out loud. It's my dad. Jamieson, he's called. I don't know if

I've ever talked about him to you, but he and I have been estranged for all of my adult life. Although, estranged is the wrong word. That makes it sound like I chose to stop speaking to him. What's more accurate is, he just hasn't ever bothered to show up. He walked out on my mother when Charlie was very little, and the last time I saw him was . . . well, I tried to work it out the other night. I think I must have been twelve.'

Amy was nodding. 'I knew he wasn't around,' she said, 'but that's all I knew.'

'Yeah,' Birch said. '*Not around* is a good way to put it. Like, I've always known he was still alive and out there and everything. Just *not around*. Charlie had a run in with him a few years ago. I found out when . . . when Charlie came back, and was arrested. He'd apparently used Solomon Carradice's connections to track our father down. When he'd found him, Charlie and one of his pals had kicked the shit out of him. I was pretty shocked when I discovered, but – let's just say I recognised the impulse.'

Amy was quiet for a moment. 'God, that must have been hard for you,' she said. 'When Charlie went missing. With your dad already being gone.'

Birch was surprised to feel a thin seam of tears developing in her eyes. She sniffed, trying to blink them away. 'It wasn't great,' she said. 'And my mum never recovered from Charlie going, and the press stuff around his disappearance. I'm convinced it caused her cancer, or at least made it worse. When she died, I put something in all the papers – *Scotsman, Herald, Evening News*. I wanted him to see it. Him and Charlie, though I didn't believe Charlie was alive at that point. I wanted to make sure they knew, in case . . . but of course, neither of them got in touch. *That* was hard. I really thought my dad might.'

Amy reached a hand over the table, and put it on top of Birch's. Don't be nice to me, Birch thought. It'll just make me cry more.

'I've read articles,' Birch said, still trying to shrug the tears away, 'that say it's in the genes. The sons of men who walk out are more likely to walk out themselves. Though of course, I know Charlie felt he had no choice. He got in with a hell of a bad crowd and didn't realise just how bad until it was too late. Until he couldn't get out. Of course, you know all this – sorry.'

'It's okay,' Amy said. 'I asked. I'm fine to listen.'

'Well, anyway,' Birch went on, 'the short version is, my dad phoned me the other night. Completely out of the blue. I've no idea how he got my home number, not a clue. But yeah, there he was on the phone, like he thought I'd just *love* to speak to him, like he'd never done anything to fuck over my mum – like no time had ever passed. And he basically just said, Oh, I heard your brother's in prison, so I thought I'd phone.'

Amy sat back in her seat. 'Wow,' she said.

'I know. It's been nearly twenty-eight years since we were last in a room together.'

'So . . . what did you *say*?'

Birch paused. 'Okay, *that's* the part that's bothering me, really,' she said. The words came out slow and reluctant. 'I didn't actually speak to him at all. He left me a voicemail.'

'Ah.'

'I was outside,' Birch continued, 'and I didn't hear the phone right away, and then by the time I got to it, he'd gone. There was just this voicemail, and he said he'd try and phone again. No number to call back – I tried. He'd withheld it.'

'Oh, *that's* helpful,' Amy said.

'Right? I mean, it's a classic Jamieson Birch move. And now I'm on absolute tenterhooks, wondering if he'll phone back. Wanting him to, and also really not wanting him to. You know I said my phone was unplugged last night? That's because it was driving me so mad that I couldn't have slept at all if I hadn't taken it off the hook.'

Amy threw Birch a knowing look. 'I could tell there was more to it than you were letting on,' she said.

Birch grinned. 'We've known each other long enough,' she said. 'You know my poker face by now.'

Amy smiled back, but she was thinking, Birch could see.

'What are you going to do about it?' she asked, after a moment. 'Does Charlie know?'

Birch shook her head. 'That's part of what's bothering me so much,' she said. 'Charlie's in the prison infirmary. God, Kato, he's in such bad shape. That's killing me as it is. Now I have to decide – do I tell him that our father's taken it upon himself to show up again? I mean, look how agitated *I* am about it, and I've got work and Anjan and all sorts going on. He's just lying in a white room, literally handcuffed to a bed. I don't want him to go nuts, thinking about it.'

Amy gave Birch a look she couldn't quite read. 'But Charlie isn't like you, marm,' she said. 'I mean, I'm sure he is in many ways, but from what I know of him . . . he might react differently to you. Or differently to how you expect.'

Birch sighed. 'You think I ought to tell him?'

Amy did a little half-shrug. 'That's really not my place to say,' she said, 'but if you're worried about *not* telling him because of what's happened, I think you might be projecting a bit. I hope that's not me speaking out of turn. But . . . if Charlie's caught up in the midst of a prison vendetta, then honestly? He might appreciate something else to think about. Ever see it that way?'

Birch shook her head. 'I really hadn't,' she said.

Amy didn't reply, but gave a well-there-you-go sort of nod. She took a sip from her white wine.

'There's a part of me,' Birch said, 'that really wants to tell him. The most selfish part of me, I mean. I want someone to talk about this with, someone who knows all the family history and has all the same baggage. I *want* to be able to talk to Charlie about it. But that want feels wrong.'

'That's because you're routinely far too hard on yourself,' Amy said.

Birch wanted to argue, but then decided against it. For a few moments, the two women sat in silence.

'Frankly,' Amy said, having taken a couple more sips of wine, as if for courage, 'if it makes Charlie uncomfortable, knowing that your dad's back around – because he can't go out and kick his ass again, or because he can't speak to him himself and you can, or whatever macho compartmentalising reason he comes up with

– who cares? That boy *owes you*, marm. Doesn't he? Didn't he make your life bloody difficult and awful by going missing for fourteen years?'

Birch couldn't help but smile. Amy was barely ever this forthright. 'He did,' she admitted.

Amy sat back, perhaps worrying she'd gone too far. 'Well,' she said, 'get him to pay you back by being your personal therapist for a bit.'

Birch's smile widened. Amy was an only child, she knew, and probably wouldn't have understood the complex, aggravating, knows-me-better-than-I-know-myself place that Charlie occupied in her life even if Birch spent the rest of the night explaining it. However, she did also have a point.

'You're really on it this evening,' Birch said, laughing.

Amy rolled her eyes. 'It's just *men*,' she said. 'We spend so much time worrying about what they might think or how they might react – we even tailor our behaviour to it! And yet, do they extend the same courtesy to us?'

Birch raised an eyebrow.

'Sorry,' Amy said, not sounding it. 'I had a very mediocre date the other night. And to be honest, reading Phamie MacDonald's diaries isn't doing much to reaffirm my faith in men.'

21

The next morning, Birch found herself teetering on a fold-out camping stool, attempting to fully wake herself with coffee as the crime scene unfurled in front of her. She was in one corner of the plantation, with the railway tracks at her back. In front of her, trees stretched off in rows, the late morning light filtering dimly through to the woodland floor. The tent the SOCOs had erected over the gravesite on Thursday night was gone now, but a ghost of white tape remained, fluttering between the tree-trunks in a rough square, denoting where not to step. The same strange beam of light that Birch had followed to begin digging still shafted down between the pines. The wood had been completely cleared, with all personnel pulled back to the siding where more forensic tents were being erected. Only the radar technologist remained, trundling his cart over the awkward terrain of the wood floor. Birch sat with Tish Bland, watching the radar read-out on a monitor. With them were two officers who'd been shipped in from somewhere south of the border along with the radar cart and its operator. They were both men in their early thirties who'd arrived at the crime scene like little kids arriving at a theme park. They looked alike: skinny, well-groomed and wearing trendy half-rimmed glasses.

'This'll be fascinating,' one of them had said to Birch. 'It's really challenging terrain.'

Birch felt like asking them if they went shopping together. She realised she hadn't had enough coffee.

'Tell me something good,' she'd said instead. The officers' names were Larry, short for Laurence, and Ed, short for Edwin. It was Ed who'd spoken first, and now Larry frowned.

'It *is* good,' he said, 'in a way. It'll be hard work, but we'll learn so much here. We're still testing the limitations of this technology. This'll be a great opportunity.'

Now, Birch sat watching the read-out as the man with the cart – dressed in a white forensic suit and wellies – struggled his way over roots and rocks, flattening whatever feeble plants had managed to snake upward in the plantation's thin light.

The read-out looked like TV static, only denser: a grey fog that settled in waves.

Ed and Larry sat at either side of the monitor, Larry occasionally twiddling at controls that rendered the read-out more saturated, or less.

'There,' Ed said. He reached over and pointed to a peak that had appeared in the wave of the radargram. 'There's something there.'

Birch looked up over the top of the monitor, as though she'd suddenly be able to see something in the ground where the man had just passed with the cart, some marker. But of course, there was nothing. The earth was loose and loamy, a thick topsoil fed by years of fallen pine needles. As the radar operator passed over it, a rich smell of dirt and pine wafted up.

'The machine takes all the co-ordinates,' Ed said, following her gaze. 'We'll scan the whole area, and then we can mark out the spots where something appears.'

Birch gave a nod, and settled back into herself. She was in a dark mood, having slept fitfully. She'd dreamed she was trapped somewhere, with Charlie: they were in a municipal building, its rooms and corridors an endless maze. Someone or something was chasing them, and they couldn't seem to stay together. She'd woken up chilly and crabbit, having thrashed her duvet on to the floor.

Beside her, Tish Bland's phone rang, and both women flinched.

'Hello, Andrew? What've you got for me?'

Birch kept her eyes on the fizzing grey of the monitor as Bland spoke.

'You have? Oh. Oh, okay.' There was a pause.

Birch felt Bland look at her, and then look away again. They'd found something out.

'Right,' Bland said into the phone. 'Well, that makes sense now. I'm sitting with DI Birch as we speak, so we can get that in motion. Thanks, Andrew.'

Tish Bland was the sort of person who hung up without saying goodbye.

'We've got a positive ID on the body,' she said. 'Dental records have confirmed it's Suzie Hay.'

Birch frowned.

'Oh,' Bland said, 'yes, sorry, before your time. Suzie Hay was a missing person. Seventeen at the time, she disappeared in 1996, on Halloween.'

Something flickered in Birch's mind. 'The one who went missing dressed as a witch,' she said.

'That's the case. I'm afraid she's our girl.'

'I wasn't on the job then,' Birch said, 'but I remember it being in the papers.'

Bland was nodding. 'We'd actually found a thin loop of wire in the grave with her,' she said. 'It had shreds of black cloth attached, partly decomposed. We were having a good look at it because I wondered if it might have been the murder weapon, used to strangle the victim. Andrew's just identified it almost 100 per cent as the brim of the witch hat Suzie was wearing when she disappeared.'

Birch swallowed, hard. She tried to imagine a seventeen-year-old, tired from a Halloween night out, looking forward to getting home and taking off her nippy shoes. Looking forward to washing the greasepaint off her face. Somehow, she'd gone from a night out in the city to this quiet corner of Lanarkshire woodland. Birch remembered Bland's assessment that the body had been dropped down a hole. She realised what needed to happen next, and a shiver passed through her. She was about to authorise the worst thing imaginable: a thing she'd lived in fear of herself, for fourteen whole years.

'I'll radio in,' she said, the words coming out slow and thick, 'and get some uniforms to go and inform the next of kin.' She passed a hand over her eyes, the monitor's static suddenly unbearably bright in the dark quiet of the wood. 'Jesus, Tish.'

Bland opened her mouth to speak, but then paused, looking at the monitor.

'I'm sorry, DI Birch.' It was Ed, pointing at a second spike in the radargram's read-out. 'We've got another one.'

22

Amy liked being in the station on a Saturday. It wasn't empty, but it was quieter than usual, and she could put her headphones on and listen to music or a podcast as she worked. Today it was *Casefile*, a podcast she'd got into following a recommendation from Anjan, who also loved true crime. *Casefile* was strangely soothing, and the episodes featured a high ratio of solved crimes. This was Amy's preference: the unsolved cases nagged at her, got her blood pressure up. She found herself thinking of angles she'd take if only she were somehow given the task of reopening those cases. Sometimes it kept her awake nights. I shouldn't listen to these things, she'd think, I'm in the wrong job to enjoy them. And yet, here she was: in the office on a Saturday, doing paperwork and tuning in once again.

Except she wasn't really listening: she could hear the soothing Australian voice of the presenter, but realised she hadn't paid attention to the words he was saying for some time. Phamie MacDonald was getting to her, in the same way as the unsolved *Casefile* episodes did. If she closed her eyes, Amy could mentally transport herself back to Mary McPherson's room in the nursing home. She could see the light exactly as it had been on Tuesday evening, touching the net curtains at Mary's window, turning them pink. She could see the fear and contempt in Mary's eyes as George MacDonald's name was mentioned. As she described how George had attacked her that day so many years ago, how he'd trapped her in his own kitchen – her friend's kitchen, with the beautiful garden outside the window, a place Amy had been – quiet tears had run down Mary's face. Amy had wanted to hug her tightly: she was so elderly, and so vulnerable, and it was such an injustice that although her mind was slowly peeling away memories, it had decided to leave that one fully intact, clear as anything. Amy knew that Phamie MacDonald was the same age as Mary: perhaps she too was becoming confused, forgetful.

Phamie's diaries had been returned from the lab: Amy had arrived that morning to find them wrapped in their evidence bag on her desk, a note from one of the lab techs scrawled on a Post-it and stuck to the top. *Fingerprints and fibres pulled. Results likely by Monday.* She'd felt both relief and dread at getting the diaries back. It meant she'd get to read on through them. It also meant she'd have to endure more of Phamie's quiet, patient, downtrodden and deeply sad narrative. Phamie, who had endured decades of physical and psychological abuse. Phamie, who was missing without trace.

Amy flipped open the diary at a random page and read:

George has been gone for three days. I can't eat, and I can't sleep. I phoned in to the post office for the first time ever, and told them I was ill and couldn't go in. He hasn't phoned, and Donald can find no trace of him, though he's driven all over Edinburgh. He even drove all the way out to Carstairs Station, the place George always claims to be whenever he comes back from one of his jaunts. I've called up the hospitals, and there's no sign of him. I'm considering phoning the police. Even Robert is worried, and Robert is usually so sanguine. Robert calms me down when I get like this. Usually he does. Now, we're both just a bag of nerves. And of course I know that the most likely outcome is that George will eventually just daunder back into this house as though he'd just nipped out to the shop down the road. If I let him know I was worried, then I'm for it – he'll tell me to stop keeping tabs on him, stop trying to curtail his freedom. But if I act like I didn't wonder where he was, then I'm also for it – 'Don't you care about me, Phamie? Don't you care about anyone except yourself? Are you so selfish that you just don't think of me at all?'

Amy snapped the notebook shut, causing small flakes of dirt and old cardboard to flutter to the floor. She felt a little of the same frustration as Phamie must have, thinking of the merry dance George MacDonald was leading them on. Was Phamie alive, or wasn't she? Would they ever find out? Right now, DI Birch was out at Carstairs with a forensics team and ground-penetrating radar, looking for more bodies. Amy realised she hadn't been paying attention to her podcast all morning – she hadn't been paying attention to anything much, in fact – because she was too busy praying that no matter what the team found, Phamie MacDonald's remains would not be in those woods. She made the mistake of thinking about the officers who'd have to be dispatched to tell Mary that her friend had been murdered, and then wished she hadn't. How could Mary understand? How could they make her understand?

Beside her on the desk, the phone rang, making Amy jump.

'DC Amy Kato,' she said into the receiver.

'Amy, hen, it's John downstairs. Mr Robertson Bennet is here again, and he's asking for you.'

'Mr Bennet.'

Bennet was dressed down, and Amy wondered for a moment if the tailored suit he'd worn on Monday was just a part of his bid to have his plea for police help taken seriously. Now he was wearing stone-coloured chinos and a sweater, with moccasin shoes that Amy felt looked a little too much like slippers. He raised himself to his full height as she approached him, and looked down his nose at her. Amy simply turned on her sweetest smile. Bennet didn't realise that petite women dealt with this particular intimidation tactic pretty much every day.

'I'd like to ask what the *hell* you people think you're playing at.'

Bennet's American inflection was stronger, it seemed, when he was angry. Amy's smile didn't move.

'Mr Bennet, if you'd like to follow me.'

'No, I damn well will *not* follow you. I deserve an explanation, and I want it right here and right now.'

Amy glanced over at John, who was once again out from behind his desk, ready to deal with Bennet's next move.

'My father—' Bennet began.

Amy held up one hand, palm flat, and his eyes widened. 'I'm going to stop you there,' she said, 'because this is a public space. I am not going to discuss an ongoing investigation with you in public, no matter what demands you make. We can talk about this in a private room, or we don't talk about it at all.'

Amy dropped her hand. Bennet's nostrils were flaring, but he was silent.

'Your choice, sir,' she said.

She watched as Bennet's eyelids flickered, and he looked at the floor. He's going to comply, she thought. But it took him a moment: first, he looked up at John, who was now standing beside Amy. Out of the corner of her eye, Amy saw John give Bennet the slightest nod: do as you're told.

'*Fine*,' Bennet said, the word buzzing in his teeth. Without waiting for Amy's response, he began to stalk off towards the same meeting room that DI Birch had used to speak with him that Monday. Amy glanced at John.

'It's free,' he said.

By the time she arrived in the room, Bennet was already sitting. His arms were crossed over his chest, as though he were anticipating an attack, or perhaps holding himself back from attacking. His jaw was working. Amy closed the door.

'How *dare* you,' he said, 'call me in here to give my DNA. How *dare* you treat me like some common criminal.'

Amy took her time walking over to the table. As she sat down, she paused to smooth out a wrinkle in her skirt. Finally, she tucked her chair in under the table between them, and placed her hands on the table top.

'Mr Bennet,' she said, keeping her voice low and quiet. 'We have invited you to provide a DNA sample because we have lines of enquiry we'd like to be able to eliminate, that's all. You are in no way being accused of anything.'

'No,' Bennet snapped, 'but my father is.'

Amy tried not to think again of the diaries, the years of testimony they contained. Or about Mary, her description of George MacDonald, what he'd done to her.

'Can I remind you,' Amy said, 'that it was your testimony, when you first came in to report your parents missing, that began these lines of enquiry. It was you, sir, who suggested to us that your father might be capable of violent acts. That he might have done something to hurt your mother.'

Bennet huffed. 'Yes,' he said, 'but now you've found some random body in a wood, and because you know he was violent, you're trying to make out that he might have—'

'I assure you,' Amy cut in, 'that is really not the case. Since you reported your parents missing on Monday, there have been some developments, and—'

Bennet uncrossed his arms and banged one hand on the table in front of him. 'Do you think I don't know,' he said, 'where you found that body? Do you think that wasn't in the papers? It was at Carstairs Station, exactly where I told you my father used to spend time. Now you're trying to pin a murder on him.'

Amy raised an eyebrow. 'That is absolutely not what is happening,' she said.

Bennet made a snorting noise. 'Oh, sure,' he said. He raised his hand and made a *blah blah* motion in the air, opening and closing it like a mouth.

She felt her mouth pull down into a hard line. A wave of something came over her, and her hands and feet went cold. Phamie's words flashed randomly back and forth in her mind: *selfish, stupid woman.* Bennet sounded like his father, and it made Amy want to scream. 'If you will behave civilly towards me, Mr Bennet,' she said, her teeth clenched to keep the scream inside, 'then I will explain why I asked you to provide a DNA sample. If you will not, then I will terminate this meeting and have John escort you from the building.'

Bennet let out a short laugh, but when Amy did not blink, it faded on the air between them. He looked at her for a moment, as though he could see something in her face that scared him. 'Okay,' he said, 'tell me.'

Amy took a deep, slow breath in through her nose. 'So,' she said. 'We received word from our colleagues at the local police station in Lanark that a bag of jewellery had been found near Carstairs Station. It was found some weeks ago, by railway workers, and we believe it had lain undetected near the station for several years. One of the pieces of jewellery was a locket, and inside the locket there is a clipping of red hair. It is very similar in colour to your own.'

Bennet snorted again. 'What, so you're testing everyone within a fifty-mile radius who has red hair? Come on.'

Amy ignored him, and continued. 'The jewellery is not connected to the human remains we've found,' she said. 'Though it was discovered in the same area, there is no DNA link to the body. In fact, we have identified where the jewellery came from. It was through this identification that we came to suspect there may be a link with your father, and that is the reason we have asked you to provide a sample.'

Bennet opened his mouth to speak, but then Amy saw something occur to him. His face paled.

'Is it my mother's?' he asked. 'Does the jewellery belong to my mother?'

Amy paused for a moment, long enough for Bennet's mind to race a little, before replying. 'I'm afraid I can't tell you who the jewellery belongs to.'

Bennet's demeanour was transformed. He reached both hands across the table towards Amy. 'Look,' he said, 'if you've found some clue to my mother's whereabouts, then you've got to tell me. Don't you? You have to tell me. I'm her next of kin.'

Amy could see it then, the thing that was building up behind the brick wall of Bennet's facade of swagger. It was guilt: decades of it. He'd left his mother alone, knowing what his father was like. Now she was missing, and he wanted desperately for it not to be his fault. If she was found, he could absolve himself. If she was dead, then he'd see himself as accessory to her murder.

'I'm sorry,' Amy said, 'but I really can't divulge any more information about the case at this time. I'm not authorised to do so.'

Bennet's mouth was slightly open. She could see him trying to decide how to respond.

'What I can tell you,' she said, 'is that you are in no way required to provide a DNA sample. You can refuse to, that's absolutely fine. But please know that we would not be asking for this if we didn't think it could make a real difference in our efforts to track down both of your parents. We really want to find Phamie.' Amy heard the warmth in her own voice when she said the name, checked herself, and then added, 'And your father, too.'

Bennet was looking down at his hands. 'I know I told you my father was a violent man,' he said, 'but I really don't think he's capable of murder.'

Amy straightened her back. Mary McPherson suggests otherwise, she thought, but she pushed the thought away again. Bennet had retreated back behind his wall, and she could no longer tell if he really meant it or not. She wished her hands were under the table, so she could cross her fingers as she spoke. 'No one is saying,' she said, 'that he is.'

For a moment, they sat in silence. On the wall, the quiet snicker of the clock. Outside in the fleet yard, a siren started up, distant and muffled.

'Okay,' Bennet said at last. 'So what do I give you? Blood, or what?'

23

Somehow, it was Sunday again, and Birch found herself making the familiar journey to HMP Low Moss. As she neared the place, she realised she'd been driving on autopilot once again: her thoughts were still in the dim light under the crime scene's trees. Yesterday, she'd stayed while Larry and Ed triangulated the radar-gram's read-out, marking six 'hotspots', as they called them, for excavation. She'd overseen the erection of tents and lighting around those excavation sites. She'd spoken with the plantation owners – a company who described themselves as 'providers of forest products' – and got the green light to fell or trim several trees in the event that they might obstruct the digging. She'd listened while Letitia Bland briefed newly arrived officers on the discovery of Suzannah Hay's body: the state it had been found in, and what they themselves might discover. The scene had been set. Today, though it seemed somehow wrong on a Sunday, the ground would be broken. Excavation would begin.

Birch felt torn. She still hadn't seen Charlie since that day in the infirmary, when he'd been unconscious and she'd been incandescent with anger. Though he was still in his secure infirmary room, he was conscious now, and she badly wanted to see him and talk to him about what had happened. She was also afraid, because she knew she needed to talk to him about their father, and what she ought to do – and she'd need to confess to the fact that she still hadn't been able to bring herself to plug her phone back in and listen to the voicemails that might be on it. At the same time, the control freak part of her wanted to be there in the woods, waiting to see what came out of the dark, mulchy ground. She'd be largely useless – Letitia Bland's team were experts, and Bland led them incredibly well – but she wanted to be there. To bear witness, or something. To see for herself. She knew from years of experience that no debrief, however detailed, could match up to actually being there.

And yet, she found herself lining up with the other Sunday visitors to go through the security checks, and be processed through the heavy doors in the direction of the Visit Room. Tommy was nowhere to be seen: an officer she didn't recognise held her back to the end of the line, and then as the visitors filed in, Birch was whisked off to one side, in the direction of the infirmary. Only Mrs McGuire – back again with her three little children – turned her head and watched as Birch was taken elsewhere.

Charlie was propped up in his bed now, huge hospital pillows pushing him into a reclined sitting position. His face looked horrendous: a splotched canvas of purples, yellows and greens. His eyes were still swollen to narrow creases. Across his chest, the broken arm was cooried in a sling, the bulky plaster visible through its gauze. As Birch got close, she could hear his breath was shallow: he was breathing carefully, trying not to push against his broken ribs.

'Hey, Nella,' he croaked.

Birch sank into a chair next to the bed. She hadn't seen Rob, the nurse. The prison officer who'd dealt with her at reception was still in the room with them, as though he'd been instructed not to take his eyes off Birch. He was showing no sign of leaving.

'Charlie,' she said. There was a lump in her throat, and she found she didn't really know what to say. She raised the tote bag she'd brought in with her: it had been searched, scanned and cleared at the front desk. 'I brought you some books, from home.'

She watched her brother attempt a smile, and tried not to look at the state of his teeth.

'Thanks,' he said. 'I've been climbing the walls.'

Birch snorted. 'Hardly, in that state,' she said. 'What happened?'

'I know they've told you already. They said you were here a few days ago.'

'I was,' Birch said, 'and they did. But I want to hear your version.'

Charlie glanced at the screw, who'd placed himself in the corner of the room, but who was still only a few feet away.

'I'm probably not the best person to ask,' he said. 'I was asleep. Then all of a sudden I hit the floor. I'd been hauled out of the bunk, and my whole left side was on fire.'

Birch looked at the strapped-up left arm, hanging high on his chest so as not to displace the shattered ribs.

'I couldn't see who it was,' he said. 'I was just being hit and hit and hit. Punched in the face, booted in the side. You know how people talk about a rain of blows? I suddenly know what that's like. It was like there was no position I could get into where they weren't battering me.'

Birch realised her teeth were jammed together, her whole face tense.

'Then I heard the alarm go, and it all stopped. But you know, a cell's pretty small: it took them a while to get out. I sat up, and there's Billy Bigbaws at the back of the pack, sort of hustling the rest of them out the door.'

Birch nodded. 'The same kid who attacked you before, I assume.'

Charlie nodded. 'The very same.'

'And you still won't tell me who he is?'

'Nope.' Charlie nodded at the screw. 'These fuckers know. Ask them.'

Birch curled her hands into fists: her brother was infuriating. But she understood: he didn't want to live up to the nickname they'd given him. *Cucumber.* Grass.

'Do you think he's getting orders from Solomon? Did any of them do or say anything that might suggest a link?'

Charlie shrugged, and Birch could see it hurt him.

'I honestly don't know, Nella. I know you want to know who this kid is, what his deal is, but I promise I'm not trying to piss you off. Honestly, it might've been Solomon. It's quite some *thing* to spring six guys all at the same time. But to be fair, it's the jail. Guys in this place are just bams. We're all cooped up in here going fucking mental. They might just've decided kicking the shit out of me would be a good laugh of an evening.'

Birch sat quietly for a moment. She looked up at the prison officer, trying to catch his eye. He seemed determined not to look directly at her, or at Charlie, and yet she could feel him watching them, when she turned away again.

'So, the alarm went and they . . . it all stopped. Then what happened?'

Charlie tried to shrug, but only his right shoulder moved. 'I said something. I've honestly no idea what, Nella, before you ask. But it pissed the kid off enough to get him to come back and have another go. And then, when it was just me on him . . . well, I turned the tables on him, let's just say that.'

'Charlie,' Birch said evenly, 'from what I hear, you beat him to within an inch of his life.'

Charlie said nothing, but with as much theatricality as he could muster, he raised his good right hand and indicated his own broken state with a flourish.

'I gave him some of this back,' he said. 'That's all. Self-defence.'

Birch closed her eyes in exasperation. 'But he was *running*, Charlie. You could have let him go.' She swallowed. 'Should have, in fact.'

Charlie curled his lip, and this time she got a full view of his ruined teeth.

'Yeah,' he said, 'fuck *that*.'

She felt a familiar feeling, then: it was one that had come over her every so often for as long as she could remember. As a kid she'd had it, when her stupid brother had got something she'd wanted, or when he'd run to their mother to try to convince her that something he'd done himself was actually Nella's fault. She'd had it when he'd come to her for loans as a teenager, having blown his own cash on something she felt was frivolous or ill-advised. The feeling was *my brother is a fucking idiot*, and she felt it now more strongly than ever before.

'There's going to be an inquiry,' she heard herself saying, teeth gritted. 'The wheels are already in motion. They *will* extend your sentence over this. You might have added *years* here. Why couldn't you just keep your bloody mouth shut?'

Charlie was quiet for a moment, looking at her. She could see, even with his face bent so horribly out of shape, that there was mischief in his eyes. Behind the bruises, he was laughing at her.

'Oh come on, Nella,' he said at last, 'you wanted me to just lie there? What would *you* have done?'

Birch closed her eyes. She hated, sometimes, how well he knew her. They'd walked down opposite paths in life, but she was still like him, and he like her, whether Birch liked it or not. Charlie was right. She'd never been desperately good at keeping her nose clean, either. It was why she'd ended up on a disciplinary last year, over the Three Rivers case. It was why McLeod liked to keep her on a short leash whenever he could. Unlike Charlie, she'd lived by society's rules, and by the rules of her job. But if she came across a rule she could bend . . .

'Where've you gone?' Charlie asked, and Birch jumped.

She opened her eyes. 'What?'

'I thought you were away to fairy land for a second, there.' Her brother was still laughing at her.

A heavy feeling came over Birch. She was going to have to say it. 'Look,' she said. 'There's something I need to tell you.'

Charlie's face changed quickly – so quickly that Birch stopped in her tracks, looking at him.

'Is this about Da?' he said.

For a moment, Birch couldn't speak. He *knew*?

'How did you know that?' Her voice, when it did come out, was almost a whisper.

Charlie shuffled against the bedclothes, letting his gaze drop away from hers. 'He phoned here,' he said, 'asking to speak to me.'

Birch whipped round and looked at the screw standing in the corner, though she wasn't sure why. Her brother couldn't possibly be lying, couldn't have made up a story that matched so closely what she'd planned to say herself. He might know her annoyingly well, but he wasn't psychic.

'And? You talked to him?'

Charlie shook his head. 'No phone in here, is there?' he said. 'And they're not exactly going out of their way to give me privileges when I'm this far in the doghouse.'

Charlie was looking at the screw now, too. The man had fixed his eyes on a spot in the middle distance.

'But they passed on the message,' Charlie went on. 'It sounded like he just phoned for a wee chat, like *just wanted to speak to you!* As though I hadn't kicked seven shades out of him last we spoke.'

Birch winced. 'Maybe the less said about that, the better,' she said. 'You know – given your current circumstances?'

Charlie sighed. 'Yeah, whatever. But – he called you, too? I wondered if he had.'

Birch was nodding. 'I've no idea how he found my number,' she said, 'but yes.'

'The fuck did he say?'

Birch frowned, trying to remember the exact words. She'd listened to the voicemail over and over, the night it had arrived. Since then, she'd been trying to ignore it – trying not to hear her father's snickering voice in her head. Failing, but trying all the same.

'We didn't actually speak,' she said. 'He left me a voicemail. Said he'd found out you were in here, and wanted to – well, I don't think he actually finished the sentence, so I don't know exactly what he was wanting to do. Come and visit you? Talk to me about it? Say sorry for being the world's crappiest father? Who knows?'

Charlie finally looked back at Birch's face. 'I'm just amazed he's forgiven me, for' – Charlie glanced again at the screw – 'what went down last time I saw him. From the sound of the message, it's like it never happened.'

'From the sound of his voicemail,' Birch said, 'it's like the last thirty years never happened.'

For a moment, they were both quiet. The clock on the wall ticked. Birch realised how annoying that sound must be for Charlie, largely alone in this white box all day and all night.

'Do you remember that day he came back?' she asked, the sound of her voice jarring after their silence. 'I think I was twelve. He came to the house, and we went somewhere in the car.'

Charlie thought for a moment. 'You did,' he said. 'You went with him. I wouldn't go. Just flat-out refused.'

Birch blinked. Another chunk of that day fell into her head all at once, like a chunk of iceberg sloughing off into the sea. She remembered her father walking into the living room, their mother behind him, fixing her with a look. *Play nice, give this a chance.* Charlie hadn't noticed: he was sitting in his favourite spot, his nose about two inches from their tiny TV, some rubbish 8-bit video game spitting its inane theme music into the room.

'Hello, Helen,' Jamieson Birch said.

She remembered Charlie turning round to see who'd come in. She remembered seeing something come over him: something dark passing over his face like a shadow. She remembered him dropping the games console on to the carpet, not even bothering to hit pause, and standing up. He can't have been older than nine, she thought, but he'd raised himself to his full height and squared up to the big man their father still was then.

'No,' Charlie said. He'd said it quietly, but more firmly than Birch thought she'd ever heard him say anything. Then, he'd charged at the two adults in the doorway, so fast and so unexpectedly that they'd just flinched aside, as though getting out of the path of a speeding car. Their mother had made a sort of sorrowful noise as he'd passed, but she didn't call after him. Birch remembered hearing her brother's footsteps thump up the stairs, across the landing and into their shared bedroom. She'd heard the door slam. Now it was her problem. She'd have to deal with it on her own.

'Typical,' she said quietly.

'What are you going to do about it?' Charlie asked, as though he hadn't heard.

It's always me, Birch thought. It's always me who has to *do something about it.*

'I dunno,' she said. 'I'm not sure what I can do, to be honest. He withheld his number. I mean, I've been agonising over it, but really, I guess all either of us can do is see if he calls again.'

Charlie frowned. 'He left his number for me,' he said.

Birch swallowed hard. She felt her pulse speed up, just a little. 'He what?'

'Yeah.' Charlie leaned over towards the little cupboard next to his bed. He didn't get far before he winced, and fell back on the pillows. 'Fuck,' he said.

'I'll do it,' Birch said, getting up from her chair. 'Where am I looking? And what for?'

Charlie waved vaguely with his good hand. 'In the drawer at the top,' he said. 'There's a slip of paper. It looks kind of like a receipt. That's how they take messages for us in here.'

Birch opened the little drawer. There wasn't much there: she snatched up the slip of paper.

'Tell him I want to talk,' Birch read, aloud, from the message. 'I know he might not want to hear from me, but I'd really like it if we were in touch. If he needs some time to think about it, I understand.' Then came a phone number: 0131, the local Edinburgh area code.

'Wow,' Birch said.

'See what I mean? Like he just wants a chat.'

Birch crumpled back into the chair, staring down at the string of eleven numbers. For the first time in her life, she had a direct line to her father. She could call him and say whatever the hell she wanted. But – what was that, exactly?

'Can I take this?' She made herself look up at Charlie.

He squirmed. 'I mean . . . I *am* thinking about it,' he said. Her face must have done something, because he added, 'I'm sorry, Nella.'

'You're thinking about speaking to him?'

Charlie nodded. 'Thinking about it,' he said again. 'Maybe. I don't know if they'll even let me when I'm in here. But when I'm back out in the hall? Maybe.'

Birch looked down at the slip of paper. 'So you want to keep this, then.'

Charlie laughed at her again. 'Oh come on, Nella,' he said. 'You're not telling me you haven't already memorised that number. You'd done it before you even sat back down.'

Birch screwed up her face. He really did know her too well.

Edinburgh Evening News

Carstairs body identified as missing Suzie Hay

EMMA BLACK
Email

Published 09:12
Monday 9 September

Share this article

Police Scotland have this morning released the identity of the human remains found in woodland close to the villages of Carstairs and Carstairs Junction, in South Lanarkshire.

It has been confirmed that the remains, which were discovered by police late last Thursday night, are those of Suzannah Hay. Known to friends and family as Suzie, Hay was reported missing in October 1996 following a night out with friends. Hay's family have been informed.

In a statement released today, Police Scotland said that they were now treating Hay's death as murder, and had fully reopened the investigation into her disappearance.

Forensic teams are still on the scene at Carstairs, with disruption to trains between Carstairs and Carluke stations expected to continue for some days.

24

For the first time in days, it was raining. Birch had woken to the sound of it prickling at her window that morning. She'd known without opening the curtains what sort of rain it was: the persistent sort, that falls from an iron-coloured sky and feels like it'll never stop. Drops of water thin as pins, and yet after two minutes out in it, you're drenched. Something about the change in the weather made her get out of bed, walk downstairs, and plug in her landline at last. Her hands shook as she dialled 1571.

'You have –' the robot woman said, and Birch held her breath, 'one – saved message.'

Deflated, Birch had listened again to the same voicemail her father had left, mouthing along with parts of it. Discovering he hadn't called her again gave her more feelings than she'd expected it might. She was kicking herself for having been so afraid, for having kept the phone off the hook for so long, all for nothing. But she was also disappointed, and that surprised her. If he really wanted to talk to her, he wasn't trying all that hard. And that made her angry: he was still the same person, after all. She realised she'd been hoping for some sort of miraculous character change: he'd had a near-death experience and changed his ways. He'd finally gone to therapy and figured out he'd been a shit. Of course not. But now the joke was on him: Birch looked at the notepad she'd placed on the coffee table, her father's 0131 number scrawled in big numbers that took up half the page. She hadn't even taken her coat off the day before: she'd walked straight into the house and written it down. The ball was in *her* court now, though that didn't do too much to diminish her anger. The same thought came back to her from yesterday, sitting with Charlie: it's always me who has to do something about it.

As she drove towards Carstairs, she tried to push her father out of her mind. She thought of her crime scene, the trees drinking up the water. She thought of Suzie Hay, imagined her ghost hanging in the still air among the branches. A pale, thin ghost in a costume witch hat. Birch had made the image so clear in her mind by the time she arrived that she struggled to shake it, even as she pulled up and parked at the crime scene perimeter.

'Okay, catch us up.'

They were gathered in Tent A, the first of the forensic tents set up in the disused siding. Birch, Tish Bland, and a handful of other officers: SOCOs, forensics, uniforms. The rain hissed on the tent roof.

'I'm afraid,' Tish Bland said, 'that five of the six sites identified on the radargram yielded human remains. That wood is a burial ground, or has been. Your hunch was right, DI Birch.'

Birch winced. 'I wish it wasn't so,' she said.

Bland pointed to the same long table Birch had stood over with McLeod only a few days before. There were more trays, more evidence bags. A tablet had been set up with crime scene photos.

'We're processing the victims separately,' Bland said, waving vaguely in the direction of the other tents, 'so this is by no means everything we have. This is what we've processed so far. Right now, I can tell you that we believe all the victims are female. They're all in a similar state to the remains we found on Thursday, which means they've all been here a good long time.'

Birch immediately thought of Phamie. 'How long are we talking?' she asked. 'More than five years?'

Bland nodded. 'By quite a long way,' she said, 'yes. The bodies are skeletal. I'm happy to tell you that Phamie MacDonald's remains are not here.'

Birch let out a sigh. The information didn't make her feel any better.

'However, one of the gravesites was different to the others,' Bland went on. 'Our killer got sloppy.' Bland leaned in to one of the trays and fished out a bag that contained what looked like a solid rectangular lump of mould. 'The victim's purse,' she said. 'The purse itself isn't in great shape, but inside there are plastic bank cards that look practically good as new. They belonged to one Maisie Kerr.'

Birch closed her eyes. 'Shit,' she said. She felt a couple of the junior officers' eyes on her, and righted herself. 'Sorry, Tish,' she said. 'Carry on.'

Bland nodded. 'We'll obviously still go through all the proper channels to ascertain the victim's identity without doubt,' she said. 'This victim also still had her clothes on at the time of her burial: she was wearing a coat that included plastic sections, and those have survived. We've also recovered fragments of her trainers, and some metal rivets and other bits and pieces that we believe would have been part of her jeans.'

Birch was nodding. The mood in the tent was sombre and still. It felt like a funeral.

'The person who buried these women,' Bland went on, 'was meticulous and repetitive. They were all buried the same way, wrapped mostly in supermarket carrier bags, and in deep graves that would have taken a fair bit of digging. That said, this was decades ago, and the woodland is made up of plantation trees which grow rapidly. I suspect the roots were a lot less developed when our killer began using this place as a burial ground. It's possible he moved on from here when Maisie's grave – which we believe is the most recent – proved more difficult to dig than his previous efforts.'

Birch shivered. 'Moved on?'

Tish blinked, and then shook her head a little. 'Sorry,' she said, 'forgive me. I didn't mean to impose a narrative. He could have stopped for any number of reasons. Given the historical nature of these killings, it's very possible he died, or became too old to continue.'

Birch thought of George MacDonald, now eighty-three and likely still at large. Before she had a chance to say anything, an officer behind her, one of the SOCOs, coughed.

'He?' he said. 'Can we know that for sure?'

There was a general turning of heads. Tish Bland eyed the young man.

'You're quite right,' she said coldly. 'In the interests of equality I certainly mustn't rule out the possibility that a woman might have had the physical size and strength required to dig six eight-foot pits in difficult ground, in order to insert her young, female victims into them.'

The officer gave a small nod, and then looked at his feet. Bland, meanwhile, looked at Birch.

'I feel hopeful,' she said, 'about the discovery of personal effects on and around the body we believe to be Maisie Kerr's. It gives us more items to pull a possible DNA profile from.' Bland was still holding the evidence bag with the purse inside, and she gave it a small shake. 'It's a long shot, but the inside of this purse has been quite well preserved. If the killer ever opened it, then it's possible we might be able to get a fingerprint. You never know.'

Birch shrugged, and tried to smile. 'Positive thinking,' she said.

Outside, the rain seemed to have thickened. Birch trudged over to the wood, trailed by a few of the SOCOs. As she stepped into the tree-line, her breath caught in her chest: the scene had changed a lot since she'd sat watching the radargram monitor on Saturday. There were now six white tents huddled together under the trees: the tent over Suzie Hay's grave had been reinstalled ahead of the forecast rain. The identical white tents were close together, and the effect was strange: Birch felt like she'd stumbled on some sort of ethereal campsite. A couple of trees had indeed been felled to accommodate the excavations, but the wood felt as dark as ever under the wet, glowering sky. The rain did not fall under the thick canopy, but seemed to have invaded the wood nevertheless: everything felt wet and spongy, and the trunks of the nearby trees glistened.

The other officers plodded past Birch, splitting into twos and threes to head to their allocated areas. Birch stayed at the tree-line, where she'd have a better phone signal. She flicked her phone awake, and dialled Amy's number.

'Morning, Kato.'

'Marm,' Amy said, 'I'm glad you've called.'

'Oh yes?'

'Yes – I was going to ring you shortly to tell you that we have a DNA match on the hair from the locket.'

Birch held her breath. 'Robertson Bennet.'

'The man himself. Now, let me read off the email the lab sent.' There was a pause, and Birch could hear Amy's mouse-clicks. 'Right. So they're saying it's not the *most* robust result, because the hair in Maisie's locket was cut, and so no follicle or skin particles were present. Something about low copy number? You can read it yourself when you get in . . . but anyway, there was a close enough match to Robertson Bennet's sample to show that the hair in the locket came from a blood relative of his. Basically, it's George MacDonald's hair in that locket.'

'Damn fine work, Kato,' Birch said. 'So now we know Ginger George knew Maisie, which means we can make him an official suspect.'

Amy let out a low whistle. 'Bennet will *not* be pleased. He was pretty belligerent when he came in on Saturday.'

'Oh yes?'

'Said he thought we were trying to pin a murder on his father.'

Birch snorted. 'Well guess what,' she said. 'We are. In fact, we're now trying to pin six murders on him.'

On the other end of the phone, Amy went quiet.

'Oh God, sorry,' Birch said, 'you haven't heard. I've just been briefed by Tish Bland. They found five more burial sites. All like the first one.'

'Shit,' Amy hissed. 'That bad feeling of yours.'

'Yep. Sadly it was right on the money.'

Both women were quiet for a moment, then Amy spoke.

'Have they identified any of the bodies?'

Birch winced. 'Not with certainty,' she said, 'but one of them had personal effects on her. A purse and some clothing. We believe it's Maisie Kerr.'

She heard Amy try to stifle a small, deflated sound. Birch realised what it was she'd really been asking.

'That's the bad news,' she said, 'but the good news – if there's any such thing in a situation like this – is, none of the bodies is Phamie MacDonald.'

On the other end of the line, there was quiet, but Birch could imagine the look of relief on Amy's face.

'Well,' Amy said at last, 'that's something.'

The line went quiet again. In the distance, Birch could hear the sounds of the bullpen where Amy was sitting.

'I'm sorry, Kato,' Birch said, 'but once we get more of a solid confirmation that this body is indeed Maisie, then ... I think it would be really good if you could be one of the officers who goes out to inform Hazel Kerr. She knows you. I think she might take it ever so slightly better if you're there.'

Birch held her breath. It was the worst job in the world to have to do, to have to ask someone to do.

'Of course, marm,' Amy said, after only a couple of seconds' pause. 'Now, what would you like me to do about Ginger George?'

Birch blinked. 'We should probably stop calling him that,' she said, trying to insert a laugh into her voice. 'From now on, he's George MacDonald. That's what's on his birth certificate, after all.'

'Understood,' Amy said.

'I think we need to put the word out,' Birch said, 'ideally by the end of today, unless forensics come back with anything that puts another suspect in the picture. We need to make MacDonald our prime suspect and get everyone in on this. I'm talking a UK-wide public appeal through Crimestoppers for any info on the MacDonalds' whereabouts. I'll get in touch with McLeod for clearance, but I'll need you to prepare me some wording. The press will want an official statement about the appeal, as well as the briefing we'll give them to let them know we've found more remains.'

'I'm on it,' Amy said.

'Can you see who's around who could work on trawling through some historic CCTV footage?' Birch asked. 'MacDonald must be on plenty of it at Waverley and Carstairs stations. We might not get an immediate response to a public call-out, but if we can keep feeding them visuals of the guy, it'll help.'

The pause on the other end told her that Amy was making notes.

'Sure thing,' Amy said, the words slightly drawn out as she wrote.

'Oh,' Birch went on, 'and get in touch with Marcello or one of the other analyst types. I want them to take a look at the crime scene photos and draw up a proper profile on MacDonald. That way we can get a TIE strategy up and doing.'

Amy paused, but this time she was thinking, not writing. 'Marm,' she said, 'I know you've been waiting for a chance to go after MacDonald, but . . . McLeod's going to approve this?'

Birch raised an eyebrow. 'Don't worry, Kato, I won't let you get in any trouble. As far as I'm concerned, we need to find MacDonald whether he's our man for these murders or not. He was known to one of the victims but claimed in the past that he wasn't, even though he was caught trying to flog her jewellery. We know he hung around these parts a *lot*, that he was arrested round here for trespassing – which, if he was doing a recce on where to bury his victims, might be related to this investigation. *And* his DNA is at the scene. I know that stuff won't put him in the jail, but I think it makes enough of a case for finding the guy. We need to talk to him, if nothing else. I think McLeod will agree.'

Amy was nodding: Birch could hear the rattle of her earring against the phone.

'You're right, marm. And . . . there's Phamie, too. She's still missing, and I keep thinking about her.'

'I know,' Birch said, 'me too. I said we'd find them together, but looking at this crime scene I'm becoming increasingly certain that we won't find her alive.'

'Oh, don't say that,' Amy said. 'I've been reading her diaries, and they're – well, horrendous, to be honest. I just *feel* for her, you know? And I keep thinking about Mary McPherson, how frail she was. Phamie might have been getting like that, back in 2013, when he put her in the hospital. What sort of bastard would hurt some-one that age?'

Birch gritted her teeth, and looked at the huddle of white tents. 'A really mean one,' she said. 'The only silver lining here is we've yet to find any remains that are even vaguely fresh. Tish put it to us in her briefing that the killer might have started to find it too hard to dispose of bodies any more. MacDonald was sixty-three when Maisie went missing. Let's hope that was his retirement age?'

'He's eighty-three now,' Amy said, 'and still capable of hospital-ising his wife.' They were both quiet.

'He's our guy,' Birch said, into the dripping quiet of the wood. 'I'm absolutely certain of it. Now all we have to do is find him.'

25

By the end of the day, being in the wood had begun to get to Birch. The rain thickened as the hours wore on, and the tree-trunks turned blackish and slimy. Birch was damp: her clothes, her feet, her hair picked out with tiny droplets of moisture. All day she and the other officers tracked back and forth between the excavations under the trees and the white tents in the siding. Birch felt largely surplus to requirements, watching the suited and gloved forensics officers. She observed the way they lifted and handled the bones with such care and reverence, placing them in plastic evidence bags as though they were precious treasure. Slowly but surely, every item was inspected, bagged, labelled and boxed, and then a SOCO would appear with more items. Rocks, rubbish, bits of plastic. Anything that came out of the ground within the excavation area had to be individually dealt with. Birch was in awe of the operation, reminded of how small she was when considered as part of the machinery of the crime scene, how practically useless. The other officers ignored her, mostly, apparently content to have her watch their comings and goings. She knew she was mainly there so McLeod wouldn't need to show up: he'd told her to stay throughout the day.

'Keep a close eye on things,' he'd said. 'I'll want to be briefed in full.'

There was something else to being there, though, Birch thought. She spent a little time standing beside each of the gravesites, rain dripping off the trees on to the tent roofs. She looked down into the deep, cordoned-off holes: the soil was dark, shot through with gnarled roots. Where a spade had cut into them, those roots were scraped white as bone. In her head, Birch said a few words for each of the victims, four of them still nameless. I'm sorry this happened to you, she thought. I'm sorry you ended up in this lonely place. I'm sorry for whatever hurts he inflicted on you, I'm sorry for whatever you suffered. Loudest in her mind was the thought, I'll find him. I promise you, I will find him.

That afternoon, Amy had sent her a text. *Visited Hazel Kerr. She took it hard. Drove her in, she's with Tish now doing formal ID of the purse etc. Hope all is okay there.*

Birch wrote back: *Kato, you're a star. Thank you for doing that, I know it must have been hard. I really appreciate it.*

Around Birch, the wood ticked and dripped.

No problem. This aft I'll email you the wording re: George MacDonald Crimestoppers appeal. We should prob let Bennet know?

Reading this, Birch winced. *God yes, forgot about him. Are you OK doing that?*

You could do it yourself, Helen, Birch thought. You're just a coward. It was true: being in the woods, watching dead people come up out of the ground in bits, was pretty draining. She really wasn't sure she had the strength to be yelled at over the phone.

Happy to, was Amy's reply. *I'll call him.*

Again, Birch wrote, *absolute star. Thanks v much.*

Amy sent back a smiley face emoji, and its cheeriness made Birch shudder. She realised no one at the crime scene had smiled all day. No one had made small talk, no one had cracked a joke. Everyone was dutiful, their eyes downcast. It seemed wrong, somehow, to treat this place as anything other than hallowed ground.

Birch drove home with the car heater turned up high, trying to dry out. It didn't help: in fact, all she managed to do was make herself and the car's interior smell like wet dog. She could feel that inside her wet boots and damp socks, the pads of her toes had wrinkled. As she drove through the city, past steamed-up buses and businesses already shuttered for the night, Birch zoned out. She'd get into her PJs as soon as she got in, maybe treat herself to a takeaway. Run a bath, extra hot. She wanted desperately for the weight of the woods to lift from her shoulders. She wanted to stop thinking about George MacDonald, even just for an hour or two, but whenever she tried, she found herself thinking about her father, or about Charlie, broken in his hospital bed. Besides, tomorrow, the appeal would go out and the search for MacDonald would begin. Then there'd be no escaping the thought of him.

'Not until I've personally put him in a cell,' she said quietly, easing the car to a halt. Home at last.

She hadn't made it to her front door before her phone rang. Fishing it from her pocket, she saw it was Anjan, and swiped to answer.

'Hello, you,' she said.

'Hello, Helen,' he replied, and she could hear an edge in his voice, something not quite right. 'Are you still at work?'

'Just getting home,' she said. 'About fifty yards away. Is something up?'

As she waited for Anjan to answer, Birch squinted out in the direction of the sea. The tide was out, and the water wasn't visible: fog swirled on the beach, and the sand looked grey and dull. Normally, she could see the far shore of Fife, but now there was just a shifting wall of weather.

'All's well,' Anjan said. 'I just wondered if I could see you tonight. It's been a few days.'

Birch thought back. She hadn't seen Anjan since Thursday morning, when she'd sat eating toast in his kitchen, and the prison had phoned to tell her about Charlie's attack. She'd stormed out of the flat in a panic, barely saying goodbye.

'Sorry, Anjan,' she said. She closed her eyes, trying to decide: if she invited him over, that meant no bath, no vegging out. She'd have to run in and tidy up, in fact, and she realised she hadn't shaved her legs in over a week. Birch sighed. 'I'm not really up to going out anywhere, and the weather's filthy. But if you want to come round . . .?'

Anjan knocked at the door just as Birch finished her rapid hoover of the living room. She'd had just under an hour, which she'd spent hunting for discarded coffee cups, unloading and re-loading the dishwasher, changing her clothes, and blow-drying the rainwater out of her hair. She couldn't seem to shake the feeling of that place, the crime scene's dark dread feeling. She was conflicted about Anjan coming over, annoyed at having to do housework after a long day, and then guilty about having those feelings. She was alive, she was safe, and Anjan was a good man who wouldn't hurt her. She couldn't stop thinking about the six women in the woods.

Anjan let himself in. Birch watched from the living room as he shook out his coat in the hallway, and hung it up.

'Long time, no see,' he said, crossing the room to kiss her. 'Or, it feels that way.'

Birch put her arms around him and nestled in for a hug. It wasn't as relaxing as a hot bath, she thought, but yes, it was good to have Anjan around.

'I know,' she said, into his shoulder. 'Sorry about the way I left your place the other day.'

'Don't mention it,' Anjan said. He stepped back a little, and studied her face. 'How are you doing? I saw the paper this morning. Another body found.'

Birch sank on to the sofa. 'Between you and me,' she said, 'another five bodies, we think.'

Anjan blinked. 'A serial killer?'

She nodded. 'It's looking like it, yes.'

'Your hunch about MacDonald . . .'

'Yep. Tomorrow we go public: he's our prime suspect.'

Anjan was still standing.

Birch shook herself, and got back out of the sofa. 'Sorry,' she said, 'what am I like? Do you want tea? Glass of wine? I don't know if you've eaten, but . . .'

Anjan laughed, and followed her as she headed to the kitchen. 'I can take care of myself,' he said, 'I know where the kettle is.'

But Birch was already filling it at the sink. 'Tea, then? Sorry, I'm just . . . my head's mince.'

She set the kettle on to its base and flicked it on, then leaned back against the worktop. Anjan slid along to lean next to her, and slipped an arm around her waist.

'That's totally understandable,' he said, 'given everything you've got going on.' He paused, and then said, 'Five new bodies? All in that same place?'

Birch nodded. 'We've ID'd one. Maisie Kerr. She went missing in 1999, aged nineteen. I was only just at her mother's house, asking about MacDonald's alias. It was her mother whose emerald jewellery MacDonald tried to pawn all those years ago. He said he'd just found it under a bench, the bastard.'

'Can you tie him to the burial site?'

'We can now,' Birch said. 'We found a locket in the wood that belonged to Maisie. It had a lock of George MacDonald's hair inside – or rather, a lock of hair that's a blood-relative match to his son's DNA, which is the same thing. We can't prove he killed anyone yet, but I'm hoping we'll find more – forensics are holding out for a fingerprint from the inside of Maisie's purse. And it's enough to make him a suspect.'

Anjan was frowning, looking at the floor. 'It's a long time ago, 1999,' he said, half to himself. 'The forensics team must be up against it, to find anything more than you already have. Anything admissible, I mean.'

Birch prickled a little, but tried to ignore it. Playing devil's advocate was just how Anjan was wired.

'You're right,' she said, 'which is why we have to find MacDonald. If we can extract a confession then we'll be less reliant on all that stuff.'

'Any leads on his whereabouts?'

Birch sighed. 'Sadly not,' she said. 'The family home was sold at auction, with no forwarding address. His son has no idea. And of course, his wife is missing, too. We're pretty worried about her safety, for obvious reasons.'

'You've ruled her out as one of the burial site victims?'

'Yeah – we know she was alive in 2013, because of that news report, you remember. Police attended a domestic disturbance, and Phamie MacDonald was taken to hospital. She didn't press charges, more's the pity. But anyway – these remains are too old. We still need to find Phamie, too. So we're going public with it tomorrow, like I say. Fingers crossed someone out there will know something, or remember something.'

The kettle boiled, and the switch flipped off. Birch crossed to the mug cupboard, while Anjan reached over to the fridge for milk. The unspoken synchronicity made her smile.

'A big day for you tomorrow, then,' Anjan said. There was the same edge in his voice as Birch had heard over the phone.

'It will be,' she said. As she set the mugs down on the worktop, she raised an eyebrow at him. 'What's up, Anjan? Don't say it's nothing.'

Anjan was still for a moment, the carton of semi-skimmed slightly raised in his hand, as though he'd been frozen mid-motion.

'Tomorrow's going to be tough for you,' he said at last, 'so it can wait.'

Birch felt a stab of panic. 'So there is something,' she said. 'Just tell me, will you? It'll be much worse if you leave me to worry about what it is.'

Anjan cocked his head at her, a sign he knew she was right. 'Fine,' he said. 'I suppose this is why I wanted to come over. We need to talk about the situation with Charlie.'

The panic Birch had felt ebbed, then was replaced with a different one. Oh, it's only that. Oh wait, it's *that*. 'You've heard something?' As she spoke, Birch felt her body stiffen in anticipation.

'The prison contacted me today,' he said, 'to inform me, as Charlie's legal counsel, that an inquiry into the incident has now been launched.'

Birch set her teeth. 'I'm his next of kin,' she said. 'Why haven't they informed *me*?'

'Because I said I'd do it,' Anjan replied. 'I thought we'd better talk about it a little. The situation is quite complex.'

'The situation is that Charlie was attacked by six men, and defended himself.' Birch knew she wasn't being honest, and she shouldn't be bristling at Anjan, but she couldn't help it. She watched his face soften. He understood.

'You know that's not quite how it is, Helen,' he said, his voice quiet.

Birch turned away from him, and began fussing teabags out of
the box on the worktop.

'The two officers who were on shift in Charlie's hall that night
have been placed on leave,' Anjan went on. 'One of them is Tommy
Swinton, who I believe you know a little. You have to know that
when I spoke to them, I was only interested in talking about the
ways in which Charlie was endangered by their carelessness. I
refused to go into any who-did-what-to-whom, any of Charlie's
own actions.'

Birch didn't look back at him: she was pouring the hot water
into the mugs. But she smiled. 'Thank you,' she said.

'It is the central crux of the matter,' Anjan said. 'Cell doors are
supposed to be secure at night, precisely so that inmates are safe
as they sleep. It was a serious failing on the part of the staff there,
and they know it could have massive consequences for them.
They're trying to keep it out of the media for that very reason. We
can really lean on that, the failure to uphold their duty of care. We
can suggest that Charlie's actions are a moot point, because no
one other than his cellmate should have been there at night in the
first place.'

Birch stepped back and allowed Anjan to splash milk into the
mugs of tea.

'Good,' she said. 'But why do I feel like there's a *but* coming?'

Anjan looked at her for a moment before returning the milk
to the fridge. 'Because there is one,' he said. 'Charlie was put at
risk, and he was horribly beaten, and that's their fault. However,
he did do more than just defend himself. He targeted one other
inmate in particular, and he caused grievous bodily harm to
that inmate, even after he knew that the violence being visited
upon him was over. He did what he did consciously – instinc-
tive, or otherwise. They'll say that *his* violence was calculating,
too.'

Birch brought the tea mug up close to her face, and leaned once
again on the kitchen counter. She could feel the steam rising and
dampening her face, ever so slightly. 'Do you think it's possible to
get him out of it? Is there any way?'

Anjan bobbed one shoulder in a careful shrug. 'I'm still think-ing it through,' he said, 'but I think it's almost inevitable that his sentence will be extended. By how much, exactly, is the real ques-tion. That's the thing I'll have more control over.'

Birch could feel the threat of tears. *My stupid, stupid brother.*

'I'm sorry, Helen.' Anjan could see her fighting the upset, and reached out once again to put an arm around her waist. 'I know this is dreadful. I know how hard it must be, seeing Charlie in the state he's in. And I know it must be doubly hard knowing he's hurt and not being able to see him whenever you want to. But I prom-ise I will do my very best for him, and for you. We could be look-ing at an extension of as little as six months, you never know.'

Birch nodded, blinking. She knew this was unlikely, and Anjan was placating her, but she went along with it.

'One thing's for certain,' he said. 'I will be fighting to ensure that Charlie's assailants receive far harsher punishment than Charlie himself. And I will not rest until the ringleader has been moved to another facility. Charlie cannot be expected to live alongside that person: that is without question.'

Birch thought about where else there was, where the young man might be put. She remembered Barlinnie, and Solomon Carradice. 'Was anything said,' she asked, 'about Solomon? Whether he might be behind this?'

'It wasn't mentioned,' Anjan said. 'I suspect the Scottish Prison Service don't want to entertain the idea that an attack of this kind could have been co-ordinated from a totally different prison. But if that angle is there, I will find it. I'm unsure what to think about it at present, as the sabotage of the cell doors must have been fairly sophisticated, but what happened in the cell itself, it seems, was simply mindless thuggery.'

Birch gave a cold laugh. 'Carradice has plenty of experience in both,' she said.

'True. But Charlie is still alive. That's the main indicator, for me, that this incident is not connected to him.'

Birch snorted. 'Perhaps he's still alive because he defended himself,' she said. It was as though she thought that if she used the words *defended himself* enough times, they'd start to become true. She wanted her brother to be a good person, fundamentally, deep down. She'd tried hard to hang on to the belief that he was – in spite of all he'd done, and in spite of where he now found himself – a good man, who'd been led astray by forces larger than himself. Charlie wasn't *like* Solomon Carradice and the goons he'd worked alongside, he was *different*. It was a secret delusion she hated herself for cultivating.

'I'm going to go and visit him,' Anjan said. He seemed to have chosen not to respond to her provocation, and she was quietly grateful. 'I've been given clearance to go to the prison infirmary tomorrow. I'll take some testimony from him, and then we'll get to work.'

'Thank you, Anjan. Really.'

Birch leaned into Anjan's body, and rested her head on his shoulder. In that moment, she felt able to pick out a particular thread in the tangled knot of anger she felt around Charlie and what had happened to him. She realised she was angry that, as a result of the attack, she was going to have to redraw the lines of her relationship with Anjan. She'd just got nicely used to him being *just* her boyfriend, to things being simple. Now, he'd revert to being her brother's lawyer, and they'd need to figure out where their boundaries were all over again. Bloody Charlie: he seemed able to mess with her emotions no matter where he was, no matter how far removed.

'There's something else,' Birch said, surprising herself. The words were muffled by Anjan's body, and he pulled back from her so he could hear. 'There's something else,' she said again.

'Go on.'

Birch took a deep breath, just as she had before talking to Amy. 'A few days ago,' she said, 'my father called. Here, he phoned the house. Last Tuesday night, it was, when you were – oh, at the charity function thing. I was outside and didn't hear the phone, so he left a voicemail. He said he'd heard Charlie was in the jail and he wanted to – something. He never finished the sentence.'

Birch felt Anjan ruffle at the last part. He was still standing close to her.

'What, he just *hung up*?'

'Not quite,' she said, 'but nearly. He withheld his number, just said he'd call back. Of course, he's never called back. Typical Jamieson. And you know me. I've had it in the back of my mind ever since. It's been driving me mad.'

Anjan pulled her back in to him, wrapping his arms around her. Birch appreciated the gesture, but felt strangely stifled by it. This was hard to talk about, and being so close to Anjan seemed to make it harder still.

'Tuesday,' Anjan said. 'I wish you'd told me.'

Birch closed her eyes. I knew you'd say that, she thought. 'I thought about it,' she said, 'when I was at your place on Wednesday night. In fact, I think I was psyching myself up for it on Thursday morning, over breakfast. But then the prison phoned, and – since then, I haven't seen you.'

Anjan was quiet for a moment. Birch listened to his heartbeat.

'I'm sorry he did that to you,' he said at last. 'I'm sorry he's added that into the mix. You're having such a difficult time as it is.'

Birch felt like she might cry. She realised she'd been waiting for someone to say that to her: waiting for someone to understand.

'Thanks, Anjan,' she said.

He gave her a squeeze, and they broke apart. Birch took a step back, grateful for the clear air.

'There's more, though,' she said. 'He called Charlie as well.'

She watched Anjan's face change from being concerned for her, to being concerned for his case. The change was subtle, but she could see it happen.

'Charlie's spoken to him?'

Birch shook her head. 'He left a message. The screws relayed it to Charlie in the infirmary. Jamieson withheld his number with me, but he gave it to the prison to give to Charlie. Charlie passed it on to me. Which means now I'm not just passively waiting to see if my dad calls me back. I have to decide if I want to call *him*, which if anything is even worse.'

Anjan was quiet again. Birch could tell he was thinking about angles: might this affect the outcome of Charlie's inquiry? Anjan knew about the incident between Charlie and Jamieson while Charlie had been in the employ of Solomon. Whatever else Jamieson was, he'd been a witness to, and a victim of, Charlie's violence. Him turning up right now – just as Charlie had to try to convince the inquiry that he *wasn't* habitually violent – was pretty dreadful timing.

'I know,' Birch said, though Anjan hadn't spoken. 'This is *typical* of my father. Minimum effort from him, maximum negative fall-out for everybody else.'

Anjan didn't seem to know how to respond. This gave Birch a little stab of panic: Anjan *always* knew how to respond.

'What does Charlie think about it?' he said eventually.

Birch shrugged. 'He said he's thinking about it,' she replied. 'As in, he's thinking about calling my father back.'

Anjan began shaking his head. 'I don't think that's a very good idea,' he said, his brow knitting as he spoke. 'For a lot of reasons, it's not a good idea at all.'

Birch felt vindicated. 'Right,' she said. 'Perhaps you can say that to Charlie when you go and see him? It might mean more coming from you.'

26

Amy watched as her boss checked her watch for around the four-hundredth time.

'Marm,' she said, and Birch looked up. 'It's still eleven o'clock. You looked thirty seconds ago.'

Birch folded her arms. 'Sorry, Kato,' she said. 'I'm being completely daft.'

The George MacDonald appeal had been live for exactly two hours: the pair of them had gone over the final wording early that morning, to allow time for McLeod to give his official okay ahead of the 9 a.m. release.

'Even if someone's already called Crimestoppers,' Amy said, 'to say, Hey, George MacDonald is my next-door neighbour! You know they have to check it over, generate the report . . .'

'I know, I know.'

DI Birch was ill-slept, Amy could see it. 'Are you okay, marm? If you don't mind me saying, you seem to be flagging a bit.'

Birch looked down, as though studying her reflection in the upturned silver wrapper on the table in front of her. Amy had suggested a chocolate break, sticking her head round Birch's office door and asking, 'Canteen? Elevenses.'

Now, her boss was trying to rally. 'I'm okay,' she said, 'just . . . this case. I have a lot of mixed feelings.'

'Such as?'

Birch ran a finger across the foil wrapper, smoothing it. 'Well, on the one hand, thank God we've found these bodies, you know? Once we ID them all, we can get some closure for their families, and they can be properly laid to rest. We've taken them back, in a way: I feel like we've rescued them. From him, from MacDonald.

But then . . . he's also still out there, the bastard. Living a perfectly nice life, too, no doubt. He did this and got away with it.' Birch swept the wrapper into her hand and crushed it into her fist. 'We *have* to find him. MacDonald. Or . . . whoever did it.'

Amy frowned. 'And Phamie, too. We have to find her.'

Birch looked up at her, and nodded. 'Phamie too,' she agreed. 'That's a whole other strand.'

Amy bit her lip. 'It's keeping you up at night, too? Or . . . I wondered if maybe there'd been developments with your dad?'

She watched her boss think about her response, Birch's nose wrinkling.

'No,' Birch said, after a moment. 'Nothing from him. He's never called back. I'm still thinking about it all the time, of course, but I haven't spoken to him or anything. There's this whole thing with Charlie too, – the plot thickens with that. But to be honest, last night, it was the case. I just . . . every time I fell asleep, I found myself back in those bloody woods. In the dark, on my hands and knees in the dirt. I was digging and digging, I knew there was something so important that I had to find, and it was like I was being watched, being appraised. Like it was a test. But then just as I was about to unearth something, I'd wake up, and feel so awake that I thought I'd never get back to sleep. Then after a while, back I'd go, into the wood in my dreams. Digging.'

Amy said nothing, unsure of what might help. She'd been dreaming about the case, too: dreaming that she was in a room with Hazel Kerr, with Mary McPherson, with Phamie MacDonald, trying to explain. Trying to tell them that the police were working on it, they were doing their best to see justice done. But it was like the women wouldn't listen, or couldn't hear. They were silent.

'It's a lot,' Amy eventually said, 'this case.' She wanted to say more: to say that cold cases represent a double failure, because not only was the crime allowed to happen, it was also allowed to lie undiscovered for so long. She wanted to point out that these failings belonged to other people, not to them: they were the failings of other officers, long ago. She wanted to tell Birch that hey, had it not been for her very bad feeling then those bodies would be lying undiscovered still. But instead she just said again, 'It's a lot.'

Birch looked at her, appearing for the first time to see the weight Amy had been carrying around. 'The diaries,' Birch said, 'have they – are they harrowing to read?'

Amy winced. She felt seen, and she both appreciated it and didn't at the same time. 'In places,' she said. 'In the places where she reports some of the things he used to say to her. About her. George, I mean.'

'What kind of things?'

Amy closed her eyes. She'd spent so much time reading Phamie's dense handwriting that now she could see it, as though projected behind her eyelids. As she began to speak, she felt like a medium, like she was channelling George MacDonald's rotten spirit into the room. 'You're a selfish woman,' Amy said. 'That's something he says a lot. Whenever Phamie has done anything even slightly nice for herself, he berates her for being selfish. I just read an entry where she'd been into town with Mary, shopping, and they'd gone for a cup of tea somewhere, just like Mary told us they used to. She'd come home and George had yelled at her for being selfish, for supposedly never thinking about *him* and *his* needs and the fact that he apparently had to know where she was at all times. That was his right, he'd said to her, as her husband. Then he'd beaten her. She wrote that she had to go to Mary's afterwards, to have Mary look at a cut he'd given her, to check whether it might need stitches. The irony was, he'd stormed out and disappeared all night after doing that to her. He'd pontificated at her about how *he* needed to know where *she* was at all times, then he'd up and disappeared. That's what really gets me about reading these things. He was clearly an arrogant, violent bully – but he was also *such* a hypocrite.'

Birch's expression was somewhere between concern for Amy and sadness for Phamie MacDonald.

'And you know, marm,' Amy added, 'she never once writes about leaving him. Not once, in all the pages I've read. It's like it never even crosses her mind.'

Birch shook her head. 'It's a depressingly common tale,' she said. 'And you know, I was thinking about that very thing the other night. Thinking about people whose partners are abusive, and who don't leave – who feel like they can't leave. It's a weakness of mine, that I really struggle to understand it.'

Amy was quiet for a moment. 'To be perfectly honest with you,' she said, 'the more of the diaries I read, the more there's a part of me that hopes Phamie *is* dead. Simply because, if she's dead, then she's away from him. She's finally out from under George MacDonald.'

Birch opened her mouth to reply, but on the table between them, her phone rang. Both women leaned over slightly to look at the caller ID.

'Oh great,' Birch said, 'here we go.'

Amy shook herself. She'd been doing this more and more over the past few days: it was as though Phamie MacDonald's ghost were following her around, whispering into her ear.

'You want me to stick around, marm?'

Birch lifted the phone, one finger hovering over it, ready to answer. 'No, I've got this. You've been on the receiving end enough times. It's my turn.'

The caller was Robertson Bennet. Birch picked up.

'Good luck,' Amy mouthed, and as her boss began speaking, she gathered herself up from the table, and left.

When Amy reached her desk, there was a Post-it stuck to the space bar of her keyboard. *Amy, can you come to front desk when you have a minute? Something to run by you. Ta, John.* She didn't bother getting settled: indeed, she appreciated the opportunity to do something other than sit back down with Phamie's diaries. She was well into the third one now, and nearly finished. She both did and did not want to get to the final page, and hand the diaries over to DI Birch. Amy plucked the Post-it off the desk and turned on her heel to go and find John.

She found him at his usual post, with Klara, the front desk receptionist on shift, talking on the phone nearby. John looked up as she approached, and she could see he was pleased to see her.

'Morning,' he said, raising a hand in greeting. 'You got my note.'

'I did,' Amy said. 'What can I do you for?'

'Funny thing,' John said. He skirted along to where Klara was just putting down the phone, and picked up something from her side of the reception desk. 'This letter came,' he went on, 'addressed to *MacDonald Investigation*. We haven't opened it – we've tried not to handle it – but we think it might be a tip.'

Amy frowned.

'It came in the general mail,' Klara said, 'and I wasn't sure what to do with it. I showed it to John and he suggested we ask you.'

'You're working on that case,' John said, 'right? That's the case with the aggro American guy who keeps coming in.'

'I . . . guess so?' Amy looked at the envelope in John's hand. It was handwritten, the writing small and spidery. 'I don't know of any other active investigation that would be called the *MacDonald Investigation*. It's just weird, because we only sent the appeal out today.'

John held the envelope out for her to take: a this-is-your-problem-now sort of gesture.

'Wait,' Amy said, 'we don't know what this is. John, you have gloves somewhere?'

'Oh, hang on.' Klara held up a hand, *stop*, then began rummaging in a drawer. After a moment, she pulled out an open box of single-use white latex gloves. Amy's face must have registered her surprise, because Klara shrugged and added, 'Hey, you never know.'

Amy pulled a pair of gloves from the suck of the box, and shimmied them on. It had always made her cringe, the powdery feel of them against her skin. Now, she allowed herself to reach out for the envelope. John was blushing, she realised.

'Sorry,' he said, nodding at her gloved hands, 'I should have thought.'

'It's fine,' she said, 'it's probably nothing.'

Amy put the envelope down flat on a clear stretch of the reception desk. She ran her fingertips over it, checking for lumps or grooves, for the feeling of powder – or anything else besides paper

– inside the envelope. The paper was thin, letter size, the sort of cheap, basic stationery one could buy for a few pence at the post office. Amy could feel that there was only a single sheet inside the envelope, folded once.

'Right,' she said, 'I'm going in.'

It was tricky with the gloves on, but the adhesive on the envelope's seam was not strong. Amy fumbled open the envelope, and drew out the piece of paper inside.

Unfolding it, she noted the same spidery hand, the pen pressed hard against the paper, forming grooves she could feel even through her gloves. There was one sentence, written in the very centre of the page, right where it had been folded: *Look under the flagstones*. As Amy's eyes scanned the rest of the page, her breath caught in her throat. Lower down, below the fold, and slightly to one side, the paper was signed: *George*. Above the name, the writer had drawn a straight line, which wavered like the line on a polygraph read-out. The word was not underlined, but overlined. *George*.

'Holy shit,' Amy whispered.

For a moment, no one spoke, and then Amy shook herself.

'John,' she said, 'I need you to get me an evidence bag for this thing. Fast as you can.'

When Birch arrived at her office door, Amy was already inside. She heard her boss knock, and laughed.

'Marm, it's *your* office.'

Birch's face appeared round the door. 'I know,' she said, 'but your text sounded so serious, I was afraid to come in.'

'Sorry,' Amy said, as the other woman opened the door properly, walked in and then closed it behind her. 'I didn't mean to alarm you.'

Birch crossed the room and sank into her chair, across the desk from Amy.

'I just hope it's nothing too terrible,' she said, 'I've just done ten rounds in the ring with Robertson Bennet.'

Amy winced. 'It was bad, then?'

Birch rolled her eyes, and smiled. 'He's going to sue us, apparently,' she said. 'For defaming his family's good name. Bringing him into disrepute. We've made him look bad, he says. I think he reckons the British justice system is one very long episode of *Judge Judy*.'

'You're not too worried, then?'

Birch shrugged. 'He doesn't have grounds for a defamation claim,' she said, 'and he seems to have forgotten that we also know he doesn't have the funds to lodge one. To be honest, I think he just wanted to have a bit of a shout. I could have done without being his verbal punching bag, but it's over with now.'

'You'll tell DCI McLeod?'

Birch looked at Amy for a moment, and Amy saw a glint in her boss's eye.

'Perhaps,' she said. 'It's the sort of behaviour that'd enrage him, I'm sure. *I'll sue* is McLeod's second biggest bugbear, after . . .'

'After *I'll go to the press!*' the women chimed in unison. Amy laughed. Birch was smiling, but she looked a little perturbed.

'I just hope I handled him okay,' she said. 'I don't want him to become a recurring problem. We've got enough to deal with.'

Amy shook her head. 'I'm sure you were great, marm,' she said. 'Diplomacy is your middle name.'

Birch snorted. 'Oh, *hard*ly,' she said. 'You know me and my big mouth. I feel like I'm in a constant battle these days, trying not to snark people off. I tell you, living with Anjan is a struggle. He's always so bloody *right*.'

Amy raised an eyebrow. '*Living* with Anjan?'

Birch swatted at her. 'No, not that. Just . . . oh, whatever. You know what I mean.'

'I do,' Amy said, her eyebrow still arched. 'And I also know you think the sun shines out of him, so don't think you've got me fooled.' She watched her boss colour slightly, and grinned.

'Oh shut up,' Birch said. 'I'm just saying . . . he's great, but he's such a bloody *lawyer* sometimes.'

Amy was smiling, but she could feel anxiety rising in her. This wasn't what they were here for. 'I'm sorry, marm, but . . .'

'Yes, shit, sorry. There was a serious thing, and I'm just wittering.' Birch settled back in her chair. 'Let's have it,' she said.

Amy lifted the evidence bag from her lap, and passed it over to Birch. 'This arrived in the general mail this morning,' she said. 'Klara and John downstairs intercepted it and passed it to me.'

Birch took the bag and held it up to look through the plastic. Amy had put the letter back inside its envelope.

'Obviously I'm not certain,' Amy said, 'but it appears to be a tip. And it's signed *George*.'

Birch's eyes widened. Her mouth opened a little, but it seemed she couldn't speak.

'You've got gloves?' Amy asked, and Birch nodded, mute. 'Take a look.'

As her boss rummaged in one of her desk drawers, Amy went on speaking. 'The note reads, *Look under the flagstones*,' she said. 'That's the only wording except for a signature: the name George, written underneath a straight line. When I saw it, I almost had a heart attack, I have to admit.'

She watched as Birch struggled a glove on to her right hand, which was shaking slightly.

'It's too soon for the letter to have been sent in response to this morning's public appeal, obviously,' Amy continued. 'The stamp shows it was sent first class, so there's a chance it was posted yesterday. But it's more likely it was posted on Saturday, or even Friday of last week.'

Birch had opened the bag now, and was drawing the letter out of its envelope.

'The fact that it's addressed to MacDonald Investigation is what freaks me out,' Amy went on. 'Because the case has been in the papers, but we've only publicly linked it to MacDonald today. No one knew last week that we were interested in him, except for folk on the inside, and Robertson Bennet.'

Birch looked up for a moment. 'I doubt Bennet's behind this,' she said. 'This is out of the serial killer playbook: the guy contacts police, wanting to show how fucking smart he is. Bennet's livid about this whole investigation. No way he'd add fuel to the fire, right?'

'That's what I thought,' Amy said. 'And look at the handwriting. It's the writing of an elderly person, no?'

Birch held up the letter, her head cocked to one side. 'I'd say so,' she said. 'But we'll get it analysed. It's possible to fake a tremble like that, I imagine.'

Amy realised she was shaking her head. 'I just don't know who else could have done this,' she said, 'but MacDonald himself. *He* would know we'd be looking at him. And if he saw in the papers that we'd found Suzie Hay . . .'

Birch was nodding. Amy watched her eyes, could see her mind working, trying to think of other options, other ways it could have been, other people who might have sent the letter, who might have known. After a short silence, she pulled her eyes away from the letter, and retrained her gaze on Amy.

'It certainly looks that way, doesn't it?'

The two women sat in silence for several moments. Birch was still holding the letter in one gloved hand. Amy could see her eyes moving, reading the one line over and over, then looking at the signature, then going back to read the line.

'Okay,' Birch said. 'Let's say this *is* the work of George MacDonald. What do we make of it? What's he telling us?'

Amy felt her forehead crease. 'Well,' she said, 'Tish Bland said in her briefing that the burial site in the wood was last used in 1999. Maisie Kerr was the last to be buried. She said Maisie could have been the last victim, *or* the killer could have just started putting his victims elsewhere. Maybe he's telling us where the *elsewhere* is.'

Birch was nodding, but slowly, perhaps reluctantly. 'But if there are more bodies somewhere,' she said, 'why tell us? Why help us find them? The more we unearth, the more chance we have of finding incriminating forensic evidence.'

'Perhaps he wants to be caught? Perhaps, after all these years, he thinks he ought to be punished?'

Birch snorted. 'People say that about serial killers, don't they?' she said. 'They want to be caught. I don't think I believe in that. I get that they have a compulsion to show off, to illustrate how they pulled it off. But . . . no. If MacDonald wanted to be caught, why wouldn't he write more? Be more specific? This is pretty vague. I mean, *what* fucking flagstones?'

Amy said nothing. Her boss had a point.

'I suppose,' Birch said, after another pause, her words drawn out slow as she thought them, 'it doesn't have to be a body, under the flagstones. Five of our six victims were buried without clothes, without personal effects. Only Maisie Kerr had anything with her, apart from Suzie Hay's witch hat. It could be MacDonald telling us where to look for those things. But again, he'd be leading us to a forensic goldmine.'

'Maybe it's where Phamie is,' Amy said.

Birch looked at her. 'Maybe,' she said. 'And does under the flagstones necessarily mean *buried*? Could he be holding Phamie somewhere – a cellar?'

Birch had leaned forward in her chair, and Amy realised she had mimicked the movement.

'Are we getting into the realms of wishful thinking?' Birch asked.

Amy sank back. 'Maybe,' she said. 'It's not much to go on.'

Birch was once again looking at the sheet of paper. 'He's not trying to be caught,' Birch said, 'so . . . could it be that he thinks he's untouchable? He thinks he's somewhere where we'll never find him? Sending this is a pretty gallus act.'

Amy nodded at the envelope, now resting on top of its evidence bag on Birch's desk. 'The letter is postmarked locally,' she said, 'it wasn't sent from far away.'

Birch switched her attention from letter to envelope. 'You're right, Kato,' she said. 'And you know that the first thing I'm going to ask you to do once you leave this room is follow up on that. I want to know exactly where this letter has been, every single pair of hands it has passed through.'

'Yes, marm,' Amy said. 'I'm on it.'

'Of course,' Birch said, 'there are other possibilities. One is, he's trying to throw us off. We've found his burial spot. He wants to send us off on a wild-goose chase, so we don't discover anything more.'

Amy nodded. 'That seems a pretty logical move,' she said.

'And of course,' Birch went on, 'it could be a hoax. But as you say . . . the appeal only went out today. I was bracing myself for crank calls, fake tips, the usual. But this is too early. It's weird.'

They sat in silence again. Now, Amy could see Birch's lips moving, *flagstones, flagstones*. It was as though her boss thought this were a riddle she could solve, if she only looked at those same four words enough times.

'So . . . what do we do, marm?'

The silence didn't break right away: Birch sat for a few more seconds, not acknowledging the question. But then she looked up at Amy.

'Right,' she said. 'Obvious things first. We need to find out as much as we can about where this letter has been – then we can decide more easily if it's a hoax. I'll leave that with you, Kato. The other obvious thing is, we need to get this off to the lab, see what forensics can pull off it. For all we know it might be covered in fingerprints. And it's the sort of envelope you lick, so that's something. I'll get that ball rolling. And I'll get myself into McLeod's calendar, see what he makes of it. I'll maybe let him decide if we start digging up flagstones or not. I'm already in his bad books for going off down the garden path of a hunch that ended in six bodies.'

Amy raised an eyebrow again. 'Now, marm, surely you're not saying DCI McLeod would prefer if people got away with murder?'

Birch shrugged. 'No, no, of course not. Just that he'd prefer it if I stuck to the proper channels. I think he gets sick of telling me.'

Amy smiled. 'You're just good at your job, marm,' she said. 'Can't argue with that.'

Edinburgh Evening News

Body of missing nursery teacher Christine Turnbull found as police hunt for serial killer

EMMA BLACK   Published 15:01   Share this article
Email   Tuesday 10 September

SIGN UP TO OUR DAILY NEWSLETTER

The hunt is over for missing nursery teacher Christine Turnbull, who disappeared from her aunt's house in Glasgow over fifty years ago.

Police Scotland confirmed today that Christine Turnbull's remains were found in woodland close to the villages of Carstairs and Carstairs Junction, in South Lanarkshire, where a grisly crime scene is unfolding.

Turnbull was last seen on 1 June 1965, having travelled from her home in Edinburgh to visit her aunt in Glasgow. At the time of her disappearance, she was 23 years old. The discovery of her body, which was identified using dental records, brings to a close a 54-year police investigation into her whereabouts.

Police have also confirmed the identity of Maisie Kerr, whose remains were found not far from those of Turnbull and missing teenager Suzie Hay. Maisie Kerr was 19 years old when she left her house in Carstairs Junction in

April 1999. Her case was reopened just days ago when police came across jewellery belonging to Kerr in the same patch of woodland where her body was later discovered.

A source close to the investigation commented that still more remains had been found in the woodland, and that further announcements pertaining to the identity of these remains would be made in the coming days.

In a statement released this morning, a spokesperson for Police Scotland said: 'For several days, our forensics teams have been excavating a stretch of woodland near the villages of Carstairs Junction and Carstairs. We now believe that this woodland was used as a burial site by a serial murderer, and we have begun a full-scale investigation to identify this person and bring them to justice.'

Police are appealing for members of the public who may have information relating to the murders of Hay, Turnbull or Kerr to come forward. They are particularly keen to speak to one George MacDonald, now aged 83 and believed to be from Edinburgh. Anyone who can provide information relating to the case should report to their local police station, or call Crimestoppers.

The Crimestoppers telephone number is anonymous and any information passed on is treated confidentially. The number to call is 0800 555 111.

27

Birch drove home that evening, but couldn't settle. The rain of the last two days had finally lifted, and if she stood at her living room window she could see the clouds being pushed eastwards over East Lothian and out into the North Sea. Blustery sunshine took over: on the beach below her house, dogs appeared, accompanied by people in wellies. Even from inside, Birch could tell that the weather felt autumnal: the change of season perceptible somehow for the first time. She sat on her sofa, doing nothing other than listening to the wind buffeting around the chimney of her little house. Occasionally it wheezed in the slats of the gas fire. Roughly every thirty seconds, Birch glanced at the phone: plugged in, ready for her father to phone again. It had been exactly a week since he'd last called. Should she mark that anniversary, and call him back? Anjan had warned against it, and she'd agreed that her father appearing at this precise moment was really not ideal. She also had no idea what she would say, other than asking him what the hell he thought he was playing at. What the hell had he been playing at for the last thirty years? Hell, for the whole of his life? No: she couldn't trust herself not to yell at him, not to get out of control. Birch glanced at the mantel clock: 6.34 p.m. There'd be a little light out, yet, and she couldn't sit here all night staring at the phone, wondering. She stood up, grabbed her coat, and headed out of the front door.

Birch didn't really realise where she was going until she found herself waiting at the traffic lights on Sir Harry Lauder Road. A young woman had chanced the crossing and made it halfway: now she shivered on the central traffic island, her arms folded around her. She was wearing a short skirt and heels, with no tights, and the silver bomber jacket she hugged herself into didn't seem to be doing much good. She must be going for a bus, Birch guessed: nothing round here merited being dressed that way. She felt a pang of concern that hurt, somewhere below the breastbone. The girl would be maybe eighteen, nineteen. She looked so frail as a gap came between the cars and she made a dash for the other side: deer-like, wide-eyed and vulnerably beautiful. Birch felt her fingers tighten around the steering wheel. Just George MacDonald's type. Just the type to be picked off for precisely that vulnerability.

When Birch reached the crime scene, the sun had just begun to set behind the horizon. The light was gold and pink and everywhere: even the State Hospital, up on its hill, looked appealing in this golden hour. She parked on the run-on, amid tatters of police tape clinging in the fences like streamers. At the gate that led on to the tracks, a neon-uniformed scene guard was stationed.

'Evening, marm,' he said, as she approached. 'Bit late to be working, isn't it?'

'It is,' Birch said, 'but I won't stay long, don't worry.'

The policeman gave a none-of-my-business smile, and said, 'Take your time.'

Birch picked her way across the tracks, and entered the wood.

The effect was like turning off a lightbulb: the golden light didn't reach under the thick pines. The tents were still clustered there, glowing unreal white between the black trunks. Birch found she couldn't approach them, not at this hour, and not alone. She imagined she could feel the six women's expectant ghosts watching her from some safe distance, realising she'd found out nothing, she'd come here empty-handed once again. She shivered, and turned her back on the tents. They weren't the reason she was here.

Birch walked the path – now well worn by many pairs of police-issue wellies – from the tents to the tree-line, at right-angles to where she'd entered the wood. She paused at the line of shadow the trees cast into the evening, remembering how she'd entered here that first time, to scrape in the soil with her baton based on nothing more than a hunch. Then she went on, following the path towards the disused siding. Ahead of her, she could see another scene guard waiting there, his back turned, facing towards the station.

As soon as her feet hit concrete, she stopped, and pulled the crumpled print-out of a map from her pocket. On it was the terrain she now knew by heart: the crucial near corner of the wood, the gravesites marked with tiny squares. The railway tracks beside her, the run-on layby she'd parked at, and the siding, cutting a flat rectangle into the map. The tip of the station was pictured, too, and she thought of its paved platforms, the flagged concrete floor of the waiting room.

But she'd start here. Between where she stood and where the gravel of the railway tracks began, there was a flank of flagstones. Fat grey oblongs half swallowed by grass and rosebay, each one was perhaps two and a half feet long and looked like it weighed as much as she did. Her whole body felt weak: this was only the first patch. She fished a pen from her pocket, and drew a line around the area on her map.

Birch walked further into the siding. The ground was a patchwork of different surfaces: broken concrete, gravel, patches of bare earth where grass and weeds grew. She veered right, towards the nearest of the derelict buildings. It was choked with rosebay, the stalks almost as tall as she was, crowned with fluffy seed heads. Morning glory scrambled over the jagged walls. But below the undergrowth, she could see the floor was flagged: the plants pushed their way between the stones. Birch drew a circle on the map over the little square that represented the building. She then picked her way through tall grass, nettles and more rosebay. The other structures, set further back, also had flagstone floors. She circled them in red, too, her heart heavy. There was going to be a lot more excavation here before they were done.

The light began to fade suddenly, as the sun's last sliver disappeared behind the treetops of the wood. Birch felt cold, and upped her pace, striding towards the station. She hailed the scene guard whose back was still turned to her, and saw him jump before he registered who she was.

'Is everything okay, marm?'

'Yes, everything's fine. Just doing a recce ahead of tomorrow.'

The uniformed officer gave her a look.

'I'm a workaholic, okay?' Birch tried to insert laughter into her voice. 'I want this case solved, and sitting at home in front of the TV isn't going to help with that.'

It worked: the officer smiled. 'If you say so,' he said. 'I'm just glad you're not a marauding reporter. Thought I was going to have to rugby-tackle you for a second, there.'

Birch grinned. 'Sorry to have caused alarm. I'm heading off in a minute, as the light's going.'

'Good idea.'

Birch glanced down at the ground below the scene guard's feet. More flagstones.

Driving home, Birch thought about Christine Turnbull. That case had been in the news on and off for as long as she could remember: every so often, some new lead would come up and the disappearance would bob to the surface of public awareness once again. The Find Christine appeal had outlived Turnbull's parents and the aunt who'd been the last person to see her alive. It had been taken over by the next generation of the Turnbull family, and moved on to social media in the early 2000s. Birch recalled her mother saying to her during her own teenage years that if she stayed out after her curfew, or walked places on her own at night, she'd end up like that Christine Turnbull lassie. It was one of those cases: everyone in Scotland had heard of Christine Turnbull. A girl with a life so ordinary, you could have been forgiven for calling it boring. No tragic past, no violent boyfriends or exes, no money to speak of, no reason to disappear. There were even online message boards that posited alien abduction theories. Birch rolled her eyes at such things, but she could see why they existed: it was as though Turnbull had literally taken flight, leaving not a single clue behind her. And the whole time, Birch thought, she'd been in that wood, buried standing up, under the trees. For over fifty years, Turnbull had been there in the cold and

damp, as many thousands of slow trains from Glasgow or
Edinburgh rattled by.

Birch rolled through Juniper Green, approaching the City of
Edinburgh Bypass, her least favourite road in the world. Darkness
was falling now, and the streetlights were on. As she passed, Birch
caught glimpses into the living rooms of the sandstone villas on
Lanark Road. She spotted big TVs, fringed lamps, a white cat on
a windowsill waiting to be let in. The world seems cosy and safe,
she thought, if you don't scratch the surface. If you don't stop to
think about how easy it is for one person to prey on another. How
easy it still is, even now, to disappear.

As she took the A720 slip road, Birch did the sum in her head.
In 1965, when Christine Turnbull vanished, George MacDonald
would have been twenty-nine years old. She recalled the photograph Amy had shown her of MacDonald aged forty-five, standing next to his awkward-looking son. He'd been handsome then,
younger-looking than he was. At twenty-nine he'd not been
married long, and his son was only a small child. Christine had
been in the wood the longest: unless he'd had a previous burial
site, then she'd been MacDonald's first victim. Birch could feel
herself frowning. What made a young man who'd just started a
family go out and murder an innocent young woman? She made
a mental note to have Amy check out any connection between
MacDonald and Christine Turnbull. Were they known to each
other? Was Christine his mistress? Or did he want her to be, and
she rebuffed him? Birch's head hurt. Those were only a couple of
possible scenarios. Christine could have been a total stranger. She
could have done or said something to MacDonald in passing that
he took offence to. She could have reminded him of someone. Or
she could just have been a conveniently petite, vulnerable young
woman who was in the wrong place at the wrong time.

The bypass was quiet, and Birch zoomed past Dreghorn,
Fairmilehead, Straiton. The road was almost the same purple-blue
as the evening sky, dotted with pink brake-lights instead of stars.
The Hillend ski slope was a white gash in the grey hillside, lit up
by floodlights. Birch didn't really want to go home, didn't want to

be alone with the circling thoughts of MacDonald, of Phamie, of the women in the woods and the things that must have happened to put them there. But she drove on regardless, merging on to the A1 and then back along Sir Harry Lauder Road. She thought of the deer-like girl she'd seen earlier, at the crossing, and wondered where she was. She thought of that girl's mother, sitting watching TV in a safe-looking living room just like all the ones Birch had driven past that night. She thought of that woman looking at the clock, counting down the minutes till her daughter came back. Waiting for the familiar sound of the key in the lock: the sound of *everything's okay, she's back. She's here.*

Edinburgh Evening News

Victim's mother makes heartfelt plea as more Carstairs bodies are identified

EMMA BLACK   Published 12:33   Share this article
Email   Wednesday 11 September

SIGN UP TO OUR DAILY NEWSLETTER

The mother of murdered teenager Maisie Kerr made an impassioned statement to members of the public today, as Police Scotland named more victims in the Carstairs serial killer case.

Hazel Kerr, 60, of Carstairs Junction, spoke to reporters at her home this morning, making a heartfelt plea for information relating to her daughter's case.

'My daughter was not perfect,' she said, fighting tears, 'but I still love her so much, and miss her every day. If anyone saw her before she disappeared, or if anyone knows anything about what happened to her that day, then I'm begging you, please come forward and tell someone. Tell the police. Help me find justice for my little girl.'

Police Scotland revealed today that a total of six bodies have been unearthed from the makeshift burial site in woodland near Carstairs Station. Three bodies were identified previously as Suzie Hay, Christine Turnbull and Maisie Kerr.

Today, a further two women were identified. They are Marta Zajac, who disappeared in 1992 at the age of 25, and Fiona Mandel, who is believed to have disappeared some time in the 1970s, when she would have been in her mid to late twenties. Uncertainty over the date of Mandel's disappearance is down to the fact that she was never reported missing, having been estranged from her family for some years. Police have also not been able to connect Zajac to a missing persons report: according to one source, her Scottish neighbours believed Zajac had moved home to her native Poland.

The identity of the sixth body is likely to be released in the coming days. Meanwhile, forensic excavation and examination of the site looks set to continue for the rest of this week. Carstairs Station remains closed to the public, and rail passengers can expect ongoing disruption in and around the area.

28

Birch sat in the passenger seat of McLeod's recently valeted Vauxhall Insignia. It *had* to have been recently valeted, she reasoned, because there was no way the inside of someone's car was ever just this clean. She flipped through the crime scene photos on the iPad in her lap, trying to find her wonky scan of the map with the red pen marks. The rain had returned, and smattered on the car roof. McLeod was parked at the very bottom of the run-on layby: the car faced the tracks and the dark smudge of the woods beyond. Every so often he flipped on the wipers, and the trees came into sharp focus before disappearing once again behind the wall of rain.

'Here we are, sir,' Birch said, passing the iPad over to him.

McLeod leaned it against the steering wheel. 'Each of these marks is a proposed excavation site?'

'Yes, sir.'

McLeod pinched at the screen to zoom in. 'There are a lot,' he observed.

Birch nodded, deciding to ignore the edge in McLeod's voice. 'We can walk down and take a look, if you'd like,' she said, 'but I assumed, with the weather . . .'

'Perhaps not,' McLeod agreed. 'This is really a lot of digging, Birch.'

She winced. 'I'm afraid it turns out that there are a lot of flag-stones around a railway.'

McLeod swiped backward through the photos: he'd seen her scan of the tip-off note among them, and he paused at it now. 'This could turn out to be an extremely costly hoax, Birch.'

She nodded, as he pointed at the screen, his finger hovering over the signature. *George.*

'I know, sir. I promise, I'm very aware of that. But as I explained, the letter arrived before the public appeal went out. I wouldn't be giving it as much credence as I am, if not for that.'

'The team are working on tracing it?'

'Yes, sir. I've got Amy Kato on it. I'm hoping she can tell us which sorting office it went through, if not the specific postbox it was mailed at.'

McLeod made a face: he never wasted an opportunity to remind Birch that he wasn't keen on Amy. Birch stared out at the woods, and pretended she hadn't seen.

'Okay,' McLeod said, after a pause. 'I'll sign off on these excavations, but I can't give you long. I'm getting some real pushback from the rail companies. We can't keep this stretch of line closed indefinitely.'

Birch raised an eyebrow. 'People are complaining? Isn't there a diversion in place?'

'Yes, but if you live in Carluke and work in Edinburgh, I'll admit that I can see how annoying it might be to have to get the train to Glasgow Central, walk to Glasgow Queen Street, and then get on *another* train to Edinburgh Waverley, just to get to work in the morning.' McLeod swished the car's wipers and pointed vaguely westwards to illustrate his point. 'Carluke is only over there.'

'I know what you mean. But surely the public can understand . . .'

McLeod let out a short laugh. 'You're giving *the public* far too much credit, Birch. Apparently, there are individuals out there who genuinely would have preferred our murder victims stay missing, given that finding them means disruption to their morning commute.'

Birch huffed air. She could think of nothing to say, but the image of Maisie Kerr's soil-stained belongings, laid out on an evidence table, flashed through her mind.

'And it's getting to fever pitch, apparently,' McLeod said. 'ScotRail are reporting an unmanageable spike in complaints through their website and social media. People *really* want to be able to get to Carstairs Station. Who knew?'

Birch watched him flip back through the photos to the crime scene map. Anger flared in her like a lit fuse. 'An elderly woman is missing,' she said. 'Phamie MacDonald is in her eighties, sir. Our prime suspect is her husband. We know he threatened her life in the past. I'm very worried that this note is his way of telling us that he's killed her, and where she is buried.'

McLeod didn't look up.

'In fact,' Birch went on, 'Given the testimony of Mary McPherson, I don't really know what else the note could be.'

He sniffed. 'Apart from a hoax,' he said, landing heavily on the word, the *x* of it hard in his teeth. 'You and I both know Mary McPherson's testimony isn't fully credible.'

McLeod always liked to be right, she knew that about him. Everyone knew it.

'I'm giving you till Friday to get these excavations done,' he said, pointing to the line of pen drawn nearest to the railway tracks. 'Then over the weekend, we need to get the woodlands sealed up. I want the crime scene site reduced to just these buildings, and you only have until Friday.' He pointed at her cluster of red biro circles. 'The siding is easy to manage: we'll keep the public out, and redirect all access in and out of the crime scene to the other side of the railway. That means there should be no more need for access to the tracks or the track-side. I've said to the railway people that they can start running services again first thing on Monday.'

'But sir,' Birch said, 'we don't know if we're *done* in the woods yet.'

McLeod handed the iPad back to her. 'You'll have to be,' he said. 'That's the timeframe we're looking at. We need to get those trains running, and we could do with pulling some personnel back to their regular duties, too. I've already agreed it, Birch. This is what you're working with now.'

Birch looked down at the map, the red circles. She could feel McLeod watching her.

'Ground-penetrating radar was a good call,' he said. He'd knocked some of the edge out of his voice. 'Your hunches have all been right up till now – you've done some fine police work. But this letter could well turn out to be a wild-goose chase, and I can't allow public opinion to turn any further against us with this case. After all, we've got nothing to go on in relation to apprehending George MacDonald, the bastard seems to have disappeared. So we need someone to come forward with a lead. This is not a time to be alienating people.'

Birch shrugged. He was probably right about that.

'It was never going to be a good look for us,' McLeod went on. 'After all, we've allowed someone to kill at least six times, and get away with it for decades. I mean, the man hours that have been poured into Christine Turnbull alone. Entire officers' careers were spent working that case, Birch. Never so much as a sniff that this might be where she'd ended up. It's embarrassing. We failed these women, fundamentally. The police failed them.'

'We did,' Birch said. 'We have.'

'And the families will be in the press,' he said, 'you just mark my words. There'll be a lot of accusations thrown around. Why did no one investigate x? Why was y ignored? If only the police had done such-and-such, etcetera.'

'Hindsight is twenty-twenty, and all that,' Birch said.

'Yes,' McLeod replied, 'but *all that* is coming, whether we like it or not. We're going to have to answer for the mistakes of our predecessors, come what may. So I really don't want us sliding any further down the slippery pole of public opinion, if you don't mind. We need to get this railway line back open.'

Birch looked down at her map. Each red line was a challenge, a taunt. 'Okay,' she said. She put her finger over the long line of flagstones that skirted the edge of the railway track. 'We'll break ground here, this afternoon, and focus on this section, so we can get it closed up again by Friday. But sir, if we find another body there, then forensics may need longer.'

McLeod shook his head, just slightly. 'I honestly think there'll be nothing under those flags but dirt and railway detritus,' he said. 'I just don't like this letter, there's something about it that's not quite right.'

Birch bit her lip. 'Understood, sir,' she said. 'But we do still have at least one missing woman unaccounted for. We need to find Phamie MacDonald: whether she's dead or alive, we need to know where she is and where she's been. And I've got officers back at the station looking into other historic missing person cases involving young women. We don't know how many times MacDonald might have struck. He was at it for decades, after all.'

'Yes,' McLeod cut in, 'and *that's* a PR problem for us, too. Every family in Scotland who's waiting for the outcome of a missing person case is going to be phoning us up, asking us to investigate a possible link. They've already started. You know yourself, Birch. You remember what it's like to have a loved one missing. Anything that might connect, and they're all over it. This case is in danger of getting completely out of hand.'

Birch was silent. He was right: had Charlie still been missing, she'd also have been wondering if perhaps MacDonald were responsible – even though Charlie was completely outside the young, female and vulnerable pattern they'd established for his victims. Yes, she remembered that feeling, that strange excitement: *what if this is the lead we've waited for?* McLeod knew her only too well: she'd have been the first on the phone, asking for Charlie's file to be reopened.

McLeod leaned over to look at the map again. Birch's finger still rested on the line of red pen beside the tracks.

'You have until Friday,' he said, 'and then the weekend is for clean-up. It's Wednesday now, so I suggest you get everyone mustered and get digging.'

Birch looked out at the rain, running in fat streaks down the windscreen. 'Yes, sir,' she replied.

29

Amy hadn't slept well, once again. She'd woken in the middle of the night feeling too hot, but hadn't wanted to get up and open the window. She'd dreamed that an impossibly lithe man – who she knew with certainty was George MacDonald – had scaled the front of her tenement and got in through that very same window. He'd stood in her hallway, in the dream, blocking the flat's only exit. His face had been indistinct, but she knew it was him. He was old, but tall, fast-moving, and his hands were huge. She'd woken to her own heart stuttering in her chest.

Robert has gone, Phamie wrote. Amy's hands shook as she read, the bedside light turned on to shine away the dream, the sky outside still pitch black.

> *I didn't want it to be true, but it's true. It's happened. My baby has gone, and he might never come back to me. My only son. He finally had enough of being in this house, of being with George and his moods. He's taken his father's money and he's run away. It's revenge, I know it is, and I feel like I let it happen. I don't blame him, not at all. In fact, now it's happened, I'm amazed it didn't come sooner. Of course he wanted to punish George, to make him pay for all the times he's held Robert back, tried to keep him small – tried to keep him on a short leash, the way he likes me to be. No, I only blame myself. I should have done something. I tried to protect my boy and I didn't do enough. I probably deserve this. That's what George would say, and he's right. I didn't deserve Robert. I don't deserve anything good.*

Amy felt a tear run down her face, then another. She turned the page, but the following leaves were blank. The rest of the book – the third and final diary – was empty. Phamie had stopped writing, and presumably never begun again. The day her son had left was the day she'd given up hope.

The morning felt too bright, the sky a matte white, spitting rain. Amy hadn't slept again after that: she was too upset by the final diary entry, and too afraid of her bad dream repeating itself. The morning had been a slog of reading emails, reading documents, ticking things off lists. Her tired eyes were sick of looking at screens. At lunchtime, she'd left the station and walked through Inverleith Park towards Stockbridge, a thing she rarely did, though the shops and cafés were only five minutes away. She stopped beside the boating pond, where an elderly woman was feeding the ducks and swans with seeds from a plastic bag. Overhead, seagulls swooped and yelled. Amy picked a bench, sat down and decided she needed to get to the bottom of this case, the reason it was affecting her so much. Was it because thinking of Phamie made her think of her Granny Kato, a woman she'd seen very little of as a child but loved fiercely? She watched the cygnets – nearly swans now, really, almost free of their dirty grey plumage – dip their heads under the smooth water of the pond, then surface again. Granny Kato had died in Japan: it was too costly for their little family to fly back, at the time. Her father had travelled there alone, and planted a full-moon maple for his mother. Amy thought about the seed pods that might now be falling on her grandmother: Amy's Scottish mother called them helicopters, for the way they whirled in the air before they hit the ground. The old lady beside the pond was out of seed, and stood back to watch as the ducks snuffled up the last of their food. Amy frowned. Had she switched Phamie MacDonald for Granny Kato, in her head? Was that why George MacDonald was haunting her?

She walked back to the station slowly, chewing over the idea. She thought of DI Birch and the team, imagined them levering up flagstones in the railway yard, stacking them to one side like dominoes while they dug underneath. Amy both did and did not want to get the call to say they'd found remains. She wanted to believe Phamie was still alive. It was still possible: less than two weeks had passed since Robertson Bennet first reported his parents missing. It was only forty-eight hours since the public appeal into the MacDonalds' whereabouts had gone live. Phamie might still see herself on the news and call Crimestoppers to say, *I'm okay, it's fine.* But realistically, Amy knew there was more chance that Phamie was somewhere in that railway yard. George MacDonald had kept up his life for nearly fifty years after Christine Turnbull. He'd been questioned, as Ginger Mack, in relation to Maisie Kerr, and hadn't gone to ground. Something must have happened to make him disappear. Something different. Something – Amy was sure – that involved his wife. And hadn't she said to DI Birch only two days ago that a part of her hoped Phamie was dead? Thinking about it made her head hurt, made her chest hurt, made her want to cry.

Back at the station, she stood over her desk in the bullpen, watching the photos on her screensaver play through. She hadn't changed her PC set-up for years, so the photos had become like background noise she barely noticed any more. Now, she realised one of them was a photo of her father, standing next to that newly planted full-moon maple. The tree was around shoulder-height: its thin, whippy trunk still wrapped in white felt. Her father leaned on a spade and grinned out of the picture, though he was standing in a cemetery and the sky above was low and bowed with coming rain. She couldn't help but smile back, before the photo faded into another: a picture of Amy herself, shiny-faced, holding up a medal from a 10k she'd run. If a camera came out, everyone in her family grinned: it was just one of their unspoken rules.

She couldn't face sitting down at that computer again. There were people she had questions for, and though email would be quicker, Amy found herself turning away from the desk again, and heading off to look for her colleagues in person.

She tried Marcello first. As always, she heard him before she saw him: his loud laugh filtered out into the corridor, making her smile. Marcello was one of the geek squad: criminal intelligence, profiling, cyber-crime. They were all housed on the same floor, moved around the building together like a pack, and used terms that Amy often had to surreptitiously Google. There wasn't much these guys didn't know, and they seemed to have elected Marcello as their de facto leader.

He was on the phone when Amy appeared in the doorway, but as soon as he spotted her, he raised one hand and waved a flappy hand.

'You've come to see *me*?' He put down the phone and pressed both hands to his chest, as though her seeking him out were some great honour.

'I have,' Amy replied, still smiling.

'Well, good!' Marcello scooted backward in his office chair, and retrieved another, identical one from a neighbouring desk. He dragged it over to her, and gestured for her to sit. 'Because I have a few things I can tell you.'

Amy settled into the chair and leaned forward, ready to listen.

'Now then,' Marcello said. He rummaged among the papers on his desk, before pulling out a document she recognised: a photo-copy of the tip-off note. *Look under the flagstones. George.*

'It does not take a genius,' he said, 'or even a handwriting analyst, to know that this letter was written by an older person. The tremor you see here' – Marcello pointed at the weird, waver-ing straight line above the signature – 'is not faked. This is hand-writing that fits with a person of eighty-three, George MacDonald's age. I can't tell you much else from the writing, except that the person is right-handed. However, I did find something else.'

Amy tilted her head as Marcello looked up at his monitor and began to scroll through files. He opened up an image, which Amy recognised as a fingerprint: smudged, but discernible, blown up to fill the screen.

'Only a partial,' Marcello said, 'but we found it about here.'

He pointed to a spot on the photocopied letter, and Amy fancied she could see something in the place he indicated, though of course she could not.

'I ruled out prints from John and Klara downstairs,' Marcello went on. 'They both touched the letter before they knew what it was, but this partial doesn't belong to either of them. I ran it against the fingerprints we have on file for Ginger Mack, George MacDonald's alias. He gave fingerprints at Gayfield Square many years ago, when he was brought in for trespassing.'

Amy looked up from the letter. 'And?'

'This partial isn't a match,' Marcello said. 'Which doesn't mean that Ginger George wasn't the person who wrote the letter. It just means he was careful, because there's no sign of his prints on the paper. But he might not have been the only person who touched it.'

Amy raised an eyebrow. 'I assume you've . . .'

'Checked against Phamie's fingerprints? We have. We got plenty of hers off the diaries you gave us, clear as day. This partial isn't hers. So, having exhausted the obvious options, I ran it through the database. No matches. Whoever it belongs to has had a nice, quiet life.' Marcello was grinning. 'Never been arrested, anyway, or had cause to be fingerprinted.'

Amy was nodding, looking at the smudgy image on the screen. 'So it wasn't Phamie,' she said. She didn't know why it would be, but she realised she'd been hoping for something.

Marcello shook his head. 'Honestly,' he said, 'it could just be the person who sold this letter-writing paper, handing it over in the shop. It could be the letter was left lying somewhere, and someone moved it or touched it. Or, of course, it could also be the case that someone wrote it who *isn't* George MacDonald.'

'It could be that it's a hoax,' Amy said.

'Yes,' Marcello replied. 'That's a possibility. A hoax, but written by an elderly person.'

'Do you buy that?'

Marcello fixed Amy with a look. 'There are bad apples in any age group,' he said. His voice was serious, but he winked.

Amy tried to smile back. The idea of the letter being faked made her queasy: she thought again of DI Birch, the team at Carstairs, their hurry to excavate as much as they could before McLeod's deadline. Instinctively, Amy touched her hip, where her phone nestled in her pocket. Birch might have texted her an update. But she tried to keep her attention focused on Marcello.

'We're going to keep working on it,' he was saying. 'I also looked at the envelope, briefly, before it went to the lab. There was a piece of cloth fibre, attached to the adhesive where the envelope had been sealed. They might be able to tell you more, if you head down there.'

Amy straightened up. The letter could still be genuine. 'Thanks, Marcello,' she said. 'What else can you report?'

Once again, Marcello began scrolling through files on his screen. 'Well,' he said. 'We obtained a warrant to access some of George MacDonald's personal details, as you know. I've been able to see his recent banking history. Or rather . . .' He settled on a file icon, and clicked it open. 'There is none. George MacDonald hasn't made a transaction of any kind in four years.'

Amy frowned, and leaned forward to look at the monitor.

'You see.' Marcello hovered his cursor over the final transaction on an internet banking screenshot. 'He made a series of withdrawals, from the cash machines at the bank at Morningside Station. Three hundred pounds per day, which must have been his cash machine withdrawal limit. He did this for two weeks, which means by the end of that time, assuming he didn't spend any of the cash, he'd have amassed over four thousand pounds. Then, it's as if he just disappeared off the grid.'

Amy could feel her frown deepen. 'Why didn't he go into the branch,' she said, 'if he wanted that much? He could have withdrawn it all at once.' She felt a shiver go through her. Four years fitted with the rough timeline they'd been working from for Phamie MacDonald's disappearance. 'Unless he was scared,' she said quietly. 'Unless he'd done something that meant he didn't want to draw attention to himself.'

Marcello looked unperturbed. He was still staring at the numbers on the screen. 'Could be,' he said. 'But it's odd, no, that he's never resurfaced? Not a single transaction: he's never bought anything, never withdrawn any more. His pension has been coming in, piling up. But it's never been touched. Four thousand pounds in cash can't keep you going that long.'

Amy felt cold. 'It might be enough to get away, though,' she said. 'Say you'd murdered your wife. If you wanted to get out of the country, disappear . . .'

Marcello shrugged. 'I can't pretend to know,' he said, 'what goes on in the criminal mind.'

Amy allowed herself to laugh at this: Marcello was a pretty good profiler.

'No, seriously,' he went on. 'You're right. That might be what we're looking at, a deliberate disappearance.'

'No other bank accounts we know of?' Amy asked. 'What about in Ginger Mack's name?'

'We're still looking,' Marcello said. 'The warrant – it was easier to check out MacDonald's stuff first. But I'm on it.'

'You'll let me know—'

'If the smallest thing comes up,' Marcello said, 'you will be my first phone call.' He winked at her again. 'Promise,' he added.

Amy was aware of someone standing at her shoulder, and she turned. It was one of Marcello's colleagues whose name she knew but couldn't recall. He was holding a canteen coffee cup, and looking at her.

'I'm sorry,' he said, 'but I think you're in my seat.'

Amy flinched up out of the chair, and allowed the other officer to wheel it away.

'Sorry,' she said. 'And thanks, Marcello. I'll let you know if there's anything new at my end, too.'

Marcello threw her a salute, and his trademark grin. 'Always a pleasure,' he said.

As Marcello had suggested, Amy headed in the direction of the lab. Tish Bland was there, along with some of her team, though the place was quiet. Fingers tapped on keyboards, and occasionally someone coughed. The lab felt peaceful, compared to the rumble of the bullpen with its constantly ringing phones.

'Hello, DC Kato,' Bland said, as Amy approached.

'Hello,' Amy said. 'I hope you don't mind me coming down in person?'

Bland smiled, and gestured vaguely around her. 'As you see, we're not exactly rushed off our feet,' she said. 'We're sort of waiting to hear if any more of us are going to be needed out at Carstairs. I assume you're not here to give us an update?'

Amy shook her head.

'Hmm. I don't know how to feel about it,' Bland went on. 'Obviously, dead bodies aren't good – we don't want any more of them, ideally. But at the same time, if that letter turns out to be a fake . . .'

'I know,' Amy said, 'I've been feeling conflicted myself. There's Phamie MacDonald, too. If we find her body, we'll have found her. I know that's a daft thing to say, but . . .'

'Not at all,' Bland said. 'If we find her, we'll have done our jobs. Closure.'

Our jobs ought to be about keeping people alive, Amy thought, but she nodded. 'Yes,' she said. 'Closure.'

Bland seemed to have a thought, and then shook her head a little to clear it away. 'Anyway,' she said. 'I suspect you may have come to see me about the envelope?'

'I have,' Amy said. 'I've just been to speak to Marcello. He said there was a cloth fibre?'

'Stuck against the adhesive strip,' Bland said, 'yes. A rather coarse fibre, grey in colour. To the naked eye it looked like it might have been animal hair, a dog hair or something. But it's actually sheep's wool, and it's been processed and dyed. I suspect it's from a glove, simply because of the lack of fingerprints on the letter. I'd guess that our writer handled the paper and envelope with wool gloves on.'

Amy nodded. 'That would fit,' she said.

'However,' Bland said, 'it could also be from a jumper or cardigan. It's hard to say with certainty, beyond the fact that it's from clothing.'

'Okay.' Amy tried not to look disappointed. She'd hoped, when Marcello suggested she follow up with the lab, that the fibre might have yielded something more exciting.

'But here's a thing,' Bland said. 'We've lifted DNA from the envelope.'

Amy blinked. 'You have?'

'Yes. Someone licked it, to seal it up.'

Amy felt a kick of excitement, but Bland was frowning.

'I'm afraid it plays into my fears that this letter is a hoax,' she said. 'The DNA doesn't match anything from the database. It doesn't match what we lifted from Phamie's diaries, and it doesn't match the hair from Maisie Kerr's locket, either, so it's not George MacDonald's. In fact, all we know is it belongs to a woman. Not what we were expecting.'

Amy remembered what she'd thought when Marcello had shown her the partial fingerprint. 'And it definitely isn't Phamie's DNA?' she asked. 'I know you couldn't get much off the diaries. DI Birch is sure that if Phamie's alive, then she and George are together. There's no way he could have got her to lick the envelope?'

Amy felt her face flush. She knew Tish Bland wouldn't have ruled Phamie out if the science hadn't been certain. She was too close to this case, she knew. Too involved. But Bland was looking at her kindly, shaking her head.

'I did think of that,' she said, 'and I wanted to be sure, so I ran this DNA alongside the sample provided to us by Robertson Bennet. As Phamie's biological son, he'd have been a partial match. But there was no match at all. I'm afraid we're looking at an unknown woman. As I said, it doesn't look good for the letter's legitimacy. But it doesn't rule MacDonald out as the sender, either, as he may be in the vicinity of other women. We're kind of still at square one, I'm afraid.'

Amy realised she was nodding repetitively. Her chest was hurting again, like it does when you want to cry, and have to try to stop yourself.

'Anything else?' she asked, after a moment.

'Well,' Bland said, 'nothing you don't already know, really. We've proved beyond reasonable doubt that George MacDonald was the person who buried the six women from the woodland. Traces of DNA came up on those carrier bags, like I'd hoped, and there was more on Maisie Kerr's personal effects. It all matches the hair from the locket, and the hair from the locket is a blood-relative match to Robertson Bennet. George MacDonald is our man, we're now absolutely sure.'

Amy tried to smile. 'You've done a great job, Tish,' she said. 'Your team have worked so hard on this.'

Bland smiled back, but the smile was like Amy's: tight and businesslike. 'Thanks,' she said, 'but we still haven't caught the bastard. I for one won't sleep properly until we have.'

Amy blinked. She considered, just for a moment, telling Bland about her own wakeful nights, the nightmare about MacDonald standing in her hallway, and all the thoughts she'd had just that day about Granny Kato. But no: it would be inappropriate and only waste a smart woman's time. Amy pushed her smile wider.

'I really appreciate the update, Tish. Keep me posted if anything else comes up?'

'You know it,' Bland said, and turned back to her work.

Amy stepped outside. She just needed five minutes, she told herself: she could feel that headache pressing harder now, the bulge of it behind her eyes. Outside, the light was lengthening, and the big trees on the Fettes Avenue side of the building were throwing dark green shadows across the grass. This case was maddening. In many ways, they'd solved it, open and shut: they knew whodunnit, for sure now. They just couldn't *find* him.

'How does an elderly man just vanish into thin air?' Amy said quietly to the car park, the empty smoking shelter. The thought of those cash withdrawals bothered her: four thousand pounds wasn't much, but it would buy you a plane ticket to anywhere in the world. She thought of George MacDonald sunning himself in the garden of some retirement community somewhere, and felt sick. That money could be significant, she thought, it could mean something. She pulled her phone out, and dialled her boss's number.

'Hey, Amy.' On the other end of the phone, DI Birch sounded weary.

'Hello, marm,' Amy said. 'How are things going down there?'

She could practically hear Birch shrug. 'Still nothing,' she said. 'And I'm getting pretty sick of hefting concrete slabs around. You got news to cheer me up with?'

Amy paused, thinking of what Tish Bland had said: *we're kind of still at square one*. But the money and the clothing fibre. Yes, she had something to report.

'Well,' she said, 'it's nothing earth-shattering, but ... listen to this.'

30

Birch clattered in, kicked off her boots and headed straight for the shower. It had been a long day: her limbs were sore from moving stone and rubble, and there was black dirt caked under her nails. She'd lifted as many slabs as anyone there, perhaps more, working with a fervour that she knew was rooted in fear. McLeod *wanted* the letter to be fake, *wanted* her to be wrong, she was certain. Another body was more bad PR, more disruption to the trains, more angry members of the public. He wanted it to come to nothing. But the letter couldn't be ignored.

Birch stood under the warm water, watching as streaks of grey dirt ran into the plug hole. She soaped the sweat from her hair, scrubbed the back of her neck, stayed in the shower until the skin on her fingertips puckered. She was spaced out, thinking about George MacDonald in an endless, blank loop. Eventually, a snarl of hunger pulled her out of the warm grip of the water. She pummelled her hair with a towel, then pulled on a pair of yoga pants she didn't think had ever seen a yoga class, in spite of her good intentions. Anjan had left a plain white T-shirt at her place, and she'd taken to wearing it in bed when he wasn't around. It had smelled of his cologne at first, but now it smelled of nothing really, other than her familiar washing powder. She put the T-shirt on, and stomped down the stairs.

The fridge needed a clean-out: Birch eyed the sprouty garlic, the once-fresh chillies now withered into dry curls. She reached past them, grabbing a pack of Aldi pasta parcels, her old faithful. In the door shelf, there was an open jar of pesto: Birch unscrewed the lid to check for mould, but it looked okay. This would do.

As the pasta cooked, Birch retrieved her laptop and George

MacDonald case file from her bag in the hallway. If she couldn't turn her brain off, she figured, she might as well keep working. There was a lot of stuff she needed to look over: the new details on the letter that Amy had told her about, but also a whole load of information from Crimestoppers. Tip lines were, in many ways, a pain: people loved to call them, thinking they were being helpful, assuming that any small *could have been* or *if I remember rightly* might turn out to be of use. Back in the kitchen, Birch stirred pesto into the hot pan of pasta, and told herself off for being petulant. Sometimes those little off-chances *were* helpful. Sometimes they turned into leads. It just took a lot of time and patience to go through them all, and Birch wasn't feeling patient.

Nevertheless, she carried her bowl of pasta over to the sofa, and sank down to make a start. She spread what physical files she had across the coffee table, and looked over them as she chewed.

Robertson Bennet had sent Amy some more photographs of his father. They were all years old due to the length of time that Bennet had been estranged from his family, and as such weren't desperately useful. They'd released CCTV footage of MacDonald as part of the public appeal, and stills from that footage were also printed out and included in the case file. Birch looked from the family photos to the footage and back, easily recognising the same man in both. MacDonald walked across the Waverley Station concourse in the video, taken perhaps five years ago, making him seventy-eight. He was still tall, and moved quickly for someone of his age. He'd kept himself fit, though he'd begun to walk with a stoop. At the ticket barriers, MacDonald had stopped, just for a moment, and tilted his head up. He could have been looking at the departure boards, but it seemed as though he were staring right at the CCTV camera, looking into the lens. That was the primary still they'd released: MacDonald's face, seemingly staring out at the viewer.

She shivered. It was an uncanny thing, looking at the face of someone you know is a killer. Birch always tried to scrutinise such faces, trying to see whatever it was inside that person that made them do the horrendous things they did. She looked back at

Bennet's family photos. George MacDonald looked pretty normal
– *wholesome*, even: the pictures showed him smiling, slinging his
arm around Phamie, doing regular family things. It was Phamie
who had surprised Birch, when she'd first looked at these photos.
She'd imagined a petite woman, someone pale and fragile-looking
like Mary McPherson, and when the photos came across her desk
she'd taken a moment to examine once again her own preconcep-
tions around women who experienced domestic abuse. Phamie
didn't *look* like a woman you could bully: she was tall, too, perhaps
five foot ten, and in several of the photographs she stood with her
arms folded. Her forearms were thick, doughy, and they looked
strong. Robertson Bennet had inherited his solid build from both
of his parents.

Birch looked again at Phamie. She could see now, having
corrected her prior assumptions, that Phamie's was a defensive
stance. When George MacDonald draped his arm over his wife's
shoulders, it looked proprietary: Birch realised it was Phamie's
folded arms that completed the effect. She wasn't responding,
rather she was making herself compact, tidy. Her husband's touch
was something she protected herself from.

Birch felt such sympathy for the woman in the photographs.
Phamie had spent most of her adult life putting up with her
husband's actions: from what Amy had said about her diaries, the
abuse had been almost constant. As recently as 2013, MacDonald
had hospitalised his wife. And now, after all that time, she was
missing. What had happened? Birch remembered back to Bennet
saying his father was a little obsessed with his mother. Was that
why she'd escaped the fate of his other female victims for so long?
Was it easier to get away with murdering a stranger? Or was it
just easier to do? Birch imagined that, in his own weird way,
MacDonald *had* loved Phamie. She remembered her own mother
talking about her father: a man whose violence and alcoholism
were part of Birch's own childhood memories, and a big part of
the reason why she still hadn't been able to pick up the phone and
dial his number. *He loved me*, her mother used to say, *and he loved
you, too, but it wasn't love like other people love. It was his own version,*

all twisted and malformed. I didn't know how to give it back, I didn't want to.

Birch felt glad, for about the millionth time, that her mother had got out of the relationship, that she'd suffered relatively little in comparison to Phamie. Then she felt angry all over again at her father, the gall of him phoning her as though nothing had ever happened, as though he just wanted to get in touch for a friendly chat. Then her thoughts circled back once again to the case: if MacDonald loved Phamie, what had he done with her? Where *was* she?

She placed her empty bowl on the floor beside the sofa, and pushed the photographs to one side. Now it was time to look at the tip line stuff, and her heart felt heavy. Happily, someone had printed out the details of calls that looked most credible, and gone through with a pink highlighter to show the most pertinent details of those calls. It looked like the work of Amy, and Birch smiled a grateful smile.

Most of the calls were from people who had known or known of the MacDonalds, and who had phoned into the tip line to give information that Birch would class as contextual, rather than particularly useful. The man who owned the house next door to the MacDonald family home in Craigs Park Avenue – the house on the other side from Mary McPherson – had called. Birch read the notes: the man had said that he didn't have much to do with the MacDonalds as he had never liked George. He'd always suspected he was a violent person. For the past few years, this man had run the house as a holiday cottage, and reported that until the MacDonalds had moved out, he'd had occasional reports from people staying in the place that they'd heard raised voices through the walls. Okay, Birch thought. Confirms what we already knew. Thank you, next.

She read the notes from a call that *did* have some new information in it, though it was historical. A woman named Joyce, who'd worked with Phamie at Bruntsfield Post Office, had called in. She, too, said she knew of George's violent tendencies: things Phamie had said to her on odd occasions made her wary of him, and sometimes Phamie had bruises she couldn't really account for. She particularly remembered Phamie asking to be paid in cash, because George wouldn't allow her to have her own bank account. Birch underlined this to pass on to Marcello, who was looking into the MacDonalds' personal information. No point in him searching and searching for Phamie's bank account as this new tip confirmed what Robertson Bennet had told them: his mother didn't have one, George MacDonald wouldn't let her.

As Birch drew blue biro lines under the text, her hand shook slightly, creating a tremor that reminded her of the one in the handwriting from the flagstones letter. Her arm felt weak and shaky from the day's lifting of stones, but she was also angry, once again, on Phamie's behalf. The idea of earning money, but not being allowed to control what happened to it, was horrifying to her. Even Jamieson, for all his faults, hadn't stooped that low with Birch's mother. George had clearly controlled Phamie in every possible way. Birch thought back once again to the various training days she'd done around domestic abuse and coercive relationships. She knew how thoroughly men like George MacDonald were able to make the women around them feel helpless. Birch glanced back at the photo of Phamie standing resolute, arms folded, her smile for the camera slightly forced. Her husband had killed six women – at least six women. Birch knew better now than to wonder why this woman couldn't leave.

She read through the rest of the tip line notes. There was nothing particularly of value, though she drew a small biro star next to a couple of details. Things to flag in the electronic file, for other members of the team to follow up on. As was often the case, a sample of the prank or vexatious calls had also been added to the file, clearly marked *not to be followed up*. These were calls that, had they been genuine, could have provided huge leads in the case – but they'd been discounted as hoaxes. A man had called in pretending to be Robertson Bennet, for example, using Robert MacDonald, Bennet's old name. This man clearly knew that Bennet had gone to live in America, but hadn't realised he was back and assisting – albeit grudgingly, Birch thought – with the investigation. Another man had phoned claiming to be George MacDonald's long-lost brother, a brother no one knew about because of a painful family secret he wouldn't disclose. She read the notes on this call and wondered what these people got out of their fictions and impersonations, but often it was simply a case of greed. Some investigations had financial rewards attached to them, even if this wasn't immediately made public. Rewards were more common where the missing person was a child, but they were known to happen. These callers didn't know the complex bureaucracy that prevented such money from ever being released to a hoaxer, so they thought they'd chance it. That, Birch thought, or there was just some thrill for these people in feeling part of an investigation, even in the tiniest way, that she didn't understand.

She rolled her eyes and began to pack the paper files back into their folder. The light had completely gone from the room now: she was sitting in a stripe of illumination thrown from the kitchen door. Outside her living room window, the orange orb of a streetlight cast its stripes through the venetian blind. She heaved herself out of the chair, accidentally knocking the coffee table, and spilling the files straight back out of their folder again. They swooped out in an arc across the carpet, and Birch swore.

She fumbled the overhead light on, and then bent to gather the papers back together again. As she did so, her gaze happened to catch on a photocopy of the auction paperwork that Abe Ross had given them for the MacDonalds' house. Birch felt her memory jog: she'd forgotten all about that, and hadn't heard anything of it from any of her colleagues. She shoved the folder back on to the table, pushing it safely to the middle, but kept hold of the house papers, and sat down again.

She wasn't really sure what she was looking at, having never bought or sold a house at auction, but Birch tried to recall what little knowledge she'd picked up from buying her first and only house, the one she was sitting in. There was little for her to go on, until she got to the part where the seller's details were entered. *Euphemia MacDonald*, the document read, and gave Phamie's date of birth and address.

Euphemia MacDonald, just her. Just Phamie, no George. Birch frowned, and then wondered why no one in the team – herself included – had followed up on this sooner. Now she remembered it, she recalled how significant it felt that the house had been auctioned, meaning that it sold cheap and fast. Amy had called her earlier that day to tell her that George MacDonald had withdrawn cash in increments before disappearing. That he hadn't gone into the bank, rather gone back to the machines every day for nearly two weeks. She felt goosebumps rise on her arms. Perhaps Amy had been right, on the phone: perhaps George MacDonald had suddenly needed to disappear.

Her mind began to race. Why sell the house in only Phamie's name? Because George wanted to leave no trace of himself? Because he had a criminal record – albeit largely under another name – and didn't want the sale to be hindered? Maybe he just didn't want official people looking into him too closely: solicitors, financial organisations. Maybe there was some other reason, something the police didn't yet know.

Birch leaped up, and went back to the kitchen, where she'd left her phone next to the cooker. She dialled Anjan's number.

'Hello, Helen,' he said, 'this is a welcome interruption.'

'Hey,' Birch said, then paused. 'You're not still working, are you?'

She heard the sound of a photocopier starting up in the background.

'I'm afraid so,' he replied. 'Still at the office.'

Birch was about to tease him when she realised that she was also still working, and indeed, calling him about a work-related thing.

'Me too,' she confessed. 'Working, I mean. Not still at the office. My office is a muddy Lanarkshire siding these days.'

'Did you find anything today?'

She sighed, and heard the sigh buzz in the receiver. 'Nothing,' she said. 'Tomorrow's the last day, then McLeod's saying we need to seal the whole thing up. If Phamie MacDonald *is* buried in that railway yard, tomorrow is my last chance to find her.'

'You'll need a drink tomorrow night, then,' Anjan said, 'no matter what happens. Fancy it? I'll treat you.'

Birch thought for a moment. 'Okay,' she said, 'but we can't go anywhere too posh. I'll have been digging all day, probably, and I'm in enough of a state after today.'

Anjan laughed. 'I bet you look great,' he said, 'and I bet you're doing far too much work and putting all the twenty-something constables to shame.'

Birch grinned, though Anjan couldn't see her. 'You're too kind,' she said, 'and I don't want to keep you if you're working. I had a work-related question myself. A legal question.'

She could *feel* Anjan making a face on the other end of the line: he was extremely careful when talking to her about the legal aspects of active cases. Too careful, Birch grumbled sometimes, though she knew he was right.

'Don't worry,' she said, 'I'll keep it all hypothetical. It's a property thing, anyway, nothing juicy.'

'Well, since you've really sold it to me . . .'

Birch laughed. 'Okay. So, I'm sitting here looking at paperwork for a house auction. The house belonged to a couple, but when it came time to sell it, only one of their names is written anywhere on the paperwork.' She paused, not really sure what her question was.

'And?' Anjan said.

'Well . . . is that legal? For one half of the couple to just not declare themselves?'

'Certainly it's legal. In fact it's pretty common, in cases where only one half of the couple is listed as the homeowner, although they both live in the house. It happens less often now, but it used to be fairly normal for a married couple to live in a house that was legally owned by the husband. The husband would do all the paperwork in the buying of the house, and quite often he'd only put his own name on the deed. Perhaps his wife was very trusting – or very stupid – and gave him permission. Or sometimes, men just didn't think to add their wife's name, or didn't think they needed to, or they decided to be calculating about it in case the relationship didn't work out. It used to happen a lot, and still does. Every firm I've ever worked at has dealt with its fair share of wives caught up in divorces where they realise they've been legally written out of their own home.'

Birch was nodding. 'But it's less common for the wife to be the only person named?'

'Oh yes,' Anjan said. 'Much less common. Though again, it happens, and with greater frequency these days. Women are much more able to buy property on their own now. If they've bought a house and *then* married a man, they're under no obligation to add that man to the house deeds just because they're cohabiting.'

Birch frowned. She realised she didn't know how the MacDonalds had come by their house, but she knew Robertson Bennet had been born there, and therefore they'd lived there for perhaps fifty years. She didn't imagine Phamie had bought the house herself, not back in the sixties. Though she didn't know . . .

'Thanks, Anjan,' she said. 'I know that was a very random query.'

'Have I helped? I thought you were just getting started.'

'No, no,' Birch said. 'You've made me realise I've got some holes in my timeline. I might ask you more about this at some point, but right now I need to be asking . . . someone else.'

Anjan laughed again. 'This is the thing about hypotheticals,' he said. 'You sound terribly mysterious.'

Birch scoffed. 'The mysteries of property law,' she said, 'so intriguing.'

'Hey, some of my colleagues seem to think so. Can't say I agree, but each to their own.'

Birch was smiling. 'I'd like to go for that drink,' she said. 'I miss you. I'm sorry I've been so caught up in this case.'

'No worries,' Anjan said. 'I miss you too, but we're all good. You know me, I just bury myself in my own cases until you resurface.'

'And that,' Birch said, 'is why you're the best.'

'If you say so. I'll text you tomorrow?'

'I'll look forward to it. Don't stay there too much longer, okay?'

Anjan sighed. Birch thought it was meant to sound comic, but it sounded like a real sigh, a sad one. 'I'll do my best,' he said.

After Birch hung up, she went back into the living room and awakened her laptop. She searched for Robertson Bennet's contact details, and found a mobile number. Then she glanced at the time: it was nearly 9 p.m. Not the most appropriate time to call anyone, she thought, but what the hell. It would take five minutes. Besides, if he valued his privacy that much, he could send her to voicemail.

The phone seemed to ring for a long time, and Birch had begun to rehearse in her head the message she'd leave for Bennet. Then, at last, he picked up.

'Hello?'

'Mr Bennet,' Birch said. She knew it was him, simply from his *hello*: his weird mix of Scottish and American accents. 'It's DI Birch here. I do apologise for calling so late.'

On the other end of the phone, she felt his attention sharpen, and she suddenly realised what this looked like. 'Please don't be alarmed,' she said, 'or get too excited. I'm not calling with a lead, I'm afraid. But I am working late on your parents' case, and I have a very quick question for you.'

There was a pause. Yes, she'd got his hopes up, only to dash them immediately. Nice work, Helen, she thought. You'd better hope this doesn't send him into another litigious rage. McLeod is irritated enough with this case as it is.

'Go ahead,' Bennet said.

'Okay. I'm looking at the sale of your parents' house, and I realise . . . there are some gaps in the information here. I wondered if you could tell me when your parents bought their house at Craigs Park Avenue? I know it was before you were born, but I don't suppose you happen to know any of the details? How they came to choose that house, what they paid, etc?'

'I happen to know a fair bit about it,' Bennet replied.

Birch felt herself leaning forward to listen, the biro in her hand. She hadn't expected this.

'They didn't buy the house,' Bennet said. 'It was gifted to them, by my great-great-aunt. Isobel was her name. She owned the

place, though I can't tell you how she came to. She was very
elderly, and had no children of her own, so the house was willed to
my mother anyway. Isobel became too infirm to manage in the
house, so she moved out, and handed it over to my parents. They
were newly married then, I believe. As far as I know they never
handed over money or anything like that. I think the house just
naturally passed into my mother's name when Isobel died, which
can't have been long after. She died around the time I was born.'

Birch looked down at the auction paperwork. Well, she thought,
that explains that.

'Thank you, Mr Bennet,' she said. 'You've told me everything I
need to know. Apologies for disturbing you.'

'No problem,' Bennet said.

Birch ignored his slightly confused tone and ended the call. She
had what she needed, which was an explanation, though it gave
her little more to go on. Except . . . the house belonged only to
Phamie, so George couldn't have sold it without her. She must
have been alive, still, when the auction took place. That moved her
last-seen date a little closer.

She leaned down to make a note on the auction letter photocopy: a reminder to ask Amy to follow up with the auction folk,
the warrant. If they could track down the specific person there
who dealt with the sale, they could maybe find out if George
MacDonald was in evidence or not. Okay, his name didn't need to
be on the paperwork, but it seemed odd for such a controlling
man to simply hand the entire process over to his wife. Surely he'd
been present for meetings, for signings-over of paperwork?
Whoever had dealt with him might have talked to him, might have
been given a sense of why the sale was being done the way it was.
Why so cheaply, with the emphasis on speed of sale.

As Birch scribbled, she noticed the final line of the photocopied
letter: typed in bold print were the words *do not detach from form
381c*. She frowned. The copy Abe Ross gave them was two sheets,
photocopied for the file on to a single piece of paper. She reached
for the folder and flipped through every piece of paper, looking to
see if form 381c – whatever it was – had ended up in the wrong

place thanks to her spilling the whole lot on the floor. But no, there was only this letter.

Birch opened the electronic case file on her laptop, and scrolled through the documents there. There were a couple with ambiguous filenames, which she opened just to check, but neither was a scan of the missing form. She opened up her email client, and typed 'form 381c' into the search bar. When she got no results, she tried '381c' and 'form 381', still to no avail. She picked up her phone once again, and found her text message thread with Amy.

Hey Kato, she wrote, *sorry it's late. I have a quick Q re Abe Ross and the MacDonald house sale if you're still up?*

Birch waited for a moment: sometimes, Amy read texts right away. After a minute or so, the message was still unread, so Birch pocketed the phone and headed back to the kitchen. She filled the kettle and set it to boil. She didn't really want a cup of tea, but her brain was busy, and this was a small, mechanical sort of task she could do while it ran through those same circular thoughts about the case.

The kettle hadn't boiled when her phone pinged: Amy had replied. *Can't believe you go on at Anjan about working late*, she'd written. *But yes, happy to answer if I can . . .*

Birch smiled. *Just a quick one*, she wrote. *Can you remember what paperwork Abe Ross gave you? I'm looking at the case file and there's just a letter here. Is that it?*

That's it, Amy wrote back. *He just dug out what he could find at the time. We need more?*

We might, Birch wrote. *This auction thing is bugging me, think we need to follow up.*

She watched the little ellipsis animation as Amy typed. *Happy to go back and see Mr Ross again*, Amy wrote. *Can get in touch and set up tomorrow.*

Thanks, Kato. Birch thought for a moment, then added, *Let me know when you're going. Unless I'm tied up, I'll come with you. I feel like I've been too much at Carstairs. Need to get a better sense of the rest of the investigation.*

Will do, marm, Amy wrote.

Thanks, Kato. Have a good night.

You too.

Birch poured hot water into her mug, and stood watching the steam rise in a slow curl. The thoughts chased and chased after the same question: what had happened to Phamie MacDonald? What had he *done* with her? Through the kitchen door, Birch could see the case file, still sitting on the coffee table, her laptop open and glowing next to it. She hauled in a deep breath, and carried her tea back through. There was nothing in there, she knew, nothing new to be found. But that wouldn't stop her from looking.

Edinburgh Evening News

Final Carstairs body 'may never be identified', say police

EMMA BLACK   Published 14:12   Share this article
Email   Friday 13 September

Police Scotland made a fresh statement to the public this morning regarding the discovery of human remains near Carstairs Junction, South Lanarkshire.

A total of six bodies have been exhumed from a wooded area between Carstairs and Carluke, with further excavations being made around the area of Carstairs railway station.

In the statement, a police spokesperson revealed that, 'the remains of the sixth victim may never be identified with certainty, due to their extensive decomposition.' However, police did appeal to members of the Scottish Traveller community to come forward with any information they may have regarding the disappearance of a teenager from a Traveller settlement in Craigmillar, Edinburgh, in the mid-1980s. It is possible that the unearthed remains belong to Kayleigh Kelbie, who was reported missing from Niddrie Mains Road in the spring of 1986. However, police have been unable to make a conclusive identification and would not comment further, other than to confirm that the case into Kelbie's disappearance has been reopened.

Additional examination of the area around Carstairs station have turned up no further leads, and it is believed that excavations will come to an end today. This news comes after several days of disruption to rail travel between Glasgow Central and Edinburgh stations. Police have confirmed that travel networks will resume normal service in the area from Monday 16 September.

31

Birch had left the crime scene at 4 p.m. They'd broken all the ground they could: searches had been made in all the areas Birch had marked on her recce three nights before, though they were not as thorough as she would have liked. MacDonald's MO was to bury his victims feet first, meaning any evidence of another gravesite might be compact, easy to miss. But McLeod's word was law, and the deadline had arrived. Birch had tried to avoid the eyes of the officers she passed as she made her way back to her car. They'd worked extremely hard over the past two days, digging, shifting slabs of concrete, staying late, standing in the slick, needling rain. It had all been for nothing: they'd found nothing.

As of Monday, McLeod texted her, *we're declaring the flagstones letter a hoax.*

The words stung. It isn't one, Birch thought, it isn't a hoax. But the voice in her head sounded petulant, and she knew she had no way of proving it. She'd just used up a hell of a lot of police resources digging holes in a disused siding, and found nothing. She knew she was in no position to argue.

Birch tried not to think about Phamie MacDonald as she drove through Friday evening traffic to meet Amy at the MacDonald house – or rather the Ross house, she corrected herself. It was hard to keep Phamie out, though: the photos she'd scrutinised the night before floated in her mind's eye. Phamie, arms folded, flinching away from her husband. In a way, it was a relief to have found nothing in the railway yard: perhaps there really was nothing else in the area. But Birch couldn't shake the idea that Phamie's body might still be there somewhere, that they'd missed her, that now she'd never be found. It made her shiver, though the evening sun was strong, a bright flare in her rear-view mirror.

It was slow going, getting to Morningside: Birch picked the bypass, then regretted it as it slowed to a virtual crawl. By the time she turned right on to the rutted tarmac of Craigs Park Avenue, Amy was already parked and out of her car, standing on the pavement outside the Ross house. She waved, and then stood watching as Birch parallel-parked her Mondeo.

'Stop watching, Kato,' she hissed. 'I always screw it up when someone's watching.' It wasn't the perfect manoeuvre, but Amy didn't seem to notice.

'Evening, marm,' she said, as Birch approached. Then her face fell, and she added, 'I'm really sorry about everything. With the crime scene.'

Birch shrugged. 'It's okay,' she said. 'I mean, it's not okay, because I might just have wasted two days of police time. But we didn't find any more dead bodies, so … swings and roundabouts?'

'Totally,' Amy said. 'And it means Phamie MacDonald might still be alive.'

'Here's hoping,' Birch said, trying to believe it.

Amy jerked her head backward in the direction of the Ross house. 'We're a little bit late,' she said. She'd not said it in a pointed way, but Birch still felt her face flush. 'Shall we?'

'Sorry,' Birch said, as they climbed the few stairs to the front door. 'I took the bypass, because apparently I never learn.'

Amy laughed, and pressed the doorbell. There was a long pause, but then they heard the fumble of a lock, and the door opened.

'Mr Ross,' Amy said, smiling. 'Thank you for agreeing to see us again. This is Detective Inspector Birch.'

Birch extended her hand, and Abe Ross shook it. His handshake was dry, firm.

'Of course,' he said, 'good to meet you. Come in, both of you.'

Birch followed Amy, who knew where she was going. Abe stood outside the living room door, gesturing them in.

The living room was chaotic: the first thing Birch noticed was the huge playpen set up in the middle of the floor. Brightly coloured toys were scattered everywhere: toys inside the playpen, toys on the floor around it, toys stacked up on shelves in the fire-place alcoves. Amy moved a large plushie hippo from the sofa, and they both sat down. Abe perched on the edge of an armchair that was piled with laundry.

'I'm afraid it hasn't got any tidier since you were here last, DC Kato,' he said.

Amy laughed. 'Don't worry,' she said. 'How's Belah doing?'

Abe Ross snorted and rubbed the back of his neck. 'She's been a terror today, to be honest,' he said. 'She's down for her nap right now. Getting into danger nap territory.'

Both women laughed, and Birch wondered if Amy actually knew what this meant. She resolved to ask her later.

'We won't take up much of your time, Mr Ross,' Birch said.

'Abe,' he interrupted. 'Please.'

'Abe,' Birch said. 'Thanks. We just wanted to chat to you a little more about your purchase of this house. Specifically, we're wondering if you could look out some more of the paperwork. We're looking for a document called form 381c.'

Abe raised his eyebrows. 'Well,' he said, 'I have to admit that means nothing to me. 381c?'

'That's the one,' Birch said. 'We reckon you must have it, because it was meant to be attached to the letter you gave Amy last week. I'm not sure myself what it is. I'd just like to see it, to make sure we've gathered all the information we can.'

Abe was nodding. 'How's it going,' he said, 'if I can ask? I guess not well, if you're back here.'

Birch and Amy shared a glance.

'Sorry,' Abe said, 'I didn't mean it like, *not well*, like you're not doing your jobs well. I meant, like ... it's obvious you haven't found the couple yet. The MacDonalds. God, sorry. It's been a long week, I'm not totally with it.'

Birch laughed. 'Don't worry,' she said, 'I think we can both relate to the long week thing.'

She knew he hadn't meant it, but he was right: things were indeed going *not well*. She willed him not to ask any more questions, and it seemed to work.

'So,' he said, leaning forward as though about to stand, 'shall I go and see if I can dig this thing out, then? This form?'

'Just a second,' Birch said. 'I'd like to ask a couple of questions first, if that's okay.'

'Sure.'

Birch flipped open her phone, and opened a new note. She suspected she knew how this would go: it was likely she wouldn't need to write much down.

'First up,' she said, 'did you ever actually meet either of the MacDonalds during the course of the sale?'

Abe shook his head. 'No,' he said, 'it was all done through the firm.'

'Okay. Did you speak to either of them on the phone? Receive any letters or emails from them?'

Again, Abe shook his head.

'Were you ever given any explanation for the house being auctioned?' she asked. 'I don't necessarily mean officially. Did the people at the auction firm ever speculate, even?'

'Oh,' Abe said, 'sure. We were told a couple of times that the owner wanted a quick sale. They never said why, but they said the woman was elderly. I wondered if she was sick, you know? Couldn't manage the house any more.'

Birch nodded. 'And they only ever mentioned a woman? No mention of her husband?'

'No,' Abe replied. 'I've been thinking about this, and I realised I thought at the time that the husband had left. I've been trying to remember why I thought that, if someone had told me her husband had left her. But I can't recall, and now I think I might just have made that up.'

Birch fixed Abe with a stare. 'Left,' she said. 'You thought the husband had *left*, not died?'

He frowned for a moment. 'Yeah,' he said. 'I guess it would have made more sense to assume he'd died, now I think about it. Knowing she was elderly, assuming he must have been, too. But yeah, I had this idea in my head that he'd left her, and she was in a jam. But like I say, that might just have been my own little story I made up. You know how you do.'

Birch nodded, tapping a note into her phone.

'Have you ever received any post for the MacDonalds?' she asked. 'Anything at all? Even junk mail might be useful to know about.'

Abe's shamefaced look returned, and Birch knew what he was going to say.

'We used to get a fair bit, actually,' he said. 'Official-looking envelopes, you know, bills and stuff. But I'm afraid we always posted it back, return to sender. We wrote *no longer at this address* on the envelopes, and after a year or so, they stopped appearing.'

Birch winced inwardly, but said nothing.

'Sorry,' Abe said. 'Had I known this was going to happen, I'd have kept hold of that stuff.'

'It's okay,' Amy said, 'I'd have done the same.'

Thanks, Kato, Birch thought, but she knew her colleague was right. What Abe Ross had done was the right thing to do with rogue mail.

'When you bought the house,' she went on, 'had the MacDonalds left anything behind? Other than the diaries, which you handed over to Robertson Bennet. They're now in our possession. But did you find anything that belonged to them, at any point?'

Abe shook his head once more. 'We found those notebooks when we ripped the old kitchen out,' he said slowly. 'And a few other things – nothing significant though. Things like ... there was an ancient spatula, wedged down the back of a cupboard, covered in dust. We found some kirby grips, you know, the hair slides? A few of those under the lino when we took up the kitchen floor. But apart from those diaries, there was nothing we'd have thought they wanted.'

Birch thought of kirby grips, and remembered the photograph of Phamie, her hair styled into a bun. The look on her face.

'Right,' she said. She'd come up short, unable to think of anything else useful to ask. Abe seemed blank, deeply honest: it was clear he remembered very little, and wasn't hiding anything. 'I think that's it. If you want to have a look for those papers, we can be on our way.'

'Great,' Abe said, levering himself upright. 'It might take a few minutes, as I thought I'd given you all I had. I might have to check the loft. But just make yourselves at home.'

'Oh,' Amy said, and Abe turned back from the doorway to look at her. 'Could I show DI Birch your garden? She has one of her own and it's . . . in need of some TLC. I reckon yours could give her some inspiration.'

Birch felt a spike of annoyance at Amy, but Abe was smiling, nodding.

'Yeah, of course,' he said. 'You know your way through, and the back door's unlocked.'

'Thanks,' Amy said, then turned to Birch, whose face was obviously not as neutral as she'd thought. 'Sorry, marm. We can stay put, if you think it's inappropriate. It's just . . . it's a hell of a garden.'

Birch rolled her eyes at her colleague. 'It's fine,' she said, pushing herself up off the sofa. 'I'm just in a bad mood with myself about the crime scene. Let's have a look.'

As they entered the kitchen at the back of the house, Birch's breath caught in her throat. The room was flooded with dappled green light. Outside, the garden was a gift box of colour. Amy pulled open the back door, and they stepped out. Somewhere, a blackbird was singing. Birch stood on the back doorstep and took in the garden.

'This was Phamie's garden,' Amy said. 'The Rosses didn't do any of this, apparently. It was all Phamie.'

Birch looked around. The garden sloped steeply up from the back of the house, but had been cut into terraces, with stone retaining walls bolstering each one. At the top, fruit bushes and trees drooped low with heavy fruit, green netting slung over them to keep off the birds. On the higher terraces Birch could see canes with beans and sweet pea plants curling around them. Trellis had been attached to every flat surface, crowded with the last of the summer's honeysuckle. There was plenty of greenery she couldn't identify, as her gaze followed the garden's lush cascade. On the bottom terrace, there was a small patio, complete with a round café-style table, and two wire-backed chairs.

Amy was halfway up the stepped path and bent over to examine a flowering plant. Birch was vaguely aware that Amy was speaking, but she couldn't focus on what her colleague was saying. She was staring at the patio, its blue-painted terracotta pots, its scrubbed flagstones.

'Flagstones,' she said aloud. Out of the corner of her eye, she saw Amy jerk upright.

'Sorry, marm?'

'Flagstones,' Birch said again, not taking her eyes off the patio.

Amy followed her gaze. 'Okay . . .' she said.

Birch climbed the first few steps up to the patio, and stood at its edge. 'How old does this patio look to you?' she asked. Amy appeared at her side. Birch didn't need to look at her to know she was frowning.

'Look, marm, I know that . . .'

'Seriously,' Birch said. 'It's not old, right? These stones are pretty clean. There's no moss, no frost damage. You said the Rosses hadn't done anything to this garden?'

'Right, but . . .'

'So, if this patio was laid right before they moved in . . . that would be what? Four years ago. Give or take.'

Amy glanced back towards the house. 'Helen,' she said, quiet but urgent.

Birch spun to face her. 'Come on,' she said. 'Humour me. George MacDonald wanted us to look under the flagstones. We assumed he wanted us to look there because that's where he put Phamie, right?'

'Right . . .'

'So,' Birch said, 'what if we were looking under the wrong flagstones?'

Amy opened her mouth to speak, but then stopped. She looked down at the patio.

'Four years ago,' Birch said, 'MacDonald was seventy-nine. He killed Maisie Kerr when he was sixty-three. What if he no longer had the strength to get a body out to that wood, and bury it among all those roots and rocks? What if the best he could manage was a short trip out to the back garden?'

Amy said nothing. She was still looking down at both of their feet, the flagstones below. 'Okay, marm.' Amy was speaking slowly. 'I'm just going to be the voice of reason for a minute, okay? I'm not saying that theory doesn't make sense, because it does. But I'm just going to be DCI McLeod for a minute.'

'If you must,' Birch said.

'So . . .' Amy risked a look at her boss's face, from under her eyelashes. 'I know how much you want this letter to be genuine. We all want it to be genuine. It's the biggest lead this case has got, so far. But . . . with all due respect, marm, I really don't think that you can go around digging up every stretch of flagstones you see until you find something.'

Birch was quiet for a moment. 'Well,' she said, 'that really was an uncanny McLeod impression.'

Amy shrugged. 'Sorry,' she said. 'But he does usually have a point.'

'Is everything okay?' Abe Ross had appeared at the back door, framed in the doorway. He was looking up at the two of them and frowning.

'Mr Ross,' Birch said, 'I don't suppose you can tell me when this patio was installed?'

The man blinked.

'Sorry,' she went on, 'I'm going to ask you a few questions now which may make me sound like a madwoman, but I promise there is logic behind them.'

'Okay,' Abe said. 'I can't tell you much other than we didn't install it, it pre-dates us moving here. But as I told DC Kato the other day, I think the old couple who lived here were in the process of making the garden more manageable for their old age. I suspect this patio was part of that. I mean, it looks pretty new.'

Birch made a conscious effort not to meet Amy's eye. 'Right, so my second question,' she said, 'is, would you object to my lifting a couple of the flagstones in this patio, if I ensured they were put back exactly as I found them?'

On the edge of her vision, she saw Amy's mouth fall open.

'I mean' – Abe was trying to ride the wave of his own confusion – 'I guess so, but . . .'

'It's possible,' Birch said, 'that something may have been buried under here by . . . the house's previous occupants. We have a time-line that I think roughly matches with the installation of this patio.'

Birch could feel her own pulse racing. She couldn't stop talking now, or Amy might jump in and walk everything back.

'Of course,' she said, 'it may be that I'm wrong, and there's nothing there at all. If that's the case, you'll have my sincere apologies, and, as I say, I'll ensure everything is left as it was.'

She stopped, waiting for his answer. For a moment, there was quiet.

Then Abe Ross shrugged. 'Fine by me,' he said. 'You want to look right now?'

'If that's possible,' Birch said.

Abe nodded. 'Sure.'

'Great.' Birch still couldn't bring herself to look at Amy. 'Do you by any chance have a shovel, or—'

Abe waved up and back, in the direction of the little wooden shed that sat at the top of the garden, among the fruit trees. 'In the shed,' he said. 'Hang on.'

For a moment, he disappeared back into the kitchen.

'Marm,' Amy hissed, 'this is—'

'Here you go.' Abe reappeared at the back door. He brandished a small ring of keys, and gave Birch a nod. When he realised she had understood, he flipped the keys to her with a smooth, under-arm throw.

'Thanks,' Birch said, catching the keyring in both hands. 'We'll be as fast as we can.'

Abe's head flicked to one side: he'd heard something inside the house.

'That's Belah waking up,' he said, 'I'll be back shortly.'

Birch barely heard him: she was already climbing the steps towards the little shed, leaving a stricken Amy on the patio behind her.

The shed lock was scabby with rust, and there was clearly a knack to opening it. By the time Birch had jimmied the door, Amy had shaken herself and begun following her up the garden steps. Birch ignored her, stepping into the small, musty space. Out of the corner of her eye, she saw a spider shudder itself into the safety of the eaves. The shed smelled like compost and creosote and wood shavings. In the back corner, there was an old tea-chest, out of which poked a variety of long-handled garden tools.

'Oh God,' Amy said, still outside the door, 'that's the biggest centipede I've ever seen.'

Birch shivered, but didn't turn: instead, she began lifting items out of the tea-chest and inspecting them in the dull light.

'Please tell me it isn't climbing up my leg, Kato?'

'Oh no, sorry,' Amy replied, 'it ran out from behind the door, and out. Great whiskery thing.'

'Lovely,' Birch said. She tried to lift the items out gingerly, suddenly afraid that one wrong move might dislodge a nest of crawling things.

'Jackpot,' she said, and began to back out of the shed. The instrument she drew out with her was heavy, and she could feel rust flaking off it, sticking to her palms. Once she got out of the shed, she could see it was a long, flat, cast-iron strut. She found herself looking around for the fence it must once have belonged to.

'Hold this,' she said to Amy, and Amy obliged. 'It's a lever.'

Amy opened her mouth to protest, but Birch dived back into the shed. She re-emerged with a shovel, its blade caked with old dirt.

'Right,' she said, looking Amy in the face for the first time since her colleague's DCI McLeod impression had ended. 'Let's do this.'

Amy didn't move. She stood holding the iron bar, fixing Birch with an expression that was hard to read. 'Okay, look,' Amy said. 'If I go along with this, you majorly owe me one, right?'

Birch lifted the shovel, and grinned. 'This is why I keep you around, Kato,' she said. 'You're the only one who humours my hunches.'

Amy rolled her eyes, and set off back down the stepped path. 'Let's just get on with it,' she said, 'before I change my mind.'

Birch followed her, strode to the centre of the patio, and took the slim iron bar from Amy's hands. Amy swapped it for the shovel, which she leaned against the retaining wall while she began to move the little table and chairs.

'You need help with that?' Birch asked.

Amy lifted the table, testing its weight, and shook her head. 'All good, marm,' she said. 'You just get on with the demolition.'

Birch snorted, watching for a moment as her colleague wobbled down the bottom few steps to deposit the table in the flat space beside the back door. Then she looked down, and inserted the end of the iron bar into a crack between two flagstones. She eased it downwards, feeling it scrape against the stone, and then when it was deep enough, she pushed all her weight down through her arms and levered the stone out of its bed. It came up fairly easily: another sign that the patio hadn't been in place long. Underneath, Birch saw woodlice scurrying away, back into the darkness. Sand had been spread over the soil before the flags were laid, and the area below the stone was yellowish and damp.

'Give us a hand, would you, Kato?'

Amy hopped to Birch's side.

'Grab the shovel,' Birch said, 'and slide it in under the stone. I'll take the weight on the bar, and then when I count to three, we'll both lift and see if we can't get it properly out, okay? Move it right.' She nodded vaguely at a spot on the ground. 'We'll start a stack there.'

'A stack? I thought we were just moving one or two.'

'Two's a stack,' Birch said. She could feel sweat starting to prickle around her hairline. 'Right, ready? One, two, three.'

The two women staggered a little as the stone crunched up out of its space, but together they managed to transfer it a few feet to the right, and lower it into the rough spot Birch had pointed out.

'One down,' Birch said.

'And one to go,' Amy replied, her voice firm.

'Fine,' Birch said, 'for now.'

Amy narrowed her eyes, but moved into position, ready to help lift the next flagstone along. Birch repeated the lever and the lift, and the second slab landed on top of the first with a shallow crack.

Amy held out the shovel. Birch realised for the first time that the younger officer was in high heels, and didn't seem to have broken a sweat.

'Okay, marm,' Amy said. 'Do your worst.'

Birch looked down at the space they'd created. It was right in the middle of the patio, about four feet long, and two feet wide. She aimed the blade of the shovel at the middle of the space, and pushed it in.

Amy watched, running a strand of hair between her fingers, as Birch dug. Birch could see her colleague was wincing, as the sandy soil piled up on the otherwise pristine patio next to her feet. The soil came up easily: it was mulchy and full of worms. It felt like a joy to dig, in comparison to the packed, rocky earth at the crime scene.

'Stop!' Amy shouted.

Birch jumped. She realised she'd got into a rhythm, zoned out with each stroke of the spade.

'Stop, I think I saw something.'

Amy bent down, not to the hole Birch had dug, but to the pile of soil she'd made. She pushed her manicured fingers into the soil, and for a moment, seemed to rummage. Birch had begun to frown, wondering what her colleague was playing at. But then Amy drew out a small, pale object. It looked like a wonky sort of stone. Amy put one palm out flat, and laid the object on it. With her other hand, she dusted off the soil, and prodded it this way and that.

'Kato, what—'

'Shit,' Amy hissed. She flinched hard, almost dropping the object. 'Look at this.'

Birch stepped over the hole she'd made, and peered down at the thing in Amy's hand. Amy prodded it again.

'Look,' she said, 'look how it bends. It's articulated. I think it's—'

'A knuckle,' Birch said. The sweat on her face had gone cold, and she felt suddenly sick.

Amy was staring down at the bone in her hand. 'Of course,' she said, 'it could be . . . I don't know, they could have buried a dog out here. It could be—'

'Do dogs have knuckles?' It was cruel, Birch knew, and when Amy looked up at her, her face was pale. 'Okay,' she said, softening her tone, 'you're right. Let me see if I can see anything else, before we get too excited.'

Birch abandoned the shovel, kneeling down next to the hole and peering in. She'd dug about three feet down, so she rolled up the sleeve on her right arm, and reached down into the cavity, where the soil was wet and fragrant.

'Give us a bit of light, would you?'

Birch waited while Amy laid the bone down on the path, and then dusted her hands off to handle her phone. The torch made a little beam of light that darted around the hole whenever Amy moved.

Birch began to crumble earth with her fingertips, moving it this way and that. Once a small pile had accumulated, she pushed both hands in and lifted the soil out with cupped palms. Then she began again, feeling around, trying not to recoil at the touch of a worm.

'Maybe we should take up another slab,' Amy was saying.

But Birch wasn't listening: she felt her thumbnail snag on something hard. 'Bring that light closer in, if you can,' she said. Whatever it was she'd touched was wedged in the wall of soil that the shovel had cut. Birch spat on one filthy thumb, and then rubbed at the hard thing until the soil came away and she could see that this object, too, was white. Her fingernails were barely recovered from digging at the crime scene, but Birch twisted her hand around and tried to pincer the object between the nails of her thumb and index finger. She felt the object shift a little, so she kept pinching, rocking it back and forth as a gap widened around it, a millimetre at a time. Suddenly, the thing came free, and as Birch loosed it from the earth's clasp, another object fell out in its wake, as though the two pieces had been held together precariously until then. Birch scooped both up out of the soil, and brought them into the light. They were both small, not much bigger than a marble, and though they were caked with dirt Birch could see the careful shape of them, the way they locked together. She looked up at Amy, whose eyes were wet.

'Get on the phone, Kato,' Birch said. 'We've just found Phamie MacDonald.'

Edinburgh Evening News

BREAKING: city crime scene could be linked to Carstairs serial murder hunt

BREAKING NEWS TEAM   Published 08:49

Email

Saturday 14 September

Share this article

Live updates

BREAKING NEWS: Police Scotland have set up a crime scene at a house in Morningside, according to reports from local residents.

A large number of forensics officers were seen attending a property in the Craigs Park Road area at approximately 7 p.m. yesterday evening, and uniformed scene guards have closed off public access in and around the affected street. Drone footage released on Twitter shows that crime scene tents have been erected in the back garden of the property, which is a private residence.

Sources close to the ongoing Carstairs investigation report that this new crime scene is linked to that case. Police are continuing their search for a serial murderer after the decomposed remains of six women were unearthed in woodland near the villages of Carstairs and Carstairs Junction, South Lanarkshire.

Police Scotland have yet to make a statement, and the exact purpose of this new crime scene has not been confirmed.

More details here as they come in.

32

Birch stood on the stepped path behind the Ross house, waiting for her first coffee of the day to kick in, and reflecting on her weekend thus far. The night before, she'd stood cupping the two small bones in her palm: she'd watched as Amy clambered to the top of the garden, where the mobile signal was better. She could only half hear what her colleague was saying, so she'd crossed to the path where the knuckle bone was laid, and placed the two other bones down gingerly beside it. Looking at them, she'd tried to see a shape, a pattern. To the untrained eye, the dirty white objects could have been stones, pieces of quartz, the dug-up tubers of some weird plant. She'd stood staring down at them until Amy held the phone away from her face and shouted her name, and Birch had climbed the garden herself, to brief the police dispatcher.

Toni Ross had arrived home from work, and Amy switched into family liaison mode. The Rosses stood with her just inside the open back door, Toni balancing Belah on her hip, while Amy explained to them what procedure the police might follow, what they could expect to have happen. Toni was a compact, athletic woman whose face fell ever deeper into a frown as Amy told the family that they'd have to vacate the house. Birch saw the woman's eyes following the white-suited forensics officers as they moved back and forth through her garden. Belah laughed and played with the beaded necklace her mother was wearing, as Amy explained that they could go to family, or have Police Scotland cover the cost of a hotel for as long as the excavation went on. Birch had felt glad, listening in, that her task was out in the garden, directing the arriving officers as they went about securing the scene, setting things up for the following morning.

Systematically, the slabs of the patio were lifted. It didn't take long: the total area was roughly the size of a large hearth rug. The bones Birch and Amy had found were bagged and recorded, and the shovel and iron bar they'd handled were tagged and taken away. Birch watched as a tent was erected over the hole she'd dug, and another, smaller tent put up on a small patch of lawn at the other side of the path. Once Amy had dispatched the Rosses, the kitchen was commandeered: officers cleared and disinfected every surface, packing the family's jars and utensils into plastic storage boxes. These were moved into the living room, so the kitchen table and worktops could be used to store evidence if necessary. By 9 p.m., the Ross property had been fully prepped for excavation to begin. Birch had watched it all play out, as she paced around the garden on her phone, trying over and over to contact DCI McLeod, without success. The voicemails she left became increasingly terse, but the calls went unreturned.

Eventually, the forensics team declared they'd done as much as they could, and Birch's final task of the night had been to brief the uniformed scene guards who'd keep an eye on the house overnight.

She hadn't wanted to leave. Amy and the forensics team were long gone, but Birch lingered in the street outside the Ross house, looking up at its darkened first-floor windows. The streetlights had come on, and the house looked creepy in their thrown orange light. So this was where Phamie was, she thought. Where she had been all along, unlooked-for. The words from the tip-off letter rang in her head: *look under the flagstones.* It made so much sense now. Birch had sleepwalked back to her car and driven home without paying much attention. She hadn't been long in the house when her phone rang, and she leaped to answer it, hoping it was DCI McLeod at last. But no: the caller ID read *Anjan.* It was only when she'd let it ring out that she realised she had seven unread texts from Anjan, too. She'd forgotten about their plan for drinks, and now it was late and all she wanted to do was sit alone on her sofa and think about Phamie MacDonald. How had she ended up under the patio? The patio – *really*? Birch realised she felt angry, thinking what a cliché that was. What had MacDonald done to her, and why? Was it an accident, one of his usual assaults gone wrong? That would explain the panicked cash withdrawals, the sudden disappearance. But it was Phamie who sold the house. Did that mean it was planned? That he got her to sign off on the sale, and then murdered her once the deal was done?

Birch had texted Anjan back, explaining in as much detail as she could muster what had happened, why she hadn't been in touch. The reply she got managed to be kind, while also suggesting he was still vexed, but she didn't have the headspace for it. Why had George MacDonald sent the note? Why tip the police off, when – if it hadn't been for that letter – they might never have looked at the Ross house? MacDonald had to believe he was somewhere safe, somewhere he couldn't be touched. Somehow, Birch had ended the text conversation with Anjan; somehow, she'd made herself some food and settled in. Those actions were a vague blur behind the endless noise of questions upon questions, theories upon theories that built up in her head. It was only as she was brushing her teeth that Birch had realised she hadn't thought about her father all day, and Charlie barely at all. She'd slouched back downstairs in her pyjamas and dialled 1571, but there were no messages. She felt too tired to care.

Now, she was back at the Ross house, standing beside the stack of displaced slabs, blinking up at the sky. It was one of those typical Edinburgh days where the weather might do anything: a stiff breeze was blowing, and though the clouds above looked dark and threatening, they were moving fast. Every so often there'd be a brief gap and weak sunlight would illuminate the garden, rendering the stark white tents almost too bright to look at. But then the gap would close again, and Birch would squint back heavenward, vigilant against rain.

The forensics officers milled around, chatting, wandering back and forth from the kitchen to the garden. They were waiting for a senior officer: Bland, or McLeod, who Birch had finally reached early that morning.

'I'm at Machrihanish,' McLeod had said, and then, in response to Birch's baffled silence, he'd added, 'it's in darkest fucking Argyll, Birch, it's hard to come by a signal in these parts.'

Birch had apologised for the many calls, and explained the situation.

'Well.' McLeod huffed into the receiver. 'I suppose I'd better set off. It *was* in my calendar, I should say. I'm here for the golf.'

Tish Bland was also away, though her team had reached her the night before. She'd been at a conference in London, and had left immediately, boarding the Caledonian Sleeper from St Pancras just before midnight. She ought to be with them at any moment, and Birch realised she was excited for Bland to arrive. She itched for the excavation to begin: the sooner it did, the sooner some of her questions might find answers.

When Bland turned up, Birch knew it instantly: she felt the forensics officers around her check themselves over slightly, the way she did herself when McLeod walked into a room. She resisted the urge to head into the kitchen and accost Bland while she climbed into her white protective suit. Instead, she positioned herself beside the tented patio, and waited.

'DI Birch,' Bland said, as she climbed the first few steps of the path. 'You're like a bloodhound, you know that?'

Birch laughed, but Bland's mouth was a straight line. This was serious business.

'I'm somewhat briefed,' Bland went on. 'I understand you got a bit gung-ho with a shovel?'

Birch nodded. 'Sorry,' she said. 'It was a sort of *let's just check* situation. Scratching the itch of a hunch, you know? I wasn't sure we'd find anything at all.'

'Well,' Bland said, 'you found the best part of a human thumb, a trapezium and a scaphoid bone.'

Birch frowned.

'Pieces of a wrist,' Bland explained.

Birch let out a long breath. She felt as if she'd been holding that breath all night: this was the first confirmation she'd had that the bones were definitely human.

'We'll get to work,' Bland said. 'I suggest we roughly sort what we excavate here, but make our priority to get everything to the lab. I'm not desperately keen on working out of the family's kitchen, and I'm sure they wouldn't love the idea, either.'

'Absolutely,' Birch said. She glanced at her watch: 9.30 a.m. 'It might be another two hours before DCI McLeod gets here, but the site is fully prepped and you have the all-clear to get started.'

'Great. Let me have a quick look over everything. I'll brief the team in the house in fifteen minutes. You'll be around?'

'Of course,' Birch said. 'I'm waiting until McLeod arrives, at the very least.'

Bland nodded, and turned towards the tent.

'Is there anything I can do to be useful?' Birch asked.

Bland looked back over her shoulder, and after a pause, replied, 'If you wouldn't mind, I'd love a cup of tea.'

McLeod arrived at around midday: Birch heard his voice inside the house before she saw him.

'Why the hell did no one warn me about that bloody road?'

She'd been in the smaller of the two forensic tents, where newly excavated objects were brushed down and bagged before being placed in boxes and moved into the kitchen. She ducked out through the flap as McLeod appeared, outlined by the back door.

Birch had to stifle a laugh. Her boss was dressed in full golf regalia: tartan trousers with an Argyll jumper, crosshatched with purple and blue. He'd been wearing a cap, too, she could tell: his hair was flattened on top.

'Don't look at me like that, Birch,' McLeod said. 'Did you want me to waste time going home to change?'

'Not at all, sir,' Birch said. Stop it, she thought. This is no laughing matter. 'I'm very glad you're here.'

McLeod sniffed. 'Well,' he said, 'that makes one of us. I'd been looking forward to that trip, Birch. Machrihanish is one of the most picturesque courses in the world.'

'I'm sorry, sir.'

'It is what it is,' McLeod replied. 'I just . . . I'm struggling to understand what happened here, frankly. Lead me through the chain of events.'

Birch squared her shoulders slightly. 'The tip-off letter,' she said, 'was genuine. MacDonald really did send it, he really was serious about the flagstones. We were just looking at the wrong flagstones. I was here with DC Kato, following up on some details about the MacDonalds' sale of the house. We happened to look outside, and . . . well, it suddenly seemed obvious.'

McLeod raised an eyebrow. 'You're a lucky woman, Helen,' he said.

Birch thought about the two days she'd just spent scrabbling around in railway debris, completely in vain. 'Not always,' she said. 'But we got there eventually.'

McLeod nodded. 'Still,' he said, 'nothing is set in stone, yet – if you'll pardon the expression. I maintain there's something not right about that letter. We all have our hunches, and that is mine. The other shoe will drop yet, mark my words.'

Birch gritted her teeth. He was like this, she reminded herself. You just had to go with it. 'It is odd, sir,' she said. 'MacDonald must feel very confident, to send a letter like that. He must think he's put himself beyond our reach.'

'No,' McLeod said. 'I mean I'm still not sure that George MacDonald was the author of that note. I'm still not sure it's not some sort of distraction.'

Birch blinked. 'Sir, if I may,' she said, 'we've literally cracked it. We've found the body under the flagstones, just like he said.'

'We've found *a* body,' McLeod corrected her. 'At this point, we still don't know who it once belonged to.' He raised his voice slightly. 'Am I right about that, Dr Bland?'

From inside the excavation tent, Tish Bland's voice could be heard. 'You are, DCI McLeod. But we're working on getting an ID as fast as we can.'

McLeod fixed Birch with a hard look. 'All we know right now is we've found a body in someone's back garden. I've dispatched a team to take the Rosses into custody, as a precautionary measure until we know more.'

'You've *what*?' Birch realised she was being insubordinate just a moment too late.

'You heard me, Helen,' McLeod said. 'If I find a dead person at your house, I'm not just going to operate on the assumption that you had nothing to do with it. This is police work 101.'

Birch thought of Toni Ross's face, the deep frown she'd worn as she'd watched the officers pull up her patio. 'Has a Family Liaison Officer been organised? They have a small baby with them.'

'I called your DC Kato,' McLeod said.

Birch allowed herself to breathe. Amy would be horrified that the Rosses had been taken in, but she would, at least, look after them.

'The Rosses have nothing to do with this,' Birch said, 'I assure you, sir. I interviewed Abe Ross just yesterday. This patio pre-dates their moving here, so the body had to have been—'

'You only have *their* word for that,' McLeod said. 'I'll say this once more. When a body is found on someone's property, that person has to be investigated as a matter of priority. If you're right, then the Rosses will be eliminated from the enquiry and we'll all carry on about our business.'

Birch closed her eyes for a moment. 'Sir,' she said, 'George MacDonald—'

'Let me stop you, Birch.' McLeod's tone was sharp, but not malicious. His face looked a little pained. 'You've been running at ninety miles an hour on this case ever since it was opened. You've overstepped on numerous occasions, and I've looked past it because you seemed to be making progress. But let me just remind you, shall I, of how things have gone thus far. I told you not to get into it: you put Kato on it, and as far as I was concerned, that was it. Then I hear you've been down at Waverley Station, putting ideas in the heads of these lunatic trainspotters. Order disobeyed.'

Birch opened her mouth to speak, but McLeod held up a hand.

'Next, you misused your authority to get information from our colleagues in Lanark,' he said. 'On what I can only describe as a whim, you went on to private property and began an unauthorised excavation. That's not just an order disobeyed, it's a total bypassing of proper channels. You know I'd never have signed off on you digging around in those woods.'

'But sir, I found—'

'Yes, you found the remains. You got lucky. But as you know, you opened a real can of worms for me and others in terms of PR. There are all sorts of questions being thrown around about Christine Turnbull, *and* about Maisie Kerr. Kerr's house is half a mile from that woodland, and we've got journalists demanding to know why we didn't search them at the time.'

Birch's face was burning. 'To be fair' – she could hear the recklessness in her voice – 'that's a reasonable question, when—'

'Birch,' McLeod barked, 'I am not *finished*.'

Birch closed her mouth, but she could feel annoyance rising inside her.

'I told you I was up against it,' he went on, 'but you pushed for more time to excavate, on the grounds of this flagstones letter, and found absolutely nothing. Then I discover you're out here, spending your Friday evening ripping up someone's garden. Again, you didn't go through the proper channels, because again, you knew I'd never sign off on this. You may think it doesn't matter, because you found another nice big can of worms. But it *does* matter, Birch. Procedure is procedure. You have *got* to learn to do as you're told.'

Birch stood for a moment, watching McLeod, checking he was definitely done. Against his ridiculous purple collar, one fat vein stood out in his neck.

'What I've done,' she said quietly, 'is my job. I have investigated the Phamie MacDonald missing person case. And what's more' – she waved towards the tent – 'I've found Phamie MacDonald.'

McLeod passed a hand across his face. Birch realised that most of the forensics officers had carefully positioned themselves in spots around the garden that meant they could listen in. It felt like everyone around her was holding their breath. She felt McLeod notice it, too.

'I've heard enough,' he said. 'Like I said, you've been taking this case at ninety miles an hour, and standards have been allowed to slip. I'm sending you home.'

'Sir—'

'No arguments, Birch.' This time, McLeod held up both hands, and Birch saw how soft and pale his palms were. 'I'm taking over here. I want you to go home and spend a bit of time cooling off, do you understand? Have some down time. Take the rest of the weekend, for God's sakes, and we'll talk again on Monday.'

Birch felt her hands curling into fists, her fingernails digging in. 'Sir, really—'

'I said no arguments,' McLeod said. 'You can claim the day as overtime, as I know you had an early start. But I want you out of this crime scene now. That's an order.'

For a moment, Birch couldn't move. She could feel her face was bright red with anger, with embarrassment, with knowing that a whole load of junior officers had just watched her get thoroughly bollocked. Even Tish Bland had poked her head out of the tent's opening. Birch allowed herself to look at Bland, and saw she was frowning at McLeod. Somehow, Birch opened her mouth, forced her lungs to inflate.

'Yes, sir,' she said, with as much strength as she could muster.

'Thank you, Birch,' McLeod said. 'Like I said, we'll talk again on Monday.'

Birch looked down at her feet, trying to make them move. Mechanically, she picked her way down the steps to the back door of the house. As she passed into the kitchen, she saw on the sideboard an evidence box containing the small bones she'd held in her hand the night before. She could still feel their powdery dryness, the barely there weight of them.

'Drive safe, Helen,' McLeod called after her.

He was already sorry, she knew: he realised he'd overdone it, five minutes too late. She didn't turn around, but walked through the shadowy house and out to her car. At the steering wheel, she considered letting herself swear, or shout, or cry. But instead, she fastened her seatbelt, peeled out of her parking space, and drove home.

33

'I'm just saying, I do see where he's coming from.'

They were sitting in the car park of HMP Low Moss with the engine turned off, Anjan in the passenger seat. They'd argued about the case, and McLeod, for most of the journey. Birch felt crabbit and tired: after she'd left the crime scene, she'd wandered listlessly around her house for most of the day. She'd punched her father's number into the keypad of her phone several times, then hung up without dialling. She realised it wasn't a good idea for her to be alone. When evening came, she'd called Anjan and asked him to come over.

'Please just don't ask me about work,' she'd said. 'Or about my father, if you don't mind.'

Anjan had promised. When he arrived, he'd set her up on the sofa with a bottle of wine, and then disappeared into the kitchen to cook her dinner. Later, as she curled into him in bed, she'd thanked him for being the best man in the whole world. But even as she fell asleep, she knew she'd have to tell him, once the morning came, what had happened with McLeod, and why she was in such a weird, quiet mood. She'd waited until they were in the car, setting off to go and see Charlie. Now, she regretted it.

'Of course you see where he's coming from.' Her tone was weary, rather than snappy. 'Of course you do.'

It was a gloomy, Scottish Sunday: turning off the motorway, Birch had noticed the trees beginning to loosen their first dead leaves into the sift of the rain. She remembered the sound of that same sort of rain on the roof of the forensics tent at Carstairs; thought of the officers slowly lifting Phamie MacDonald's body out of the soil of her own garden. The rain would make things difficult, she knew: the garden's steep slope would sluice water in under the skirts of the tent. The soil would get heavy with moisture. They'd have to work hard. She could imagine McLeod, sheltering in the kitchen while boxes of evidence piled up around him. You ought to be pleased, Helen, she thought. Rather him than you. But the thought was hollow: she was kidding herself.

'Look, I'm sorry,' Anjan was saying. 'I know that was hard for you, hearing that. He was wrong to say it all in front of everyone. I'm sorry that happened, I really am.'

He reached over the gear lever and put one hand on Birch's knee. She thought about flinching it away, but she'd always liked the warm weight of Anjan's hands.

'But we're here now,' Anjan went on, 'and we have important work to do today. I think it's important that we're able to focus on Charlie while we're in there, don't you agree?'

Birch nodded. Underneath her embarrassment and annoyance over McLeod, she also felt a thin seam of guilt: she'd let the case get bigger than Charlie, in spite of what had happened to him. He needed her right now: the internal inquiry into his assault was under way, and he'd been called before the panel, the date only days away. Yet in the last week, she'd thought more about Phamie MacDonald – and more about her worthless father – than she had about her little brother.

'I do agree,' she said, though she still didn't want to look at Anjan. Instead, she looked out across the car park, at the cars of other visitors beginning to arrive, and at the rain. 'You're right. I'm sorry for getting so upset. I'm just . . . this case has really got its teeth into me. I know you understand how that is. It happens sometimes. But I've been neglectful of a lot of things.' She paused. The words were tumbling out, surprising her. 'Like due process, as McLeod says. But I've also neglected Charlie. I've neglected you.' Finally, she made herself turn to look at Anjan. 'And I'm sorry.'

Anjan met her eye, and smiled. He squeezed the knee his hand was resting on. 'You don't have to say sorry, Helen,' he said. 'Not to me.'

Birch smiled back. She reminded herself, for about the thousandth time, that Anjan *got* it. He understood what it was to be married to the job.

Birch unfastened her seatbelt, leaned over and put her arms around him. It was a wonky hug, but she didn't care. 'Thank you,' she said. She breathed in the smell of him, his star anise cologne. She could feel he was still smiling, glad the argument was over.

'Just promise me,' Anjan said, his words fuzzy this close to her ear, 'that you'll never change, okay? That you'll always care about people as much as you do.'

Birch blushed, and kissed him. 'Give over,' she said, unwinding her arms and righting herself in the driver's seat. 'You'll have me forgetting I'm in the professional doghouse at this rate, and McLeod would *not* be happy with that.'

'Forget McLeod for now,' Anjan said. 'Let's go in and talk to your brother. See if we can't sort out some damage limitation.'

Charlie was still in the infirmary, but Birch knew it was only a matter of time before he'd be pitched back out into the push and shove of his hall. As they walked in, she could see he was sitting up, looking stronger than he had been, more upright. His face was still a mess, but it was a different kind of mess than before: the swelling around his eyes had gone down, and now she could see that the whites of them were shot through with blood. His bruises had begun to turn yellow and green, the colours so vivid in places that he looked like he'd been daubed with face-paint. His arm was still hanging in its sling, the plaster-cast around it jutting out from his chest. When she reached the bedside he smiled, and she could see that some of the gaps in his teeth had been filled.

'Pretty smart, eh?' Charlie had seen her looking. He did some kind of trick with his tongue, and the new teeth jiggled out of his mouth. Birch could see the fine wires holding them together.

'Dentures,' Charlie said, lisping slightly as he reinstated the teeth. 'I'm like a fucking geriatric.'

Birch smiled, feeling a lump in her throat. Charlie still looked so battered, so vulnerable, and yet soon he'd pass the medical examination that would put him back into the general prison population. He'd be out there on his own again, having to survive.

'Want me to sign your cast?' Birch said, trying to keep her smile going. 'I brought a Sharpie specially.'

Charlie laughed. 'Lots of love, DI Helen Birch,' he said. 'That'd go down a treat in the hall, wouldn't it? You can draw me a nice big weed leaf, though, if you like.'

Birch rolled her eyes. 'It's like you were put on this earth just to troll me.'

Charlie was grinning, and now she knew they were there, Birch could see the silver fixtures of the denture glinting at his gumline.

'You only just realised,' he said.

Anjan had been speaking quietly with the screw who'd seen them in. Somehow, he'd managed to persuade the man to wait outside the door. Now, he crossed the room, and reached out to shake Charlie's good hand.

'Good to see you, pal,' Charlie said.

Anjan looked him up and down. 'How are you feeling?'

Charlie shrugged. 'Still shite,' he said. 'Every time I wake up it's like I've just crawled out of my own grave. But they tell me I'm mending.'

Birch shook off a shiver: the word *grave* made Phamie cross her mind again.

Anjan was still looking down at her brother, assessing his physical state. 'I'm going to put in for an extension to your time in the infirmary,' he said. 'They're angling to move you out, claiming they need the bed, but even having looked at you just now, I think you need a bit longer to recover.'

Birch threw Anjan a grateful smile.

'In the meantime,' Anjan went on, 'I need you to get ready to go before the enquiry next week. You're going to have to give your testimony to them in person. I've already passed on my understanding of what took place on the night of your attack, so part of what they'll be doing is checking that the stories match. The prison will generate a report on your character and conduct since you were brought here, and of course they'll also prepare testimony relating what happened that night, based on their knowledge of events. But the panel will want to get the measure of you themselves. This will be an important moment in the enquiry: it will be a big factor in whether they decide to be lenient, or strict.'

'Got it,' Charlie said. 'So, what do I do in there?'

Anjan was still standing, Birch having taken the only chair. She thought about offering it to him, but she could see that his brow was slightly creased, that he was focused intently on Charlie. Anjan was in work mode, and she knew better than to interrupt that flow.

'We'll need to lean away from your past misdeeds, as much as we can,' Anjan said. 'The fact that you spent fourteen years doing criminal and often violent things is what goes against us, obviously. They'll be ready to see your actions on the night of the attack as the natural reaction of a man who's become desensitised to violence. A dangerous man, who needs to be in prison.'

Birch saw Charlie wince, and she waited for him to deflect Anjan's words with a smart comeback. She was surprised when all he said was, 'Okay.' He was deferential with Anjan, she remembered: she'd found the only person in the world around whom her brother wasn't sure of himself.

'What we'll do,' Anjan went on, 'is remind them that you were coerced into a life you didn't want, fourteen years ago. That you did what you did because you were afraid of what might happen to you if you walked away. We'll point out that, when you got the chance, you blew the whistle on Solomon Carradice and his gang: you sacrificed your freedom in order to take down the firm. That illustrates that your moral compass remains intact. You are, fundamentally, a good person.'

Charlie grinned. This time, Birch could see, he couldn't resist. 'Damn right,' he said. 'I'm a hero.'

Anjan held up one hand, a *settle down* gesture. 'What we don't want,' he said, 'is for you to get cocky.'

Birch looked at Anjan. His tone was firm but not sharp, and his face wasn't far from a smile.

'Sorry, chief,' Charlie said.

'Humility,' Anjan went on, 'is the way to go. Remorse for your past actions, and humility around your current state. You're a smart man – degree-educated, fluent in Russian, an avid reader. We'll lean on the fact that you've worked hard since you got here, that you've spent a lot of time in the prison library. I'll be pointing out that your primary assailant has nothing like that sort of track record. You're a good man who lashed out in a perfectly understandable way. You've been working to build a life in prison, and they were trying to take that away from you. They targeted you based on your good actions in the Solomon Carradice case, your informant status as part of Operation Citrine. They spread lies about you throughout the prison: they smeared your name. Who wouldn't be angry in that situation? I'm going to paint your reaction that night as a natural one, your actions as understandable, if not pardonable. I'll just need you to back me up. Look and act in accordance with those sentiments.'

Charlie was nodding again. 'I can do that,' he said.

Anjan smiled. 'Good,' he said. 'I trust you, Charlie. I think you'll know how to play things once we're in the room. But I'll come back and brief you some more in the morning, on Monday, before we go in. There might be unexpected questions, and we need to be ready to think on our feet. Just spend a bit of time mulling over what I've said, okay?'

'Sure,' Charlie said. 'I will. Good use of the time, right?'

'Right.' Anjan reached down and placed a hand on Birch's shoulder. He was speaking to both of them. 'I'm going to excuse myself now. I'm going to speak to the warden about all this, and try to get the infirmary stay extended. Helen, I'll meet you down in the lobby when you're done.'

Birch put her own hand on top of Anjan's, feeling his thumb resting against her collarbone. 'Sounds good,' she said.

Anjan bent down and planted a kiss on her head, before pulling his hand away.

'Jesus,' Charlie said, once Anjan had pulled the door closed behind him. 'You two need to get a room.'

Birch rolled her eyes. 'Whatever, you big jerk,' she said. She realised, almost with a start, that she was happy to be here: happy to be in a totally sealed room, away from the outside world and misery of the MacDonald case. She glanced at Charlie's bedside cabinet. 'How're you liking the books I picked for you?'

Charlie followed her gaze. 'Not a bad selection,' he said. 'So far, I've liked *Manhattan Beach* the best. Gotta love a book with gangsters in it.'

Birch screwed up her face: it had been a while since she'd read the book, and she'd forgotten.

Charlie laughed at her. 'Didn't think that one through, did you, Nella?'

'I absolutely did not,' Birch admitted. 'All I remembered was the other storyline. The girl who learns to be a diver, and her dad who goes missing.'

Charlie's face suddenly went serious. He'd thought of something. 'That reminds me,' he said.

Birch closed her eyes. The good feeling she'd just had was gone. 'Let me guess,' she said, 'more messages from Jamieson?'

Charlie was quiet for a moment, and when he did speak, his voice came out softly. Cowed. 'Not messages,' he said. 'I spoke to him. I actually spoke to him.'

It seemed to take a moment for Birch to understand what he'd said. For a second, she had a vision of their father sitting there in the infirmary room, in the same chair she was sitting in now. But no, she thought. No way would they let him visit: Birch was only allowed into the infirmary because she was Charlie's next of kin, and her status as a police officer probably didn't hurt.

'You *what*?'

Charlie was looking down at the bedsheets. 'Look, I know Anjan told me not to,' he said, 'but it was driving me nuts, lying here all day, wondering what the old man wanted to talk about. In the end I spoke to that nurse about it – Rob, I think you met him? Explained that my long-lost Da was trying to contact me – don't worry, I left out the part about hating his guts and me battering him. I pointed out I was losing out on visiting time and I wasn't getting outside, and I wasn't getting library time or phone calls in here, and the least they could do was bring a phone in so I could talk to someone.'

Birch put her head in her hands. 'So you phoned him.'

'Yeah. And to be honest, Nella, I'm a bit fucking shocked that *you* haven't phoned him, seeing as how you've got his number. I honestly thought it would be the first thing you'd do when you walked out of here last time.'

Birch allowed herself to sit like that for a while: elbows on her knees, the palms of her hands pressing into her eye sockets, turning her vision into a swimmy purple dark.

'I've thought about it,' she said at last. 'A lot. I got as far as dialling the number. But I realised I might just yell at him. I might just tell him exactly what I thought of him.'

'And? So what?'

Birch thought for a moment. A realisation came to her, and the feeling was like finally finding the word that's been on the tip of your tongue for days. 'So if I did that,' she said slowly, 'he might never call back again. He might go away again and never reappear. I was worried I might just blow it, for good.' She looked up. There were spots on her vision.

Charlie was nodding. 'I get that,' he said.

'Did *you* yell at him?'

Charlie shrugged. 'Didn't feel like I needed to,' he said. 'But then, I had my chance to show him what I thought of him, didn't I? I guess I got all my aggression out.'

'So what did he say? How did the conversation go?'

'It wasn't long.' Charlie said it as though he were downplaying, worried his sister might be jealous. 'Phone calls never are in this place, you know that. And of course I had Rob and a screw sitting right next to me the whole time. Basically the old man said he's recognising his own mortality. He's realised he might not have all that many years left. Apparently he's been to the GP and had a bollocking about his drinking, about his smoking, all of that. Get this, Nella: he says he's been going to meetings. AA, I mean. He's trying to get sober.'

Birch blinked. She struggled to remember any memory of her father that didn't somehow involve the drink. Another memory from that twelve-year-old day fell into her head: a wine shop. They'd stopped in at a wine shop on the way home. She remembered sitting in the car outside – Paul Simon singing on the stereo – and waiting for what seemed like a very long time.

'He's for real?' she said. Her voice was a flat line: she didn't believe it.

'Who knows?' Charlie said. 'That's what he said, though. That he's turning over a new leaf. Wants to get to know his kids, before he runs out of time.'

Birch sat very still, trying to process this. I'll believe it when I see it, she thought. But the very next thought that followed was, But how will you see it, Helen, if you never call him?

'I think you should do it,' Charlie said. 'I think you'll regret it if you don't.'

Birch swatted a hand at him, though she was nowhere near enough to touch him. 'Stop that,' she said.

'What?'

'That weird reading my thoughts thing. That psychic sibling thing.'

Charlie grinned. 'I'm right, then. You want to.'

Birch rolled her eyes. 'Just stop it, I said. I got used to the privacy of my own head, the fourteen years you were away. I don't appreciate you reappearing and claiming to know everything I'm thinking, thank you very much.'

Charlie was delighted by this. 'Oh, the power,' he said, then threw back his head and let out a pantomime cackle.

Birch let her gaze rest on her brother. He was laughing at her out of his broken face, enjoying as he always had any opportunity to tease her. A feeling struck her, hard: an electric shudder down her neck and then her spine. She realised, for the first time ever, that Charlie was going to be okay without her. That he'd been okay without her all that time he was missing: fourteen whole years doing stupid and dangerous things. He'd survived that, he'd survived this attack, and he'd survive the inquiry, no matter what happened. He'd survive in prison, with his huge arms and tattoos and his fast mouth. He didn't need her – or Anjan for that matter – to tell him whether it was a good idea that he speak to his own father or not. He didn't need anyone. She'd still worry about him – she'd always worry about him – but he didn't *need* her. He was his own daft, impulsive, hot-tempered person.

She almost laughed aloud, amazed that she'd never quite seen this before. In her head, they'd always been a unit, one-third of the Birch family team, until their mother died and made them even halves. Birch realised she'd never stopped thinking of them that way, even when he was missing all that time and the logical part of her brain said he was dead; even as she sat through his trial and heard the horrendous things he'd seen and done. Now, he'd eased the dentures out of place again and was rattling his loose teeth at her like a laughing cartoon skull.

'I love you, you absolute daftie,' she said, and reached into her pocket for the fat black pen she'd been allowed to carry in.

'I love you too, Nella,' Charlie said, flipping his teeth back into place in order to speak. He shoogled the plaster-cast arm under its sling, and Birch uncapped the pen.

'I'm drawing you a love heart, then,' she said, watching his face to see if she could make him believe it. 'And I'm putting Anjan's initials in it. How d'you like that?'

Birch had expected Anjan to be in the lobby by the time she got down there, but he was nowhere to be seen. She retrieved the few belongings she'd left in the locker and then sat down on one of the scratchy, upholstered chairs to wait. She felt a prickle of anxiety: was Anjan struggling to get the prison staff on the same page? She hated the idea of Charlie being put back into general population with his ribs still tender and his arm all strapped up. He'd look like a walking target. And even if no one decided to take advantage of his vulnerability, she had the horrible feeling it would only take one hard jostle in the canteen queue to undo so much of the healing he'd done in the infirmary. She tried to remind herself that Anjan was a master of persuasion – and he was a stickler, too. No

doubt he's just making sure every t is crossed, she told herself. No
doubt he's got it all under control.

Birch wasn't convinced. She patted herself down for the phone
she'd just pulled out of the locker, and opened it up, hoping to
find something to distract her. It worked: she had five missed calls
from *Amy Kato Mobile*.

Birch glanced up at the reception desk. Taped to the wall above
it was a printed-out sign that read: *Please keep mobile phones
switched off in this area*, but the desk was unmanned. Outside, the
rain was blowing around the car park in rattling squalls. She
decided to risk returning Amy's call from here, turning her back
on the reception desk and the sign so she could pretend, if chal-
lenged, that she just hadn't seen it.

Amy answered after two rings. 'Marm. I'm so glad you've
called.'

'What's up, Kato?'

On the other end of the phone, Amy sounded breathless. 'I've
been working to narrow down the origin of the tip-off letter, like
you asked,' Amy said. 'The sorting office sent me a list of all the
postboxes in their catchment. The box numbers, and their loca-
tions. And there's one that's pretty significant.'

Birch frowned. She wasn't sure why Amy was working on this
– or indeed on anything – on a Sunday. She could only imagine
the younger officer had been spurred into action by McLeod
ordering the arrest of Abe and Toni Ross.

'The postbox they believe the letter was posted at is literally
on the end of the street where the Ross house is. It's only yards
away.'

'Wait,' Birch said, 'you're saying the Rosses sent the letter?'

She heard the sound of Amy's earring against the phone: she
was shaking her head.

'No. I thought that, at first, and it gave me a bit of a fright, I'll
admit. I realised that it would check out: Abe Ross was the first
person to know we were looking for George MacDonald. He
would probably have told his wife, which could have explained the
female DNA from the saliva on the envelope seal. For a horrible

minute there, I thought McLeod was actually on to something. So I decided to look into it, and went back to my notes from that first meeting with Abe at the house. As I scanned down, my memory was jogged. Marm – what *else* is just off Craigs Park Road, apart from that house?'

Birch glanced over at the reception desk – still no one there, but now she could hear voices approaching. 'I've no bloody idea, Kato,' Birch said. 'What *is* this?'

Amy went quiet, and Birch realised she'd snapped at her: she was still reeling a little from her conversation with Charlie, from the news about Jamieson's supposed new leaf.

'Sorry, marm,' Amy said, though it was Birch who ought to be apologising. 'It's the nursing home. The one where Mary McPherson lives. It is *also* only yards from that postbox, and I realised—'

Birch's eyes widened. 'That Mary McPherson knew,' she cut in. 'Before the public appeal went out, Mary McPherson knew we were looking for George MacDonald.'

'Exactly,' Amy said. 'We went to see her. Do you remember her knitting? It was sitting right there in her room. Grey wool.'

Birch slapped one hand against her forehead. 'Wool like the strand that was found stuck to the envelope.'

Amy was nodding now, Birch could hear the clatter of the earring once more.

'Right,' she said. 'And a very good reason to hate George MacDonald. I think Mary McPherson is our letter-writer.'

Birch swayed on her feet. This is information overload, she thought, I can't keep up. The tip-off letter that Birch had believed in so fervently had been sent not by MacDonald himself, but by an old lady who'd seemed utterly innocent when she and Amy had spoken with her. Birch and her team had spent hours digging in a railway siding for absolutely no reason, all because of that letter. McLeod was going to hear about this, and she knew he'd be a foul mix of pissed off and triumphant once he did. She realised she'd now need to arrest Mary McPherson for – at the very least – wasting police time. Because how – *how* – did Mary know that there was a body under those flagstones? Most likely the body of her own best friend, Phamie. Had Mary actually been an accomplice to George MacDonald's disappearing of his own wife? Had she made up the whole story about George attacking her in his kitchen?

They'd need to get to the bottom of all of that, and Birch knew they'd need to do so before this new development hit the press. Questions would be asked about the resources wasted in the siding search: the stopped trains, the police manpower, Birch's dogged belief in the veracity of the tip-off, her certainty that George MacDonald was its author. In that moment, she wanted the cheap carpeted floor of the reception area to open up and swallow her, so she wouldn't have to untie the fiendish knot this case was about to become. But she could feel Amy on the other end of the line, waiting for her to speak.

'Okay,' she said slowly, hauling in a deep breath. 'I'm sorry, but I'm at Low Moss right now. Are you actually at the station?'

Amy paused for a moment before admitting, 'I am.'

Birch made a mental note to chastise Amy for working the weekend. But later, that could wait.

'It might take me an hour or so,' Birch said, 'but get yourself ready, and I'll pick you up. We're going to go and speak to Mary McPherson.'

34

Birch hated the convoluted traffic system in the West End. As she turned into the bottleneck of Torphichen Place, a boy racer in a low-riding Honda Civic cut her up, and she put her hand on the horn.

'If we weren't going somewhere,' she yelled, 'I'd pull you over, sunshine!'

On the edge of her vision, she saw Amy's eyes widen, and moderated her tone. 'Sorry, Kato.'

Amy laughed. 'Don't mind me,' she said. 'I just hope you know that he can't hear you.'

Birch rolled her eyes. 'Not over that so-called music he's blasting, no. Jesus, I've become such an old granny.' Just saying it made her shiver. Mary McPherson. How could they have overlooked Mary McPherson?

'Do you think she could have killed someone?' Birch asked. 'Or helped to kill someone?' It was a question out of nowhere, but Amy didn't flinch.

'I've been wondering the same,' she said. 'Was the forgetfulness just an act? All the sweet little old lady stuff?'

Birch thought back to the evening they'd visited the nursing home: Mary propped up in her chair, her skin translucent, the knuckles of her small hands thick above stacked, sparkling rings. 'It was convincing, if so,' she said. 'But whether she was acting or not . . . she's tiny. I doubt she'd ever have had the height or strength to even hurt someone. Not seriously.'

'Or even,' Amy said, 'to dig a grave. Surely she can't have been involved?'

'But she knew,' Birch said. 'If she wrote that letter then she knew about that body, and she knew where it was buried. She *knew* that when we were sitting there in the room with her.'

Amy was twirling a piece of hair around one finger: a thing Birch had noticed she did whenever something perplexed her.

'But she did tell us,' Amy said. 'That was the whole point of the letter. She tipped us off. I'll admit, she did it too late, anonymously, and it was pretty vague—'

'If not unhelpful,' Birch cut in. She thought about the word *George*, written on the tip-off. She thought about the railway siding, the talking-to she'd get from McLeod later.

'Right,' Amy said. 'But she did tell us. She wanted us to find it. Doesn't that also imply she didn't do it?'

'Sure.' Birch sighed, pulling up to what felt like the five-hundredth red light in a row. 'I don't think she *can* have: she's not capable, and wouldn't have been going back years, either, I don't think. But if she knew where Phamie MacDonald – we assume – was buried, then she must know what happened to put her there. She must know who did it. She must know if it was George. And she didn't tell us *that*, even when we were right there, asking her to her face.'

Amy tugged on the piece of hair, her shoulders curled inward. She didn't like this, Birch could tell.

'But that might be because the forgetfulness *isn't* an act,' Amy said. 'If she really does have dementia, then maybe at that moment, when we were there, she genuinely didn't remember what she knew. She might only have figured it out later, and not remembered our names. Hence the letter addressed to *MacDonald Investigation*.'

Birch cocked her head at Amy. That would all make sense.

'If that's the case,' Amy went on, 'then she might still know where George is, and everything that happened to Phamie. She just might not always remember.'

Birch sighed. She had to hand it to her colleague: Amy could see the bright side of just about anything. In her own head, Birch was struggling to make sense of this case: it started as a double missing person, but led to the discovery of a serial killer. Now they had another murder on their hands, and their only lead was an elderly woman who was either very confused, or very manipulative. If she didn't murder Phamie herself, did Mary McPherson help? Did she witness the murder, or at least the burial, and tell no one? It felt like months ago that Birch had first picked her way along the railway line at Carstairs, following the weird invisible breadcrumb trail of a hunch. In truth, it was only ten days since she'd scratched about in the loamy darkness of the wood, and found the body that would turn out to be Suzie Hay. Then Maisie Kerr. Then Christine Turnbull. Then Marta Zajac. Then Fiona Mandel. Then the Jane Doe who was most likely Kayleigh Kelbie. Birch realised she'd been doing this, ever since they were all found: running through their names in her head, in the order they were found, like a rosary. Did Mary McPherson know about these women?

'This might be a difficult interview,' Birch said, after a long silence. 'You ready?'

Amy didn't speak at first, but nodded her head emphatically once, twice. 'Trust me,' she said, 'I want to get to the bottom of all of this as much as you do.'

Birch smiled. I doubt it, she thought.

When they arrived at the door of the nursing home, Birch didn't bother with the niceties of waiting at the desk. She could feel Amy scuffing behind her, wanting to follow the home's procedure, but everything felt too urgent: Mary McPherson had key information that might join the dots in a murder investigation. Birch walked straight into the corridor they'd been led down on their last visit. Staff in blue tunics looked up from their tasks in the adjacent rooms, and she registered surprise on their faces, but didn't stop walking. She climbed the stairs, not turning to check if Amy was still with her, and paused outside Mary McPherson's room. The door was closed. Was the old lady sleeping? Was she dressed? Birch hung back, listening, until she realised she could hear the dim babble of a television inside the room. Amy was at her shoulder now, and Birch felt her boldness return. She knocked sharply on the door, and then pushed it open without waiting for an answer.

Mary McPherson was sitting in the same place she'd been when they'd last visited. The light in the room was brighter, and the TV was on, playing some mindless daytime TV show. But otherwise, it was as though the two weeks that had passed in the world outside hadn't touched this room or the woman who lived in it. Mary McPherson looked up at Birch with the same trusting expression as before. The woman's face said, *I have no idea who you are*, and Birch believed it. Now she was back in Mary's presence, it was much harder to contend that her dementia symptoms might be some sort of elaborate act. The woman hadn't even spoken yet, but whatever suspicion Birch had been carrying was melting away fast. Mary was even smaller and more bird-like than she'd remembered. There was no way this woman was a killer.

'Come away in, come away in,' Mary said. 'I'm glad someone's come. I'm honestly gasping for a cup of tea.'

Birch sidled into the room, with Amy following. She remembered now how uncomfortable she'd felt the last time she was here. It worried her, being in the presence of Mary: a woman so vulnerable that she had no choice but to trust anyone who came near her.

'Mrs McPherson,' Birch said, stepping closer, 'I'm Detective Inspector Birch. This is my colleague, Detective Constable Kato. We came to visit you a couple of weeks ago, do you remember that?'

Mary frowned. 'Just a cup of tea,' she said. There was confusion in her voice.

Amy reached around Birch, bent down and plucked up the buzzer from the coffee table in front of Mary. She pushed the call bell. 'Don't worry, Mary,' she said, 'someone will sort that for you in just a tick.'

Mary McPherson threw Amy a small, watery smile. When she looked back at Birch, her face clouded again.

'You do this,' Birch said, nodding to Amy. She stepped back to let her colleague through. 'You're much better at this than I am.'

Amy looked at Birch for a moment, as though she might be about to object. But then she moved forward, and the two women did an awkward dance to reposition themselves in the small room.

'I know you, hen,' Mary said, as Amy came more clearly into view. 'You're one of the nice ones.'

Amy beamed. 'Thank you,' she said, 'I'm glad you think so.'

Mary glanced past Amy at Birch, who'd taken up a sort of sentry position by the bedroom's open door. 'They're not all nice,' she said.

Birch bit her lip.

'Oh,' Amy said, 'my boss is really nice when you get to know her, I promise. She's a really good person. You've just caught her on a difficult day. You see, she's very worried about something.'

Mary blinked, as though trying to focus properly on Amy's face. 'Oh yes?'

'Yes,' Amy said. 'Mary, we're looking for someone who's missing. You might remember we came and asked you about it before. Your friend, Phamie MacDonald?'

Birch saw the name register with Mary. Yes, she knew who Phamie was.

'Phamie is missing,' the woman said. It wasn't a question: she was trying to retrieve this information, trying to place how and why she knew it.

'You remember,' Amy said. 'We came to talk to you, and you told us about how you used to live next door to Phamie and George.'

'Oh yes,' Mary said. Her eyes seemed to brighten, as though something had clicked. 'Of course. Phamie's next door! She lives just next door.'

Birch squeezed her eyes closed. Come on, Helen, she thought. How did you think this was going to go? You thought you were just going to walk in here and get her to tell you everything?

'Right,' Amy said, 'that's right, Phamie used to be your next-door neighbour, before you moved here. She used to live next door.'

Mary made a sort of clucking sound in her teeth. 'That George, though,' she said, 'that husband of hers. That man is a *brute*.'

Amy nodded. 'You told us a bit about George,' Amy said, 'the last time we were here. Then I think you remembered some more things that you'd missed out, so you wrote us a letter. You sent it to us at the police station. Do you remember doing that, Mary? You wrote a letter and had someone post it for you, at the postbox at the end of the street.'

Mary was watching Amy's lips move. Her brow was creased. 'A letter . . .'

Amy reached into her jacket pocket and pulled out Birch's battered photocopy of the tip-off letter. 'Here it is,' she said, holding it out to Mary. 'I brought it with me.'

Mary reached out a small hand and took hold of the paper. It shuddered in her grip. She laid it down flat on her lap, and smoothed it out with a careful stroking motion. Birch thought she looked as though she were stroking a cat. Then she placed the pad of her index finger over the word *George*, scrawled under the thin, shivery line.

'There's George,' she said.

'Where is he, Mary?' Amy asked.

Birch held her breath.

Mary didn't look up immediately from the paper, but when she did, her eyes looked somehow clearer, less milky than they had before. 'There,' she said, pointing to the paper again. There was an edge to her quiet voice. 'Where he belongs.'

'Who's this, Mary?'

Birch jumped. A short, stocky woman in a blue tunic had appeared in the doorway. She was peering into the room, looking Amy up and down. Birch fumbled for her badge.

'Who's come to see you *outside* visiting hours?' The woman turned her keen, dark eyes on Birch, and Birch flashed the ID at her.

'Detective Inspector Helen Birch,' she said, trying to match the woman's pointed tone. 'Police Scotland.'

Across the room, Amy was also holding up her badge. 'Detective Constable Amy Kato,' she said. 'We came to visit Mary a couple of weeks ago, and we're following up.'

The blue tunic woman shrank back slightly, but her voice didn't change. 'It's standard procedure,' she said, 'for visitors to report to the welcome desk downstairs.'

Birch drew herself up to her full height. 'We're investigating a murder,' she said, 'Ms . . .?'

'Dalvey,' the woman said.

'Ms Dalvey. I hope you'll forgive us for skipping protocol.'

In her chair, Mary was squirming. The tip-off letter was still on her lap: Birch could hear the static swish as it rustled against her skirt.

'Murder?' Mary said. 'What murder? What's happening, Donna?'

'You're right to ask, Mary,' Donna Dalvey said. Her voice was loud: she'd be heard in the corridor outside, Birch knew. 'I don't think it's right to come in here and frighten an old woman like this, I really don't.'

Birch glanced at Amy.

'It's all right, Mary,' Amy said. 'You're not in any danger, I promise. We're here because we need your help. Because we believe you have some knowledge that could help us.'

'Knowledge!' Donna Dalvey practically spat the word. 'This woman needs twenty-four-hour nursing care for Alzheimer's. I'm amazed she knew my name just then, and I see her most days of the week. What knowledge, exactly, are you referring to?'

Mary McPherson raised her hands to her face. The letter slipped off her lap and on to the floor, as she began rocking in her chair.

'Please, Mary.' Amy looked up at Birch as she spoke, her face anguished. 'Please don't get upset, I promise it's all okay . . .'

'See!' Donna Dalvey stabbed a pointing finger towards Amy, though it was clear she was addressing Birch. 'See what you've done? Coming in here and intimidating an old woman – I'd call that bullying, quite frankly. You ought to be ashamed of—'

Birch held up one hand, palm first. 'Ms Dalvey,' she said, 'I'd like to point out that Mrs McPherson was speaking to us quite happily until you came into this room. We haven't done anything to harm or upset her. If anyone has done that, it is you.'

The woman spluttered. On the other side of the room, Amy had placed her hand on Mary's shoulder, though the woman was still rocking.

'Amy here rang the buzzer for Mary,' Birch said, 'because she was asking for a cup of tea. I think that might be just the thing to calm her down right now, don't you?'

Donna Dalvey's eyes narrowed. 'If you think I'm leaving you alone with her,' she said, her words sharp and spitty, 'you've got another thing coming, Madam Polis.'

In her chair, Mary had begun to make a quiet, high-pitched sound. Beside her, Amy had tears in her eyes.

'All right, Donna. I don't think we need to resort to hostilities.'

The voice came from outside, from the corridor beyond the bedroom. It was a calm, steady voice with a regional Scottish accent Birch couldn't immediately place. Both Birch and Donna Dalvey turned to see who was addressing them. On the threshold of Mary McPherson's bedroom stood another elderly woman: another resident, Birch guessed. She was considerably larger in stature than Mary, though slightly bent over by age. Her hair was coiffed into a loose perm that sat on top of her head like grey foam. A small clear tube snaked out from behind her ears and plugged into both nostrils: beside her, she held a slim oxygen tank with castors and a handle.

'Let me in, would you?' the woman said. 'Let me see if I can calm her.'

Birch stepped aside, and the elderly woman moved into the bedroom, pulling the tank behind her. She walked over to where Amy was crouching beside the still-rocking Mary: her stride was slow, but confident, Birch noticed. Amy stood and moved aside without speaking, and the woman placed her free hand on the arm of Mary's chair. She bent down and put her face close to Mary's, though she was still hiding behind her hands.

'Mary, hen,' the woman said. 'It's me. You're all right, my darlin'. You're all right.'

After a moment, Mary stopped her keening noise.

'Good girl,' the woman said. 'Now, let me look at you. Let me look at you, Mary.'

Slowly, Mary lowered her shaking hands from her face. Birch had expected to see tears, but she hadn't been crying. When she focused in on the oxygen-tank woman, her face lit up into a smile.

'Oh, hello, hen,' she said.

'Hello, my love,' the woman said, beaming back at her friend. Then she looked up, towards Donna Dalvey and Birch. 'Do you still want a wee cuppa, Mary?'

Mary's smile widened. 'Oh, yes *please*,' she said. 'I think I was just saying, wasn't I? I'm positively gasping.'

The oxygen-tank woman's eyes were fixed on Donna Dalvey. 'Donna's going to sort that right out for you, aren't you, Donna?'

Birch couldn't help but smirk at the woman standing next to her as she spluttered, quietened, and then replied, 'Of course, Effie.'

The woman whose name was Effie straightened up. 'Lovely,' she said. 'One for me too, please. Plenty sugar for Mary, mind that, Donna.'

Donna Dalvey nodded, then lowered her eyes as she moved past Birch and out of the room. Birch waited until she had descended the stairs before turning back to Mary, Amy and the woman named Effie.

'Well,' Effie said. 'That was rather a lot of fuss, wasn't it, Mary? Let's see if we can't all talk a little more ladylike from now on, eh?'

Birch could see Amy blushing, though she knew the comment was very much not aimed at Amy.

'I do apologise . . . Effie?' Birch said. 'I'm Detective—'

'Detective Inspector Helen Birch,' Effie cut in. 'Yes, I heard. I've been waiting for someone like you to turn up here, one of these bright days. It's taken longer than I thought it would, so I suppose I've been lucky. But here you are. Here we all are, eh, Mary?'

Birch frowned. On the other side of the room, Amy was frowning, too.

'Sorry,' Birch said, 'I'm not sure I understand what you mean.'

The woman named Effie turned to face Birch properly for the first time. Birch felt a jolt of recognition as she spoke: a kind of electric shock that passed through her entire body.

'I'm the person you're looking for,' she said. She placed her free hand on her own chest, a kind of greeting. 'Euphemia MacDonald. Phamie. And I assume you're here to arrest me for murder.'

Amy heard herself make a strange hiccupping sound. DI Birch was standing bolt upright beside the door, her face ashen.

'Phamie MacDonald,' Birch said.

The woman who'd called herself Effie nodded. 'Guilty,' she said. 'Guilty, guilty, guilty.' She turned to look at Amy then, and said, 'You look like you've seen a ghost, young one. Have a sit down for goodness' sake.'

For a moment, Amy wasn't sure she could move, but the other three women were all looking at her. She willed her feet to carry her the couple of steps to Mary's bed, and sat down on the edge of it.

'You too.' The old woman pointed at Birch, and then waved in Amy's direction. Amy watched her boss go through the same motions, crossing the room to sit next to her. She felt the bed bow as Birch sank down beside her.

'I'll take the wee puffet,' said the woman who'd called herself Effie. She moved a pile of magazines off the footstool next to Mary's chair. Mary smiled blithely as the three women arranged themselves around her.

Amy thought the small woman looked like a tiny, pale saint, her padded chair rather throne-like, and the three of them – herself, DI Birch and this woman who claimed to be Phamie MacDonald – all gathered around her as though to partake of her wisdom.

'You are.' DI Birch spoke, the words coming out cracked and strange. 'You *are* Phamie MacDonald. I recognise you, now. From a picture your son gave us. It's you.'

Amy watched Phamie's face change as she registered the idea of her son.

'Robert?' she said. 'You've spoken to Robert? He's in Scotland?'

'He came to us.' Amy could hear a waver in Birch's voice, a note of disbelief that this was all really happening. 'He reported you missing. You and . . . his father. He's the reason we came looking for you.'

Phamie reached down from her seat on the low stool, and scooped up the photocopy of the tip-off letter from where it had fallen.

'I understand you've found a body in my garden,' she said, and then, when surprise registered on Amy's face, Phamie added, 'It was in the paper.'

Amy and Birch both nodded in tandem: out of the corner of her eye, Amy saw, and realised how funny they must look. She wondered if her own face was as pale as Birch's.

'I have some explaining to do,' Phamie said.

Outside the door, the clink of china. Donna Dalvey appeared on the threshold, carrying two mugs set on saucers. She eyed Birch and Amy with open hostility as she entered the room.

'Lots of sugar,' she said, teetering the first mug down on the coffee table in front of Mary. Phamie held up her hands, and retrieved the other mug from the saucer Donna Dalvey held out.

'No saucer for me, hen,' she said. 'I'm not as shaky as Mary is, I promise I'll not spill.'

Amy's lips were dry. She thought about asking for a glass of water, but seeing Donna Dalvey's face, she decided against it.

'You want me to stay?' the woman asked. She was standing between Phamie and the bed, the empty saucer in her hand.

'No, not to worry, Donna,' Phamie said. 'You've enough to be doing, I'm sure.'

Amy was struck by Phamie's quiet power. Donna Dalvey hesitated for only a moment before trudging back out of the room.

'Now,' Phamie said, 'where should I begin?'

Amy glanced at Birch, and found her boss looking back at her, the same sort of blank expression on her own face.

'Perhaps . . .' Amy ventured. She couldn't believe she was in the presence of Phamie: Phamie whose voice she already knew so well. 'Perhaps you could start at the beginning of your relationship with George? Tell us the history. I – we found your diaries, the ones you hid under the oven. And I read them, but . . . there are some gaps we haven't been able to fill.'

Beside her, she could see Birch was nodding again. Phamie blew on her tea, took a sip, and then wrapped her hands around the mug. Amy noticed a pale white stripe on one finger, where a wedding ring would once have been.

'Settle in, then,' Phamie said. 'It's a long tale. One Mary already knows well.'

Mary grinned, then, and reached down beside her into the folds of her armchair.

'I do love a good story,' the little woman said, drawing out a huge remote control with many tiny coloured buttons. She pointed it at the TV, still burbling away to itself in the corner, and muted it. Phamie drew in a long breath, and then began.

'The thing you need to understand about George is, he was sly. When we were courting, he showed me none of his bad behaviour, not a bit of it. He was charm personified, a real gentleman. Even my mother loved him, and my mother did not love many people. He treated me like a princess back then. I was a wallflower, you see, and now I realise that was just what he wanted in a wife. He could see I was a big girl, I didn't get asked up on to the floor at dances, just sat to one side all bashful. Oh, he knew what he was doing when he set his sights on me, did George. And of course I couldn't believe my luck, this tall handsome man showing an interest in me. At first I thought he was after one of my girlfriends and this was all some sort of front, you know? He was a big strapping boy, *so* tall. No one else could understand what he saw in me either. It shocked everyone when he asked me to marry him. And at that moment in time I'd no doubts, no reason to ever suspect he was anything other than the charming creature he claimed to be. Of course I said yes. I felt like I'd won the pools. I was twenty-three by then, and back then that was old to still be unmarried.

Some of my girlfriends had babes in arms already, but oh my, the single ones were jealous when I paired off with George. We married in 1959. Coming up sixty years ago. Nearly sixty years I spent with that man, didn't I, Mary? What a mistake I made that day, letting him put that ring on my finger. What a mistake.'

Phamie's face had clouded over, and her words stuttered to a stop.

'He was violent,' DI Birch said. It wasn't a question: everyone in the room knew it.

Phamie nodded. 'As soon as it was legally binding,' she said. 'From the first day of the honeymoon onward, I saw the change in him. At first it wasn't so bad: cross words, you know, and I thought, Well, it's an adjustment, he'll settle. We'd moved into the house together, and I assumed he was just getting used to living with me. It was a shock for me too, after all. I'd lived with my mother until then, I didn't really know what I was doing.'

'The house,' Birch said. 'You mean number 23, along the road?'

Phamie nodded again. 'Yes, that was our house,' she said. 'My great-auntie Isobel's house. George didn't like that, mind. He would have preferred us to find a house of our own, he didn't like that the place was in my family. But we were poor, then, and he didn't want me to be working. In the end we married and nothing else had come up and we needed to live somewhere. I was delighted of course, I loved that house. Loved that I had my own garden. I'd have died in that house, if I'd had my way, had things not . . . gone how they did. I'd never have left it.'

Beside Amy, Birch cleared her throat. 'Is that why you never left George,' she asked, 'even though he abused you?'

Phamie fixed Birch with a look. 'These young ones,' she said, nudging Mary's elbow, 'they don't know what it was like, do they, Mary?'

Mary was hanging her head a little, but now she shook it. 'They do not,' she agreed.

'In those days,' Phamie went on, 'you didn't leave your husband over such things. Especially not a woman like me. As I say, I was considered old when we married. I had always been plain, ungainly, all of that. My mother thought I'd die an old maid. She was over-joyed when I married George, everyone was. I couldn't disappoint them all by walking away, now could I? She might not have taken me back in, my mother, and then where would I have gone? It was much harder back then, much harder. And within the year I had a bairn on the way.'

'Robertson,' Amy said, then corrected herself. 'Sorry, Robert.'

'Robert,' Phamie repeated. 'I thought a wean around the house might soften George. I thought it might stop his bad behaviour. He made me think it was all my fault, whenever he flew into one of his rages. He'd speak to me so gently afterwards, say how sorry he was, how he just couldn't help himself when I aggravated him, and if I'd just try to be more douce and good and respectful then it wouldn't happen so much. I honestly thought it would be better if we had bairns. I thought I'd be what George wanted me to be, I thought he'd forgive me.'

Amy could feel her pulse quickening, a now familiar anger at George MacDonald rising in her. 'But of course,' she heard herself say to Phamie, 'it didn't help.'

Phamie shook her head. 'It made things worse,' she said. 'At least when it was just the two of us, George was at home of an evening. When Robert came along he'd say he couldn't stand to be there with all the wailing and fussing. That was when he started to disappear, at first just for a few hours, and I'd think to myself, Och Phamie, every husband goes for a few jars in the pub. But then it would be whole days, on the weekends. Then days at a time. He'd other women, I was sure of it. I told Mary here, plenty of times, didn't I, hen?'

Mary was looking at Phamie, watching her lips move. 'Wee Robert,' Mary said now. 'Where's wee Robert, Phamie? I've no' seen him in such a long time.'

Phamie smiled sadly. 'Mary's not having a great day today,' she said, putting her hand on top of Mary's on the chair arm. 'She comes in and out, these days.'

Beside her, Amy could feel DI Birch was still, attentive. She wanted Phamie to keep talking.

'The number of nights I'd sit in Mary's parlour, crying my eyes out,' Phamie said. 'And Mary's Donald out driving around looking for George to bring him home. There were other women, I know that now for sure.' The woman's face grew dark, her eyebrows knitting. 'But not in the way that I thought there were.'

Amy felt the mattress shift beneath her as DI Birch leaned forward. 'What do you mean by that, Phamie?'

The older woman shifted her eyes. 'I'll get to that,' she said. 'I'm old, you know, Inspector Birch. I'm not like Mary here, not quite yet, but I can feel it coming on. The memory isn't what it used to be. I have to keep things in the right order, or I'll lose my thread. You understand.'

Birch sat back again. 'Sure,' she said.

'The worst thing,' Phamie went on, 'was Robert up and leaving. He couldn't see, not really, what George was like. That was my fault, because I'd protected him. Times when he was a wean, barely walking, George would fly into a rage, and I'd lie on top of Robert so George could only get to me, not to him. It wasn't what I wanted for my boy, growing up in that sort of household, so I did what I could. George wanted Robert to get into all his trains, all his sitting on stations in the weather doing nothing, all his making notes and disappearing. I wouldn't have it. I sent Robert out to play with the other weans, I got him in the football team. George never forgave me for that. And then he left. Robert, I mean. A part of me was glad: he at least could get away. But oh, I felt it when he was gone. And George blamed me, said I'd made the boy too independent. When we found out the money was missing – good Lord, it was a bad time. It made George even worse. So much worse, in every way.'

'Robert left you,' Amy heard herself say. 'He left you alone with his father, when he *knew* . . .'

Phamie shrugged. 'Young men are impulsive creatures,' she said. 'And George was right, I *did* raise him to be independent. Everything that happened with Robert was my own fault. He didn't know how bad his father could be, because I protected him from it, I hid it from him. And yet he knew enough to hate George by the time he was grown, enough to want to punish him. Of course he took our savings money. Of course he did. If George had been my father and I'd been a young man with the opportunity, I'd have done the same in his place. I'm glad he went. I'm glad he lived his life, out from under George. But oh, it was the worst thing, too. The worst thing.'

Mary made a sort of clucking sound. She was nodding, squeezing Phamie's hand. 'You poor thing,' Mary said. She looked directly at Amy then, and said, 'This poor, poor thing.'

Phamie extended a watery smile in the direction of her friend. 'Mary knows,' she said. 'She's very confused these days, but she knows. Sometimes, she's right here with us, aren't you, Mary? Less often now than she used to be, but sometimes she's as sharp as a pin.' The tip-off letter was still on Phamie's lap, her hand flattened over it. Now she lifted that hand, and said, 'Like the day she wrote this letter. I suppose she knew then. Or she remembered what she knew.'

There was a moment of quiet. Amy could hear the distant sounds of the home: voices, far off. TVs in other rooms, the sound dampened. Outside, a blackbird.

'What happened,' DI Birch said, 'in 2013?'

Phamie looked up. 'Ah,' Phamie said, 'you know about that.'

She took her mug of tea off the coffee table in front of her, and took another sip. Then she gestured to Mary's mug. 'It's cooler now, Mary,' she said. 'Will you have your tea?'

Mary nodded, enthused as a little child, and Phamie passed the mug to her gently. Mary took it with both hands, holding it as though it might burst into flames.

'Good girl,' Phamie said. Then she looked back up at Amy and Birch. 'That day, I'd taken a notion to clean out the attic. We were old by then, both George and me, and though we weren't doing badly, I felt as though we needed to take some steps. Make life a little more manageable. I was still out in my garden every day, still doing the housework and all of that. But I realised I might not have so many days left where I could get up that ladder and into the attic. I hadn't been up there in years – decades, I suppose it must have been. It was George who always went to get anything from up there. But I thought, He'll not have thought to clean it. He'll not have thought to bring things down we might need as we get older, less able. Papers, that sort of thing. So I thought, I'd get up that ladder and I'll take stock. See what's up there after all this time.

'So I climb up and sure enough, boxes of papers. Notebooks of George's, all his train paraphernalia going back years and years. I get up there and I'm out of breath, so I sit down and start to go through a shoebox. Envelopes, handwritten to me and George. Sent from America, I could see from the stamps. But though they had my name on them, I'd never seen them before. I imagine that you might know what they were, but I had no idea.'

Amy's heart fluttered. 'Letters from Robert,' she said.

A thin seam of tears appeared in Phamie's eyes. 'Letters from Robert,' she said. 'Letters from my boy, telling me how sorry he was. Telling me he felt like he'd made a mistake. Telling me he'd made the money back, the money he'd taken from his father's account. Offering to send us that money and more, offering to take care of us. Telling us what a success he'd made of himself in America. Telling us he'd like to visit, he'd like to have us visit him there, see the life he'd made for himself. These letters had dates on them. He'd sent them over twenty years before.'

When DI Birch spoke, Amy could hear the anger in her voice. 'George had never told you?' she said.

'No,' Phamie replied. 'He'd opened them, he'd read them, and then he'd hidden them from me. Hidden them for all those long years. And I assume he never replied, because there were five or six of them, and then Robert must have stopped writing. He must have assumed we didn't want him.'

Now, the tears thickened and fell down Phamie's face. Amy curled her hands into fists.

'Sitting in that attic,' Phamie went on, her voice thick, 'I realised I'd been sleepwalking for far too long. I'd got so very used to George that . . . well, I'm ashamed to say his rages rather washed over me by then. I realised that when Robert left, I'd become numb. I didn't feel it any more. I stopped writing in those diaries, the ones you said you'd found, young one. I'd forgotten all about those, though they felt like my lifeline for a while. But I stopped needing them, or at least, I stopped feeling like they did me any good. I'd even started to feel *lucky*, if you can believe it, by the time I found those letters. Time had settled George a little, he wasn't so stirred-up as he had been. He still flew into a frenzy every now and then, but he'd got to be more bark than bite. He was an old man, and I think he'd started to feel it. He'd been strong for so much of his life, but he'd weakened by then. And I was so grateful for that, so used to it all, that I'd lost touch with reality. With the reality of what George was.

'It hit me then, that afternoon sitting in the dust of the attic. I realised in a way I'd never done before that my husband was a monster. A psychopath. He had no feelings for other people, only for himself. He kept those letters from me because *he* wanted Robert gone, because *he* couldn't forgive him. And yet he kept them, because he knew that one day he might be able to use them. He knew he might be able to hurt me with them. I realised then that George wasn't just an ordinary man who lashed out sometimes. He was broken, fundamentally broken.'

'That George,' Mary said, in a voice so small it was almost a whisper, 'he was a *brute*.'

Amy watched as the two women consoled each other: Phamie taking back the half-empty mug from Mary, and grabbing hold of both her hands, squeezing. She wondered if Phamie knew that George had attacked Mary, too. She wondered how many times it had happened. She wondered how often Mary thought of it, how often she remembered. Amy realised her own face was wet: the tears were thin, hot and angry, but they were real.

'So, you confronted him?' That same fine seam of anger in DI Birch's voice.

'I did,' Phamie said. 'I took those letters down from the attic and I sat at the bottom of the stairs by the door until George saw fit to come home. And then I told him what I thought of him, every bit of it. I told him he was a monster, he was depraved, he didn't care about anyone but himself. I thought it might kill me to say it all, but I would die telling the truth to his face. I hadn't realised until that day that I hated him, but I did. And I told him so. I threw those letters at him and I told him I hated him.'

Amy held her breath. She thought she knew what would happen next, but Phamie's face was hard to read.

'I didn't expect him to let me finish,' she said. 'I thought he'd see the letters and snap. He never wanted me in that attic, and now I know why. So I talked fast. I yelled. I tried to get it all out in a rush, because I thought he'd stop me. But he didn't. He stood there and listened. He didn't even flinch when I threw those letters in his face. He just laughed at me. And honestly, it frightened me more than anything he'd ever done to me before. I was used to the shouting, the raging, the lashing out. But that look in his eyes that day – I'd never seen that before.'

Phamie paused. Her own eyes were wide, unfocused: Amy could see she was remembering the moment.

'Then what happened?' Amy asked. Phamie looked up, and underneath the fear the memory had stirred in her, Amy could see something else in the woman's face. Guilt.

'Then he put me in a chair,' Phamie said, 'and he told me what he'd done. So you think I'm a monster?, he said. And his voice was so cold. He said I'd no idea, I was a stupid pathetic woman and I had no idea. No idea how lucky I was, that was what he said. He told me that if he didn't love me so much when I was young, if he hadn't been dazzled into marrying me – that was the word he used, dazzled – then I'd have been dead in the ground by now, and I was lucky. I said, what do you mean, dead in the ground? You might not believe it, but for all he did to me, for all his threats, I never thought he'd kill me. Truly, I never feared for my life before that day, because I did everything for that man, and I knew he couldn't live without me. But the way he said that, dead in the ground, it chilled me. Even more than the letters had.'

Birch was leaning forward again. 'Did George confess to you,' she asked, 'about what he'd done at Carstairs?'

Phamie seemed to flinch at the utterance of the place. 'I didn't know it was there,' she said. 'Not until recently, now that it's in the papers every other day. But he told me what he'd done, yes, Inspector. He told me I was lucky, because he'd put plenty of other women in the ground – women who didn't respect him, he said. I told him I didn't believe it, and he wouldn't frighten me. I said I was finished with being frightened of him, and I was going to leave, and nothing he could say could make me change my mind, so he might as well stop with all of that talk. And he didn't like that, not at all.'

Amy bit at the inside of her lip. She knew from reading the 2013 news report what was coming next.

'As he beat me,' Phamie said, 'he told me about all those women. All those girls.' Her voice cracked, and the tears began to fall once again. 'He told me it was my fault, because of what happened when Robert was born.'

Birch was leaning so far forward now that Amy thought she might topple off the bed. 'What happened when Robert was born?' she asked.

Phamie shivered. 'It was a hard birth,' she said. 'I had to be cut, so they could get Robert out of me. *That* wasn't like it is now, either. They didn't sew me back up all that well. George always said I was useless after that. Useless for . . . sleeping with. That day he told me about the girls, the women, he said – he said it was my fault. He had to go and look elsewhere for . . . all of that.' Phamie stopped speaking for a moment, and dragged a hand across her face to wipe away her tears.

'There now, Phamie,' Mary said. 'I know it's hard, hen, I know it's hard.'

Amy was crying again, too. She knew it wasn't professional, but she couldn't seem to stop.

'I felt so awful,' Phamie said. 'So, so awful. Those women died because of me. He went and found them and . . . well, he must have done such dreadful things to them. Because of me. Because I couldn't give him what he wanted.'

Quiet fell again. Amy wished that she could say something, that someone would say something, anything. Something to comfort Phamie. But there was nothing anyone could say.

'He told me their names,' Phamie said. 'While he beat me. He told me what they looked like, what they were all wearing when he took them into the woods. He told me they liked him, that he behaved fatherly towards them so they'd trust him. He told me he offered to help them, and they thought he would, and then he—' Phamie stopped. She seemed to have seized up, like an engine left out in a storm.

'We know about what he did,' Birch said quietly. 'You don't need to tell us that part, it's okay.'

Amy let out a long breath she didn't realise she'd been holding. They didn't know what MacDonald did, not really: the bodies had been too decomposed to know for sure what their cause of death had been, whether they'd been sexually assaulted. Phamie *would* need to say what she knew. Sometime, though, Amy thought. Not now. That was what DI Birch was really saying.

'I think he told me all those things,' Phamie said, 'because he knew that knowing them would hurt me more than anything else he'd ever done. I think he really thought that I might leave that day. I'd never threatened to before, though Mary here tried to persuade me a lot of times. I think he saw that it was a possibility, that day. So he stopped me, by telling me all of that.'

Beside her, Amy heard Birch make a sound in her throat.

'You could have come to us,' Birch said, 'to the police. You could have told us he'd confessed to murder.'

Phamie laughed a hollow laugh. 'George made sure I couldn't walk, that afternoon,' she said. 'He left me in the living room, blacked out. I came to hours later, and found there was a paramedic shining a light into my eyes. For the first time ever, George had misjudged things. I think he thought he'd killed me, when I didn't come round. So he called for an ambulance.'

'It was in the news,' Amy said, her voice hoarse. 'We know you didn't press charges.'

Phamie laughed again, and this time the laugh had a rattle in it. She reached behind her, to where she'd propped her oxygen canister, and fiddled with a knob on the top of it. Then she sat quietly for a moment, pulling in long breaths through her nose.

'Two very nice young policemen came to see me,' she said, 'in the hospital. They explained how it could go. They had George in custody, they said. But I wasn't convinced. I wasn't convinced they could do what they said they could. And you have to understand, I'd lived that same life for almost sixty years. I didn't know if I could do anything else.'

She looked at Mary, who was watching her friend again, watching her lips move as she talked.

'Mary's Donald had died by then,' she said, 'and I knew Mary wasn't coping on her own. I could see her forgetting things, getting confused. She'd get lost in the town for hours, sometimes. She wasn't right any more, she wasn't herself. I didn't want to get like that, being on my own. And like I say, I didn't think they could fix up George.'

Phamie put a hand on top of Mary's hand, the same way she had before, their fingers curled together on the arm of Mary's chair. Phamie's face grew dark again. 'But I knew I could,' she said. 'I knew *I* could fix George right up.'

'George,' Mary whispered, a thin echo.

'You killed him,' DI Birch said. It wasn't a question. Amy felt like she ought to be shocked, but she wasn't. As Phamie had told her story, it had become clear that this was the only possible ending.

Phamie looked down at the tip-off letter, still in her lap. 'I bided my time,' she said. 'I had to make him think I'd forgotten it, all those things he said. Or . . . not forgotten it, but filed it away. Made peace with it. I had to make him think I'd forgiven him.'

Amy blinked. The light in the room was fading, and the soft light of the TV seemed brighter now. She realised she had no idea how much time had passed since they'd arrived.

'After I came out of hospital,' Phamie was saying, 'George was like he'd been all those years ago, back when we were courting. He was charming. Grovelling, even. It had scared him, hurting me that badly. It had scared him that other people had got involved, that other people knew what he did to me. The police. That was the last time he ever raised a hand to me. I think he realised how close he'd come to his whole twisted world falling apart. He wanted to know exactly what I'd said to those two policemen, exactly what they'd asked me, word for word. He'd gone too far, hurting me that badly, telling me all those things, opening up the rotten cage he'd made for me in that house. And it was like he flicked a switch inside himself. He stopped hurting me, stopped even shouting.'

'That *brute*,' Mary hissed, and Amy believed what Phamie had said: sometimes, Mary really was in the room with you, sharp as a pin.

'It took me a year,' Phamie said, 'but I fixed him up. I organised to have the patio built. I chose two Polish boys to do it, lovely sweet boys who didn't charge too much and didn't ask me questions. I had them dig out the beds that had been there, so the earth was all freshly turned and loose. Then I went out after they'd gone, and dug a bit deeper.'

Phamie looked up then, and saw the surprised look that Amy and Birch shared. 'I know I'm an old lady,' she said, 'but I've always dug a garden. And I wasn't saddled with this thing, then.' She nodded behind her at the oxygen tank. 'I'm not saying it was easy,' she went on, 'but I did it. And George knew I was out there, working in the garden. I often was, I doubt he thought anything of it. Once I'd done the digging, I came inside and made him his dinner, just like always. I did my favourite, a roast chicken, and I tell you, Inspector, it was a damn fine meal. I savoured every last mouthful of that meal, watching George eat, knowing he'd not the faintest idea of what was coming to him. My arms and back were aching from the work of the digging, but it was wonderful nevertheless. I loved that feeling, that power – it wasn't a thing I'd ever had any of, power. So I'm not ashamed to say that I relished it, and if I could go back and live that hour of my life again, I absolutely would.'

Amy realised she was nodding, and stopped herself.

'Then,' Phamie said, 'after dinner, once it was dark, I told George I'd seen something in the garden, where the Polish boys had been digging. I said I thought they'd hit a pipe, and it was playing on my mind that maybe it was a gas pipe and there might be a leak. I said he ought to go and look at it, though it was probably nothing. Set my mind at rest. Silly little me and my worries.'

Beside Amy, DI Birch let out a low whistle. She'd worked out what happened next.

'So of course, out he went with a flashlight,' Phamie said, 'and bent over where I'd dug down.'

'What did you hit him with, Phamie?' Birch asked.

'With the handle of the shovel,' Phamie answered. Her voice was even, matter-of-fact. 'The first time, he fell on to his knees in the dirt. I hit him again, and then he fell on to his face, right in the centre of the channel I'd dug, right where I wanted him. I hit him another couple of times to make sure he was really dead. He was always a big man, George – he was always strong. I wanted to make damn sure.'

Amy put one hand over her mouth. She looked at Mary, to see if her friend's murder confession had upset her at all. If it had, Mary didn't show it.

'Then I straightened him out,' Phamie said, 'so he'd be good and flat, and not disturb the earth too much. Covering him over was easy enough, far easier than the digging had been. The Polish boys didn't have a clue when they came the next day to put the slabs down. I'd told them my name was Effie Innes, and I paid them in cash and tipped handsomely. And that was that. My back gave me grief for a couple of weeks after, but I tell you, Inspector, it was all worth it. Yes, I killed George. And what's more, I'd do it again, as many times as was necessary.'

Phamie's words seemed to echo off the walls of the little bedroom. The four women sat in silence, listening to the echoes fade. For a long time, no one spoke. Phamie sat with her eyes locked on DI Birch's face, waiting to see what she'd do. Amy wanted to know, too: would her boss get up off the bed, walk over and handcuff Phamie?

Birch seemed to sense that it was her move. 'That's why you auctioned the house,' she said at last. 'You wanted a quick getaway.'

'I did,' Phamie said. 'I felt . . . not remorse, never remorse. But fear. I realised that no one would understand what I'd done, that I wouldn't be able to convey to anyone just what it was like, living with George all those years. People don't believe women. No one would believe me and I'd be thrown in jail. I didn't feel remorse for what I'd done, but I also didn't want to end up living out the rest of my days in Cornton Vale prison. I'd no family left save Robert, and he was gone . . . the only person I had in the world was Mary here.'

At the mention of her name, Mary's face broke into a smile.

'And thinking of Mary gave me an idea,' Phamie went on. 'Mary had always said she'd come and live in this place when things got too much for her. I knew that time was coming: she was still at number 24 then, but I knew she wasn't coping. I thought, Well, I'm an old person, why can't *I* go and live in an old persons' home?'

'You moved just down the road.' Birch sounded incredulous.

'Exactly,' Phamie said. 'The house sold very quickly, of course. I figured I didn't need to sell it at market price as I wouldn't have all that many years left. I got my first bank account – in my maiden name of course – and cashed that cheque into it. I took some of George's money out of the bank, too, in cash, and then walked into this place. Sorted myself out with a private care plan, all under the name Effie Innes.'

'Effie,' Amy said. 'All that time I was running searches, looking for Euphemia and Phamie.'

Phamie laughed. 'Effie's by far the more common shortening, young one,' she said.

Amy cursed herself inwardly: she'd been so focused on George MacDonald's Ginger Mack alias, yet it had never occurred to her that Phamie might go by another name, too. And the money – George's regular cash withdrawals. They weren't him at all: they were Phamie, with George's card.

'Of course,' Phamie was saying, 'the good Lord saw fit to punish me for what I'd done. You can't take a human life and get away with it, no matter how sly you are.'

'What do you mean?' Birch asked.

Phamie reached behind her and knocked on the oxygen tank with one curled knuckle. The tank rang softly, like a bell.

'I had to have a medical,' she said, 'to determine what my care plan would include. And they saw a shadow on my lung. Cancer, it turns out. I'm at stage four now. I'll be honest, I'm not entirely sure what that means, but I'm led to believe it's not very good.'

Amy glanced at Phamie's hair, the thick grey cloud of it. 'You're not in treatment?' she asked.

Phamie raised an eyebrow. 'Young one,' she said, 'I'm very old. I've had my three score years and ten, and a little extra. I survived nearly sixty years of bruised ribs and concussion and being pushed down the stairs, and I lived to tell the tale. If my time's come now, then my time's come.'

Birch was shaking her head, in a slow, deliberate way, as though something were lodged there that she was trying to loosen.

'I'm confused,' Birch said. 'The letter. Mary's letter. How . . .?'

Phamie looked down at the photocopy, still in her lap. 'Ah yes,' she said. 'Well, Mary arrived here shortly after me. I'd told the home she was coming, that she was my best and oldest friend in the world and I was excited to see her again. They set us up with next-door rooms. It was like old times, except it was new times. When Mary arrived, I realised how confused she was. Sometimes she knew me, knew our long history together, and sometimes I was just the lady next door in the nursing home. Sometimes I was Phamie, and sometimes I was just Effie. It was difficult at first, but we worked it out, didn't we, Mary?'

'What's that, hen?' Mary leaned towards her friend.

'We worked it out,' Phamie repeated, 'living next door to each other again.'

'Oh yes,' Mary said, and smiled at Amy and Birch. 'Phamie and I have lived next door for . . . oh, how many years is it now, Phamie?'

Phamie didn't answer, but smiled. The smile had a tinge of sadness in it. 'One day,' Phamie said, 'I mentioned George. A memory of him, years ago. Mary works better in the past, she remembers more things from back then. And she suddenly got agitated, then upset. When I asked her what was wrong, she told me about a day when she'd come round and found me not at home, but George was in the house.'

Amy winced. Phamie *did* know.

'That was unusual,' Phamie was saying, 'for him to be there, and not me – and it seems George saw an opportunity.'

'Mary told us George attacked her,' Birch said. 'Last time we came here, she told us that memory.'

Phamie shook her head. 'I couldn't believe what I was hearing,' she said. 'All those years he hurt me – like I say, I got numb. It stopped upsetting me all that much. But hearing he'd hurt Mary . . .'

Phamie reached up a hand, and carefully pushed a tendril of hair away from Mary's face, tucking it behind her friend's ear. Mary smiled again, her saintly smile.

'It made me glad all over again,' Phamie went on, 'that I'd done what I'd done. In fact, it made me wish I'd done it sooner. And I told Mary that. I told her I was sorry I hadn't known about it, I was sorry I hadn't protected her from him, I was sorry I hadn't done enough. But I told her he was gone now, and he couldn't hurt either of us any more. I told her everything: George's story about the women. The shovel, the patio. All of it.'

Birch pointed again at the letter on Phamie's knee. 'You weren't worried she'd talk?' Birch asked. 'That she'd come to us, come to the police?'

Phamie shrugged. 'I could see her getting more confused by the day,' she said. 'I didn't expect she'd be able to hold on to the information. I certainly didn't think she'd ever have cause to repeat it to anyone, and besides' – Phamie looked at Mary, who was watching her friend's lips move once again – 'who'd believe an old lady with dementia? I just thought knowing, even for a moment, might give her some closure, and I didn't think beyond that.'

Birch let out that low whistle sound again.

'But it seems it made a difference,' Phamie added, 'you two coming here and asking her directly about George. I suppose I didn't expect anyone would ever do that.'

Amy felt a question push up out of her chest. It was irrelevant, but she wanted to know. 'How do you feel,' she asked, 'knowing that Mary alerted us to where George was?'

Phamie looked down at the tip-off letter again, and was quiet for a moment. When she looked back up, her eyes were damp again. 'Proud,' she said. 'I feel proud of her, for trying to do the right thing.'

Beside her, Amy felt Birch draw herself up. A long time had passed: outside, the streetlamps had started to come on.

'Does that mean,' Birch said, 'that you'd submit everything you've told us here to be recorded, as a proper confession?'

Phamie looked at Mary, who seemed to have sunk down a little in her chair. Amy could see the small woman's eyelids were heavy.

'I do love a good story, Phamie,' Mary said.

Phamie looked back at Birch, and mimicked her pose, straightening herself up too, and squaring her shoulders. 'I would,' she said.

DI Birch heaved out a long breath: relief, Amy could tell, but also something else, something painful. She watched as her boss levered herself up off the bed, and shook out her arms as though waking up from a sleep. Amy realised she too felt as though she'd been elsewhere, so caught up in Phamie's tale that she almost wanted to pinch herself.

'Euphemia MacDonald,' Birch said, taking a step towards Phamie. 'I am arresting you for the murder of George MacDonald. 'You do not have to say anything, but it may harm your defence if you do not mention when questioned something you later rely on in court. Anything you do say may be given in evidence.'

Edinburgh Evening News

BREAKING: Explosive revelations in Carstairs Killer case, Edinburgh woman charged with murder

BREAKING NEWS TEAM   Published 10:04   Share this article

Email   Monday 16 September   Live updates

SIGN UP TO OUR DAILY NEWSLETTER

BREAKING NEWS: The hunt for the Carstairs Killer came to an end this morning following an explosive press conference at Police Scotland's Fettes Avenue station.

Police had been hunting for George MacDonald, 83, the prime suspect in the Carstairs Killer case and a missing person, last seen in 2014. Following the discovery of human remains in woodland near Carstairs railway station, South Lanarkshire, MacDonald was being sought for questioning in connection with the murders of missing nursery teacher Christine Turnbull and five other women.

Over the weekend, forensics officers were called to an address in the Craigs Park Road area of Morningside, where the remains of an adult man were uncovered. A police spokesperson revealed today that these remains have been identified as belonging to George MacDonald. The property where the remains were found is the former MacDonald family home. Senior forensics expert Dr Letitia Bland was quoted as saying it is likely MacDonald was murdered and buried under a garden patio at the rear of the property some time in 2014.

Yesterday evening, police apprehended George MacDonald's wife, Euphemia MacDonald, and charged her with her husband's murder. Mrs MacDonald is in ill health and has been placed under house arrest at her current address. Until yesterday, Mrs MacDonald was also a missing person, having auctioned off the family home at around the time of her husband's murder before disappearing. According to archive news reports, Mrs MacDonald was hospitalised in 2013 following a domestic disturbance at the couple's address, but her husband was not charged with any wrongdoing. Mrs MacDonald is said to be co-operating fully with police.

Today, Police Scotland revealed that George MacDonald was their only suspect in the Carstairs Killer case, after DNA evidence linked him to the Carstairs burial site and to personal effects discovered close to the victims. Dr Letitia Bland revealed that there is no doubt in the minds of police working the case that George MacDonald murdered Christine Turnbull, Fiona Mandel, Marta Zajac, teenagers Suzie Hay and Maisie Kerr, and a sixth woman whose remains have yet to be positively identified. MacDonald's killing spree spanned over three decades.

In today's lengthy statement to the press, a police spokesperson revealed that further leads are now being followed up to determine whether George MacDonald is connected to other unsolved missing person cases involving young women.

More details here as they come in.

35

Birch sat in an armchair, looking across the room at Phamie MacDonald. Phamie had her back turned: she was fussing at the windowsill, buffing ornaments with a yellow duster in such a distracted way that Birch was just waiting for the crash, the scatter of porcelain shards into the carpet. Fine, she thought. Being ignored suits me. She was distracted herself: that morning, she'd waved Anjan off while it was still dark outside. He was headed to HMP Low Moss, to brief Charlie ahead of his enquiry hearing. Today was the day they'd find out how much time would be added to her brother's sentence. She realised she'd been praying ever since she'd woken up, the same words circling in her mind over and over, a kind of mantra: six months. Please let it be only six months. Please let it be only . . .

'Oh, where have you been, Billy boy, Billy boy?' Phamie was singing softly to herself, as though she had forgotten Birch was there. 'Where have you been, charming Billy?'

The words faded into a hum, and Birch wondered for a moment what the old lady was thinking. Then quiet fell once again.

Walking into Phamie's room, Birch had realised her six-month Charlie mantra had replaced the names of George MacDonald's victims. The night before, Birch had read Phamie her rights, and then been informed by the nursing home staff that this smooth and easy arrest was in fact going to be anything but: Phamie required twenty-four-hour nursing care and could not be moved. A doctor was summoned, and Phamie was assessed. No dice: there was apparently no way this woman could be put into a custody suite. McLeod had to be contacted, and then briefed. Paperwork had to be filed. It wasn't until almost midnight that a house arrest was put in place: now, a scene guard stood in the corridor outside Phamie's room, drawing a great deal of interest from the home's residents. A couple had even requested selfies with him.

Birch's thoughts had been filled with all of this until she'd fallen asleep in the early hours of that morning. She hadn't even thought to check her voicemails to see if her father had called. And she hadn't realised until she'd woken that something was different. Inside her head, something had changed. There was more space: she felt able to be anxious about Charlie and the outcome of his enquiry in a way that she just hadn't been until this point. She was able to think about her father more clearly: though she was still angry with him, she could make space for the idea that he might be telling the truth. He might really want to get sober, and start living a different life.

Now, as she sat in a floral armchair listening to an elderly murderess hum as she dusted her Beswick figurines, Birch realised what the change was. She was no longer holding space for Christine Turnbull and Fiona Mandel, for Marta Zajac and Suzie Hay, for Maisie Kerr and Kayleigh Kelbie. She was no longer thinking about them, wondering what MacDonald did with them before he finally planted them in the ground. The remains had been there so long, it was impossible to tell if there had been sexual assault, and very hard to know for sure their cause of death. The time of death could be narrowed down only to within a few months: in Fiona Mandel's case, Tish Bland had speculated at a possible year. Birch realised how much this had bothered her, this gap in each woman's timeline. The scant details around each of their deaths made it impossible to imagine their final hours, impossible to do a mental walk-through of how things happened, and in what order. Birch hadn't realised until this moment how important this sort of imaginary role-play was to her deduction process.

Now, they had Phamie. Phamie had promised to tell them everything she knew. Those gaps in the timeline still wouldn't be filled – the women's final hours would for ever be a terrible, aching mystery. But the case against George MacDonald would be made complete. They'd be able to go to the women's families, to tell them that George MacDonald was definitely the man responsible for their loved ones' murders, and to tell them what had happened to him. Birch allowed herself to admit, privately, that the end MacDonald had come to was really rather satisfying: the woman whose life he'd made miserable had finally had enough, and stopped his violent behaviour once and for all. She suspected that some of the families might find this idea comforting, too. They might prefer the idea of MacDonald lying under a patio with his skull stoved in to the idea of him living out his days in a prison cell on the taxpayer's dime. Birch realised she was smiling, ever so slightly, and rearranged her face. Vigilante justice isn't justice, she reminded herself. Outwardly at least, she'd need to toe the party line.

'Can I ask a question?' Birch's voice seemed overly loud in the quiet of the room.

Phamie looked up from her dusting, surprised, as though she hadn't realised Birch had come in. 'You can,' she said.

'What was George's motive,' Birch said, 'in killing those women? In your opinion, I mean.'

Birch interrupting her dusting seemed to make Phamie realise that she'd been doing it for too long: not consciously dusting at all, simply doing something with her hands while her mind worked away at whatever she was thinking about. She shook out the yellow duster, and crossed the room, pulling the little oxygen canister behind her.

'Like I said yesterday,' Phamie said, settling into the armchair opposite Birch's own, 'he blamed me. Blamed our . . . lack of sex life.'

Birch frowned. 'That wouldn't explain the murders,' she said. 'Forgive my bluntness, but – that would excuse a rape, or sexual assault. Murder is something else. Murder has its own reasoning.'

Phamie looked at Birch for a moment, blinking. Of course, Birch thought, I am speaking to a murderer right now.

'George was a violent man,' Phamie said, after a moment, 'but I think his violence was about power. He loved to keep me guessing, that was his favourite thing. He liked it if I didn't know from one moment to the next whether he was going to slap my face, or present me with a dozen roses. For a lot of my life, I've been bewildered – that's the word I'd use, bewildered. That was how he liked me to be. And that's about control, isn't it? Him always having it, and me never having it.'

Birch was nodding. She was looking past Phamie's shoulder, at a decorative floral plate that hung on the wall behind her. 'It's interesting that he began with Christine Turnbull,' she said. 'In 1965, not long after your son was born. Perhaps he felt some of his control had slipped away, with the baby being in the house.'

Phamie shrugged. 'I suspect so,' she said. 'He certainly didn't have all of my attention any more, and I know that upset him. He was on an even shorter fuse than usual, because of that, but also because of the things that come with a small baby. The crying, the disturbed nights. And honestly, I was so tired when Robert was small, I think I just zoned George out a lot of the time.'

'So he wasn't getting as much of the power and control that he craved,' Birch said. 'That makes sense.'

Phamie closed her eyes, and screwed up her face. 'It really was my fault, then,' she said. 'My fault that those poor girls died. I should have tried harder to . . . be my usual self with him. I should have tried harder to keep him in the house. I thought he was just having affairs, I didn't have a clue—'

Birch held up a hand. 'Please,' she said, 'don't blame yourself for his actions. I didn't mean to suggest you were responsible.'

Phamie opened her eyes again, but kept them focused on the yellow cloth in her hands. She worried at its red stitched edge with her thumbs. 'But that first one,' she said, 'Christine Turnbull. I remember her. I remember reading all about her in the papers, that huge manhunt.'

'It was a big case,' Birch said. 'But you had no reason to suspect George then. No one did. He went a long way to cover his tracks, didn't he?' Birch waited for Phamie to look up at her. 'Or didn't you know that George used an alias?'

Phamie frowned. She finally looked Birch in the face, and Birch could see her confusion was genuine. 'He did?'

Birch sat back a little in her chair. 'I won't discuss it with you,' she said, 'if you didn't already know. You'll likely be asked about it at trial.'

Phamie looked back down at the duster. 'I thought I knew George,' she said. 'I thought that was the one trump card I held, in the whole miserable hand that life seemed to have dealt me. As the years went on, I thought, I know that man better than he knows himself. That felt like a very small victory, sometimes – the times I predicted what he'd do before he did it, or the times he lied to me but I thought I knew where he'd been all the same. It turns out, I barely knew a thing. I only ever saw what he wanted me to see. He was more in control than I realised.'

Phamie's hands were balled into fists now, the duster pulled taut between them. 'I'd do it again,' she added, her voice almost identical to the way it had been in Mary's room the night before: steely, certain. 'In fact I think it'll be the greatest regret of my life, not killing the bastard sooner.'

Birch opened her mouth to speak, but there was a knock at the door. Phamie released her grip on the duster, and flicked it away down the side of the chair cushion. Birch could see she was suddenly on alert: she knew who was about to walk into the room.

The scene guard opened the door and poked his head round it. 'They're here, marm,' he said.

Birch nodded. 'That's great,' she said, 'show them in.'

Phamie was levering herself up out of the chair. Birch could hear the breath rattling in the old woman's chest as she straightened, put her hands to her face to adjust the oxygen tube at her nose. The door opened fully, and Robertson Bennet strode in. In his wake came a taller man wearing the kind of brash suit McLeod would have admired: Bennet's lawyer.

'Robert,' Phamie said. Her voice was small and watery. 'I can't believe you're here.'

Birch looked at Robertson Bennet, who had stopped about six feet away from his mother, the lawyer coming to a halt at his elbow. She tried to read Bennet's face, but all she could see for certain was conflict. That wasn't exactly surprising: Bennet had wanted to find out where his parents were, and now he had. But it had to be hard on a man like this – a man so righteous he'd threatened to sue the *police* – discovering that his father was a serial killer and his mother a murderer. Birch suspected that Bennet's initial desired outcome – obtaining some family money to shore up his failing company – might have been thrown into harsh perspective by the events of the past fortnight. She realised she couldn't wait to hear what Bennet had to say to his mother, or what his mother might say back to him. She stepped to one side, indicating that Bennet should come and sit in the armchair she had just vacated. The movement made Bennet look at her, registering her presence in the room. He leaned sideways towards the lawyer.

'Does she have to be here?' he asked.

Damn, Birch thought. 'As a condition of her house arrest, Mrs MacDonald does need to be in the presence of a member of police personnel for all visits,' she replied. 'So, in short, yes.'

The lawyer smirked at her. Birch had never met him before, but she could tell from the shiny gold tack on his briefcase that he was both high-priced and without scruples.

'No, actually,' he said. He had an American accent, thicker than Bennet's subtle one. Had Bennet flown him over? Or had the lawyer seen an opportunity here, and flown himself? 'A member of police personnel must be present, but it doesn't have to be *her*.'

Birch rolled her eyes at him, but Bennet was nodding.

'Good,' he said. 'I want someone else.'

'Robert,' Phamie said, 'Inspector Birch is—'

Bennet held up a hand. 'Mother,' he said. His voice cracked a little, and Birch saw surprise register on his face as he said the word. 'Can I just—'

Phamie seemed to shrink a little. The habit of a lifetime, Birch thought.

'Fine,' Birch said, trying to sound breezy about it, though inside she was thinking damn, damn, damn. 'I'll swap places with PC Leake, outside.' She indicated towards the bedroom door. 'Will that do?'

Bennet looked at the lawyer, who shrugged back at him: up to you. Bennet nodded. 'Yes,' he said. 'That would be great.'

Birch drew herself upright, and walked stiffly past Bennet, looking down at him as she went. She opened the door and stepped halfway out. 'Dave,' she said, and PC Leake turned.

'Marm?'

'I'm persona non grata in here, apparently. They've asked for someone else. Mind if we switch places?'

PC Leake nodded. 'No problem at all,' he said. 'They did offer me a chair, but I prefer to stand. I'm sure if you wanted one—'

'Don't you worry,' Birch said, shimmying fully out of the door and dancing around her colleague until they'd swapped places in the doorway. 'I'll fend for myself out here.'

'Any instruction for me?' Leake asked.

Birch shook her head. 'No,' she said, 'it's not an interview, just a family visit. The lawyer's here, so best to just say absolutely nothing.'

'Gotcha.' Leake put one foot through the door.

'Oh, Dave?'

'Marm?'

'Just . . .' Birch lowered her voice to a near whisper. 'Take some mental notes for me, would you? I'll want a bit of a debrief later.'

Leake tapped the side of his nose, then stepped through the door, and closed it behind him. Birch sighed heavily, but then rolled her shoulders and straightened up into a sentry position outside the door. She glanced at her watch: 11:03 a.m. She had hours of this ahead of her, potentially, depending how long the reunion between Bennet and his mother took. Hours and hours with nothing to do but stand still and worry about what was happening to Charlie.

Birch smiled to herself. 'Well, isn't that just business as usual?' she said. She tried to imagine where her brother might be at that moment: in his hearing, sore and struggling to sit on the hard chair they'd given him, but probably very glad to be up and out of bed, even if only for a little while. Anjan sitting next to him, upright and focused, handsome in a good suit, expensive tie. Birch realised she was looking forward to Anjan's call later: no matter what news he might impart, she was looking forward to just hearing his voice. Then, something occurred to her, and she took out her phone.

As soon as Charlie had handed her the message from their father in the infirmary room that day, Birch had committed the number to memory. Her brother had been right about that – of course she had. She'd driven home, and scribbled it down on the notepad beside the phone, so she couldn't forget it. But she'd also created a new contact in her mobile, and thumbed the number in there, too. Now, she opened that contact. *Jamieson Birch*, it said.

Birch took a deep breath, and leaned back against the doorframe of Phamie MacDonald's room. Around her, the nursing home went about its business: TVs murmured, china cups clattered in saucers, and from the kitchen downstairs came the faint smell of vegetable soup. You might be standing here for hours, Helen, Birch thought. There might be no better time than this. Before she could think about it too much more, she hit the green *call* button, and raised the phone to her ear to listen for the rings. There were four, and then a voice that was old – so much older than it had been – but deeply, terribly familiar.

'Jamieson Birch?' she asked. 'Dad? It's – it's Helen, here. It's me.'

Edinburgh Evening News

Elderly murderess who 'stopped a serial killer' dies before being brought to trial

EMMA BLACK
Email

Published 15:32
Friday 20 December

Share this article

The woman at the heart of the ongoing Carstairs Killer investigation, Euphemia MacDonald, has died of complications relating to lung cancer.

Mrs MacDonald, who was due to stand trial in the New Year for the murder of her husband, George MacDonald, was rushed to hospital on Wednesday night with severe respiratory problems. A source at the Edinburgh Royal Infirmary stated that Mrs MacDonald was unable to be revived after she stopped breathing, as she had requested a Do Not Resuscitate order. She died in the Emergency unit at Little France with her son, Robertson Bennet, at her bedside.

Mrs MacDonald has been under house arrest at her Morningside nursing home since September, when she confessed to police that she had murdered her husband George upon discovering that he was responsible for the Carstairs killings, which took place between 1965 and

1999. George MacDonald was found to be behind the slayings of six young women, including Christine Turnbull and Suzie Hay, whose disappearances in 1965 and 1996 prompted national appeals for information. Many members of the public took part in outdoor fingertip searches in the Christine Turnbull case, which remained open for over fifty years. The bodies of the six women were eventually found buried in woodland near to the villages of Carstairs and Carstairs Junction, in South Lanarkshire.

There has been widespread public support for Mrs MacDonald since the news broke that she had murdered her husband and buried him under a patio in the garden of the couple's Morningside home. Many people took to social media to express their gratitude to Mrs MacDonald for, as one commenter put it, 'stopping a serial killer in his tracks'. The nursing home where Mrs MacDonald was a resident has received thousands of letters of support for her cause, and reported that she was visited by several of the murdered women's loved ones.

Hazel Kerr, the mother of Maisie Kerr, who disappeared in 1999 and was George MacDonald's last known victim, made a statement to the press last month in support of Euphemia MacDonald. Mrs Kerr said, 'I may never be able to forgive the wicked things that George MacDonald did to my daughter and to other vulnerable young women, but I do take comfort in knowing what happened to him at the end. It feels fitting that he was also forced to lie in an unmarked grave, with no one knowing where he was, after he visited that fate upon so many who didn't deserve it. In my opinion, his wife's actions were an act of public service.'

Police Scotland today stated their disappointment that Mrs MacDonald would not be brought to trial, with a spokesperson saying, 'Although vigilante-style acts of violence can sometimes masquerade as justice, they have no place in a fair society. It is the place of the courts, not the public, to determine an appropriate and measured response to any criminal act.' The statement also reiterated Police Scotland's pledge to continue looking into other missing person cases they believe may be linked to George MacDonald, making use of DNA evidence recovered from the investigation's two crime scenes in Carstairs and Morningside. Sources from within the Fettes Avenue station suggest that over a dozen unsolved cases have been reopened since George MacDonald's body was discovered.

A public Indiegogo campaign has raised over £250,000, intended to cover Euphemia MacDonald's legal bills. Earlier today, Indiegogo confirmed that the funds would be transferred to Mrs MacDonald's son, Robertson Bennet, who is the sole executor of his parents' estate. Speaking to the assembled press outside the Balmoral Hotel, where he is believed to be staying, Mr Bennet promised to use the funds to set up a charitable trust to assist women who have suffered from domestic violence. Mrs MacDonald was hospitalised in 2013 following a domestic disturbance at the MacDonald family home.

'My mother lived with my father's wanton violence for almost sixty years,' Mr Bennet said. 'I know she would want this money to be spent on helping to make sure that no other woman has to suffer the same fate.'

If, like Phamie, you're in an abusive relationship and you're not sure how you can leave, you can seek help from the following organisations:

Refuge: refuge.org.uk 0808 2000 247
Women's Aid: womensaid.org.uk
Scottish Women's Aid: womensaid.scot 0800 027 1234
Welsh Women's Aid: welshwomensaid.org.uk 0808 80 10 800
Women's Aid Federation Northern Ireland: https://www.women-saidni.org 0808 802 1414

ACKNOWLEDGEMENTS

Thank you as always to the wonderful Cath Summerhayes and everyone at Curtis Brown; to Carolyn Mays, Jenny Platt, Sorcha Rose and everyone at Hodder who has worked on and championed this book. Special thanks to my brilliant editor Jo Dickinson – Jo, thank you for your belief in me.

I'm grateful to Ellie Hutchinson, formerly of Scottish Women's Aid and Hollaback Edinburgh: Ellie, your training and workshop sessions helped hugely in creating a narrative for Phamie. I'm grateful to Scottish Book Trust and Open Book for giving me opportunities to work inside prisons in Scotland, and deeply grateful to the men I met and talked to as part of that work. I'm grateful to my dad, John Askew, for his encyclopaedic knowledge of railways and stations. (Any errors in this book are mine.)

Thank you to my colleagues and students at the University of Edinburgh, and to my colleagues at the Edinburgh International Book Festival and Write Like A Grrrl! (Jane and Kerry, I love you) who supported me while I wrote this novel. Thanks are also due to Scottish Book Trust and Moniack Mhor Creative Writing Centre who gave me time and space to write in Spring 2019, and to everyone at Bloody Scotland for investing in and encouraging me via the 2019 Scottish Crime Debut of the Year award.

Thanks are due to the many people who've championed my work thus far, and especially the booksellers and library staff who've helped give my books to readers. There are too many of you to list, but special mentions go to Julie Danskin and the team at Golden Hare Books; Mairi Oliver and the team at Lighthouse Books; Sally Pattle at Far From The Madding Crowd; Angie Crawford at Waterstones; Kirkland Ciccone, and the one and only Jack Dennison.

I am so lucky to have such a supportive network of friends who put up with my social flakery, book-related moaning and general weird behaviour. Stella Birrell, Alice Tarbuck, Leon Crosby, Natalie Fergie, Colin McGuire, Hannah McCooke. Sasha de Buyl, I miss you. Dean Rhetoric, I miss you, too. I'm sorry – and thank you! – to you all.

Endless gratitude to Amanda, John, Ian, Danielle, Dave, Amelia, Alfie and all the Grimsby/Cleethorpes family for all their support and love. Thank you to my mum, Chris, for badgering bookshop staff about stocking my books; to my dad, John (again) for being the best proof-reader in the known world; and to Nick, the best human – Team Askew, I love you. Finally, this book is for Dom, without whose endless patience and strange curveball ideas my stories would be nothing. Sorry I didn't get the alien abduction in this one, honey. Maybe next time.